AS1

TREVOR LEWIS
A HARD SCIENCE FICTION NOVEL

Copyright ©2024 by Trevor Lewis

All rights reserved. No part of this book may be used or reproduced in any form whatsoever without written permission, except in the case of a brief quotation in critical articles or reviews.

This book is a work of fiction. All names, characters, businesses, organizations, places, events, and incidents either are the product of the author's imagination or are used fictitiously. Any resemblance to actual persons, living or dead, events, or locales is entirely coincidental.

Book cover design by Trevor Lewis and Rica Cabrex

ISBN - Paperback: 979-8-89283-099-7
ISBN - Kindle: 979-8-89283-097-3
ISBN - EPUB: 979-8-89283-098-0

First Edition, Third Printing: June 2025

Published by Books to Hook Publishing, LLC

For all those who believe

Part I

DISCOVERY

The important thing is not to stop questioning. Curiosity has its own reason for existing.

– Albert Einstein

Chapter 1

Sweat dripped onto the touchpad keyboard, causing the connectivity area of his finger to spread through the salty liquid and activate the M key for an extended period. Cursing, the young naval officer dried the surface with his blue military-issue coveralls. He noticed a slight shake in his hands. The tight walls of the Virginia-class surveillance submarine seemed to be slowly closing in on him, a constrictor squeezing the life out of its prey. Pressing his clammy fingers deep into his eyelids, he wished that when he reopened his eyes, he would be surrounded by daylight, rather than the ominous red glow that filled the interior of the top secret submarine. He focused on his breathing, an attempt to calm his nerves and reclaim his heart rate, which was beating above its normal pace.

As the lead data analyst, he had been stationed aboard the vessel for almost nine months, with only two days breached, allowing him and the small crew to open the hatch and see natural light. A sensation he never knew he could miss so much. The USS *Dark Water* was the most powerful radio communication submarine in the South Pacific. It, paired with a 9-C reconnaissance satellite, was built to intercept and communicate some of the darkest, deepest secrets being transmitted worldwide. Now, he was face-to-face with one of the strangest and startling transmissions yet.

With limited options, he began thinking of option B as option A. Protocol dictated that if an anomaly was detected and it passed both stage one and stage two verification checks, he was required to submit the report. But if he were wrong, doing so would most definitely include a demotion and a mark on his record that every ranking officer would scoff at. The bright monitors seemed to mock him, displaying a dizzying array of numbers and graphs that made no sense despite his greatest efforts.

Ashamed and defeated, he cursed under his breath, wishing he had never acquired the intel that a detected signal had interfered with their satellite—a transmission too consistent to be a bug or a natural anomaly. Holding the rank of petty officer first class on the sub, he needed to produce a report that provided a quantifiable explanation for the occurrence. Focusing on the screen again and realizing that over an hour had passed since the initial log report was opened, the R0-121 regulations for the US Navy surveillance division required all findings to be reported within ninety minutes of discovery. He had nothing, no clue how a signal of this nature could be interfering with their satellite. No clue how a signal could appear to be coming from a place outside of a typical Earth orbit. No clue why the signal didn't seem to have any logical patterns or typical frequencies.

Wiping his brow, he knew there were less than thirty minutes left to provide his results. At this point, they would not be complete and likely deemed "inadequate—more analysis required." He shouldn't be sweating this much. Too many weeks in a row in the cramped quarters were getting to him. Or maybe it was the weight of the decision? Spinning his chair to check the radar screen, he placed his hand on the cool, refreshing interior wall of the sub. He closed his eyes and sucked in a long, deep breath of stale recycled air.

The damp coolness of the metal brought him back to the present moment. He had to send the report. But how could he do this in a way that didn't make him look paranoid? Just two weeks ago he had reported on an anomaly. That one had been an apparent mistake. But this, this was different. This was actual data. It was a genuine signal, or at least it appeared to be, until someone else could verify it with the other satellites. But that could take weeks.

He sighed and stared at the screen again. The sixty-foot carbon-reinforced fiber optic cable was still deployed. At the end of the cable was a small beacon floating at the surface, communicating with the reconnaissance satellite via binary direct laser communication. He wished for some new information, something that would help explain what they were dealing with, but the air was silent.

There were only two choices: either classify it as a nonsignificant finding and close the case or escalate it with a level three emergent report, triggering an alert to the highest command. Although every part of him wanted to sweep this one under the rug and close it out as nonsignificant, instincts wouldn't allow it. There was something here, something in this data that needed to be understood. With a swift movement of his hand, he punched in a sequence on the tablet, cutting communications from the surfaced beacon, and began the retraction sequence. Submitting this report would surely put them into lockdown and cause them to stay dark for weeks until the Pentagon analysts could better grasp what they were dealing with. After a moment of pause, he submitted the report of level three emergent findings with the simple words, "More analysis required."

He expected relief from his anxiety to come after submitting the report. However, he couldn't shake the pit in his stomach telling him that something was deeply disturbing about this anomaly.

Chapter 2

Rays of pink light painted the empty white walls, giving the colorless room some life. The computer lab was nearly empty, just several scientists and lab techs remained scattered throughout the sea of computers, faces lit up by the glow of the monitors. Gideon had been in the lab since 6 a.m., and the thought of missing sunset after arriving in the morning darkness put him in a bad mood. Days had passed in this fashion for almost a week now; the only thing keeping him going was genuine excitement and curiosity.

He ran a hand through his thick mop of blond hair, fingers catching on a long strand in his bangs. Noticing it was nearly long enough to fall into his eyes, he wrapped it tightly around his finger and gave it an annoyed tug, as if he thought it might pull right out. With an exhale of breath, he peered over the row of computers.

"I'm taking off. Will you lock up today when you leave?" Gideon asked.

Dan, Gideon's colleague, replied with an unenthusiastic thumbs-up. Dan never seemed overly passionate about the research; this rubbed Gideon the wrong way. The two of them had been partnered last year, working as a team on the signal boosting of the 4 mm frequencies. The goal was to find obscure radio signals and enhance them, hopefully into useful information, often picking up disruptions from pulsar stars over six billion light-years from Earth.

Once they had gotten into the research, it became clear to Gideon that Dan and his undergraduate degree in computer science from Harvard were simply there for a new "gold star" to slap on a résumé. Dan was always going on and on about his "next move" at NASA and the CIA. Initially frustrated with Dan's lack of engagement, Gideon slowly began to appreciate it, as it allowed him to dive deeper into the research and do things his way.

And now, while Dan was running around kissing ass, Gideon was beginning to think he may have found something worth noticing. A new energy filled him.

Striking the keys of the faded, off-white keyboard, exerting extra emphasis on the space bar, which only worked about 50 percent of the time, the macro program began running in the background. He observed as the computer worked autonomously, tirelessly making computation after computation. Gideon reached into his left jean pocket, finding a 5/16-inch copper washer, a habit he used to focus his busy mind. He spun it vigorously with his thumb around his forefinger; his brain was making computations that could put the old computer to shame.

"Do I need to reboot you?" Dan raised his head so just his eyes could be seen over the top of the computer screen.

Snapping out of his trance, Gideon replied tiredly, "Man, yeah, I'm out of here."

Grabbing a sticky note, Gideon wrote a message: *Please do not shut down, running an overnight program*. He powered down just the monitor, leaving the computer awake to continue its computational quest, and with more force than necessary, slapped the note to the now black screen.

"See you tomorrow," Gideon called out as he left the shadow-filled room.

Walking out of the lab took only a minute, following a small hallway to the fluorescent green sign indicating the exit. He opened the heavy metal door with his shoulder.

The evening air was still warm as the sun dipped below the trees. Venus was visible in the bluish-pink sky as it chased the sun into the forested horizon. Walking to his small Airbnb-rented house would take twelve minutes, thirteen and a half if he chose not to cut through the grass when there was too much dew on the ground. Tonight, the grass was dry. Walking gave him time to reflect on how it all started ...

Originally from a small town in Idaho, Gideon graduated high school a year early. He was a finalist in the MIT THINK Scholars Program with the development of a 5G NR radio that transmitted on a 240 kHz frequency band. After receiving scholarships and high praise, he was accepted into MIT.

Most people from his high school considered acceptance into the local diesel mechanics apprenticeship a massive accomplishment, but his acceptance to MIT went largely without notice. His mother had complained about the high costs of the school, even with the scholarships. She showed him that a career electrician made far more money than the average research scientist. Despite her best efforts, Gideon enrolled in classes and excelled in astrophysics and computer programming.

Two years later, his brother's accident altered the course of his life. While changing the family truck's oil, the block of wood shifted, dropping the 4,300-pound Dodge Dakota and putting his brother into a coma. Gideon flew home that night, never to return to MIT. Six months of difficult times dragged on, countless nights spent in the hospital, helplessly hoping for a miracle that never came. After his brother's death, Gideon's mom chose to move in with her mother, and Gideon moved to Seattle, hoping to land a job at one of the big technology companies like Google, Boeing, or Blue Origin.

Soon, the harsh reality hit that an MIT dropout paired with a handful of impressive research studies did not make up for his incomplete educational résumé. Working thirty-six hours a week delivering sandwiches for Jimmy John's had rescued him from unemployment, but not dissatisfaction. There, he finally received the news he had been dreaming of—his acceptance into the Green Bank internship program in Arbovale, West Virginia.

Gideon remembered that phone call back home.

"Green Bank Observatory is the most advanced telescope in the United States, Mom." He had tried to explain this amazing opportunity—reaching for his dream at last. "It can operate from meter to millimeter wavelengths with a one-hundred-meter diameter collecting dish with an actuating surface. An *actuating* dish surface! Can you believe that?"

"English, please, Gideon." Her scowl was felt even over the phone.

"Mom, this facility has the most advanced radio telescopes in the United States; some argue in the whole world. We're talking about technologies that you don't find anywhere else."

"That's nice, sweetie; I'm just worried about you. You already struggle to make friends … I just googled Arbovale; Jesus Christ, Gideon, there isn't even cell service there?"

"There are plenty of workarounds to not have cell service. And being in the middle of the National Radio Quiet Zone, a thirteen-thousand-square-mile area with strict radio broadcasting restrictions, is what allows the telescope to work so well. And the geography here, it's perfect; the telescopes have a completely unobstructed view of the sky with almost no interference."

"What about the town, son? Any nice women there?"

"How would I know?" Gideon replied, rolling his eyes and blushing at the same time.

"It's a quiet little town, but it's beautiful, surrounded by rolling forests. It has a bank, general store, church, small café. I think you'd like it here …"

Gideon found his thoughts back to the present, walking home. This was a quiet town. The only consistent sound came from the auto shop right next to his house. Lacking a vehicle, Gideon had only left the town twice since his arrival. This was something most outsiders thought was crazy, but the locals found the concept of ever leaving even more foreign. Everyone here noticed you, but nobody really saw you. Smiles were rare; pursed lips and head nods were common practice.

But he didn't tell his mom that part.

From the beginning of his research at Green Bank, things had been mundane and straightforward. With the lack of oversight and his partner's lack of interest, Gideon had been able to follow his own path while still accomplishing the requirements of his contract. He had begun running searches of different frequencies and slot durations. After some time, he began picking up so much space noise and chatter that he created his own computer program to sift the data into categories, making it easier to digest.

Eight days ago, his program led him to his recent discovery. He quickly went to the head of his department with his findings but was met with a lecture that he should stick to his assigned tasks. Bemused by the fact that everyone had been uninterested in his findings at a facility that had been expressly established for searching for the unknown, Gideon took it upon himself to dig into it more, and after just a few days, he knew he had found something … abnormal.

Once home, Gideon cracked the only beer left in his fridge, a bitter porter from a variety six-pack he had bought several weeks ago. The house was about twice the size of his apartment back in Seattle but rented for a third of the price. Being an Airbnb, the house was minimally furnished but had all the basic needs covered. Pots and pans, an ancient coffee maker that seemed to produce more steam than coffee, and a few old pieces of furniture.

The living room sported a maroon sofa and what had been a television stand, now standing empty and forlorn, waiting for something to hold. Although no attention had been paid to the aesthetics of the place, it was tidy and clean.

While unintentionally warming the beer in his hand, Gideon's mind raced.

The signal was like none he had ever seen. When he initially discovered it, the signal was at 104.8 GHz and ranged in a very narrow band, making it very difficult to detect. Its origin seemed to be coming from within our solar system, closer than the typical signals they picked up, often many light-years away. Only a small number of unmanned crafts had ever covered that kind of distance, and he had checked the locations of several, including the Lucy and Psyche spacecrafts, but none seemed to be near the source of the signal. His interest was piqued but he hadn't been putting too much thought into it. That all changed yesterday.

When he went to realign the radio antenna to reacquire the signal, something that always required recalibration to account for Earth's rotation, the signal was gone. Alarmed and a bit disappointed, he assumed it had vanished for good. Perhaps it was just one of those anomalies you never get the chance to understand. However, before calling it a night, he pointed the antenna back to the last known coordinates and to his astonishment, the signal was there, still broadcasting the same pattern as before. At that moment, Gideon's heart skipped a beat.

It implied something nearly impossible. For the signal to be broadcasting at the same coordinates without needing adjustment, it had to be moving in sync with Earth's rotation. No known man-made object could achieve that from such a distance. To match Earth's rotation from the asteroid belt, an object would need to travel at an impossible velocity, faster than anything natural could sustain, without being flung out of orbit entirely.

Never had Gideon considered UFOs and folklore, but his mind was now wandering there, only to be reeled back to the probable reality that he'd likely found some type of confidential government technology or space noise anomaly.

Thinking of the computer grunting away back at the lab gave him an excited feeling, like the anticipation you get when ordering something online and knowing it will arrive the following day but don't want to wait. Gulping down the last of the warm, dissatisfying beer, he made his way to the bathroom. Grabbing a pair of scissors from the center drawer, he chopped off the bangs that were beginning to disrupt his vision. Once the final short lock of hair fell into the sink, he took a look at himself in the mirror. Dark circles hung under his blue eyes, and his beard scruff was getting long, but that could wait another day. Taking a deep breath, Gideon shut off the light, made his way to the small bedroom, and sank into the old coil-sprung mattress.

Chapter 3

Cold air bit Gideon's bare arms as he waited for his watch to display 4:30 a.m., the earliest his allotted badge would let him into the lab. Not a person or car could be seen in the dark morning fog. People would rarely show up before 6 a.m., and Dan would usually arrive around 7:20, exactly ten minutes before the head of the lab, Dr. Longsarbin, arrived. Gideon would have more than enough time to analyze the results before anybody else came in.

    Finally, the security panel buzzed, and Gideon pulled the heavy metal door open after scanning his badge. Darkness engulfed the hallway as the door shut behind him. As he neared Lab 113, his heart rate accelerated above its normal frequency. He had never felt this awake so early. Scanning his badge again, he entered the lab and heard his computer humming as it recovered from working tirelessly throughout the night. After flipping a switch on the wall, allowing the flow of electrons to begin moving back through the outdated light fixtures, fluorescent bulbs illuminated, causing his pupils to constrict. In similar fashion, the computer screen came to life, asking for a password with a blank stare. After entering the correct order of keystrokes with precision, Gideon removed his sticky note and placed it face down, leaving the sticky side up to prevent contamination in case it needed to be reused. He then refocused his attention on the data.

His face warmed as the blood vessels expanded, and his stomach dropped in exhilaration—a similar feeling to the spike of adrenaline you experience when your airplane takes a quick plunge in turbulence. The difference was that this feeling continued to grow and build as thoughts and speculation raced through his neuron passageways. After nearly an hour and a half of reviewing, the results were clear.

The signal was, in fact, broadcasting in a regular pattern—this was not random and was not a natural occurrence. But how could it be artificial? That didn't seem possible either. What other possibilities were there? Another form of … intelligent life?

The loud metallic bang of the heavy exterior door made him jump, the first sound he had heard since entering the building, alerting him that people were beginning to trickle in. Knowing he could finish the rest at home on his laptop, Gideon transferred the results and data onto a hard drive and rushed out of the lab. As he stepped into the hallway, now violated by the glare of fluorescent lights lining the ceiling, he directed his eyes to the ground to avoid eye contact with any talkative colleagues. He slipped through the back door unnoticed.

Gideon rushed home, eager to review the data. Needing a larger working space, he pulled up the large end table next to the couch, which was empty except for the single small trophy that sat near its edge. Gideon grabbed the object, one of the few personal items he had brought to Green Bank, and brushed his thumb across the gold-inscribed label, "First Place: Mathematic Olympiad."

He remembered going home after winning the award; his brother had always given him a hard time about spending time at competitions.

"What's the point? To prove to everyone how smart you are?" his brother had asked, black grease rubbed across his right cheekbone.

Gideon hadn't replied.

"Well, get your scrawny ass out here and put that brain of yours to actual work, I've been waiting for you to get home," his brother said with a wink.

Gideon followed his brother to the back of the house, where there were at least ten broken-down cars. Two of them were his brother's and the rest belonged to different folks in the town.

"Alright," Gideon's brother continued, arms crossed, "Mr. Pittman is gonna have my ass if I don't get his car back to him. I think I got it patched up; just needs oil and a filter."

Gideon perked up; he loved it when his older brother needed his help.

"Mr. Pittman's Ford is a '96 and has the 3.0L V6 engine, so you will need four and a half quarts of 5W-30 oil and a 51515 part number oil filter. Also, don't forget, the day he gave it to you he said the rear left wheel bearing was going bad, you can use a 5526-07944866 part number bearing."

His brother laughed.

"Thanks, Gid. See, you can put that photographic memory to good use out here. We gotta start up a shop together someday. With my connections and your memory, we'd be unstoppable …"

Gideon snapped back to the present, noticing he was squeezing the washer in his pocket so tightly that his hand was beginning to hurt. He quickly placed the small mathematics trophy on the floor, shaking his mind free of the relentless pull of memories.

Pulling the small table to the couch and throwing his notebook on it, he sat down and began quickly scribbling down his initial thoughts. He would reference the hard data presented by his laptop periodically, but most had stuck in his memory. After working for an hour on the cramped pages of his notebook, it became clear he needed a larger writing space to work everything out. Gideon gazed around the neglected room, noting the outdated 1970s faded orange floral wallpaper.

"This will do." Gideon jumped up and ran to his bedside table, retrieving several Sharpies from the old drawer. He removed the cap from the black and placed the red and blue pens on the TV stand. Gideon then pressed the Sharpie against the wall of his rented home and began scribbling what he knew. Soon, the wall was covered in equations, assumptions, and theories. Standing, he smiled at his work, thinking the mess of writing looked better than the tired, faded wallpaper.

However, he knew that upon moving out, he would have to peel the walls and repaint them, presenting it as an offer of gratitude rather than the act of concealing possible vandalism. A stern look pulled his smile down as he refocused on his conclusion.

"This is it ..." Gideon ran his hands through his hair. "The signal is—without a doubt—artificial."

His hand, still tangled in his hair, closed into a fist, pulling on his scalp. "How can it be?" he whispered.

Gideon pulled out his laptop and began typing up his findings:

> *The signal is confirmed to be artificial in origin. Its narrowband frequency ranges from 104.8–105.2 GHz, something not found in natural anomalies. I am confident it is coming from within our solar system; due to its intensity and interferences, I'll need greater time intervals between measurements to get a better location fix. I am VERY startled to find that the signal origin appears to be in some sort of massive geosynchronous orbit centering around Earth. Which, due to the Earth's relatively zero gravitational pull on an object that far away, is an impossible trajectory without some type of alternative thrust.*

Rain began tapping on the single-pane window behind him as the wind picked up. The room darkened slightly as the clouds piled above the humble house in the midst of its momentous discovery.

Gideon walked to the small floor lamp and flipped on the switch. He stared at the wall of illustrations. Now that he understood the origins and general properties of the signal, he knew he had to see if he could decipher it—was it really a message?

"What are you trying to say?" he pondered out loud, ignoring the intrusive weather pressing down upon the house.

From the moment his computer first indicated the results back in the lab, he had a strange sensation that it might be a message. It followed a dynamic time division multiple access frame structure, also known as DTDMA, and featured a type of preamble. He knew this preamble was important because, as with most signals looking to have an acknowledged receival, the preamble is a way for a radio signal to get a receiver's attention. He remembered one of his professors explaining it to the class: "*If you need to address a large room of chatty people at a wedding, a common method is to ding your knife against your glass to gain the attention of your audience, which then allows you to broadcast your message to listening ears. This is what a preamble does for the radio signal.*"

By having a preamble, the signal clearly was trying to get found, which was particularly inconvenient for many of his original theories. What undetected signal *wants* to be found? Gideon had only once come across something similar. It ended up being a transmission from an Israeli satellite. Those findings had escalated quickly up the chain and Gideon had never been given the privilege of knowing what the purpose of that satellite was. However, what was clear was that Israel had tried to make the signal undetectable.

Moving his attention back to the task at hand, Gideon noted that the preamble took about 20 milliseconds of the four-second repetitive frame. Thus, he was sure that the 3.98 seconds of repetitive cycle contained some type of message.

The 3.98-second frame appeared to be broken up into three subframes, each 1.23 seconds long with a similar split between each. Gideon assumed that these frames, per a typical DTDMA signal, would contain tens of thousands of binary bit packets, ultimately representing a coherent message.

After rubbing his eyes and the blur of regaining visual focus dissolved, Gideon noticed something intriguing. Something familiar caught his eye. Grabbing the blue Sharpie, he went to the printed frequency chart, now stapled to the wall, and traced a line from each spike. The action reminded him of playing "connect the dots" as a kid. After completing the action, he took several steps back, processing the new shape.

He had seen it before. Finding the washer in his pocket, he spun it slowly, relaxing him into deep thought. Where had he seen this graph? Then, with a hard squeeze on the copper washer, he remembered. The electromagnetic absorption by water! Pulling out his phone, he searched Google, and sure enough, the graphs lined up nearly perfectly.

Recognizing that this message contained logical information, Gideon diverted his attention to the only two plausible explanations he could come up with for the signal's source. He fluttered the marker in his fingers as he talked out loud.

"First, it is plausible this is some sort of unmanned craft that somebody or some country managed to send into space, like the Voyager or New Horizons."

He took a step back.

"But I wonder ..." His voice made a slight echo in the bare room. "All of these crafts were designed to travel *away* from Earth and explore the solar system. This is clearly being used for a different purpose and has technology that is unprecedented, nearly unfathomable, in terms of thrust capabilities, allowing it to have a location in a geosynchronous orbit like this." Gideon looked around out of habit, almost as if making sure nobody was watching or listening. He then turned back to the wall confidently, knowing he was in a space that contained only himself and his own mind.

"Second, the signal could be of extraterrestrial origin. It doesn't seem to be coming from any planetary body, which would indicate that it is originating from some type of craft."

Gideon's adrenaline pulsed as he realized his most plausible explanation seemed to point toward some type of artificial non-earth-based originator: extraterrestrial intelligence.

What else could it be?

"What am I missing? There must be a third plausible explanation. Perhaps some new classified technology I don't know about?"

Desperate for answers, Gideon decided to allow the scientific community to weigh in. Reviving his laptop from sleep mode, he navigated to a science forum he'd been involved in since his MIT days. The forum contained a core group of nearly two thousand experienced scientists, each of whom had to complete a rigorous application to ensure that ideas would not be stolen, reproduced, or leaked. The community was committed to providing unbiased opinions on complex science topics, perfect for Gideon's application.

It took nearly an hour to translate his scribbled walls into a coherent problem statement and theory, complemented with attached data. The text proved to be longer than he expected, but after a thorough review, it was ready. Hovering the cursor over the post button, he pondered if he was making the right decision, posting this for others to see …

He clicked.

His post soon topped the list of diverse topics. He sent the link to a professor he had formed a close bond with at MIT, and another to his friend, Kyle, whom he had met in Seattle through the group. In the subject line, he wrote: "You have to check this out and tell me I'm not crazy."

Adrenaline lost the battle to exhaustion, and Gideon threw himself down on the uncomfortable maroon sofa and closed his eyes.

Chapter 4

Jerking awake, Gideon noticed the rain had subsided and the sun seemed to have fallen below the horizon. His windows were no longer visual portals of the outside world but reflected back the interior of his dimly lit room. Gideon snatched his laptop from the TV stand. Several notifications inhabited his inbox, and many people had liked or commented on the post, although not nearly as many as he'd expected. Topping the list of emails were replies from both his teacher and friend.

He opened the first one.

> *Good to hear from you, Gideon. Hope all is well. Impressed to hear you are out at Green Bank, what an impressive step. By the way, the link you sent doesn't seem to be working, please resend, I would love to see what you've been working on.*
>
> *Sincerely, Dr. Moran*

Annoyed, Gideon opened the second email.

Link doesn't work … Hope all is well. – Kyle

Confused, Gideon clicked the link within each email, and each time, the browser displayed "*Page does not exist.*"

Opening the website, he clicked on the notifications, noticing with mounting suspicion that all had occurred in the first five minutes of the post. When clicking to see the comments, he was again brought to: "*This page does not exist.*"

"What? They removed my post?" In frustration, Gideon copied his findings from the Word document and pasted them into a fresh post. After pressing "publish," a new page was displayed, this time a bit more startling.

"*Your IP address has been banned; we apologize for any inconvenience.*"

Heat filled his face once again. Had the government, or whoever was making the signal, somehow found his post and shut it down? Was this dangerous? Determined to share his findings, he explored another option. Having no issue assigning a fake IP address, he created a new account and went to post, this time anonymously, tweaking some words to make it a little more obscure and perhaps harder to find.

Clicking the post, the title, *Science Bloggers – Intriguing Discovery Made, Need Opinions,* now topped the list of topics by an anonymous poster. He smiled at his victory.

Hitting reply to Dr. Moran and Kyle, Gideon reposted the link and decided to double-check before sending. To Gideon's shock, the link brought him to the same:

"*Page does not exist.*"

Gideon could hardly believe it, and for a few brief moments, while he stared at his computer screen, he wondered if he was making a mistake.

He almost laughed at the situation. This is like something out of a movie, he thought. But the signal he had picked up was real, and so was the fact that his posts about it were disappearing and his IP address had been banned. It was no coincidence, he knew, and no laughing matter, either.

Still shocked at everything that was happening, Gideon decided to go for a walk to clear his mind. Gideon quickly grabbed a jacket and tossed it around his tall, slender frame. Stepping outside, he noticed the morning sun just beginning to light up the sky, pinks and blues fighting off the black of the night. Walking kept his mind going forward, jumping from his solved equations and back to the fact that he had not been able to successfully post his links.

And then a bit of despair crept in, and Gideon considered that maybe, just maybe, he was on his way to ruining his future. Life had given him a number of good chances to get ahead—being accepted into MIT and then the Green Bank program. But what if one little mistake, one turn down the wrong path saw all of his efforts negated?

And then it's back to wrapping sandwiches, Gideon thought bitterly.

But he couldn't just ignore what he had found—and the fact that it really looked like some powerful entity was trying to suppress it. So, as he walked through the still-sleeping town of Arbovale, he decided that he would not run away from his findings, whatever they were. He would, however, be as careful as he could.

I'll tread carefully, he thought, trudging over a cluster of stones on the sidewalk in front of him and stepping softly over them. When he made it back to his place, Gideon found that he had walked up an appetite. He opened the fridge, the food scattered meagerly across its shelves looking unpromising. Some bread, a few slices of cheese, a pickle jar with one single pickle remaining. A mayo jar that looked to have just enough to scrape out for a single sandwich.

He spooned out the last dregs of mayonnaise from the jar, threw on a couple of slices of cheese, and garnished the scanty plate with the last pickle in the fridge. Then he plopped down and got ready to eat.

As he looked down at his meager sandwich, he thought about his next steps in life, about a time in his future when there would be more food in the fridge than some bread and a few slices of cheese. He thought about when he would find success in life, when his schooling, hard work and intelligence would pay off. He wondered if they ever would. He'd seen people work harder than ever and never seem to get anywhere, and then others who seemed to hardly work at all who had everything they wanted and needed.

Gideon refocused his thoughts and began searching for sites to buy a new VPN. If someone was messing with his ability to post, maybe hiding his IP address and bouncing that trail across a few different continents would help buy him some time. It would also allow him to run a test. Having a post blocked was one thing, but having your entire IP address blocked was something else altogether.

He clicked on the VPN service that he had heard good things about, excited to get started. But the page came up blank. What the—? He clicked back, and his computer froze. His Internet was gone. He checked his modem and the connection. Nothing.

A noise outside caught his attention, the sound of heavy boots just outside the door. His heart began to race. He sat, frozen, sandwich clenched in one hand as if he might be able to use it as a weapon. Never had Gideon had a visitor at his doorstep, especially not at 6 a.m. Now realizing the limp sandwich would have no contribution to battling an intruder, he dropped it on the table and stood, trying not to move one more muscle than required. He held his breath and closed his eyes, listening. Silence.

He began to relax; was this all making him overly paranoid?

BANG … BANG!

Someone was pounding on the door. Gideon took several steps back, mind racing. Another bang on the door, loud and abrupt, followed by a deep Southern voice.

"West Virginia State Troopers. Gideon J. Haas, open the door."

Startled and confused, Gideon held perfectly still. His breathing sounded too loud in the tense silence between the shouts and pounds on the door. Time crept as he stood motionless in the small room. The scribbled walls now gave the room an ominous look. Three more bangs came with impressive force; Gideon wondered how many more the flimsy door could take.

"Open on up, Gideon, we'll be comin' in there invited er not."

Unable to derive any alternative options, Gideon took the five steps toward the door and reached for the handle. After trying to turn it, he realized it was locked. Right hand still firmly grasping the cold copper knob, his left hand reached and turned the small lock in the center of the handle, making an inconveniently loud click as it released. His right hand slowly began turning the doorknob an—

WHAM!

The door flew open with outrageous force, striking Gideon's forehead and causing his vision to flicker. Somehow, he was able to remain on his feet, only to be thrown to the ground by the sheriff. Without attempting to struggle, he was forcefully flipped over onto his stomach and hands swiftly cuffed behind his back.

"Gideon, we, the West Virginia State Troopers, hereby place you under arrest for suspicion of the murder of Ms. Alexandra J. Hewitt. You have the right to remain silent."

Chapter 5

Last-minute travel arrangements typically frustrated Robert Waller, but tonight was different. Word that a potential information leak may have occurred worried him greatly. Not only could this cause worldwide panic, but the United States would also be under intense scrutiny for hiding it. Luckily, the individual, a young astrophysicist named Gideon Haas, who had attempted to leak the information, was safely detained and sitting in an interrogation room at the West Virginia Sheriff's Office. The three-and-a-half-hour drive from DC to West Virginia gave him time to consider the last month.

Long days and weekends at the office or traveling dominated his life. After the news, although unable to share it with his wife and two sons, he moved his family out of DC to their vacation home in a secluded area near Sugarloaf Ski Resort in Maine. Nothing was more difficult than trying to explain to his wife that they had to go without giving her a real reason. She knew much of his work was confidential, but that didn't make it any easier.

She had looked him directly in the eyes, reading him. She was frighteningly good at that, and without saying a word, she only nodded and started helping the kids pack.

It felt safer there. But safer from what, he wondered? Was there even a threat? These questions had been pulsing in his brain since the call from the five-star general, John Higgens.

Waller had worked for the United States government for the last twenty years. His roles ranged from public relations to head of top secret military programs. He was close with many high-ranking individuals and had an influential voice in the Oval Office. Experience like this should lead someone to be prepared for anything. But nothing could have prepared him for what was occurring now.

The white lines of the roads zoomed by, reflecting the light coming from his government-issued C-Class Mercedes headlights. Only the skeletons of crops in the fields could be seen in the dark as he sped by. His thoughts shifted. Who was Gideon, and how did he fit into all of this?

He flipped open the manila folder resting on the passenger's seat, trusting the car's autopilot. A photo of Gideon sat on the cover page of the intel packet. In the passport-size photo in the corner, Waller didn't see a wild-eyed old man, thug, or stereotypical scientist. He saw a young man with a slender but lean-looking frame wearing a gray zip-up hoodie over a loose-fitting white tee. Gideon had messy blond hair that didn't seem to be much of a priority. His bright blue eyes were intense, portals into what was clearly a sharp mind.

Having only an hour to review his profile before hitting the road, Waller replayed the audio file that repeated what he had observed on paper. Gideon was an impressively bright young man who had been through a string of bad luck, which had brought his promising future at MIT to an abrupt end. He had since moved to Seattle, only holding a job at a sandwich shop until beginning work at Green Bank.

No ties to any terrorist groups, hacking organizations, or even a traffic ticket. Waller knew who he would be meeting, a confused geek who had stumbled upon something, by accident, that was much bigger than he could imagine or cope with.

Waller was an expert at being prepared for these kinds of meetings. The more information he knew about someone, the more likely they were to cooperate. It was like it impressed them, intimidated them, or both, knowing so much about their personal lives. Information that ordinary civilians wouldn't be able to come up with so quickly.

Waller focused on committing the intel to memory: *from Idaho … the MIT THINK Scholars Program … scholarships … his brother's accident … Green Bank.*

His cell phone rang, and Waller answered the call via his Bluetooth earpiece.

"Did you do some digging?" General John Higgens asked him.

"I sure did."

"And what do you know about him?" the general asked.

Waller sighed, reflecting on all the information he had taken in over the last hour. "Everything."

Chapter 6

Gideon leaned back against the cold cement wall, neck aching from the strain of holding up his head. With his hands cuffed behind him, there was no relief, no way to ease the discomfort. His thoughts twisted into dark spirals of hypothetical *what-ifs*, each one more suffocating than the last. They had thrown him into the back of a squad car, disregarding his frantic pleas that this was clearly a mistake. After arriving at the local sheriff's office, he was searched a second time and then escorted to a holding room without the opportunity to make a phone call or ask any questions.

New voices could be heard from outside the holding cell. The door latch twisted along with Gideon's stomach, revealing the same trooper who had brought him to the room just hours before, but it felt like a year ago. With no new information and only the original accusation that he was up for a murder, Gideon's emotions flipped quickly between fear and anger. He had never heard the name Alexandra Hewitt and from what he understood about the law, he was also clearly being illegally detained and denied his phone call.

"The detective is here. He's going to ask you a few questions."

Gideon pondered everything he knew about situations like this. Everything he had read, everything he had heard from the rougher kids back home. What are my legal rights here? he wondered.

"I want my phone call," said Gideon, knowing that was definitely a right of someone who had been arrested.

The trooper hesitated, looking slightly confused.

Gideon wondered about the trooper's apparent bewilderment. Why would asking for a phone call throw him off? Was he not the one in charge here?

"You'll get it after you answer a few questions. Now follow me and I'll take you to see the detective."

Gideon stood; the trooper grabbed the chain linking the two cuffs around Gideon's wrists and pushed him through the doorway. Armed with no knowledge or real understanding of how the legal system worked, Gideon obliged, feeling like a cow being prodded toward its butcher. The walk down the sterile hallway felt like an eternity. Gideon's heart pounded in his chest and ears, unsure of what this next phase would entail.

He was led into what he assumed was the interrogation room and forced to sit down at the stainless-steel table. The sheriff released the cuffs to Gideon's relief … only to realize it was just to re-cuff his hands in front. Still, better than the previous configuration.

The room looked as though it hadn't been used in years, which was no surprise considering they were still somewhere deep within rural West Virginia. The room had a musty aura about it, with a faint smell of bleach or some other cleaning solution. Maybe from cleaning up blood, Gideon thought morbidly. In the corner sat an old fan, far from any outlet, perched atop a weathered cardboard box. Clean streaks across the dusty floor indicated larger items had recently been pulled from the room. The only other objects remaining in the obnoxiously brightly lit room were two metal folding chairs flanking the metal table. A large mirror occupied the adjacent wall. Gideon wasn't sure if he was supposed to pretend like he didn't know there were people looking in from the other side.

Several minutes passed before a new individual walked into the room. This man was different. Dressed in a freshly pressed black suit wrapped around a perfectly white shirt colored with a dark red tie. The man had a persona about him that oozed experience and confidence. His high-quality yet heavily worn leather briefcase matched his brown shoes and belt. Clean-shaven, with hair that appeared too perfectly black to grow from a man of his age, around fifty.

He entered the room smoothly and comfortably, closed the door, and gave the room a quick scan with dark brown eyes, which sat deep in his skull. He turned and stepped to the table, promptly sitting down while laying the briefcase on the table at the exact same moment. After opening the briefcase to remove several documents and a sophisticated tablet, he finally locked eyes with Gideon for the first time.

"Hello, Gideon."

Gideon replied with a faint smile, lifting his cuffed hands slightly off the table as if to say he had already surrendered.

"My name is Robert Waller, and I am here to explain the situation you have gotten yourself into."

There was a short pause, a fake smile, and then the man continued.

"Alexandra Hewitt is a real, young woman who was found dead several days ago. The autopsy report indicates murder. You see—"

"Sorry, uh, shouldn't these … this … conversation be recorded?"

The man's facial expression did not change in the slightest.

"Would you feel better if I came in here with a little tape recorder that had a 'for evidence' label slapped on it? Press the record button when we start talking? Come on, Gideon, you're a smart kid; let's just recognize that we are not operating under typical protocol. May I continue?"

Gideon nodded, beginning to question the legitimacy of what was going on. Why would they not be following typical protocol? Was he being set up?

"So, you're admitting you're not following protocol?" Gideon demanded. "I'm telling you, I'm not the right guy, you don't even know who I am!"

Waller squinted; his lips twisted in a prim smile. "I don't know who you are? Well, let's see. You're from Idaho. From an itty-bitty town no one's ever heard of." Waller brought his thumb and index finger together to indicate the small size.

It didn't impress Gideon that the man knew he was from Idaho. It didn't seem like that would be too hard to find out.

"You were too smart for high school, weren't you? Graduated early. Then there was that scholars program, MIT THINK. You did pretty damn good there. Got a scholarship, accolades, and then it was off to MIT."

Gideon began to worry about where this was going. The man did know who he was. But how?

"I won't talk about the tragedy that made you leave MIT," said Waller, his face unmistakably solemn in the overly bright room. "But let's end on a high note with you being accepted into Green Bank. Congratulations, Gideon."

Gideon was paralyzed under the weight of all the information he had just heard—information about himself. Especially the personal bits. But Waller wasn't done.

"And now you spend your days in a lab studying radio signals with your colleague, Dan." Waller leaned forward over the table. "But his heart's not in it, is it?"

Gideon had no words.

"I'll cut to the chase. The point I am making here is we know *everything* about you. And we have all the evidence we need to convict you for the murder of Alexandra Hewitt."

"If you really knew everything, you'd know I didn't murder anybody!" Gideon was beginning to feel desperate.

Waller's eyes sharpened like a cat about to pounce on its prey.

"Allow me to paint you a scenario. You would be walking into a courtroom with overwhelming evidence supporting your murder of Ms. Hewitt, who refused to go home with you last Wednesday evening after meeting her at a bar. She was strangled behind Hoot's Sports Saloon at approximately 2:45 a.m. and left next to the dumpster."

Waller paused, studying Gideon's reaction before continuing.

"Sure, you will tell everyone how you didn't do it and that you're tied up in some government conspiracy to cover up an unidentified signal you found. And hey, maybe that'll get you some slack and sent to a psych ward for life instead of prison, but the point is, either way, you will get convicted."

"This is related to the signal!" Gideon gasped, remembering the data he'd been studying all night.

A look of knowing passed over Waller's face, but the man simply shrugged and shook his head grimly. "Have fun in jail."

With that, Waller left the room, and two officers came in and escorted Gideon to a tiny jail cell. It had gray concrete walls and a small toilet in one of its dusty corners. The bed was a comically thin mattress lying atop a metal frame, and it hurt Gideon's back just looking at it.

"Hey!" said Gideon as the officers shut his cell's gate. "I didn't do anything!"

But they walked off disinterestedly, leaving Gideon alone to think about everything that had happened. He plopped down on the bed, his shoulders sinking as low as the flimsy mattress he sat on. He looked around at the austere cell's walls, the lack of comfort and outside light, the bars of the gate that served as a door.

Minutes turned to hours as they passed. Gideon felt around in his pocket constantly out of habit, only to remember that the copper washer was still resting back at his Airbnb on his table. There was no one coming to rescue him, and the terrible bed beneath him really was where he was going to sleep. A guard came by and tossed a single sandwich wrapped in cellophane into his cell. When Gideon unwrapped it, he saw that it was the most unappetizing food item he had ever seen. The bread was hard and rubbery, with a single piece of sandwich meat pressed between. There were no condiments to be seen, and if Gideon wasn't famished from not eating in what felt like days, he would've tossed it on the ground and ignored it. Instead, he bit into the curiosity, surprised that it could actually taste worse than it looked as he forced it down.

More hours passed by, and Gideon grew tired, wondering what time it was. Disoriented from the lack of windows and clocks. Even the pathetic excuse of a bed he sat on seemed more and more comfortable as he lay on his side and curled up. If he didn't assume the fetal position, the mat wasn't even long enough for him to lie on without his feet hanging off the far end.

Gideon recited his conversation with Waller, who had made it clear that they weren't following protocol. He began breaking down the situation. Who was Waller and what organization did he represent? FBI perhaps? Gideon wondered if he would be seeing him again or if that was really it, he was going to jail. It didn't make sense, a man like Waller would come all the way out here, violate protocol, just to meet with him for several minutes. There must be something else going on, something they needed from Gideon. Did they really think he killed Alexandra Hewitt, whoever that is … or was. And how did that connect to the signal he had detected?

Gideon curled up even tighter, noticing the temperature had dropped. And there he lay in the cell, scared and cold, harrowed by the reality of this new nightmare.

Chapter 7

"Top of the morning to yah, sir."

Gideon sat up in his bed, rubbing at his tired eyes with no idea how long he had been asleep. Waller, still in the same suit that he had been wearing before, stood leaning his right shoulder against the metal bars of the cell that held Gideon captive. There was a guard standing in the aisleway, but Waller motioned with his head for him to come over.

"Yes sir," the officer asked.

"Open the cell, I need to take Gideon back to the interrogation room," Waller said.

"I'll need to check with the commanding offi—"

Waller interrupted.

"Just open the fucking cell, I can handle it from here. I am your commanding officer today."

Confused and visibly startled by Waller's aggression, the young officer unlocked the cell and pulled open the door, which let out a loud squeal of metal on metal.

"I can handle it from here," Waller reiterated with a raised voice, keeping eye contact with Gideon.

The officer turned on his heels and walked away.

"Let's go, Gideon," Waller said, still locked with Gideon's gaze.

Gideon rose to his feet but nearly fell to the ground as he found his legs had fallen completely asleep from the stiff mattress.

The two walked back down the hall to the same interrogation room that they had sat in before.

"Just help me … please?" Gideon felt a stinging sensation in his nose, he was close to tears at this point.

Waller walked to one of the chairs and sat, swiftly laying his briefcase on the table at the same time. "Well, that all depends, Gideon. Please sit." Waller gestured toward the remaining open chair at the opposite side of the stainless-steel table.

"Yesterday, I gave you option A, conviction leading to jail." He looked around the small cell and chuckled. "And today, I present to you option B."

"Option B?" Gideon repeated.

"Gideon, what you found and attempted to post is, let's just say, a big fuckin' deal. I will not, and cannot, provide any more information than that. The fact that you were able to detect, boost, and then locate the signal, especially from Green Bank, was impressive. Not many have done that. But the fact that you were able to recognize what it represents, now *that*"—Waller pointed a finger right at him—"was astounding. Because of this, we had t—"

"Who are *we*?" Gideon blurted.

"The United States government, Gideon. That is who I represent. Because you are clearly capable of deciphering and understanding more about this … situation. I, and a panel of individuals, believe you could become a valuable asset to the project. Thus, option B is that you join us in an effort to learn more about this signal. You will inform your friends, colleagues, and family that you were offered a job at the Department of Defense and will be working on confidential communication methods for the navy. You will then be placed under strict supervision while you work for us, and all of your outside communication will be monitored."

The man's facial expression remained unchanged as he looked at Gideon in silence. Mind swimming and unsure how to reply, Gideon slowly worked out the words. "Wait a minute," said Gideon, scratching his head, "if you had this option the whole time, why let me spend the night in jail?"

Waller gave a sigh. "We're shooting from the hip, Gideon. As of last night, there was no option B. We needed you contained so you couldn't recklessly post any more of your data for the world to see. I made some phone calls to the Pentagon last night."

"OK," Gideon replied flatly, feeling the pain in his shoulder from the less-than-sleep-worthy mattress.

Waller only shrugged. "What's it going to be?"

"I guess … I'll take the job. Right? Like you're literally giving me two options? Jail or work for the government on some type of foreign signal detection?"

"I am happy about your enthusiasm, Gideon, but please take a moment to realize that, although it seems like option B is a much better alternative, this decision *will* alter your life indefinitely."

He looked at Gideon as if he expected him to grasp everything that was to come.

"Understood. I accept ... What happens now?"

"First of all, you will have to sign several documents." The man opened the briefcase and produced a very large stack of papers. "And then undergo training on secret clearance while we establish your new position—do you want me to go over each of these in detail?" Waller checked his watch.

Gideon hesitated, assessing the size of the stacked papers in front of him, wondering what more to expect. Was this all? He nodded his head. "Yes. Doesn't sound like I have much choice, but I want to understand all the details. And ..." Gideon lifted his hands cuffed together.

"Officer!" called Waller. And after a few moments, the same officer moseyed into the room.

With a nod from Waller, he walked up and uncuffed him. Gideon rubbed his wrists.

"That will be all, please leave us," Waller said. The officer gave Gideon a hard stare, and then left the cell.

Waller placed a pen in front of him, then explained what to anticipate in his new role and life, going over each document. The process took over an hour and Gideon committed each spoken word to memory. Once the papers were signed, Waller gathered them up crisply, put them into his case, closed and locked it, and stood.

"Great, we will be in touch very shortly. Thanks for your time, Gideon," Waller said, leaving Gideon in the interrogation room by himself.

Following Waller's departure, the silence pressed down on him. Gideon had always preferred quiet, it allowed him to think more clearly. But now, the silence was torturous, as if forcing him to try and think about something he did not understand. Now that he knew the US government was in on the signal, he was less concerned about its origin and purpose and more concerned with how it was going to affect him personally. Why the secrecy? He couldn't piece together what technology could be contained in this signal that was so proprietary that they would go through this kind of effort to stop it from being found. He wondered if this was some type of cybersecurity attack on the United States. Terrorism? Muted minutes rolled on and on. Gideon lost track of time.

Voices could be heard again and sounded like the state trooper that had originally arrested him. He could also make out the voice of Waller. Gideon closed his eyes, focusing on deciphering the words coming through the room's walls.

"Mr. Waller, I am understandin' that you work for the F-B-I, but I am not understandin' how you can have the authorization to remove a potential murder suspect from holdin'? Not none of this agrees with protocol round here."

"You have the documentation and I assure you this is, in fact, strictly following protocol. He is a national security threat and is wanted back in his home country. We will take him back to DC for questioning, and then deport him to Israel. This discussion ends here. If you continue to resist, I will cite you for inhibiting a government operation."

"I'll be followin' up with you," the trooper grunted.

"That is fine."

The door opened and Gideon pretended to be occupied rubbing his wrists. The trooper, face red with beads of sweat forming on his brow, strode into the room.

"Hands," he shouted as he removed the cuffs from his black belt. In a series of powerful yet elegant moves, the trooper had Gideon's hands once again cuffed behind his back before he had time to react. Gideon grunted, not expecting this.

"Piece of shit, I hope they get yah good," the trooper breathed in his ear, smelling of booze and Kodiak.

Gideon looked to Waller, who gave a small nod, indicating for Gideon to play along. There didn't seem to be much choice.

The three men walked into the parking lot, Gideon directed from behind by the trooper. The sun was just starting to rise into the cold air. Though the circumstances were far from ideal, being outside was a welcomed sensation, hearing the birds singing and morning traffic beginning—as if nothing had changed.

His enjoyment was quickly cut off as he was roughly pushed into the back seat of a black Mercedes. Waller slammed the door so hard behind him that Gideon's ears popped from the pulse of pressure.

After a few last heated words with the trooper, Waller smoothly moved into the driver's seat, gracefully sending his briefcase into the passenger seat simultaneously. The interior of the car was immaculate. Small details led Gideon to believe the car was a personal car rather than a government-assigned vehicle. Stuffed into the backseat pocket was the top of a magazine, a travel brochure, and a Chinese restaurant menu. It lacked the safety precautions found in squad cars, which Gideon was now all too familiar with.

Waller's car had no screen separating him from the driver. There were door handles on the inside, and he assumed the windows rolled down, although with his hands still cuffed, he was unable to validate that assumption.

Without saying a word or even acknowledging that Gideon was sitting in the back seat of his car, Waller accelerated, clearly knowing exactly where and what the next phase of this process would be.

Chapter 8

The digital alarm clock jerked Gideon from his sleep. His blurry eyes did not check the time, as he had been required to wake at 6:00 AM for the last four days. Lifting himself from the bed, he made his way to the plastic set of drawers, the only other piece of furniture in the minimalistic room, besides the twin bed and small plastic nightstand. Gideon mused at the fact that most people would consider this a poorly furnished room. But to him it had all the required necessities.

    Dressing in the clothes provided in the drawers upon his arrival, Gideon checked himself in the mirror. The snug-fitting white collared shirt and light brown khaki pants looked as uninteresting as they had the day before. It felt surreal. Just several days before he had been working in an outdated computer lab at an observatory most people had never heard of. Now, after a night in a jail cell, he stood in a small room within the heart of the Pentagon, stripped of all personal identity, with only a temporary badge displaying an ID number and an unflattering picture of his tired face. He checked his standard-issue mobile device, his own was confiscated, along with all other personal items, but per usual there was nothing besides the calendar reminders that helped him track his busy day.

After leaving the state trooper's station back in West Virginia, Waller had taken Gideon to his home to retrieve his laptop and information regarding the signal, which he was required to turn over along with all personal belongings. Gideon had desperately tried to retrieve his copper washer, which he had not left behind since his brother's accident. He was met with a wrath from Waller he hoped to never see again. Watching them place it into a clear ziplock bag gave him more anxiety than he had experienced throughout this entire process. When they left the house there was a group of four men waiting outside with several cans of paint, some large pieces of electrical equipment and other miscellaneous items. Gideon assumed they would turn the house upside down looking for anything left behind and prep the house to be turned back over to the owners.

On the drive to DC, Waller explained a bit more about what to expect, but would not provide any more information on the signal and its relevance. Upon arrival at the Pentagon, Gideon was required to complete a series of scripted calls and texts to inform family and friends of his new job. This job, an alias of course, was supposed to be at the Department of Defense in which he would be working on confidential communication methods for the navy. He explained that it would be a month or two of security clearance in which he would not have access to public communication.

His mother hadn't shown much interest and just made some jokes that if he kept moving around so much, people would start to assume he was homeless. She asked when she'd see him again to which Gideon replied, "I don't know."

A loud knock on his door regained his attention. He checked his watch.

"Yup, 6:30 a.m., right on time," Gideon said under his breath.

After inhaling a deep breath, he opened the door.

"Morning, Gid," said Adam Fangman, a large, redheaded man who was Gideon's "facility escort," and accompanied him at all times.

Gideon forced a smile but failed to make eye contact.

They walked shoulder to shoulder without exchanging a word. Although similar in height, Adam probably had eighty pounds on Gideon, resembling a mountain man who had been trapped in a suit and tie. Once he had a cup of coffee, Gideon checked the emailed itinerary of his day. Similar to his last few days—a series of training sessions from 7 a.m. until 6 p.m. But today he noticed a meeting set with Waller, whom Gideon had not seen since the day after he met him.

Most trainings consisted of how to handle classified information, use software, and follow protocol commonly utilized within US government organizations, along with information concerning what his life would now be like.

After leaving his press deflection training, he and Adam headed to Waller's office. Gideon walked through the door, but for the first time in the last four days, Adam did not follow. Sometimes Gideon actually felt bad for Adam. Though he occasionally tinkered on his phone, Adam sat through every boring meeting with Gideon.

Waller's office had more decor than anything Gideon had seen inside the building so far. It revealed a space that had been occupied by the same person for many years. Although tidy, the numerous awards, letters, and other small mementos throughout the room made it feel cluttered. After presenting an awkward smile, Gideon took a seat.

"How have you been doing, Gideon?"

"Well, so far all training pretty much just seems like common sense with a few technical details."

Waller smiled. "Yeah, I wouldn't wish that training on my worst enemies. Glad you're making it through everything. Unfortunately, time isn't on our side."

"When will I understand why that is?" Gideon's voice rose slightly.

The signal had not been mentioned once since his first day in the Pentagon, where he was questioned about his findings, resources, and technical questions regarding the blog he posted. After the interrogation, Gideon was ordered not to talk about the signal to anyone, as the information was highly classified, even from most people within this facility.

"Soon, Gideon. Your discretion is of the utmost importance, and I appreciate your cooperation. Once your training and background checks are complete, in what, four days now?"

"I think so."

Waller checked his phone.

"Yes, in four days you will be officially sworn in and granted top secret security clearance. You will be held under oath to keep all confidential information just that way, confidential. We will then hold a briefing with you and several others going through a similar process, to bring all of you up to speed."

"Others have detected this signal, too?"

"Some, yes. But we are primarily pulling in others for their various expertise in an array of technical fields, not because they had discovered the signal like you had."

"So, will I be meeting them?" Gideon asked.

Waller shrugged a shoulder and pouted a corner of his lips.

"Soon. The process of assembling a new team for a project such as this is challenging and does take time and patience. Many of them are undergoing the same training and background checks as you."

"How many others have picked up the signal? Did you throw all of them into jail too and threaten them with charges of murder?" Gideon wasn't sure if he was finding this amusing yet.

"Our intel tells us that a handful of other scientists have detected it. It is difficult for us to know exactly how many. That said, nobody, as far as we know, has been able to decipher the signal like you did and therefore didn't pose much of a threat leaking anything that would catch the public's attention. What you were able to figure out in such a short amount of time with limited resources was pretty astounding. My team still doesn't understand how you did it and is hesitant to believe you were working alone … I, however, believe you did. An impressive mind you have there, kid."

Gideon thought about the mass of writing that had decorated the walls of his last home, the data that his macro-program had uncovered. He wondered what other secrets lay in the details that he had not had time to uncover.

"Will I be getting my data back? I want another chance, there must be more there."

Waller smiled.

"That time will come, trust me. You will be in the middle of this whole thing very soon."

"Can you at least confirm who is responsible for the signal? Is it US or foreign?"

Waller sighed. "Gideon, you are persistent, I'll give you that. Your question is *the* question we are all trying to figure out. But there are a couple things you need to understand. First, the US government is not in control of this situation. If we were, you wouldn't be here. You're on the inside of something with lots of question marks. This is uncharted territory for us; we are creating new protocols every day and digging up old ones some of us didn't even know existed. This operation has two very important factors: confidentiality and getting answers quickly."

Gideon nodded. Waller's face was serious, and Gideon could tell he wanted to say more but there were obviously restrictions keeping him from telling Gideon too much.

"This isn't the first time the government has had to deal with something like this before?" Gideon asked. "Like after 9/11 when you had to create the entire Department of Homeland Security and the Patriot Act, what makes this unique to that?"

Waller grimaced. "Yes, but there was a lot of work that went on behind the scenes from what you saw on the news. This is—" He paused and looked around. He looked like he wanted to say more. "I'm just saying this could be a far more complex situation than 9/11 and it's the unknown that is causing the highest levels of concern."

Waller paused and held up two fingers.

"And secondly, you're working with the federal government now. Things take time and patience. We have to get politicians to work with private sector experts. We have to get major institutions to play nice with each other, share information. And we have to do all of this without providing details into what it is we are actually working on. As you can imagine, this is proving to be vastly more difficult than we imagined."

Gideon thought long and hard; he was frustrated that Waller seemed more concerned, or at least more willing to share the details of political and policy changes than he was the science.

"I have one last question," Gideon said.

"You are a kid with many of those, I am learning," Waller said and Gideon felt himself blush.

"Once I do get my data back and I am allowed to start working on this … project. Will I get my personal belongings back?"

"No, Gideon, your phone and laptop will not be returned. But if you need data from them, we will have a team that can transfer that to you upon your request," Waller replied.

"More specifically, there was a small copper washer …," Gideon said, in a quiet voice.

Waller gave Gideon a puzzled look.

"What is up with you and that damn washer?" Waller asked.

"The day of my brother's accident, I flew home. They had already cleared out the garage and pretty much everything in it. But I found the copper washer from the oil drain bolt lying in the middle of the floor. I'm pretty sure it was the last thing my brother ever touched, and I have kept it with me ever since. It helps me think and find clarity in my thoughts." Gideon felt a small lump in his throat.

Waller paused, thinking for a moment.

"Yes, Gideon, we will get that back to you."

Chapter 9

The conference room had a lofty air to it, as if only the most serious of business was conducted there. The long table that ran through the middle of the room was immaculately clean, glistening under the bright overhead lights. The air-conditioning was set cooler than Gideon thought it should be, and the crisp room became even colder with each frigid breath he took. It looked more bare and grim than any room he'd ever been in, completely empty besides the table, chairs, and the handful of people sitting in them. As Gideon thought about it, he supposed it made sense in a way: a cold, bare room for serious times and dire discussions.

The space contained seven people, including Gideon. Most noticeably was the man at the front, standing while his dark eyes scanned the room with intention. Gideon felt as though he recognized him but couldn't place a finger on why. The tall man had a broad chest, and his meaty neck was as wide as his head. His short gray hair was nearly nonexistent on the sides and grew to only a short buzz cut on the top. Based on his iron-pressed dark green suit, heavily decorated with medals and rank insignia, it was clear the man's involvement was military, not science.

To Gideon's right sat a man and a woman, each wearing the same white shirt and khaki pants, leading to his assumption they were there under the same conditions as himself. The man was short and had a darker complexion. The woman had thick, shoulder-length hair, brown and a little frizzy. Several silver curls were sprinkled throughout.

All three of them exchanged glances. They seemingly were suspicious of Gideon just as he was of them. Gideon wanted to introduce himself, hoping to learn from his colleagues. However, the tone of the room told him this was not appropriate.

Directly to his left, per usual, was Adam Fangman, who still monitored Gideon closely even after being sworn in. Gideon made note that the other two did not appear to have a security guard watching their every move.

Across the table sat Waller, who nodded in his direction. Somehow the simple gesture settled Gideon's nerves. The man in the military suit clapped his hands together hard to gain the attention of the room. Gideon noticed the skin wrapping his thick fingers was weathered and rough, resembling the hands of a mechanic or other labor trade.

"Welcome, I am General John Higgens." The booming voice matched his masculine features.

"I flew in overnight from a secure location that you will soon be very familiar with. You are all here because of certain circumstances and you have been given the chance to work in conjunction with a very special team. The unprecedented nature of why we are here today has forced us into some—unusual recruitment practices. The specific nature of who you are and how you became a part of this team does not matter at this point. Time is of the essence. You will have plenty of time to get to know one another in the near future. So, please, pay attention and we'll make the most of our time today. I oversee Operation SD: Signal Decipher, code-named San Diego."

Higgens cleared his throat and continued.

"On June 13, a United States Navy surveillance submarine, the USS *Dark Water*, picked up an unexpected signal. This signal was immediately classified as a URF, unregulated frequency. After logging it, our team confirmed it as artificial in nature, meaning not your typical space noise. Furthermore, our team was able to show that the URF was originating from a location within our solar system. Whoever is producing the URF is using advanced technologies and does not have any registration with the Federal Communications Commission or the National Telecommunications and Information Administration to broadcast within the discovered frequencies, which automatically makes this a highly classified objective and an escalated priority for the US government. A team of radio frequency engineers has worked diligently to intercept and decode the signal. We were unsuccessful in understanding the meaning or communicating with the URF. That is, until Mr. Haas, here"—he gestured toward Gideon—"got involved independently and recognized the pattern as a representation of molecular properties of elements."

Gideon was surprised to hear his name mentioned and sat up straighter in his chair.

"Now, we are calling the origin point of this signal, X0-5. We have not been able to confirm *what* X0-5 is but hypothesize it to be some type of spacecraft or probe. What is very startling, is that X0-5 is not moving away from us, as you would expect with any craft launched from Earth. Its location, in fact, is in a massive geosynchronous orbit with Earth meaning it appears stationary from our orientation."

Gideon felt a sense of pride that he had correctly determined this back at Green Bank.

"For those of you unfamiliar with geosynchronous orbits, they only occur naturally at thirty-six thousand kilometers from Earth where they are in perfect balance of the Earth's gravitational pull and orbital velocity. The orbit we are seeing is just past the Asteroid Belt, a region of asteroids in our solar system over 650 million kilometers from Earth."

The general paused, then spoke his next sentence with slow staccato, emphasizing every word.

"This means that X0-5 must be utilizing *constant thrust* to keep its location steady."

An outrageous amount of thrust, Gideon's thoughts responded.

"No known spacecrafts or probes of the United States, NASA, or any other known missions across the globe have come close to the thrust ability it would take to travel out to the Asteroid Belt and then change its trajectory from moving away from Earth to a geosynchronous orbit around Earth. An orbit like this does not happen naturally, as Earth's gravitational pull on an object that far away is negligible."

Everyone shifted uncomfortably in their seats.

"The possibility that another country or company could have developed this technology and launched it into space, completely undetected for its entire journey, is highly concerning and seemingly implausible. With the ambiguity surrounding Operation SD, we have an executive order from the president of the United States to bring in a much wider range of professionals, which is why this team sits here today. You all are here to bring in fresh minds specializing in radio frequency, astrophysicists and linguists."

There was another stir in the room after the word *linguists*.

"No, we are not looking for ET out there, but per protocol, we will be prepared for anything that could come our way."

Anything, thought Gideon, as his mind reverted back to the plausible explanations he had written across the walls of his Airbnb. One of which was exactly that: "ET," an intelligent being, not from Earth.

The words hung in the air like a thick fog. Everyone sat frozen this time, digesting Higgens's words, trying to logically conclude what the implication could mean. Trying to process.

Higgens went on to explain, for the next thirty minutes, the overall goals of what they were trying to do. He went over all data expressing what the government had already done, had already tried to do and was currently trying. It became clear to Gideon why he was involved; most of the data was directly from his very own findings.

"We must reach a conclusion soon, and that means we need facts. X0-5 is too far away to observe with telescopes, so we must find a way to prove what it is, where it's coming from, and what its purpose is. Then, we must find a way to interfere or communicate with it. We need answers and we need them now."

"Your first assignment"—Higgens put down his notes and looked at each of them—"is to provide logical explanations to this mess of chaos. We currently have over seventeen different committees going in a variety of different directions. We need to start with getting some outside eyes, your eyes, on all the data and providing a clear path forward. We are confident you can come up with some solutions or at least some theories. But we cannot waste time on fanciful options. We're not looking for creativity. We're looking for solid solutions from hard data. If we detect you are wasting time, you will be cut from the program."

 Gideon swallowed.

Chapter 10

The Gulfstream IV ascended steeply into the morning sky. The day was clear and presented an incredible view of DC. The rising sun danced across the water of the Lincoln Memorial Reflecting Pool. Gideon leaned forward, expanding his view out the window, watching the ground slowly pass by. The Washington Monument cast a long shadow on the green grass. He could just make out the city's early risers heading out on their morning jogs and errands.

The interior of the small jet was elegantly upholstered but surprisingly worn. The walls were an off-white with dark wooden borders throughout. It contained ten navy blue leather seats, all with the ability to swivel 180 degrees to face toward or away from each other. Seven of the ten seats were filled, including the two other individuals Gideon recognized from yesterday's briefing, plus Waller, a security officer, and two men near the front who had been engaged in a deep conversation since the beginning of the flight.

The jet leveled out and set course for San Antonio. After yesterday's meeting, the team was notified they would be leaving the next day for Lackland Air Force Base in Texas, home of Operation SD.

Waller swiveled his seat to face Gideon and the man and woman, gesturing for them to turn toward him.

"So, tell me," said Waller with a grin. "How does it feel?"

Gideon sat there in silence for a moment, not sure what Waller was talking about nor how to respond. A quick glance at the man and woman next to him told him they were just as puzzled.

Waller winked. "Don't worry, it's a compliment. What the three of you are involved in now is one of the most high-profile projects the US is working on. Consequently, your government saw fit to assemble a select group of exceptional civilians for this task. And guess what? That group is none other than you, my friends."

Gideon and the two others glanced around at one another.

Gideon wondered how his two new colleagues felt about all this. He himself was surprised, proud, and just a little bit scared. There was a feeling of pressure and responsibility on his shoulders. The US government was taking a chance on him, expecting results. But what if he wasn't as helpful as they thought he'd be? What if he let his entire country down?

Gideon looked around. "But there are more of us, right?"

Waller nodded. "Well, yes and no. There are plenty more government staff working on this, yes. But as far as the outside experts, you're it. And to be quite honest, the other experts and leaders in this field who have already been working with the government are not exactly excited to see three outsiders come in and get all this access."

"What do you mean?" Gideon asked, quickly feeling uncomfortable as a person who didn't particularly enjoy conflict.

"People have been working around the clock, trying to make progress. Bringing in new people can give the impression they failed." Waller paused and then held up a hand. "That is why we have a chain of command in place. You three need to do your thing. Don't worry about anything else. I'll handle all of that."

"What about the others?" the woman asked. "I was under the impression there were others in the private sector who had detected the signal and were involved."

"About that." Waller looked down. "Let's just say not everyone passed the background check if you know what I mean. We do have other civilians working on different levels, but it is safe to say that you three are the best of the best. Congratulations." He held out his hands.

The three looked at one another. The woman nodded.

"I'd pop a bottle of champagne for you if I had one." Waller was chuckling.

"But that might give you the wrong idea. Consider yourselves special, but not lucky. It's not all going to be fun and games. Your lives, as you know them, are over. And that can be good or bad, depending on how you see it. But your new lives"—Waller cleared his throat—"are all that matter now. And you're really living for something now. Something bigger than yourself. Something more important than the very air you breathe."

"And, what's that?" Gideon dared, regretting it as soon as the words left his mouth.

But Waller only shrugged.

"Ensuring the safety of humanity."

Gideon and the two others nodded.

"Good. I have a folder for each of you. Most of each folder contains identical information. This information, of course, is highly confidential and for your eyes only. Packet A gives a summary of Higgens's briefing yesterday and contains a link to the audio file if you would like to listen to it again. Packet B highlights all additional data that we know at this time. It may be overwhelming at first, and admittedly we don't know what everything means within the data. That is why you are here. Packet C gives details of your own personal objectives, ID numbers, living quarters, etcetera. Finally, the appendix in the back gives you details of all team members currently working on Operation SD. This information has also been sent to the email address that has been assigned to you and can be found in packet C."

Gideon thumbed through the immense folder, slightly amused that it really did have a big red *Top Secret* watermark across every page, just like in the movies. Reaching the back of the packet, he noticed the long list of names; at least one hundred people were assigned.

"More people than I was expecting," he remarked.

"Like I said, lots of people are involved but there are many different levels. You three are at the top level. You will have access to all the data you need but we are keeping it compartmentalized so no one person has access to everything. This is a strategy we use on top secret programs to limit the possibility of a whistleblower."

"So, that means we'll be working in silos?" Gideon asked.

"No, as I said, compartmentalizing. You three will have access to essentially whatever you need. Everyone else, not so much. Intel leakage and operational security are our top priorities here. As mentioned yesterday, we are in a serious time crunch to make sense of all this. President Helland is not going to support keeping this from the public much longer; she is ready to pull the trigger on informing SETI and UNOOSA, per established protocol. Once that happens, this investigation goes public, spawning organizations specializing in the search for extraterrestrial life … well I'll let you use your imagination on how that'd work out in the public arena. That said, Higgens and I will continue to throw people and resources at this until we can get an understanding of what we're dealing with. We'll be landing in about two hours. Get to work." He nodded at the packets.

"Oh and, Gideon," Waller said.

Gideon looked up and saw Waller reach into his chest shirt pocket and pull out a small flat object, flicking it off his thumb in Gideon's direction, like flipping a coin. Gideon caught it and felt a sense of ease come over him as he saw the small copper washer, now resting in his palm.

"Thanks," Gideon said with a nod. The other two scientists looked puzzled by what had just happened. Waller simply nodded, rose from his seat and took another near the front of the aircraft. Gideon turned back toward the others and made an attempt at a confident smile, but his face did something different. Fortunately, the others looked equally uncomfortable.

"I'm Gideon," he finally said.

After twice speaking over each other and then immediately stopping, the man gave his name.

"Rajit, originally from India, but I've been living in Tennessee the last six years." His warm smile immediately gave Gideon a feeling of trust.

Rajit was a shorter man with a round face, no more than five foot six. His black tight-fitting jeans gave his legs an unusually thin look in relation to his relatively pear-shaped upper half. His jet-black hair was deliberately parted and combed with what seemed like an excessive amount of gel. He wore a large gold watch on his left wrist.

The woman spoke next. "Linda, grew up in LA; I work as a linguist professor at Stanford." Linda carried a very professional demeanor. Her wavy dark brown hair was thick and wiry, held up on one side with a bobby pin and revealing her prominent cheekbones. Her skin was lighter than Gideon would have expected from someone who lived in California and her frame was thin.

Both Gideon and Rajit perked up.

"So, you're the linguist … what do you take from all this?" Gideon asked. "Do you really think people could be considering this to be nonhuman in origin?"

Gideon noticed Rajit shift uncomfortably in his seat and shift his gaze to the window.

Linda shrugged. "My job, I suspect, won't be to determine whether this is or is not a nonhuman. But if it is, I would imagine my role would be learning how to communicate with the being, assuming that it does not know any Earth languages." Linda paused, clearly deep in thought.

"Which I must say, is pretty hard to wrap my head around. And I suppose, Gideon, if I did have to take a guess on whether I think people really are considering that this could be nonhuman in origin, I would have to say yes. If not, I'm not sure they would be spending the money and resources to fly me on this ridiculous private jet to a military base." She paused again.

Gideon appreciated that she spoke slowly, carefully choosing her words. Fitting for a linguist.

"Waller has made it clear, however, that no contact has been made. So, Gideon, I think that's your role, right? Where are you from?" Linda shifted her gaze in his direction.

Gideon explained his history and how he had detected the URF from Green Bank Observatory. Both showed intense interest.

Rajit spoke up next. "Last couple years I've been performing research at Vanderbilt University—"

"Wait a minute," Gideon interrupted. "Aren't you the one who was awarded the recent Nobel Prize in Physics? For the ...what was it again?"

Rajit's light brown face flushed a shade of red. "Yes, I've been conducting research in theoretical physics and its effects on organic matter for many years. I actually started the research in India, seeing if I could take Dewey Larson's material further, trying to understand gravity and what we are calling 'n' dimensions. The Nobel was awarded for my paper regarding the kinetic theory of matter."

Gideon and Linda sat in silence for a few minutes, digesting this as Rajit tried to explain the basics of his research.

"What about you, Linda?" Gideon shifted the conversation after Rajit had clearly lost momentum in getting them to understand the influence of a vacuum on antigenic particles.

"Well, I haven't won any Nobel Prizes, that's for sure." Linda smiled. "As I mentioned, I'm a professor, but really just in my spare time in order to keep my research privileges at Stanford. My primary goal is to understand and find ways to teach languages to non-speaking persons. These could be individuals who don't speak because of mental limitations or those who have never been introduced to modern language, which you may be surprised is more common than you may think."

"A linguist—how many languages do you speak?" Rajit asked. "Hindi, by any chance?"

"Haan, main hindee bolata hoon, kya app?" Linda replied with a bit of a smug smile.

Rajit laughed in delight. "Hann!"

"I speak thirty-seven different languages fluently; I've studied them my whole life. It's funny, since I was a little kid, I was fascinated by all the different ways people and even animals communicate with one another. Now, I travel around the world decoding and learning about Indigenous languages and communication. I've been creating automated programs for teaching language with a new technique engaging the subconscious mind, just as children learn. Similar to the way I first learned when I grew up in Brazil as a missionary kid, mastering English and Portuguese by the time I was four." Linda smiled. "The method is pretty straightforward, but it's been challenging creating a learning program effective for everyone."

Rajit rubbed his chin in an animated fashion.

"Out of curiosity, where do your grants come from? Finding the money to conduct research is one of the hardest parts, and from what I've heard, linguistics is a sector that is struggling."

Linda paused for a few seconds.

"Well, perhaps that is the most interesting part. About five years back, I was approached by a member of DARPA. They as—"

"Sorry, but who … what is DARPA?" Gideon asked.

"DARPA, or the Defense Advanced Research Projects Agency, is a division of the Department of Defense that conducts advanced research and development projects, including some related to space exploration and technology that could have implications for detecting or communicating with extraterrestrial civilizations."

Linda paused, collecting her thoughts. Again, Rajit seemed to be uncomfortable at the mention of extraterrestrials.

"As I was saying, a representative from DARPA contacted me asking if I would accept a grant from DARPA under certain conditions. I was, of course, confused at first. Why would a division of our government, military at that, care about my linguistics work? Well, long story short, they wanted to provide a large grant in exchange for a signed retainer stating that in the event of contact with intelligent life outside of our planet, I would support efforts by establishing contact using what I had gained from my research."

Gideon and Rajit digested this information. The Department of Defense had a linguist on retainer? Was the possibility of this being alien actually being considered?

"Do you … really think that's why you're here? Because DARPA wants to use your linguistics research?" Rajit said quietly, almost as if he didn't want anyone else on the small aircraft to hear.

"I don't know. I asked Waller if this was related to that agreement I signed, and he said no. But I would have to imagine that is how they got my name and involved me into this project."

Conversations flowed for some time, and Gideon was surprised when his brain's dorsal stream let him know that the plane had begun to descend. Waller looked back and tapped the seat belt across his waist. Gideon and the team took the hint and clipped their belts as they dove through the intermittent fluffy clouds. Looking out the window, he was surprised by the amount of green that surrounded the suburbs of San Antonio. As they cleared the clouds, the airplane banked to the right, and Gideon could see what he assumed was Lackland Air Force Base. A spike of adrenaline hit his nervous system.

Chapter 11

Crickets began their symphony as darkness engulfed the air force base. Gideon walked next to Rajit, confirming his short stature. They had been placed just two doors apart in their sleeping quarters.

Their assigned rooms were similar to those in the Pentagon. Each had a twin spring mattress with white linens, and a small bedside stand with a lamp and digital alarm clock.

"Warm out here," Rajit said.

"No kidding. This is my first time in Texas, actually." Gideon smiled. "Although, this can't be too bad compared to India …"

Rajit laughed.

"I think this heat would even put New Delhi to shame," Rajit joked. Even though the air temperature had cooled to the mid-eighties, the heat could still be felt radiating off the blacktop they walked across.

"Do you have a family?" Gideon asked.

Rajit seemed to bow his head a little and then lifted it again, shaking side to side.

"No, I was supposed to be in an arranged marriage; that's how things are done in India, but I got cold feet the day before and left for the city. This was taken as a huge disgrace and got me expelled from the family. I've only recently begun talking with my father again. I think that is why I got so submerged in academics; it was an escape for me. How about yourself?"

"No … not even a thought of marriage … so I suppose you're technically ahead of me." Gideon winked. "Hey, maybe some single ladies on this adventure?"

Rajit blushed and chuckled. "I always did want to go to the YMCA summer camps. Maybe I need to start looking at this thing a different way."

They both laughed before noticing the guard tailing them. They were immediately impressed with the seriousness of the situation again. After arriving at the base, with the exception of being inside his room, there was always a security officer, fully armed with what looked like an M-16 and a combat helmet, within eyesight.

A figure, slightly silhouetted in the darkness by the fluorescent white light from one of the nearby buildings, walked toward them.

"Gideon? Rajit?" a woman's voice called out. Gideon lifted his hand and waved as Linda joined them, looking uneasy.

"Headed to the mess hall?" she asked. Gideon and Rajit nodded.

Once they had gotten settled in at the base, the group had been escorted to a conference room where they were briefed on the protocol of Lackland Air Force Base. One of the rules was they were not allowed to leave the base without an escort, which meant strictly enjoying the widely acclaimed excellence of the base's "mess hall," or cafeteria.

After dishing himself some refried beans, slightly wilted Caesar salad, and a bowl of chili, which seemed a bit redundant with his refried beans, Gideon followed Rajit and Linda to one of the metal tables. Linda had chosen to fill both her plates with salad, and after giving the chili a second look, he figured that would have been the safer option.

"So, Linda, Rajit here was almost married and I haven't been lucky enough yet to come close," said Gideon with a laugh. "How about you? Married? Any kids?"

Linda speared her fork through a wilted lettuce leaf. "Yes, and yes. I met my wife when I studied in Ecuador; we fell in love right away, but it took us years to act on it. She moved up to LA just seven years ago and we got married the day she arrived."

"And you said you have kids as well?" Gideon asked her.

"Do dogs count?"

"Oh, absolutely," said Rajit, and Gideon nodded in agreement.

Linda chuckled.

"Well, we have a daughter named Matilda, and I've got two rotties: Roxy and Bear." A solemn look passed over her face, as if maybe she was considering, for the first time since she'd gotten into this top secret affair, that she might not see them for a very long time.

"Wow, rottweilers," said Gideon.

"Big, scary dogs!" Rajit added.

Linda sucked her teeth. "They're both big babies, wouldn't hurt a fly. They only look scary, trust me."

"At least they look the part," said Gideon, eyeing his chili and noticing it looked more questionable the more he examined it. "A nice deterrent if anyone thinks about breaking in."

"Yeah, and if anyone did, Roxy and Bear would probably lick them to death," said Linda.

The three shared a laugh.

"So, Gideon, tell me what made you notice this particular signal? What made it classified as a URF, as they are calling it?" Linda asked.

"For me, it was really three things. Firstly, the signal is narrowband; second—"

"I'm a linguist, Gideon, I need you to make me understand why these things are important … pretend I know nothing about radio frequencies."

Gideon's face flushed, but he continued. "Well, narrowband is very interesting because it almost definitely rules out that it comes from a natural source. For instance, typical space noise coming from natural sources like stars, black holes, and other cosmic phenomena produces a large range of frequencies. However, artificial or 'man-made' technology has allowed us to be able to produce and send data on very narrow frequency ranges. A great example of this is radio stations." Gideon took a bite of chili.

"So basically, natural frequencies are more sporadic and irregular compared to artificial sources?" Rajit asked.

"Essentially, yes. So, when I picked this signal up and saw it was running in an incredibly narrow frequency range, it piqued my interest." Gideon paused to ensure Rajit and Linda were following along. Linda's fork, still loaded with some sagging lettuce, hadn't moved since he started talking; he figured this was an indication of her engagement.

"I was able to tell, through some refinement and creative computer algorithms, that the signal was not local. Now getting the exact location of where something is coming from requires triangulation, but I was able to use some techniques to determine a rough approximation of location and distance, which revealed two things: A—it is not coming from a planetary body and is just outside the Asteroid Belt; and B—it appears to be in geosynchronous orbit, meaning its orientation to the Earth's surface is not changing. This is huge, as literally nothing is in geosynchronous orbit relative to Earth that far away. There was no way this was a natural phenomenon."

"Don't we have tons of satellites in geosynchronous orbit?" Linda teased herself with the first bite of salad.

"Absolutely, a great example is satellite television or the Internet. That is how we are able to point the dish mounted on your house directly at the specific satellite in the sky and it never needs to move. However, those satellites accomplish this by finding the perfect balance between speed and distance from Earth. As Higgens mentioned, this can only happen, without external thrust, at about thirty-six thousand kilometers. For something roughly 630 million kilometers away to pull this off … I can't even comprehend the amount of thrust that would require." Gideon put his spoon down.

"At least 2.27 million newtons of continuous thrust, not to mention, it would be traveling at 45,800,000 meters per second, which is over 15% the speed of light… more than two hundred times faster than any spacecraft we've ever built," Rajit added. "I ran some quick calculations. Obviously, I had to make an array of assumptions, like the mass of the signal-producing object — er, X0-5. I'm still getting used to these names. That amount of thrust and speed is just unheard of. Back in the early 2000s, NASA prototyped a rocket capable of nearly 9 million newtons of thrust, the highest number mankind has ever achieved, as far as I know. Although that's more than X0-5, it was only for a very short duration. X0-5 is utilizing continuous thrust, meaning it needs to produce that much force the entire time, not just a short burst like the rockets we launch. The amount of fuel alone… it doesn't add up." Rajit's brows furrowed.

"There must be some other explanation, right?" Linda asked.

Gideon shook his head slowly. "That is all I have been able to think about, Linda. I've only been able to come up with two plausible theories: either it's human technology that was kept a secret for decades, or, as crazy as it sounds, extraterrestrial." Gideon still experienced a zing of shock every time the words "extraterrestrial" were spoken.

The group of three sat in silence for a moment, thinking.

"Hard to fathom, an intelligent species that likely developed with a completely different set of rules," Linda said, finally biting the lettuce off her fork.

"If we can understand why and how X0-5 is accomplishing that orientation, it will tell us a lot," Gideon said.

"What about you, Linda? Anything new?" Rajit asked as he forked some salad into his mouth.

"Well, yes." Linda set down her fork and her eyes lit up. "Actually, the data definitely shows some strong signs of a systematic organizational structure. But there is nothing proven yet." She shrugged. "It passed all tests from the bilateral linguistics approaches and passed seventy-eight percent of all fully mathematical, psychological and sociological aspects of formalist and structuralist theory and—"

"Whoa, whoa." Gideon held up a hand. "You're going to have to break that down a bit just like you asked me to earlier. Pretend I don't know anything about linguists, which I really don't compared to you."

Linda pulled out her phone and found some notes. "Think of it this way: Our first step is to give some kind of statistical likelihood that the signal is either in the camp of structural linguistics or some other form of pattern recognition. Pattern recognition is just a relationship between stimulus and information."

"But don't we already see patterns in the signal?" Rajit asked.

"Yes, but that's what I'm saying. We have to determine if the pattern has intentional information behind it that can be decoded. Or if it is a longer, larger sample that only looks like it is intelligent. Which would place it in the Apophenia or Pareidolia theories. The problem is we need more data to confirm. We have no frame of reference right now."

"So," Rajit said, "it's kind of like trying to put together a puzzle where we have no picture on the box to see what our goal is. And all the pieces are painted solid black."

"Not only that," Linda said. "It's like we don't know if we have all the pieces or if we have parts of multiple puzzles that don't go together."

"How do you even begin that process?" Gideon asked.

"There are six primary theories of pattern recognition. And there is some hope. So far, the signal has made the most progress down the models of template matching, prototype matching and feature analysis. I'm making progress; it's just slow. It is like looking at each individual puzzle piece and calculating the probability that it could go with one of the other pieces. And you can only do that by holding it up to every single piece, one at a time."

Her eyes lit up when she found something else on her phone. "But check this out. After running a bunch of proprietary pattern detection software that Waller finally gave me access to, along with some other algorithms on the URF, I was able to decipher a pattern. It seems like there are some additional embedded patterns in the signal. We just need to figure out what they are trying to say."

All three stiffened in their seats, pushing their food around, brains clearly trying to find a logical explanation. Just as Gideon had been trying to do for the past several weeks.

Chapter 12

With Operation SD being placed at the heart of an air force base, the constant rumble of F-16s taking off for practice flights shook the small building that Gideon had spent the majority of the last couple of days in. The computer lab, which looked similar to a mobile home made out of sheet metal, had been converted into a highly confidential research center adjacent to a larger, single-floor structure—the SD headquarters.

Upon his arrival, all of his data and findings from Green Bank had been returned to him. Now armed with massive amounts of computer power, numerous other highly skilled radio frequency technicians, and the original data acquired by the navy, Gideon meticulously ran different filters to try and make sense of the URF, which was still producing the exact same frequencies since it started.

Several attempts had been made to communicate with X0-5 using the communication array on base. However, none had resulted in any change of the URF. No matter what they did, X0-5 just continued broadcasting the same message. Gideon leaned back in his chair in frustration when a bright light hit his eye, blinding him and intensifying his already pulsating headache.

Gideon leaned forward and the bright light went away. Annoyed, he looked around for the source, but the gray fabric-covered partition wall of his cubicle blocked his ability to see any of his surroundings. Looking behind him, he now saw the small patch of white light on the back wall of his cube, shifting around.

He stood and looked in the opposite direction of the light spot and noticed Rajit standing at the whiteboard, scribbling down theories. His watch, catching the sun, reflected the light directly back into Gideon's face.

"Rajit!"

Rajit looked over his shoulder.

"Your watch is killing me over here," Gideon said, half joking, half serious.

Rajit, at first puzzled until he saw the intense reflected light dancing around the room and Gideon's face, blushed slightly and removed the watch.

"Thanks," Gideon said, but he did not sit, suddenly deep in thought.

"Anything else?" Rajit tried to deduce why Gideon was blankly staring at him.

"Your … watch …," Gideon replied.

"I took it off, it's there." Rajit pointed at the large gold watch lying face down on the table next to him.

"That's it—reflection! That's the third plausible explanation. It's not an unmanned craft or an extraterrestrial signal." Gideon jumped to his feet and ran to Rajit, snatching a red dry-erase marker.

"Have you ever heard of meteor burst radio communication?" Gideon gained the attention of the room. Rajit shook his head no, but other RF engineers gave Gideon their full attention.

"Meteor burst radio communication is actually old technology, used way back in the 1960s."

"Hey now, watch what you call old; I was born in the '60s!" one of the older engineers interrupted.

"Sorry … anyway, the concept was used when needing to send a radio signal to a location far enough away that the curvature of the Earth would interfere with the direct path, or perhaps a mountain range, say from Seattle to Colorado. Instead of relaying the message through a series of tower repeaters, you can send the signal up into the meteor dust region that surrounds Earth. Due to this region's high volume of reflective particles, the radio frequency will be partially reflected back down to Earth, allowing it to reach Colorado. Just as your watch is reflecting the light of the sun to a specific location in which the sunlight can't directly reach. This technology is pretty outdated, because we now just use satellites to do the reflecting … but perhaps someone is developing a method of bouncing signals off of the Asteroid Belt instead of our Earth's smaller meteor belt?"

An older RF engineer was already working on the whiteboard, running off Gideon's concept. He looked at Gideon.

"What advantage would anyone have with bouncing signals off the Asteroid Belt? It would create a massive delay," the engineer said.

"One potential advantage could be to make contact with the dark side of planets. I read a research paper once regarding using reflection to communicate with the dark side, or radio silent, side of the moon," a thirty-something engineer named George piped up.

"I think the moon is the only celestial body that is tidally locked to Earth, correct?" Gideon asked, looking around the room. Hoping one of the astronomy experts was nearby.

"He's right; the phenomenon known as tidal locking occurs when a celestial body's rotation period is equal to its orbital period, causing the same side of the object to always face the body it is orbiting. The moon is tidally locked to Earth, which is why we always see the same face of the moon from Earth. I don't believe there are any other planets or celestial bodies that exhibit this orientation toward Earth."

"But why would you need to send a signal to the dark side of the moon? Maybe they know we aren't looking for these signals, who knows?" Gideon scratched his head. "But it's the only thing that makes sense, right? The URF is not actually originating from X0-5, but simply being reflected from that location. This explains why it would be in geosynchronous orbit; something that is pointed at the sky from a fixed location on Earth is always pointing to the same spot in relation to Earth, just as a TV satellite dish is always pointed at its associated geosynchronous satellite." Gideon looked satisfied.

"I'll get Higgens in here. Let's run with this." The older engineer capped his marker. "George, start searching for similar frequency patterns at surface-level planes. If that signal really is a reflection, then it is being sent from somewhere on Earth."

"Or a satellite," Gideon said.

"True, nice work, Gideon." The older engineer took his leave.

"And if it is a reflection …," Gideon pondered aloud. "What could it be?"

Rajit glanced over at Gideon, and the two locked eyes for a moment, their minds searching for answers. Gideon's thumb began rubbing the smooth surface of the copper washer.

"If the signal is coming from Earth …," Gideon started.

"And the United States obviously doesn't know who's responsible for it, or we wouldn't be here," Rajit picked up.

"Then that means it must be coming from another country," Gideon finished.

"Then why would another country …" Rajit trailed off, his eyes falling to the floor as he thought. "Some of the possibilities are a bit unnerving."

Gideon nodded.

The two stood there quietly for a moment, perhaps considering the gravity of the words they had spoken. Gideon's mind raced. He pondered what this could mean, what other findings might be on the horizon. Had they really just solved the root of this discovery, or was it the complete opposite? Could it be, Gideon wondered as he glanced at his colleague Rajit, that they were just getting started?

There could be so much more going on here. He wanted more answers. He wondered what was more threatening to the world: aliens or some human organization potentially communicating to the dark side of the moon or some other celestial body, potentially a secret military base that nobody else could ever see or discover. Both gave him the feeling that this could be the biggest threat to national security the United States, maybe the world, had likely ever faced.

Chapter 13

Looking out the window, Higgens noticed the heat waves rippling across the tarmac, making him relieved to be sitting in the air-conditioned conference room. He was the only one occupying the small space. His attention was drawn back as Waller's voice emerged from the phone speaker in the center of the brown laminate table. Waller and Higgens had known each other for many years, originally meeting almost twenty-five years ago. Still, over the years, the two seemed to be in a constant state of flux as to who was in charge of whom.

"I told you there was a good reason to keep Gideon engaged in the project." Waller sounded arrogant.

"I'll buy you a beer," Higgens replied only half sincerely. "What is the word now?"

"You first."

"I debriefed the MOPSD team; they have concluded that this new development has only complicated the situation. We will continue the top secret security level until we gather more information, are able to prove the theory, and locate who it is working on this technology."

The phone was silent for five full seconds. Waller always took his time to respond when he was thinking. Higgens let out an audible sigh, loud enough for Waller to hear.

"The White House isn't pleased. At least not about the amount of wasted resources and risk of exposure to hiding a secret like this …" Waller paused. "I think we are all a bit relieved, and perhaps laughing at ourselves for having thought this could be … aliens." Waller let out a gentle chuckle.

"Fuck, I hope we will look back at this shitshow and laugh someday."

"Don't you dare call my operation a shitshow, Waller," Higgens spat back.

Waller again allowed there to be an obnoxiously long pause before continuing, unapologetically.

"That said, the potential that this is a human organization escalates the potential of malintent. Not to mention how they were able to get this far without us detecting anything. From a strategic standpoint, continuing top secret is approved; we cannot afford to make any more mistakes. The White House needs answers and proof beyond doubt that meteor burst reflection is, in fact, how the URF is being produced. The main questions being asked are: Who is testing this technology, why are they testing this technology, is this technology malicious, and why has the US not pursued this ourselves?" Waller stated.

"One theory being developed is that using a reflection point far away, like the Asteroid Belt, allows you to send a signal to the 'dark side' of any planetary body," Higgens explained the illustrations that had been drawn up for him just thirty minutes before.

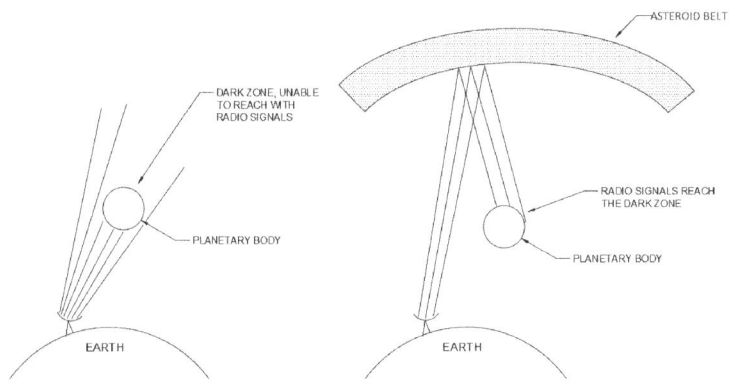

"But who and why, Higgens? Nobody has communication stations on the dark side of any planetary bodies," Waller barked through the phone.

"Not that we know of, Waller; that is what we are working to figure out. The team is running simulations to determine which planetary objects are moving between the Earth and X0-5 and rotating in a way that one side always faces Earth; currently the moon seems to be a likely option. The concern is that if someone is building a planetary base, this would give them a huge military advantage. There is nothing protecting us from strikes coming from space."

"What on Earth are you talking about? How could somebody possibly be building a fuckin' moon space base without anyone knowing?" Waller was getting frustrated by the continual barrage of what felt like far-fetched science fiction answers to this anomaly.

Higgens let out a long sigh, clearly disturbed by the same feelings.

"I don't know, Waller, but until we can find a way to disprove a theory, we have to consider it possible." Higgens paused for a moment and Waller knew there was more to come.

"Were you involved in the Alcântara Escalation?" Higgens asked, his tone more quiet than before.

"You're talking like ten or more years ago?" Waller asked.

"Yes," Higgens replied.

"No, I was never given clearance. You think they could be related?"

"Too soon to tell but during the Alcântara Escalation, the US discovered the Indian Space Research Organization or the ISRO was sending large packages to Brazil off the books. More specifically, they were sending them to Alcântara where the Brazilian Space Agency has the ability to launch rockets into orbit or beyond. We intercepted several communications between Brazilian leadership and India that indicated there was a level of pay-off and corruption happening. Long story short, Brazil launched several rockets we believed were carrying the unknown ISRO payloads. We raided Alcântara and had to work hard to keep that from becoming public but were never able to uncover the nature of what the payloads were." Higgens's face had a stern look.

"Jesus, do we have a way to see if anyone has landed something on the moon?" Waller asked.

"It's not as easy as you would think; we're working on it," Higgens replied.

Waller was silent for a moment. "Well, we will keep confidentiality high. We are not able to ask Canada, Mexico, or India for that matter, directly if they are the originators, since we are keeping this top secret. The White House has authorized you to broadcast a signal back to X0-5 with a message stating we have intercepted and must have confirmation of origin. I'll send the full details over SecuraMessage."

"Roger that," Higgens replied, glad the decision had been made to confront versus take a back seat and let the researchers run in circles.

"Anything else?"

"Nope, talk soon, no doubt." Higgens hit the red hang-up button.

After leaving the small conference room, Higgens walked into the relentless sun. Beads of sweat immediately formed on his brow. He cursed under his breath and released the top clasp of his white pressed shirt.

The walk between buildings took several minutes but felt longer. When he finally reached the mobile home of the research lab, his shirt was speckled with droplets of perspiration.

As soon as Higgens entered, the well-trained team snapped to attention. Higgens scanned the room; just his presence in the room gained everyone's diligent focus.

"Team, as you know, a recent development has produced a new theory on the URF and how it is being produced. Possibility and likelihood point toward this being a long-distance meteor burst reflection. We do not know who is responsible nor why, and that is now our primary mission. Once we are able to confirm who the originator is, then the intention of this operation will be concluded, and it will be transferred to our internal relations division of the military. With that said, we will keep all staff on site until we secure this confirmation. We have a time slot for a deep space communications antenna at Goldstone Observatory the day after tomorrow at 0130 hours to send a message back; this will be our first time authorized to use an antenna of this size. Let's hope we are able to get this message to stick. The contents of the message will be provided by our international relations department. Your main job here is to encode the message and get everything lined up for the send. Further details to come. Questions?"

Chapter 14

The energy shifted through the facility after the conclusion of Higgens's briefing on the meteor burst theory. Much of the confusion and distrust that filled the air at the beginning had begun to dissipate. People began to settle into their roles now that they understood the scope of how they could help in each of their areas of expertise.

The team became laser-focused now that there were clear objectives. First, encode a message to contact the signal originator acknowledging that the United States had intercepted it. Second, using triangulation, discover where the original source was coming from on Earth. Third, research who and what this technology was currently being used for or experimented on, and whether it could be used to contact the dark side of planetary bodies.

Gideon had been encoding all day. His primary task had been creating new code to lay the foundations for a more user-friendly interface for anyone on the team to interact with the new software that would be needed. He had just finished the UI code when he received an email from the head engineer.

"Finally," he muttered under his breath.

He had thought his colleagues back at MIT were slow in group projects, but working with government entities gave him a whole new definition of slow. Especially, for the type of project they were working on now, Gideon was shocked by the number of hoops they had to jump through and the lack of urgency from some of the stakeholders. He reminded himself that this was his first take and that most of these people were career government employees; this was probably just a typical Wednesday for them.

Gideon shook his head and pinched the bridge of his nose. Things were so much easier back in his own room, working by himself, at his own pace. When you worked alone, you didn't have to wait on anyone. And you didn't need anyone's approval.

The compartmentalization of this project and the red tape the government kept creating was astounding. It was like they were their own worst enemy, even with people being pulled together with a singular mission.

Gideon looked up from his screen, feeling confident in his encoding skills, when he noticed Rajit still sitting at his desk.

"What're you doing here, Rajit?" Gideon sat back and stretched his arms high over his head with a sigh. "Not much investigation for a materials scientist at this point, is there?" Gideon walked over. He noticed the focus and slight concern on Rajit's face.

"Well, maybe …" Rajit paused for a few moments. "After you explained the concept behind the meteor burst reflection, I wanted to better understand the physics behind it. After doing some research, I discovered that really, the radio waves are reflected from the ionized meteor trails, not the actual meteor or meteor dust. Gideon, ionized particles are created when the meteor starts to burn up by hitting our atmosphere."

Gideon already knew where this was going, and they said the last statement in unison.

"No atmosphere in the Asteroid Belt …" They both looked at each other, wondering what this meant. Before Gideon could say anything, Rajit continued.

"There are lots of compounds or elements that can reflect radio waves. But the Asteroid Belt is primarily composed of small rocky and metallic bodies, remnants from the early solar system. While some of the more distant objects may contain frozen volatiles like water or ammonia, the majority are composed of silicate rock, carbon-rich material, and metals like nickel and iron. More importantly, the overall density of these objects is extremely low, meaning the Asteroid Belt is mostly empty space. Which leads to where I am now, trying to figure out what could be reflecting the signal."

Rajit was sharp and he thought outside of the box, which made Gideon like working with him. They both had the advantage that they were not government-trained and restricted by the federal government's way of thinking. They didn't have those bad habits to unlearn, and they didn't care what others thought. They just cared about results. Making them a perfect team.

Gideon rubbed his chin and walked over to Rajit's desk, leaning in to see his screen to look at the data.

"Seems odd, doesn't it? I've reached out to a few colleagues of mine asking for more details on the gases and elements found out there, but I'm fairly confident it's not much," Rajit said. "Once I have the results, I will cross-reference them against the 104.8–105.2 GHz frequency range and see what kind of reflection we get."

"Have you notified anyone of this yet?" Gideon asked.

"Not yet; I want to better understand before coming forward with it. The last thing I want to do is show up without my i's dotted and my t's crossed, you know."

Gideon nodded his agreement.

"I should hear back from everyone by tomorrow morning. But my mind is spinning. I can't help but think of what the other possibilities could be. I mean—" Rajit rested his forehead in his palm as he put his elbow on the desk. "There is just so much going on here. Surely, someone else could have seen this too, right?"

Gideon shrugged. "Not necessarily; this is a new theory. It takes time to gather all the supporting data. I think you should bring this up, even if you don't have all the details?"

Rajit shook his head. "I don't know."

"Rajit, think about it." Gideon folded his arms. He wanted to encourage Rajit's progress. Before continuing, Gideon began to see how Rajit wasn't completely confident in his abilities. Maybe he was still too intimidated by the white coats and big-name government agencies. He had to build him up.

"You have something here; you can't sit on it. We don't have time to backtrack and if you have something legitimate that they need to know, something they are missing, you have to speak up about it. This could save us days of going down the wrong path. This is why you're here, to help in this way."

Rajit looked up with a smile and a hint of satisfaction.

"Right. The next step is to send a message back, correct?" Gideon nodded.

"So, maybe before we do that, I'll put something together in the morning. I'll just propose what I have." Rajit went back to his computer and started typing. "It doesn't have to be big, just a simple presentation lining out the problem statement."

There was a new excitement in his voice now and Gideon could see something renewed in his eyes now too.

"Maybe at that point, when we eliminate these other variables, we learn who and how they are doing this." Rajit slowly rubbed his temples and then went back to furiously typing at the keyboard.

Chapter 15

Blood flowed to the back of the fighter pilot's skull as he pressed the throttle to the full forward position. The F-22 roared to life as it rocketed down the runway. He checked the gauges, which showed acceptable speed, and a hard pull back on the joystick aggressively lifted the aircraft off the ground. He held the steep twenty-three-degree ascent, checking over his shoulders to ensure his two wingmen were in tow. The three jets powered into the sky, leaving Lackland Air Force base behind, soon resembling nothing more than a small speck among the rest of civilization.

After achieving twenty-five thousand feet of altitude, the jets leveled off and reduced thrust. The pilot released the buckle on the right side of his helmet, allowing his oxygen mask to fall to the side. He preferred to breathe the air within the small cabin instead of having it forced down his throat from the mask. Fuck the rules, he thought in his head.

"This is Skid speaking. Rabbit and Jig, you guys good?" the pilot said over his radio.

"Rabbit is ready to rock and roll," replied one of his wingmen, voice coming in through his earpiece.

"Jig is A-OK," said the other.

The pilot, Skid, again checked over his shoulders to view the two F-22s locked on to his left and right flank.

"Roger, rerouting to coordinates in three ... two ... one."

Skid slammed the joystick hard to the left. Goddamn he still loved this feeling. The others followed suit.

"Never fail to ... hick ... put us through a hard ... hick hick ... puulllll huuh?" Rabbit said in between his sips of air. A trained technique to help fighter pilots' bodies withstand the intense G-forces. Skid only smirked but didn't respond.

Once they were redirected toward the coordinates they had been provided, Skid leveled out the F-22 and took a deep breath.

"Rabbit, Jig, let's go find out who is hanging out on this empty patch of ocean."

Skid thought about the briefing they had been given, only about an hour ago. It had come straight from the mouth of General John Higgens. Not something you see every day. The general had told them the US Air Force had used triangulation to find an area, about twenty square miles, in which they thought would be inhabited by some type of non-US ship, station, or beacon. This area was about 1,700 miles off the west coast of Mexico in which there was no known occupation.

Skid and his team weren't given any other information than the order to conduct a series of flybys over the area to confirm whether or not it was inhabited. If so, take as many hi-res pictures as possible and return home. It wasn't typical for Skid and the team to not get more details and it raised the hair on the back of his neck. But whatever, a job's a job.

Skid brought his mind back to the present as his HUD helmet lens indicated they were closing in on the location. He checked his left and right. Two jets and a bunch of clouds.

"Boys, let's bring 'em down, I gave the general my word that we would find what our satellites couldn't; we're gettin' low for this one. Bring 'em down to thirty-five feet, and switch to thermal," Skid commanded.

"Thirty-five feet? Over open ocean like this? There could be swells bigger than that."

"Rabbit, you sure talk a lot, don't you? Look alive, boys, dropping in three ... two ... one."

Again, the team of fighter pilots slammed the joysticks in perfect synchronization, this time pitching the front of the aircraft down into a steep dive toward the North Pacific.

Skid was going to have some fun with this one. They sliced through the thick layer of clouds and the ocean came into view. He could now make out the actual shape of the waves, moving slowly across the dark blue waters. His hand held firm on the joystick, holding it forward and commanding his jet to continue its trajectory downward.

"SKID?" Rabbit said, sounding both worried and annoyed. Skid ignored it; the more Rabbit bitched, the tighter they'd cut it. The waves were now clear; he could see the white water spraying from the top crests of the larger peaks.

"SKID?"

A little closer ….

"BACK!" Skid yelled. All the pilots pulled back hard. His calculations were perfect as they leveled out above the water. He could see the wake of swirling water vapor clouds spiraling behind them as they screamed across the vast blue.

"You're fuckin' crazy, Skid … don't forget how you got your name." Rabbit laughed.

"You like it. Jig, you good?" Skid replied.

"Jig is A-OK," he replied.

Skid smiled; that man was all business.

"OK, let's put a hundred and fifty feet between us, wingtip to wingtip. Let's find these fuckers," Skid commanded.

The jets quickly maneuvered into their new formation and began methodically surveying the area. Minutes rolled by until the entire area had been scanned.

"Where are you?" Skid mumbled under his breath.

According to Higgens there had to be something there, something transmitting some type of beacon or signal. It could be small, but still, there was no way the thermal vision would have missed it. These pilots could find a hot piece of sand from two hundred feet away if they had to … and with the cold ocean to contrast it … There was nothing out here.

"We're calling it, boys. Pull up to reach altitude; steady climb for this one."

The pilots began a gentle ascent, back into the clouds.

Skid reached forward and flipped a toggle switch on his dash, connecting his mic to Lackland Air Force ground control.

"Skid here, squadron alpha alpha six. We have scanned the area and returned negative results … there ain't a fucking thing out here."

Skid was shocked to hear the general's voice reply.

"You sure? Nothing? Anything to report? Anomalies?"

"Negative," Skid replied.

"Roger that, bring 'em home," the general replied. Skid couldn't help but notice the sound of worry in his voice.

Chapter 16

Gideon, Rajit, and Linda found themselves sitting together again for dinner in the mess hall. The air-conditioning had broken earlier in the day and the Texas heat was stubborn to leave the large metal building. The hot air did not make the spicy pork brisket and cornbread look any more inviting. Gideon chose to stick with just the fruit salad and a cold Gatorade.

"I'm sure you guys heard. They were unable to find a source?" Linda asked once Gideon sat at the table. Both Gideon and Rajit nodded their heads.

"An error in the triangulation?" Rajit asked.

"No, I went over the formulas. They are perfect, amazing to be honest," Gideon replied.

"Then how? It doesn't make sense," Linda pushed.

"Nothing on this project has made sense. Did you see the result of the planetary study?" Gideon asked.

Linda just smiled and pointed to herself. "Linguist here … so no I didn't dig into the science reports."

"Every time it feels like we're making headway, something else proves us wrong." Gideon had found himself frustrated.

"The two most important pieces of data that we needed to back up the meteor burst theory—particles capable of reflecting radio waves and triangulation pointing to some sort of base sending the signal—have been a bust." Gideon tossed his fork down in frustration.

"This isn't your fault, Gideon. Meteor burst is still the most likely explanation; they've just found a way not to play by the rules we know of," Rajit said, wiping the perspiration from his receding hairline. Gideon wasn't sure if it was the gel or sweat that was holding his hair in its firm combed posture this afternoon.

Linda chewed her fingernails, as if holding back something. Both Gideon and Rajit looked at her and waited. They knew each other too well at this point to withhold information.

"Higgens gave the team the OK to move forward with sending a response," she said.

"OK, I guess I'm not surprised; we still need to contact whoever is sending the signal," Gideon replied.

"Yeah, I suppose so," Linda said, doing her typical long pause between statements.

"But, if the data is showing that meteor burst may not be the correct theory, is it possible we are sending this message to …" She trailed off, something Gideon had never seen her do.

"Aliens?" Rajit said flatly. "Aliens aren't real, you guys. I understand that the human brain jumps to wild conclusions to answer for the unexplainable. Why do you think there are so many different religions in the world? To help the human brain comprehend something that we can't comprehend."

Rajit seemed firm on this, and Gideon was surprised. He had assumed Rajit didn't seem like the type that wanted to believe in the concept of life outside of Earth, but this made it clear.

"I know, but ... what if the first words we say to an alien race are the military jargon that we plan on sending? It just doesn't sit well with me."

Linda brushed a lock of frizzy brown hair behind her ear, paused and continued.

"But I suppose they wouldn't be able to understand our words anyways, would they?" she finished.

"They?! Who is *they*, you guys?" Rajit stood, grabbing his unfinished plate of food and left.

Gideon looked at Linda, feeling lost for words by Rajit's reaction.

"You're doing great, Gideon. This is an environment that none of us are comfortable or familiar with navigating. We must continue to follow our hearts, best judgment and pursue all possibilities. You have continued to provide fresh ideas and perspectives to the project; that's what is important," Linda said in a compassionate tone.

Gideon felt himself relax back into his chair.

"You know, Linda, you remind me of my brother. He always had a way of making people believe in themselves. He had this ability to find the good or the hidden talents in people long before they recognized these virtues within themselves," Gideon said.

"Your brother sounded like a good man, Gideon," Linda replied.

With a slow nod, Gideon stood, grabbed his unfinished plate and left the table, urgently needing some rest.

Chapter 17

Gideon felt a surge of adrenaline coursing through him as his heart rate began to climb. He looked to his right; Shelly, the only other tech in the room, looked back at him, her face also showing disbelief. Gideon checked his watch: 14:52. His mind raced, searching for logical explanations.

Shelly slowly rose out of her chair, staring at the main screen on the wall, eyes fixed on the new oscillating signal pattern.

"This can't be," Gideon said.

"Well." Shelly chuckled. "It is. It can because the data is right there." She pointed at the screen.

Gideon leaned in and blinked, repeating the numbers in his head. "I mean—do you think it's a coincidence?"

Shelly shrugged. "It doesn't matter at this point what I think," she said. "I'm just gathering the information."

"But how— How can this be? This would imply the signal is not—" He hesitated to say the rest. He looked back at Shelly.

"Not originating from Earth," she finished for him.

"I'll call in support." Gideon reached for the wired phone that would connect him to Higgens.

"What is it?" Higgens's voice sounded on the other end.

"The URF changed."

Silence on the line.

"Sir?"

"How? How long since we sent our package?" Higgens asked.

"One hour and eleven minutes, sir. By our calculations, this is almost exactly half of the duration we were expecting."

Silence on the line again.

"I'm calling everyone in, this must be a coincidence. But if it's not, I'm assuming this means, with the known delay, there is no way someone on Earth could have received our message and already updated theirs for acknowledgment."

"That's right." Gideon was still trying to understand the only possible explanation: the signal was not originating from Earth.

Within fifteen minutes, the room was filled with personnel, Higgens at the whiteboard. The monitor was still showing the new signal being received.

"Attention!" Higgens called, then began drawing on the whiteboard. One big circle for Earth and one smaller circle a few feet away for the signal's originating point, X0-5.

"OK, as we all are now aware, approximately one hour and eleven minutes ago, we sent a signal from the GDSCC to X0-5. Given the approximate distance from the GDSCC to X0-5, our analyst calculated thirty-five minutes for our message to travel from the GDSCC to X0-5."

Higgens drew a line from Earth to X0-5 and labeled it "35min."

"It will then take another thirty-five minutes to travel back to the true source of the signal here on Earth."

Higgens drew another line from X0-5 back to Earth and again labeled it "35min."

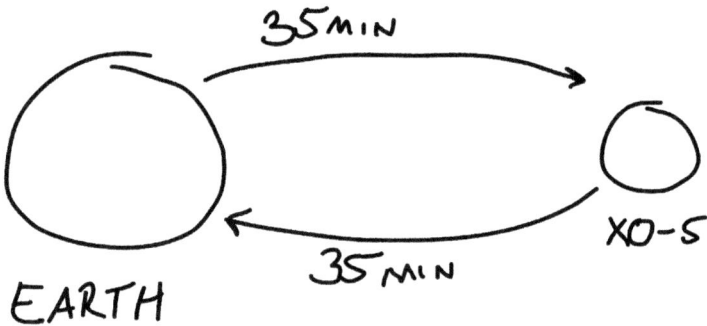

"At this point, we would assume the originators of this signal and technology would receive our message. The total time of thirty-five minutes out and then thirty-five minutes back is a total time of approximately seventy minutes, or one hour and ten minutes."

Higgens paused, as if checking his own math.

"Once our message reached back to Earth in one hour and ten minutes, we anticipated one of two things to happen. We would either be contacted directly by the organization creating the URF, to acknowledge receipt of our message. Or the URF would be revised to show acknowledgment. If the URF were to be revised, it would then take another thirty-five minutes for the new signal to reach X0-5 from Earth."

Higgens again drew a line from Earth to X0-5.

"And then another thirty-five minutes for the URF to make it back to us. This total response time is a *minimum* of two hours and twenty minutes."

Higgens took a step back, looking at the whiteboard.

"As we all know, we have just seen the URF update in one hour and eleven minutes. This leaves two options. Option A: this is a huge fucking coincidence, and the signal happened to change for the first time in two months. Or option B: X0-5 revised its signal as soon as it received ours, never needing to communicate with Earth." Higgens looked around the room. No one was brave enough to say anything.

He continued. "This would leave us to believe that X0-5 is in fact an object capable of receiving, understanding, and responding to our message." He snapped the marker on the metal tray with a loud clap to finalize his point.

Someone raised their hand.

"Yes." Higgens pointed.

"It appears the updated message is an attempt at replicating our message. The file is fairly jumbled but shows a high level of similarity," a tech called out.

"Could this be some sort of feedback?" Higgens asked.

"I don't think we can rule anything out at this point, but just looking at the data here it appears intentional. It is clean, no frequency spikes like you would see with interference. Almost like it took our message and just rearranged certain parts of it," Gideon replied.

"We need more data," Higgens said.

"In what way?" Gideon asked.

"I want to see another test." Higgens turned back to the whiteboard and placed his hands on his hips. "My gut tells me this is not a damn coincidence. But my head needs to see the data. There is too much riding on this. I want repeatable data. I want something I can point to on a graph or read in a spreadsheet."

"You want us to do it again?" someone asked.

"Yes!" Higgens spun around on his heel. "Yes, send it again. And then we'll send it again and then we'll send it again if we have to. Something out there is playing with us." He pointed dramatically up into the sky.

"And our job is to know exactly what it is, and I don't care what it takes."

"Well, it won't take us that long to resend the same data," another tech said.

"Good, get it going," Higgens said.

"Sir." Linda had entered the room just minutes ago.

"What?" Higgens barked back.

Linda paused and cleared her throat.

"I don't think we should be sending the same package." The room went silent again. Everyone stared at her. Gideon had always respected her confidence. She didn't care about the authority of the men around. When she had something to say, she would say it.

"What are you talking about?" Higgens began to look annoyed.

"Why would we send the same package again? We already know what it will do."

Higgens was listening.

"Why are we all sitting here afraid to say it?" she asked, now walking slowly to the center of the room.

"I know I'm not the only one thinking it. Our job is to make progress, to get answers and fast. And I'm sorry but we're not going to do that by playing it safe, by being fearful and making small plays. We have to take a shot. That's what we're here for, right?"

The room had never been this silent. Gideon gulped, wondering how Higgens would respond.

"What are you talking about, Linda?" Higgens asked.

She turned and locked eyes with him.

"If X0-5 is nonhuman, then they have no idea what our words are. Our message is just a random set of data to them, it means nothing. The only thing they could possibly do with it is exactly what they did, reorganize it in an attempt to let us know that they received it." Linda, with eyes still locked with the five-star general, was now walking toward him, standing tall.

"You're the damn linguist here, Linda. What do you suggest?"

"We must switch to the only universal language. Math and numbers," she replied confidently.

She paused.

"And give them a message that they can respond to." She finished her sentence, now standing face-to-face with Higgens.

Chapter 18

Higgens rotated the Styrofoam cup of steaming black decaf coffee on the polished wooden table. He had switched to drinking decaf several years ago after finding that the caffeinated stuff caused his already stressed heart to flutter with arrhythmia. Now just the thought of drinking decaf put him in a sour mood, yet he still chose to pour the cup of pointless fluid every morning. Sitting around the table were several other distinguished individuals, including Larry Whitfield, secretary of defense and Alexander Veltri, secretary of Homeland Security.

Finally, at 1038 hours, Robert Waller walked into the room and took a seat, floating his briefcase gracefully to the seat next to him.

"I had to travel fifteen hundred miles to get here and you only about five hundred feet … yet I was on time, and you were late," Higgens commented. He was always annoyed with having to take trips to the Pentagon.

Waller looked directly at Higgens, smiled and then resumed rummaging through his briefcase. The room stayed quiet for several minutes as Waller systematically laid out sheets of paper in front of him on the table, taking up enough space for several people. Finally, he pulled out and propped open a government-issue tablet and powered it on.

"Alright, folks, I will start this meeting with the assumption that you have already read the pre-meeting notes?" Waller scanned the room for nods.

"Excellent. So, at this point, Operation SD has been a continuous series of fuck-ups and bad assumptions. It has gone back and forth on its proposed solution statement. It violates multiple protocols including Homeland Security article 14.25, UNOOSA agreement fucking everything, and SETI Code of Conduct section seven. We absolutely must regain control of this situation; it is a no-fail operation, and we are currently failing." Waller looked again at all the faces around him, spending an extra second on Higgens.

Higgens's jaw muscles pulsed, but he remained silent.

"I come directly from a briefing with President Helland and her chief of staff. She is giving us a direct order to shift our attention to pulling this operation back into compliance. She d—"

"Shift our attention to paperwork?" Higgens now interrupted.

Waller's eyes sharpened; his pupils seemed to expand.

"Fall in line, Higgens, this is not the time for your shit," his voice quivered.

In his many years of working with Waller, Higgens had never seen the man in this state. He nodded his understanding. After taking a deep breath, Waller continued.

"From the White House's point of view, we are working with something that we know nothing about and doing so in a silo, which puts us at risk not only for slipping up on how we resolve this unknown, but also puts us at high risk of damaging external affairs. What this means is we have fourteen days before we declassify this information and seek counsel from the United Nations."

"I have an exceptionally strong resistance regarding taking this information to the public without us having a clear understanding of what is going on," Alexander Veltri said, changing his gaze to Larry Whitfield. "Public speculation could potentially be *the* most dangerous thing that comes out of this. People are scared of the unknown and when they learn that there is a signal coming from outer space that the United States has known about for several months and still has no idea what it is. I'm telling you, that will be the biggest threat Homeland Security has seen in years."

"My stance stays the same, this is not a military concern until there is conflict, and at this point this looks like some space noise that we have picked up and does not show any sign of requiring military engagement. That said, we have heightened security at multiple locations, and when this does go public, we will support Homeland Security in tightening up border control." Whitfield had a stern voice and an even more stern face.

"Look"—Alexander Veltri scooted to the edge of his seat—"public panic is the biggest threat. We are facing disclosing this information at a time when governmental suspicion is at an all-time high. We can't have the American people feed on any more distrust. If we tell the public that we don't know what this is, there will be no end to the misgivings and suspicion from the people."

"That is not an option," Waller said. "You may be right, but we have no choice."

"We always have a choice," Alexander Veltri said. "Our job is to protect the people; it always has been."

"We don't want to escalate anything," Whitfield said. "We need to know more before we can classify this as anything other than some space noise."

"It is most definitely more than space noise," Higgens said.

"Then prove it. Having your linguist claim it's aliens does nothing for your credibility," Alexander Veltri said. Several others chuckled at the mention of aliens.

Before Higgens could retort, Waller spoke up.

"General, we absolutely must have an understanding of what we are dealing with in the next fourteen days."

Higgens nodded his agreement.

Chapter 19

"Drinking that much caffeine could be lethal," Rajit said, acknowledging Linda as she walked in with a Stanford thermos, steam flowing from the top for the fourth time that night.

Linda simply winked one of her bloodshot eyes in recognition.

"We're nearly there; Stacey has been working at a lightning pace getting this stuff into the correct format," Gideon said.

Stacey, an impressively knowledgeable computer programmer, had been working around the clock taking the linguistics package known as language knowledge data, or LKD, and coding it into a transferable package that could be sent to X0-5. Linda was still desperately making final tweaks on its contents.

"I'm not worried about Stacey's pace; I just don't know if my LKD package is right for this," Linda replied.

After Higgens returned from DC two days ago, he directed the teams to prepare multiple different data packages to send to X0-5. One of which was Linda's linguistics learning package. Linda had resisted, but Higgens had reminded her of the agreement she had signed with DARPA several years back, putting her on retainer to support an effort just as they were doing now.

Rajit met her gaze but remained silent, Higgens's heightened level of security and haste had put them all on edge. He had high expectations and was rarely around for questions.

"Counter Package goes up in just an hour, right?" Linda asked Gideon.

"That's right. I'm going to head over soon to see it off, the data package is ready to go." Gideon stood.

"And this Counter Package serves what purpose?" asked Rajit.

"This is the first data package we'll send to X0-5; it is a sequence from one to ten."

"Like a pattern?" Rajit asked.

"Yes, exactly like a pattern," Gideon said. "It is an audio signal beginning with one knock, then two, then three and so on until it reaches ten."

"Then what?" Rajit asked.

"Who knows, but every intelligent being should understand a numerical sequence like one through ten."

"I can't believe we're doing this," Rajit said, shaking his head.

"There are two goals here," Gideon interjected.

"First, confirm that the URF will again return the package in the one hour and ten-minute window. This would confirm that X0-5 is in fact some type of physical object capable of returning our message. Secondly, we will get to see if it returns the message in the same way it did before, shuffling the data up. Or if it responds differently now that we are using what Linda is calling a 'universal language,' potentially confirming whether or not X0-5 shows signs of … intelligence."

Gideon made it to the lab just in time to confirm that the Counter Package had been sent. There was an eerie feeling in the air as no one wanted to discuss the different possibilities of the signal's response. The minutes dragged by as everyone waited for the large timer on the wall to reach the seventy-minute mark.

It was nearly midnight when it finally happened.

Everyone's heartbeats thumped as the counter rolled past seventy minutes. Higgens had tightened security levels and was only allowing prime and fully essential personnel to be involved. Even Gideon was being boxed out of certain conversations he was typically allowed to partake in. He figured this was a strategy to prevent any one person from knowing all the details.

The chime sounded, not a minute late. Gideon wondered how many people had dreaded this or been hoping for it.

"Seventy minutes and thirty-two seconds!" Someone called out.

"I'll be damned," Higgens murmured, staring at the incoming message. "How long until you are able to decode?"

"Sir, it's nearly a perfect match to our package."

"A reflection?" Higgens seemed hopeful.

"Unclear, but there does seem to be some added data, running it through the software now."

Higgens rubbed his temples, focusing on the screen in front of him.

"It doesn't look the same as before, it's not shuffled, just added on to," Gideon said. He spun his smooth copper washer between his fingers to calm his nerves.

"It's done. Stand by, appears to be audio, same as ours. Playing the file now."

A loud, slightly distorted "knock" was heard from the speaker. Silence … One one-hundred, two one-hundred …

"Knock, knock."

Silence … One one-hundred, two one-hundred …

"Knock, knock, knock."

The pattern had been returned. The knocks continued up to ten.

Silence … One one-hundred, two one-hundred …

"Knock, knock, knock, knock, knock, knock, knock, knock, knock, knock, knock."

Silence … One one-hundred, two one-hundred …

"Knock, knock, knock, knock, knock, knock, knock, knock, knock, knock, knock, knock."

Silence … the room froze as the group of humans digested and tried to understand the message they had just received. Clearly originating from somewhere other than Earth.

"Confirm they added an additional eleventh and twelfth sequence to our pattern," Higgens shouted.

"Confirmed," the team replied.

Chapter 20

Dark clouds loomed over Washington, DC, giving the Oval Office a gloomy feel. The computer screen sat on the conference portal site, waiting. President Katherine Helland, a fit and fashionable woman in her late fifties, was already deeply troubled by Operation SD and the lack of transparency on how it was being run. She closed her eyes for a moment to find her center, the last several weeks had been chaos. In fact, she was supposed to be in Japan right now negotiating a new trade agreement, but instead, her advisors had requested she postpone to focus on this new development. Since the day Waller had briefed her on Operation SD and this mysterious signal in space, she struggled to shake this nagging feeling that something was off. She adjusted her black Altuzarra suit jacket, feeling the American flag pin fastened firmly to the collar.

"Let me go over this again," she said crisply to her small council without needing to look at the notes in front of her.

"We know there was a signal, or URF as it's being called, that was detected a long distance out in space. Up until four days ago there had been no change or update to the frequencies it has been broadcasting. Now, after sending a message from Goldstone Observatory our experts received an updated frequency. Some sort of reshuffle of our original transmission."

Someone on her council began to speak, but President Helland interrupted, continuing her train of thought.

"This reply to our transmission also contradicts the theory that this was a reflecting signal originating from Earth?"

Linda chewed on her bright red shellac nails, a habit she had kicked long ago.

"And with all that aside, we then authorized a second message to be sent back to the URF."

Again, someone attempted to provide some context, but the president continued, in a louder tone.

"Meanwhile, this all is being kept from UNOOSA, the United Nations Office for Outer Space Affairs, and SETI, the Search for Extraterrestrial Intelligence Institute, even though SETI is *the* top organization specializing in deciphering unique signals captured from space."

"That's correct, Madam President," Juanita Perez, her main councilwoman, finally said. Juanita had shared the president's discomfort with keeping the project top secret, despite her primary cabinet members insisting on the importance of secrecy.

"As you know, the US has a clear process already established, in which SETI must be notified of any confirmed discoveries of potential unidentified objects or anomalies immediately. I sent a report of this protocol over this morning."

"Right, so for the past few months we have been violating established protocol at Waller's insistence, to give him more time to make sure this isn't a direct threat to Earth," the president concluded.

"Right," Karl Snyder said. "Operation SD is pushing for more time without disclosing their findings to outside organizations. This briefing will cover their most recent findings."

"Madam President, with all due respect." Juanita was firm. "You, as the president of the United States, will be held directly accountable for this decision. This won't go over well with the public or governments around the world when it comes out. It needs to be disclosed sooner rather than later."

"Madam President, if I may," the secretary of Homeland Security, Alexander Veltri, interrupted, sitting, legs crossed, in a large leather armchair in the corner of her office. "I strongly urge us to wait to disclose the discovery. The threat of letting the rest of the world learn of the signal and utilizing their own, potentially unregulated and likely more reckless methods of establishing contact would be a higher risk than for the US to understand it first and get ahead of this."

President Helland acknowledged his comment with nothing more than direct eye contact.

"Excuse me, Madam President, they are online, the conference is beginning," Juanita said. "Operation SD is online."

The screen switched to three serious-looking middle-aged men. Juanita pushed a button, then stepped out of the way.

"President Helland here."

"Madam President, this is General John Higgens. I have Robert Waller and secretary of defense Larry Whitfield with us." Higgens hesitated before continuing, "Madam President, we have news regarding Operation SD. We have just received a new response back from X0-5. It is confirmed to be originating from within our solar system and the response indicated comprehension and problem-solving. It's intelligent, Madam President."

Raindrops slammed against the window behind her. The room darkened further.

"What are you talking about, Higgens? Whitfield are you just hearing this?" Her voice was sharp.

"Came in just several hours ago; this is why the call was late: we were getting our facts straight," Larry Whitfield replied in almost a whisper, sounding like a little boy instead of a top-ranking military general.

Higgens continued, professional as always. "I'm sharing my screen, let me know when you see it."

"Got it." President Helland studied the PowerPoint slide.

"OK, stop me if you have any questions. As you know, last night at eleven hundred, we sent a signal back to X0-5. At exactly seventy minutes and thirty-two seconds later we received a revised signal in return. Our transmission was a series of dings counting from one through ten."

An audio file was played, emerging from President Helland's computer speakers.

"Ding … … ding, ding … … ding, ding, ding … …," all the way up to ten clicks.

Higgens continued, "Did you get that audio?"

"Yes," the president replied.

"Good, my computer skills are improving. These are the series of dings we sent to establish an audio representation of the numbers one through ten. We received the following message back. Notice that it will count one through twelve. Our on-site linguist, Dr. Linda Knibley, believes the two extra digits are a way of acknowledging receipt, then proving the ability of processing and understanding the pattern."

A knocking pattern, counting from one through twelve was played, President Helland noted there was also a change in the sound, an ominous knocking compared to the series of dings they had sent.

"President Helland, given what we know about X0-5, its location and the response time to our message, it is confirmed that the response was, in fact, sent from X0-5."

"My God," Helland replied, although she followed no particular God in faith.

Whitfield broke into the silence. "Although there is no direct threat to public safety, we have declared a state of Elevated Security. We are keeping the air force with fingers on triggers around the clock. I'm concerned that questions are going to start coming through, as most of the personnel have not been told what the mission is."

"We have to go forward with this information, per protocol. Waller, I want you to get a report typed up by tomorrow morning for my review. We will share this information with SETI and UNOOSA," Helland commanded, regaining her composure.

Whitfield abruptly cut in. "Madam President, once we share with those organizations, we no longer have direct control of the situation. The public will find out, and keeping things from spiraling out of control will be impossible. We must have a better understanding of what *this is* before going forward. For the safety of this country."

"With all due respect, Secretary Whitfield, I believe getting caught holding this secret is far more dangerous than going forward with it," the president rebutted.

There was a pause of silence.

"Waller, have there been any other leaks?" she asked.

"Fortunately, not much. Gideon's original leak was still the only instance detected, and the ripples were contained and now appear completely dead. There are a few conspiracy blogs and people pushing the increase of government activity, but it's not gaining much traction."

"What kind of increase?"

"Some have been able to find flight records and staff hours, stuff like that, but they ultimately have nothing but a handful of government officials working long hours. The majority of the population is paying no notice."

"What about globally?"

"Nothing yet, but it's just a matter of time before someone else detects the URF and gets it over to SETI or worse, goes directly to the public before we can. Even though I don't like it, I agree, we need to come forward with this information. I'll have the report typed and in your hands tomorrow first thing," Waller replied.

"Thank you, Waller," President Helland replied.

"Madam President, if I may, th—"

"You may not," Helland cut Veltri off sharply. "We are not dragging this out any further. Higgens, you said it takes about seventy minutes to send a message and get a response back?"

"Roughly, that is correct. Madam President," Higgens replied.

"Well then, you've got one more shot to figure this out before we shut down your operation. Our report goes to SETI and UNOOSA in forty-eight hours."

Chapter 21

Linda rotated the steaming Stanford thermos on the desk next to her computer. The LKD package was nearly ready to send. Her brain was swimming with mixed feelings about sending her life's work out into space. A part of her fantasized about the possibility of there being some advanced alien species, ready to digest the contents of the linguistics package and learn how to communicate, putting her work to the ultimate test. However, the logical side of her brain pulled her back to reality, worrying her that she was most likely sending it to some type of man-made station that would take her linguistics package and steal its proprietary contents.

Gideon walked into the room and slid into a desk on her left, and Rajit, sitting at a desk to her right, spun in his chair until he faced her. "How are you holding up?"

Linda noticed that steam was no longer rising from her thermos; she must have been deep in thought for some time. "Oh, as well as I can," she said with a sigh. "I've been working on this LKD package for the last eleven years."

"That's a long time," Gideon marveled.

"It's my life's work," she said, and she shook her head a moment with her eyes closed, as if sifting through distant memories.

"Well, tell us about it," said Gideon, with what seemed to be genuine curiosity.

Linda hardly knew where to start, and she wondered if her two colleagues would really be interested in hearing her nerd out about language for the next half hour. She chuckled. "How much time do you have?"

Rajit and Gideon theatrically looked around the nearly empty lab and smiled.

"I pretty much have all day," said Rajit.

"Yeah, I think I can make some time," Gideon was saying, gesturing as if he were looking at an imaginary watch on his wrist.

"All right, I tried to warn you guys," said Linda with a shrug. "It's going to be an information dump."

"Information overload is my favorite pastime," said Gideon, and somehow Linda believed him.

Linda raised her hands in front of her. She always gesticulated when talking about something. "It's revolutionizing the way language can be taught to humans with no base understanding of an advanced dialect."

Rajit shifted in his chair, finding some extra comfort.

Linda smiled and continued after a momentary pause. "Well, initially I fought hard for funding throughout the years, as the demographic of people it would support is a minority population. However, once I received the grant from DARPA I was able to conduct several very interesting cases. For example, three years ago a fourteen-year-old feral child from Vietnam was inducted into the program, and within less than a year had learned the basics of the English language. This shattered the theory that feral children, after making it past puberty with no comprehension of language, could never learn to speak and understand a complex vernacular."

Gideon rubbed his chin and squinted slightly. "Interesting."

Linda nodded. "The LKD package is a multimedia learning set, using thousands of visuals tied with audio representation to provide the building blocks to teach the language. The opening sequence of the LKD package focuses on the concept of an audio representation of an object; written language representation would come later. Pictures of common everyday objects are shown, such as a tree, and accompanied by a voice saying the word 'tree.' First, the candidate would grasp the concept that the sounds could be used to represent objects. Next, the LKD would build on this to add meaning to simple words and symbols using sequences. For example, a picture of storm clouds followed by the equals symbol and a picture of rain. Once the equals symbol is established, the subject learning would accelerate in terms of conceptual understanding of practical language."

"When the participant learns word association with shapes, such as square and circle, the word *large* is then taught, and the difference between *large* and *getting larger* is explained by a visual of the square getting larger with an equals sign and the words written out: 'Square is getting larger.' This begins the understanding of written language. Once established, the final phase of the LKD package focuses on the most challenging piece: explaining feelings and emotions."

Linda rose from her desk and walked over to the whiteboard in the front of the room. She picked up a marker from the storage bar and drew the mathematical *greater than* symbol on the board.

"At this point the mathematical term > or *greater than* is soon understood. Visuals such as 2 > 1 are also shown by size ☐ > ☐."

Linda went on, drawing the illustrations as she spoke.

"Once the understanding of the term *better* is grasped, it's shown that a larger box is *better* than a smaller box and thus, when the box grows in size it makes the box *happy.* Overall, the LKD package could teach a list with over two thousand words, enough for an individual to be able to speak and write in the English language."

Linda noticed that both Gideon and Rajit were leaning forward in their chairs, attending her presentation with a lot more interest than she'd imagined.

"Now, with the context that this package could potentially be given to an audience not from Earth, for the past several weeks I've been working to remove all items that may not be understood by an alien species, such as trees and other Earth-specific items. With the help of several mathematicians and astrophysicists, I've replaced them with what's thought to be universal science representations."

"Seems genius enough to me," said Gideon.

"Yeah well, not sure I would say that. In addition to the LKD package, a series of accompanying information will be attached, including television shows such as *Bill Nye the Science Guy* and several audiobooks. This will give the recipient of the LKD package a chance to test their new knowledge by viewing and listening to the attached media. I'm really struggling with knowing how to anticipate the learning behaviors of something I know nothing about."

"Are you really thinking of this as catering to an alien species?" asked Rajit. "Higgens seems to be fairly adamant that this is just a precautionary measure."

Linda recognized that Rajit still seemed completely unaccepting of the possibility that the URF could be coming from anything other than a human-developed technology. Gideon, she felt, was a bit more open-minded to the possibilities. He sat there, noticeably deep in thought, elbow propped up on the desktop with his head resting in his hand.

"I don't know, Rajit, but that is what this data package is about. To teach an intelligent being how to communicate with us."

Rajit shrugged, biting his lip.

"All I know is if this is really happening, I'm going to do whatever I can to give us the greatest possible chance of establishing communication." Linda shifted her thermos.

"That's the way to go," said Gideon, and he winked at her. "Better to be prepared to communicate with aliens, and accidentally get humans, than the other way around."

"Touché," Linda agreed. She wondered if Gideon was just being nice, or if he really considered that her language package might be going to extraterrestrials.

Linda took a moment to ponder the gravity of what was happening, and she wondered if all of her years of work had prepared her for this exact moment. But she quickly dismissed the thought knowing her life's work in linguistics was to teach humans, not imaginary extraterrestrials. And then she felt silly that she had ever really considered that they might be trying to communicate with aliens. What were the chances of that?

Linda had gone through most of her life without thinking much about aliens at all. Space, other galaxies, the possibility of life on other planets, these weren't things that came up very often in her line of work. But she imagined that for the likes of Gideon and Rajit, these topics were often pondered and debated. She wondered how much the two of them had contemplated life on other planets throughout their lives.

She turned her chair back to face her computer but couldn't think about the LKD package. She found herself trying to guess both men's stances on alien life, given their personalities and what she knew about them thus far. Both of them were obviously scientists, which meant they should be unbiased, at least to an extent, and eager to discover new information about pretty much anything. And while they both obviously prioritized science and data over feelings and philosophy, she knew there was a difference between the two men when it came to believing in things their eyes had never seen.

Rajit was clearly resistant to the idea that the signal could be from extraterrestrials but surely his scientific mind no doubt told him it was a possibility. Gideon, however, seemed more likely to consider that her language package could find itself in the hands of aliens. Although a scientist through and through, he seemed eager to consider all possibilities. Perhaps more philosophical in his approach at times. She couldn't be sure, but it's what her gut told her—and she decided to find out if she was right.

"Quick question, guys," she said to them. "For fun, on a scale from one to ten, one being no chance at all and ten being one hundred percent, how much do you really believe that this signal could be from alien life?"

"Nice," said Gideon who seemed delighted at the question.

Rajit looked less thrilled.

"Let's say five," said Gideon, and then he looked at Rajit.

Rajit's brown eyes darted back and forth.

"Two," he finally said flatly.

Linda smiled; she had these guys pretty much figured out at this point.

"And what about you?" Gideon asked her.

"Oh …," said Linda, surprised.

She hadn't even considered giving an answer herself, or what it would be. One part of her told her it was very likely. Of all the planets and even galaxies that haven't been explored, why wouldn't there be life on even one planet or somewhere in one galaxy? Why wouldn't there be? On the other hand, her more skeptical side told her it was a crazy and far-fetched idea. Much like Earth is the only planet in our solar system where humans can actually breathe, an outlier compared to other planets when it comes to atmospheric pressure and oxygen, our galaxy is likely an outlier among all the other galaxies.

"I'll say a seven," said Linda, contemplating her own question a lot more than she'd expected.

Earth as an outlier among nine planets was one thing, but among every planet in every single galaxy was another matter entirely. And that's only based on the premise that alien life would need to breathe oxygen or require the same conditions to live as humans.

It didn't take long for her to convince herself even more, and before a minute passed, she had already bumped her answer up to an eight. But she didn't tell her colleagues. She was sure both Gideon and Rajit could put together very intelligent arguments to defend their positions. But all she could say to justify *her* answer, which had now jumped to a nine, was that there were just so many planets they didn't know about.

She thought about asking them to explain their positions, which she imagined they would be happy to do, but she decided against it. They had work to do, after all, and speculation meant nothing against cold, hard proof. And the proof would be in sending out her language package. That is, if anyone—or anything—responded.

Not to mention, both men still looked to be mulling over the presentation she had given, their eyes still occasionally scanning the whiteboard.

Rajit's eyes were darting around the whiteboard, and then he glanced at Linda, a pensive look in his eyes. "How long was your expected learning duration with human subjects?"

"Gosh, with Trẻ hoang dã, the young Vietnamese girl I told you about, it took nine and a half months for her to understand about a seventy-five percent comprehension rate, which is considered enough to be fully capable of communication. She was our quickest. After trying several other candidates, the next quickest was an eighteen-year-old boy who learned in just ten months but was never able to get above a sixty-percent comprehension rate. However, due to the intense mental trauma he experienced in the past, I believe that was the predominant factor in preventing his further understanding."

Rajit nodded, clearly deep in thought, and Gideon bit his lip and let out a long, "Hmmm."

Linda continued. "The challenge is, as it is with anything nonhuman, the concept of language is so vastly different from species to species. Ours is so specific to our way of thinking…" Linda fell back into thought.

"That's right," said Gideon. "Who's to say they process language the same way we do, or that they even learn the same way?"

"But any advanced civilization must have a complex language," Rajit said.

"That is the most widely accepted theory, but again, we have no idea what other forms of communication can be out there. Although it sounds crazy, there are possibilities of telepathy, using tools, rhythms or a visual language technique comparable to sign language."

Rajit's eyes widened. "I never thought about that," he admitted.

"Me either," said Gideon. "At least not until today."

Linda grinned. There was a small part of her that relished the fact that she had made these two brilliant scientists consider something they never had before. "Well, *if* we really are attempting to communicate with an intelligent unknown species, I suppose there are two questions. Will they even be able to understand the LKD package? And if so, how long will it take them to learn human language?"

Chapter 22

"Incoming message!" a tech yelled. Higgens stood from his computer terminal and looked around. It was Johnson, the young technician who had been at Operation SD since day one.

"What is it?" He began walking over.

"It's what we've been waiting for," the tech said. People all over the lab began standing to see the large screen at the front of the room.

It had been nearly two hours since the LKD package had been sent, the first time that X0-5 hadn't replied with the typical seventy minutes. The team speculated this was because X0-5 was trying to understand the LKD package. The pulsating red light confirmed the tech's claim. The lab had been manned with a full staff every hour of every day in anticipation of how X0-5 would react to the new, highly complex LKD package. Tensions had been high with anticipation.

"Status update please!" Higgens yelled back.

"I'm running decryption right now." The tech was typing away at the keyboard, looking back and forth between two monitors.

"Turn on the signal drive," another tech said as she fought for position by the terminal. "It will process faster from there."

Higgens stood and crossed his arms, knowing he was running out of time to come up with an answer for this damned signal. He had never failed a mission and he didn't intend to now.

"How long before the data is displayed?" Higgens pushed.

"About seven or eight minutes," the tech said.

"Well, which is it? Seven or eight?" Higgens barked back.

Another technician rolled up in a chair and leaned into a screen to read some numbers. "It depends on how fast our processors can download," he said.

"The returned data package is completely different from what we sent, not a modified version of our message like we have seen in the past," Gideon stated, clicking away at his keyboard.

Higgens grimaced and tried to control his breathing. He couldn't lose his cool. All of his emotions inside him were balling up and ready to explode. He needed to know. But he had to remain in control. He couldn't let the team see him in such an undisciplined state, they needed a strong leader.

"Well, what is the next step?" Higgens asked.

"Alpha five to complete in under sixty seconds," Johnson said without taking his eyes off the screen.

Higgens rolled his eyes. Why couldn't these comm techs speak English? Everything in him wanted to bite someone's head off.

"Tell what's his fuckin' name to shut down the B drives, push all the juice to the mainframe," Higgens yelled.

"Yes, Chuck is working on that as we speak."

"Holy shit … it's done, it's looking like it's a very small file, perhaps just some text," someone said in the back.

Higgens gulped. What were they about to see? No way was he about to read a message from some alien, was he? Fuck that, no way. Probably some scathing message from some country saying to back off and stop sending fucking language packages. Higgens dreaded the embarrassment that would bring to his operation.

"I'm processing now and it will only take a moment." The original tech hit a few more keys.

"Process the file." Higgens rubbed his hands together. "And put it up on screen three when you're done." He wanted everyone to be able to read it at the same time.

"Screen three up," someone else said.

"Downloading and converting the message now. It will read out on the screen three automatically," Johnson said.

Everyone shifted and turned to the main large screen on the front wall. The screen was pure black with a white blinking cursor in the corner.

"How much longer?" Higgens asked.

"Fifteen seconds," someone answered.

The wait felt like it lingered for far too long. No one spoke. Higgens sighed and cracked his knuckles. One tech tapped his foot on the linoleum floor. The female tech chewed her fingernails. Everyone had a different way of processing the wait.

One of the computers beeped, signaling that the transfer had completed.

And then they all saw it.

Text began to appear on the screen.

Higgens read the response.

```
--
-
A B C D E F G H I J K L M N
O P Q R S T U V W X Y Z
0123456789
.!?,()+-=><*
-
Hello. Thank you for data.
Us learn data. Correct
errors in words from us.
-
Acknowledge you understand
following messages.
-
We are alien. You are alien.
You name your species human.
You may name us what you
choose in your language.
We are not enemies.
-
--
```

Higgens read the last couple of lines again just to confirm what his eyes were seeing. He stood, motionless. His weathered tan face appeared white and ghostly. Moments of silence passed.

Without warning, the silence was sliced by a high-pitched "fuck this" from the back. A young man jumped from his station and ran for the door.

"Nobody fuckin leaves!" roared Higgens. One of the armed guards blocked the exit. The young man crumpled to the ground, pulling at his hair and mumbling different phrases.

Moving faster than a cat jumping on its prey, Higgens snapped back into action and ran over to the nearest secure line and grabbed the phone receiver. There was no need to dial as it was a direct line to General Whitfield.

"Higgens?" the familiar voice said, a sense of concern already present.

"Sir, we have what appears to be open communication with the signal. It was an intelligent response."

"So, what's the category?" Whitfield asked.

"It's a Code Black."

"Black?" Whitfield asked. "Are you sure?"

"Yes, sir. I've confirmed it. It appears we have communication from an intelligent life form that is not from Earth."

Higgens felt the stare of every person in the room bearing down on him. He tried to focus, trying to listen to Whitfield's response, but his mind was swimming. No amount of military training could have prepared him for this. He clenched his teeth hard, forcing himself to calm down.

"Yes sir, right away, sir." Higgens replaced the phone, ending the call. He raised his hands in the air to get everyone's attention. He looked out at the room of worried faces.

"I need you all to shut down your machines immediately and report directly to the K building, you will be escorted by security. Leave all cell phones, iPads, flash drives, everything here. No technology leaves this room until it's been cleared. I don't want as much as a smartwatch on your person. Let's go."

No one moved. They were still in shock.

"NOW!" he yelled.

Everyone in the lab began moving like the building had caught on fire.

Chapter 23

The base of the glass award was now perfectly flush with the edge of the polished wooden desk. Declan Wilter buffed the residual fingerprint left behind on the clear surface. Observing it for several moments, he slid it back to check its width against the other trophy occupying the desk.

Rarely did nerves get to him when waiting for a conference call, but today his heart thumped noticeably beneath his neatly pressed collared shirt. The California heat assaulted the room's AC, slowly winning the battle between hot and cold. Sweat formed just below his graying hairline.

Declan was what most would consider a highly accomplished man for his age, and he made sure that was known to his visitors. His desk and walls were littered with various plaques, trophies, and certificates. By educational standards, he fell below most of those surrounding him, with an undergrad degree in mechanical engineering from a college nobody had heard of, and a master's in astronomy from UCLA. Once he graduated with his master's in 1982, he joined NASA and took immediate steps toward making the journey to the International Space Station. By the young age of twenty-six he became the second youngest person to ever go to space, serving a three-month research grant on the space station.

Upon returning from his scientific voyage, he became disgruntled with the lack of funding for space programs. He got involved in politics with the goal of expanding scientific research programs, particularly space exploration. His political endeavors consumed almost fourteen years of his life as he spent time on multiple different councils and panels.

He would have continued his political progression if he hadn't gotten married and started a family at the considerably late age of forty-five, though his wife was fifteen years younger. His friends had given him a hard time, saying his attractive young wife had only married him because of his good looks, often referring to him as a doppelgänger of various movie actors. Regardless, the life of a politician had far too much travel and dedication to the job to support also being a family man. Just two years after his son's birth, he slowly began to withdraw his involvement, which landed him his dream job.

As acting president of SETI, the Search for Extraterrestrial Intelligence, Declan spent most of his days reviewing small potential discoveries that almost always led to nothing and dealing with the never-ending battle of obtaining funding for the many ongoing programs. Although he found himself missing the adrenaline of high politics, he greatly enjoyed his work.

Throughout his life Declan had talked and engaged with many important people and been involved in many high-pressure situations. But today took the cake.

The phone receiver sat silently with an open line for eleven minutes now. When he had first dialed the secure line, described in the email he received yesterday, he was greeted by a younger-sounding woman who asked him a series of questions to confirm his identity. The process felt similar to talking to a bank about credit card fraud. Once he successfully completed the questions, she told him he would be on hold until all parties were present and then the conference call would begin. In this eleven-minute silence, his mind raced in many directions—why was he getting this call? Perhaps SETI was getting its funding pulled. He dreaded the thought.

Without warning the speaker embedded within the desk phone sprang to life. For several seconds all he could hear was the sound of soft voices in the background, papers being shuffled, and a cough. Breaking through this pattern was the voice he had been most anticipating, having only ever heard it on the news.

"Declan, do we have you on the line?" said the voice of the president.

"Yes, I am here."

A different voice. "Please state your first and last name and where you are currently located, this call is being recorded for US government records."

"Declan Wilter, calling in from Mountain View California, SETI headquarters."

There was a long silence, broken again by President Helland.

"Declan, I'm accompanied by the head of internal affairs, Mr. Waller, and the secretary of defense, General Larry Whitfield. We thank you for taking the time to accept this phone call."

"Of course," Declan replied, feeling starstruck.

"I and the individuals in the room with me this afternoon would like to share with you some news. This news is going to be startling."

His heart sank as he had come to learn *startling* typically meant *bad*. Must be funding.

"As a man in your position, acting president of SETI, I hope this comes as good news," she continued.

Good news? Curiosity and excitement pushed the bad feelings out. A soft "OK" escaped his lips, not likely heard over the speakerphone. The president continued.

"Fourteen weeks ago, the United States government detected a unique signal originating from within our solar system. Declan, we will formally brief you with all details soon, but in short, we have strong evidence pointing toward this being extraterrestrial in origin."

Declan was unable to formulate a response as his brain was instantly overwhelmed with emotions and thoughts. He had always believed in life outside our solar system, and since joining SETI those beliefs had become even stronger. But now, hit with the actual reality, it seemed impossible. The line remained silent, as they allowed the information to sink in.

Finally, Declan found his mental ground and spoke into the microphone, trying to hold his composure. "OK, this news is incredible … Are we, are you certain?" His brain was swimming in excitement and awe.

As if the words had restarted his brain's ability to process information again, he quickly followed up. "What has happened in the last three months? Was the original detection what led you to believe it is extraterrestrial, and why am I hearing about this now and not when you first detected the signal?"

"When the signal was detected, it was clear to us it was abnormal, but did not lead us to believe it was … nonhuman. We pulled together a tiger team of scientists to try and better understand what we were dealing with," General Whitfield explained.

"What do we know? What led you to believe it is extraterrestrial? Is there reason to believe that we could be dealing with an intelligent being?" Declan kept his voice professional, and calm.

"Yes, given the research and findings, we believe we are dealing with an intelligent being," a new voice replied.

Declan focused on keeping his thoughts calm and collected, as the president of SETI should. But his mind was rapidly filling with questions and actions.

"OK, oh my, this really is difficult for me to digest … and do we believe they know that we have detected the signal?" Declan asked.

"Yes, they have responded to a linguistics package sent."

Declan was taken aback by this statement.

"What linguistics package? You've established communication without engagement of SETI?" His curiosity cooled from welling frustration. "That violates Section 7 of the SETI code of conduct, as I would hope you know."

"We will brief you more soon, we really cannot discuss any more details on this line. C-37B is en route to Moffett Federal Airfield as we speak; you have been provided a pass in your email to get through security, from there you will be escorted to the aircraft. Be there in four hours."

"Four hours, OK yes, I can make that happen. I need to check with my wife an—" Declan was interrupted by another voice.

"Declan, you absolutely cannot tell your family the reason for this trip. This is of the highest level of classification. Under your oath to SETI, you must abide by this confidentiality."

"What am I supposed to say?" he replied, again feeling overwhelmed.

"I'm sure you will figure something out. This is your moment, Declan. We will see you in DC tonight." President Helland's voice was soothing.

"Yes, Madam President. I'll be there." The line went silent.

Declan let out a long exhale, stood from his desk, grabbed his laptop bag, and left the room in haste.

Chapter 24

Declan glanced back at the white Gulfstream G550 resting on the tarmac, also known as C-37B, wingtips illuminating brightly against the night sky. It had brought him here to DC from California in just four hours. The engines hummed, as if eager to lift the small powerful jet back into the air for its next mission. Declan hastily pulled his rolling suitcase across the airstrip toward the black SUV parked less than a hundred feet away, only the soft glow of its running lights guiding him.

The last several hours were a blur. He only had two rushed hours at home before leaving for the airport. His wife hadn't even said goodbye out of frustration over his unexplainable rapid departure, which in the past had been a product of his latest affair. Countless sessions of couples therapy had only begun to regain her trust in him. What made Declan feel even more uneasy was he didn't even care at this point; all he could think about was the fact that he was on the cusp of learning and communicating with an intelligent alien species.

This was really happening. He couldn't get to DC fast enough.

Once he arrived at the black GMC, a man in a black suit with a coiled wire running from his collar to the back of his ear took his bag and loaded it into the trunk of the vehicle. He then opened the rear passenger door for Declan to enter. The interior of the SUV reminded him of a small limo, and he found himself sitting facing a man he recognized but couldn't place his finger on where from.

The man looked at him calmly, then offered a firm handshake.

"Robert Waller. Nice to finally meet you, Declan. I will escort you to the White House for today's meeting. Accompanying us today will be President Helland, the secretary of defense General Larry Whitfield, General John Higgens who has been in charge of Operation Signal Decipher, and myself. There are two primary objectives to this meeting. First, develop a plan forward for communicating with the AS1, and second, develop a strategy to inform the public."

"AS1?" Declan inquired.

"AS1, alien species first occurrence, this is what we will be calling … them." Waller looked uneasy saying the final word of his sentence. The rest of the car ride was mostly silent. Waller viciously clicked away at his iPhone giving Declan time to think about what he planned to talk about at this upcoming meeting. Soon, the SUV pulled off the main street and stopped at a gate guarded by several Secret Service guards.

This was the second time Declan had been to the White House. His first time was a meet and greet with President Obama to accept a grant for the International Space Youth Scholars program which, being predominantly a publicity stunt, brought with it hundreds of cameras and spectators. Today, they entered in complete secrecy. It was of the utmost importance that nobody knew that the director of SETI was meeting with the United States president.

Once parked in the secure underground lot within White House grounds they walked to a large elevator, big enough to fit a small car. Declan's balance was thrown off when the elevator dropped instead of moving upward toward ground level. Stepping out of the lift, Declan immediately noticed the lack of windows and, paired with the elevator's descent, assumed they were now deep underground. The hallway walls and ceiling were a vibrant white, while the floor was a velvet red carpet runner. Historical pictures and awards decorated the walls.

As they made their way down the narrow passageway, Declan whispered to himself quietly, rehearsing some of the important points he planned on making at this discussion. After taking several turns, they walked into a large room with a long wooden table and chairs placed around it. Several others were already seated. Waller motioned his hands toward one of the black rolling leather chairs, Declan took a seat.

President Helland and Whitfield walked in shortly after, engaged in a hushed but heated discussion. The exchange ended abruptly the moment they took their seats and looked toward Declan, who was becoming more and more restless—why had he and his organization been kept in the dark all this time?

Waller stood from his chair and began. "The goal of today's meeting is to discuss the logistics, impact, and timeline on bringing the knowledge of the AS1 to the public."

Declan interjected, his frustration trumping his nervousness, even in the presence of the president.

"I would like to jump in here, Mr. Waller, Madam President, and others," Declan said with a respectful nod.

"And remind us all of the ground rules and expectations. Please note, these are not 'my' rules, they are legal agreed-upon terms that were vetted and established years ago. The Declaration of Principles set by SETI, agreed upon by the United States government and endorsed by the United Nations has defined steps to follow when dealing with coming into contact with an unknown, such as the AS1. Allow me to summarize the nine steps concerning activities following the detection of extraterrestrial intelligence."

Declan surveyed the room and was happy to see he had everyone's attention. He then flipped open his brown leather folder and retrieved his printed copies of the SETI protocols passing them out to each of the attendees.

"Firstly, the discoverer of potential extraterrestrial intelligence evidence should rigorously confirm its plausibility before public announcement. Second, before public disclosure, the discoverer must inform other parties for independent verification and continuous monitoring. Third, upon credible evidence confirmation, the global astronomical institutions and the UN secretary-general must be informed. Fourth, a confirmed discovery should be disseminated promptly and openly through scientific and public channels. Fifth, all necessary data for confirmation should be accessible to the international scientific community. Sixth, the discovery and related data should be permanently recorded and shared for further analysis. Seventh, parties should seek international agreement to protect relevant frequencies if evidence is in electromagnetic form. Eighth, sending any response requires international consultation and agreement. And finally, ninth, establish a committee for ongoing review and coordination of evidence analysis and information, involving international institutions and experts."

There was a sense of unease in the room, Declan continued before anyone could ask questions.

"The first two steps have been completed. Unfortunately, after that it appears there have been some drastic deviations from these guidelines. Most notably, step eight in which we have communicated with the extraterrestrials, or AS1 as you have named them, *without* any international consultation or agreement."

Declan looked around the room. He was pleased to see attentiveness and now several nodding heads with the exception of one unimpressed-looking military general. He assumed this was John Higgens.

"With all due respect, Declan, the discovery process was not as smooth and clear as the neatly outlined steps in your document," Higgens stated flatly.

"*Our* document, sir, this is *our* Declaration of Principles in which we will begin to abide by. If I may, I'd like to highlight my recommended next steps." Declan looked toward President Helland and Waller.

"Please, Declan, this is why you are here, and I appreciate your preparedness," President Helland replied.

"Good. Step three of the Declaration of Principles has one important key aspect with which we are not in compliance at the present time. I quote, '*a signal or other evidence due to extraterrestrial intelligence, the discoverer shall report this conclusion in a full and complete open manner to the public, the scientific community, and the secretary-general of the United Nations.'* In our case, the discoverer would be the United States military division. Thus, my recommendation for the most immediate next step is to alert the UN secretary-general and request an emergency special session to develop a strategy for public education," Declan stated firmly.

"President Helland and I have already made contact with UN secretary-general, Jamal Uddin, requesting an in-person meeting. This will take place tomorrow at 0930," Whitfield replied.

"Excellent. Additionally, I request all data be transferred to the International Astronomical Union, IAU, so a team from the international scientific community may examine the data. Can you please provide me with more information as to the type of signal we detected, and what leads you to believe it to be of intelligent extraterrestrial origin?"

Waller and Higgens explained the details behind the steps taken from the first time the signal was detected to when the LKD package was sent, and the response received. They also explained the physics behind the signal's orientation and how it defined all current technology's abilities.

"One of the higher-level concerns I would like to address is the fact that the AS1 appears to now understand English. They should also be able to conclude that we have recognized and responded to their presence," Higgens said.

"There is a reason 'Response to signals' is one of the final steps of the process, Higgens," Declan replied sharply.

"I'm not here to have you lecture us on what we should have done, Declan. Please help us look forward." Higgens's voice rose slightly.

"Yes, sir." Declan knew that getting the General in a state of anger would be counterproductive. "You are correct; by establishing first contact with the AS1 in which they are now awaiting our next step or response, we have initiated what I would call a 'communication pause.' Theoretically, this is how the AS1 would view our behavior of reaching out, receiving their reply and then not returning a response. This can be dangerous as it can lead to wrong assumptions from the AS1. Some of the most likely assumptions would include. One, that we did not receive their last message. Two, that we did not understand their returned message. Three, that we do not have interest in communicating with them. Or four, that we received their response and are planning something that we do not wish to communicate. The list of assumptions is long, and this is just a few of the possibilities. So yes, Higgens, I agree, formulating and sending back a response will be our top priority."

Chapter 25

The General Assembly Hall echoed with the sounds of people quietly chatting and moving about to find their seats. Located in New York City, the United Nations headquarters was chosen as the meeting point for the UN Emergency Special Session.

Tensions could be felt hanging in the air; only Jamal Uddin, the United Nations secretary-general, knew the true nature of the meeting. Jamal nodded to the security guard who stood by the back door. He adjusted his tie as the guard motioned him in. His throat was dry. Inside the small staging room, Jamal found a cold bottle of water in the tiny fridge and gulped down a swig.

Although he had addressed the UN many times, never had it been a special session ... and for the topic of discussion to be aliens?! He wiped his brow, feeling dizzy from the weight of the news he was about to share with the council. He took another sip of cold water and closed his eyes, taking in one last deep breath of air.

Jamal walked out onto the stage and took his seat in the line of chairs in the back.

The attendees were silent. The room was not in its usual swing of dignitaries shaking hands and warming each other up. The usual face-to-face politics that were normally here were gone. Everyone knew something big was to be shared.

Rumors had been kept at bay, though people were beginning to believe the United States had been hiding something important. President Helland's presence at the meeting cemented these rumors and the press, though strictly regulated, was already beginning their own theories.

For the first time in history, the meeting would be held without media coverage; this was enough to cause the public to take notice and begin speculating. Security was at an all-time high to prevent any media leaks or interruptions.

The General Assembly Hall was completely filled with the 193 country delegates. The stage was flanked on both sides by the iconic curved wooden tables. In front of the stage were the stair-stepped rows of desks. Each delegate had a computer screen, country name tag and a lamp. Everyone sat motionless, ready to hear what was about to be said.

Opela Hermadi, the elder statesman from Indonesia took the stage. Jamal knew her well, but today she avoided eye contact with him. She stepped behind the podium and adjusted the mic down and took a deep breath.

"Ladies and gentlemen, delegates of the UN, thank you for attending this emergency special session of the United Nations General Assembly. As we all know, these sessions are nontypical, and this will be the twelfth session in the history of the United Nations. The primary objective of such sessions is to make urgent recommendations on a particular issue.

Such recommendations can include collective measures and may require the use of armed force when necessary to maintain or restore international peace and security. Due to the urgent and unprecedented nature of today's meeting, normal beginning procedures will be waived. At this time, I would like to invite our secretary-general, Jamal Uddin of Bangladesh, to take the stand."

Jamal stood and walked to the center of the stage as Opela stepped away. A polite applause grew throughout the hall as he reached the podium. Once he did, the room went silent again.

He checked his notes as he laid them on the small stand. He rested both hands on the side and took a deep breath.

"Ladies and gentlemen, it is my privilege today to announce the commencement of a truly historic moment in the history of humanity. Approximately, nineteen weeks ago, the military branch of the United States detected a unique signal originating within our solar system."

He paused for everyone to take that in, noticing several people looking around with confused looks, clearly not expecting this special session to start off mentioning "our solar system." Jamal licked his lips to ensure the next words came out clearly and confidently.

"We have compelling grounds to suspect that the detected signal originates from extraterrestrial intelligence."

The room was silent, Jamal could hear his own heartbeat pulsing within his inner ear. The eyes staring at him were all wide and filled with worry and disbelief. Within moments a few voices could be heard throughout the audience, and the tension in the room began to rise with the increasing chatter.

Jamal raised his hand.

"Please, I ask that you all remain attentive and focused. This news was just as shocking to me as it is to you now. Allow me to provide you with some information before we begin to speculate."

The giant projection screen behind him came to life, displaying a graphic of the solar system, zooming out from Earth.

"The origin point of the signal has been named X0-5 and currently rests at 632 million kilometers from Earth, just outside of the Asteroid Belt."

The video highlighted the region in scale to the solar system.

"We will release all details of the physics, but what captured the experts' eye was that X0-5 is stationary from our orientation here on Earth meaning it is in a geosynchronous orbit with Earth. This tells us two things. Firstly, it is using thrust, beyond what we are capable of generating with modern-day technology, to maintain its location. Secondly, it has clearly oriented itself with respect to Earth, leading us to believe this was a targeted and planned contact." Jamal paused, to survey his audience.

"The US government has initiated contact with X0-5 and successfully delivered a linguistics package, enabling X0-5 to respond in written English. In a remarkable development, X0-5 returned a message marking the first written response we have received."

Jamal turned to the screen and the readout of the signal was displayed, just how it looked to the original scientists who read it for the first time. Jamal reread the final lines.

We are alien. You are alien.
You name your species human.
You may name us what you choose in your language.
We are not enemies.

He turned back to the mic.

"For the first time in the history of humanity we have confirmation of communication from an extraterrestrial intelligence."

This time when he stopped, people began speaking all at once. It took some time to get everyone calmed down. But Jamal was finally able to get the representative from Brazil to take the floor.

"The United States should never have hidden this information from us for so long. This communication and its existence should have been immediately reported to the United Nations and partnering organizations!" The woman's voice quivered slightly.

"SETI was brought in first for their expertise and the United Nations Office for Outer Space Affairs, with what I would assume will be agreed upon by this council, will be brought up to speed next. Yes, the United States may have held this within their own control for longer than protocol states. However, it was not clear what the nature of the signal was for the majority of the time."

The prime minister of Albania began next. "An event such as this cannot and should not be confined to the discussion at the UN. This is something that changes all of humanity as one. This event needs to be shared with the people of our world. We can no longer hold this back. We must tell the public today." Some murmurs followed.

"I'm afraid I do not agree with my colleague from Albania," the president of Malta said. "This is of great importance. There is much to be discussed. There is much we do not know. And it will be dangerous to share such a historic piece of information with the public if we still have questions. I demand that the United States reveal to us all that they know about this matter."

As Jamal tried to regain order in the hall, the president of Pakistan stood and took over with a powerful, booming voice.

"This is a sham of misinformation," he shouted. "The existence of alien beings from another planet is a false concept and is against the teaching of Allah. Nowhere in truth is this explained, and it is a deception by the United States. I urge everyone not to fall for this deception."

This harsh tone created more people yelling. Jamal was starting to wonder if he was ever going to gain control here.

"We need more proof," the president of Poland said. "How do we know this isn't some elaborate hoax? My thoughts immediately jump to AI or some type of elusive man-made technology we aren't considering."

Jamal raised his arms to get everyone's attention. "This is what the SETI experts are working on now. All current data supports that this is *not* a hoax or AI. But we are considering all possibilities and using strict scientific postulations to come up with concrete facts. We hope to declassify and release all of this information, which will be discussed, case by case, in this session."

"But why were we not informed about this earlier?" the president of Senegal asked. "Why were we forced to wait instead of being able to contribute to this historic event?"

Questions and angry comments continued. Many countries were upset they had not been communicated with earlier. Others were outright unable to process the information, some even stormed out in disbelief. Jamal had to assume they would be leaking the information, if not openly talking to the press, regardless of the NDA they had all signed. He needed to get ahead of that and get consensus before moving forward.

"I recommend we push forward with this session so we can get all of the facts in front of you," Jamal said. "Ultimately, the main objective of today's session will be to determine whether the UN will disclose this information to the public, and if so, how."

Jamal knew the only way to avoid public panic was to appear in control of this situation. And the best way to do that was to let the UN tell the world. They would have to communicate it soon. The emergency session lasted over six hours as Jamal and the council navigated the complex discussion and details of the AS1. By the conclusion of the meeting and several different opportunities to vote, the council has come to a consensus. The public would be notified immediately.

Chapter 26

Waller arrived at Lackland Air Force Base fourteen hours after the United Nations Emergency Special Session had concluded. Adam Fangman, the large security guard, greeted him at the gate. Adam was not only running internal security in the area but had become the golf cart chauffeur. Waller scanned his visitor's badge and climbed into the cramped vehicle. Adam smiled at him and took off, speeding across the vast stretch of pavement to hangar C, where Higgens had hijacked a small conference room for their use.

Higgens was waiting inside, sipping on a lemon La Croix. Upon seeing the cold beverage, Waller wheeled himself around and retrieved one from the small break room just outside. Reentering, Waller cracked his sparkling water and made the first remark.

"Well somehow you managed to get me to come down to this dump." He glanced around the room.

"It beats the zoo of DC that you call home," Higgens replied flatly.

Waller's eyes continued to scan the small room until they finally stopped at a point where the paint was peeling and bubbling off the wall from the intense humidity.

"How's your mother?" Waller asked, changing the subject but still observing all the imperfections in the outdated room.

"Don't try your bullshit political tactics on me, Waller. I don't need you tickling my balls," Higgens replied, annoyed.

Waller just smiled and tried again.

"How's your mother, John?" Waller repeated.

Higgens took a long deep breath.

"She's good, Robert. Still sharp as a tack, she wouldn't mind seeing you again, it's been a long time. Her retirement pay is covering the bills," Higgens replied, briefly remembering the time when he and Robert Waller used to get along.

"Good, good. Did she end up in Florida?"

"Got herself a nice place in Horseshoe Bay." Higgens paused, wondering if he was making a mistake telling Waller too much.

"Believe it or not, I bought a place just up the street right before this whole mess started. I haven't even had a chance to see it in person yet."

Waller looked surprised by this. "You're not retiring, are you?"

"Well, looking less likely now," Higgens barked back, thinking about all of the recent events.

Waller stretched his arms up and reached them back, linking his fingers behind his head.

"As you know, the UN held their session yesterday."

Higgens nodded.

"And, as expected, this has put a lot of different plans in motion. I've spent the last week thumbing through pages and pages of protocols when coming in contact with … aliens.

This still all sounds so absurd when I say it out loud." Waller paused.

"I know what you mean, but that is now the mission." Higgens shook his head in agreed disbelief.

"How's that affecting us here?" Higgens indicated toward Operation SD headquarters.

"Well, fortunately for you, there was no immediate request for the United States to cancel the operation, so nothing will change here, but it is more important than ever that we stay quiet. President Helland was adamant that we do our best to fly under that radar and follow all established protocols."

Higgens let out a loud groan but nodded his head.

"Additionally, Umairah Rafidi, an astrophysicist from Singapore, has been notified. She is the director of UNOOSA and holds the title of First Contact Specialist. She will be working with Linda on the communication side of things so you can expect her to join the team soon."

Both sat in silence, perhaps still needing time to fully comprehend the situation.

"Now that the UN is aware of the ASI," Higgens said. "Who do you think is going to want to shoulder in and call the shots?"

"What do you mean?" Waller asked, already knowing where this was going.

"I mean, something like this, something that is literally changing life as we know it." Higgens stood up from the table. "Everyone is going to want a piece of that action, to be in the history books, get their voice heard. Each country is going to fight for some position on some new committee; you know how it goes. They are going to drag out the process. Pretty soon we'll be having to wait for seventeen different countries' approval before we can do a damn thing."

Waller shrugged. "Yeah, maybe. But we're following the right process now, which is needed. Even you can't disagree with that."

"When are they going to make the announcement?" Higgens asked, now pacing around the room.

"Within the next twenty-four hours, but we have to assume word will start to get out before then," Waller said.

Higgens pinched the bridge of his nose.

"And once that happens, then what? When do we break the 'communication pause' that Declan talked about? We need to communicate back to the AS1."

"That will be determined after the secretary-general contacts us."

Higgens shook his head and mumbled some profanity under his breath.

"It's already starting. We wait. What if the AS1 doesn't like to wait? We're already losing control of this situation," Higgens said.

"Well, it's part of the process to get things back under control," Waller replied.

"Damn the process," Higgens said, walking toward the door.

"Higgens!" Waller called to catch his attention before he stormed off.

"Get your rest now while you can, once this all goes public, we're going to have a whole new can of worms to deal with."

Part II

DISCLOSURE

The power of the people is much stronger than the people in power.

— Wael Ghonim

Chapter 27

The clip of President Helland's red-bottomed heels echoed against the walls of the large auditorium as she walked across the wooden stage. Bright lights shone upon her; she could feel the heat they were producing. Looking ahead, she saw Jamal Uddin already standing at the center podium. He would be making the announcement today as a neutral party to all of Earth's nations. Although just a short walk, maybe only fifty feet, it seemed to take a million loud steps to reach her assigned podium, to Jamal's right. Once she finally reached her stand, she made direct eye contact with the UN secretary-general and smiled, nodding her head. Her podium, built of rich red mahogany wood, displayed the United States Presidential Seal on its front. She thumbed through the papers resting on the stand and was relieved to recognize the contents that she had worked on with her administration earlier that day to prepare.

Next, Declan made his way onto the stage, en route to the podium on Jamal's left, the SETI logo placed neatly on his podium. Helland could feel the tension in the room tighten at the sight of SETI. They knew his organization searched for intelligent life outside the solar system. Declan's smile reached ear to ear as he made his way to his stand.

All three felt the weight of the situation resting on their shoulders. This announcement was about to be broadcast live on every official news station in the world, establishing it as the largest public announcement in the history of humankind. Ads and press releases had been running continuously for the past twenty-four hours to let the public know; however, no information regarding the nature or contents of the announcement had been shared.

Almost three billion viewers, an unprecedented audience size, huddled around their televisions and computers to watch the highly anticipated statement. Radio channels broadcasted the audio, YouTube had live feed, the massive screen over Times Square began counting down, and over a hundred thousand people gathered in the cordoned streets. Snow floated down from the gray sky, leaving white accents against the black streets and buildings. The loud murmur of voices fell to almost nothing as the clock reached zero and the screen came to life.

Viewers now saw Jamal with Declan and President Helland standing by his side on a large stage. Flags from all over the world hung on the wall behind. Above the long row of familiar flags hung a larger flag, new to most eyes. It was blue in the background with a realistic representation of Earth stitched largely in the center.

Jamal pulled his mic a few inches forward before addressing the world.

"To every member of our great Earth, we thank you all for allowing us to speak with you today. My name is Jamal

Uddin, I come from Bangladesh and am the current secretary-general of the United Nations. Today, I have been given the opportunity to present to you all a very exciting moment in human history. A moment that will most definitely impact and shape our futures as humankind."

He looked down at the podium for the first time since the beginning of the speech. Millions of people were motionless, waiting for his next words.

Jamal refocused his gaze on the large bank of cameras pointed at him. A look of unease had come over his face. After a long inhale, words began filling the air once again.

"On June 13 of this year, an abnormal signal originating from within our solar system was detected by the United States military. Unsure of what was being detected, a team of scientists and analysts was brought in to study the findings. After eighty-six days, the team confirmed its origin. On September 17 it was brought to SETI's attention that a signal had been discovered and was believed to be of extraterrestrial origin."

Typically, at this point Jamal was used to an outcry of questions and cameras but today, the press box remained silent, stunned by the last sentence. Faces hollow with confused thoughts of fear, disbelief, and shock. One young reporter rose to her feet. Jamal held his breath, awaiting some sort of outcry or protest. Instead, she turned and began to walk across the front of the row of reporters, she swaggered drunkenly, reaching out at nothing to stabilize herself before collapsing to the ground. Those around her reached down to check on her; however, most of their eyes remained on the stage, locked on to Jamal. He pushed forward, focusing hard on retaining his composure and confidence as a team of medics came to aid the fainted woman.

"Moving forward, all information regarding the signal will be officially declassified and accessible to the public and nations of this world. There will be no secrets. This is bigger than governments and economies. We, as a human species, must come together and work together to choose our future. This extraterrestrial being has proven peaceful, and will likely present us with opportunities to learn more about the universe we live in. Please"—Jamal placed his hands together in front of himself in a praying position—"I ask each and every one of you to stand strong and united. Today, we are united as one, under the flag of Planet Earth and stand proud and confident in our abilities. Today, we as a human species grow stronger and closer to one another, recognizing that it is pertinent to our integrity. Today, ladies and gentlemen, we take a massive step forward in our progression through time as an always-growing and evolving race of humans. The United Nations, with the absolute support of our 195 nations and their elected representatives, will move forward with establishing communication with our new friends."

Chapter 28

~ 24 hours after public announcement of AS1 ~

Harsh echoes of beds being pushed across the concrete gymnasium floor cut into the tense air. People talked in hushed, stern voices; the lack of laughter gave the large, cramped space an apocalyptic feel. Over three hundred people had come to the guarded gymnasium, seeking safety for themselves and their families.

Darío's family had left their home the morning after the announcement. A house, just three buildings down, had caught fire and burned to the ground. Chaos in Quito had fully erupted and spread into the smaller outlying towns, which were being ransacked. The Ecuadorian military had been driving through the streets announcing through loudspeakers where the safe houses had been set up. Darío's little sister's grade school building was on the list and his family quickly fled to the location on foot, just one and a half kilometers from their house.

The family of four now sat, shoulder to shoulder on green plastic Club Lager crates, trying to watch and hear the news playing on the projector at the back of the large concrete room. His mother cried silently, head in her hands. They had been assigned one bunk bed for the four of them and had brought only what they could carry. The local news station switched back and forth from local news to world news every fifteen minutes. Much of the world news was presented in English with Spanish subtitles.

    His father, a devout Christian, refused to believe it. He said it was fake news and was baffled as to why the governments would want to instill this kind of chaos upon the people. The distressing images were uncensored and showed riots and wakes of casualties throughout the world. The death count in Ecuador alone had hit over one hundred people in less than twenty-four hours after the announcement, which had pushed the local authorities into establishing a strict 8 p.m. curfew. Dario wondered if the announcement of the new space creatures meant the end of the world as he knew it.

Chapter 29

Gideon knew the announcement would cause a stir, but he was altogether unprepared for what he saw as he stared down from the rooftop patio of the Marriott hotel. Sheer and utter bedlam. After the announcement, civilian personnel of Operation SD had been provided the option to begin staying off base. Both Gideon and Linda had jumped at the opportunity to finally sleep in a proper bed and enjoy some quality food. Rajit, on the other hand, had chosen to stay on base, worried about the safety of the outside world. Gideon wondered if he had in fact made the right choice.

Cars in the street below had clustered into traffic that was moving so slowly it was practically stopped. Several individuals had gotten out of their cars and were looking around, as if aliens might be lurking nearby. There was a hubbub of panicked voices, shouts and screams, and car horns blared through the hot Texas air. A siren wailed in the distance, the sound of its wee-woo adding another noise to the din. Then there was glass breaking somewhere, its fracturing shards sounding keen and close, even from the high rooftop.

Swarms of people shuffled about, some with their faces glued to their phones, as they scoured the Internet for all the answers. Others ran away with some purpose, whether to their own homes, to see loved ones, or even to a gun store, Gideon couldn't know.

Gideon heard someone shouting something about the second coming of Jesus, another voice yelling, "Fake news!" and a third voice, louder and more frantic than the others, yelling, "They're going to kill us all!" followed by a loud, guttural scream. Gideon saw people praying in the street, and families could be seen running out of a nearby convenience store with armfuls of toilet paper. Why is it always toilet paper? he mused.

Gideon looked down upon the city in horror. It was complete chaos and had been this way for the past several days. Gideon wondered if the AS1 had a way to see all this. He couldn't imagine the aliens' surprise, dismay, or even amusement at seeing how the earthlings were reacting to their presence.

A drone whizzed by, and Gideon wondered what its operator was hoping to find. He wondered what kind of stories people had already made up in their minds concerning these aliens. What were they imagining? And then he took a moment to consider what *he* was imagining. Based on their interactions so far … intelligent, nonconfrontational. And that's all he really needed to know, wasn't it? How long do you need to develop trust and understand intent?

Gideon closed his eyes and let the commotion wash over him. He fiddled with the copper washer in his pocket, more out of anxiety this time rather than trying to process some equations.

"Fancy seeing you up here."

Gideon turned around to see Linda, walking his way.

"How are you?" Gideon asked as she made her way over and rested her forearms casually over the balcony railing. He noticed she seemed to avoid looking down at the chaotic streets below, but instead looked up at the sky.

Linda shrugged. "Did you see the Pope made his official announcement today? Let's hope that helps the religious fanatics at least." She pulled out a cigarette and placed it in her mouth, not lighting it.

Gideon nodded; he had heard.

"And another Eastern Bloc country joined the resolution with North Korea and Iran, right?" he asked.

"It was Kosovo," Linda said. "They are calling it the Tonkin Resolution now."

"The what?"

"As in the Gulf of Tonkin. You know, the whole Vietnam War thing. The want to push the theory that everything is all a false flag by the US government to gain more international control."

She lit her cigarette and paused, still looking up at the sky.

"I don't smoke," Linda said as a red glow from the Marlboro lit up her inhale. She finally turned her gaze to the streets below. Gideon shifted his weight back to avoid the thin swirling trails of burnt nicotine gliding toward him. Confused by her statement as she clearly was, in fact smoking.

"There have been a lot of firsts in the last couple of weeks," Gideon replied.

"I used to smoke, back when it was cool. I stopped when we adopted our daughter, Matilda. Actually, both my wife and

I did. My hair was blond back then, not naturally, but I made more of an effort to try and look young." Her gaze slowly shifted back toward the clear evening sky, now speckled with stars. Her graying hair sparkled in the Edison bulb lighting the hotel rooftop.

"When was that?" Gideon now moved to her right side to avoid the cigarette smoke; Linda didn't seem to notice.

"Well, I just missed Mat's fifth birthday, so five years ago. I've never missed my daughter's birthday before."

Gideon nodded; he could sense that Linda was feeling overwhelmed.

"I'm embarrassed by the public's reaction to the news." She paused and then continued. "Although I do hold some small shred of understanding for how they are feeling. How will this impact our future generations? What will be their experience with alien life? Will it be normal for them? Just like our understanding of the planets in our solar system, will young children be taught about our neighbors on different planets? Will their picture books have illustrations of the AS1 race, with a small description going along with it?" She gave her cigarette a long hard pull, releasing a long exhale of smoke.

"Gone are the days when the existence of life on other planets was merely a theory," Gideon agreed.

"We are part of the last generation that knew what it was like before other life forms were discovered," Linda said. "There was a last generation before the printing press, before gunpowder, before the nuclear bomb …" Her voice trailed off.

The two stood in silence for minutes, deep in thought. Since the LKD package's success, an exchange of three messages had followed, each specially crafted by Linda and Umairah

Rafidi, which allowed the scientists to gather some limited information and prove the AS1s' ability to communicate.

"I'm relieved that we have broken our silence with the AS1 and we are now engaging in active communication," Linda said softly.

"Agreed, and the AS1s' claim to be nonthreatening seems to be true ... no strange requests or any signs of malicious intent," Gideon replied.

Linda nodded.

"Amazing to think there is a team of twelve aliens up there right now sitting in some alien spacecraft." She squinted up at the now black sky, as if trying to see the AS1 ship.

"They must be as excited as we are, meeting an alien race for the first time," she said.

"Do you believe that? That we are the first alien race they have made contact with?"

"I don't know, Gideon. There's no way to prove or disprove their statements yet."

Gideon digested the recent developments and created his reply.

"You know, Linda, this time was coming. Contact with extraterrestrials; most modern thinkers will agree it was just a matter of time. We are lucky to be involved and lucky the AS1 seems to be respecting our boundaries."

Linda shoved the remaining half of the cigarette into the white metal railing, bits of ash and smoke fluttering until the smothered red glow dissipated.

"But what's next? I can't imagine we will be sitting around sending messages back and forth forever."

Gideon chewed on the thought, but it didn't take long for an answer to come. There was only one thing that could possibly come next.

"The next step must be meeting," she finished, completing Gideon's thoughts.

"Agreed, and since the farthest we have ever sent a human is to the moon and they clearly have the technology to travel space, we can probably assume they will come to us," Gideon replied.

Linda raised her eyebrows in thought, her expression shifting from gloomy to thoughtful.

Gideon wondered what exactly she was thinking. Perhaps, like he, she was considering what it might be like to meet them. What the entire first meeting would be like. Pondering what the challenges would be, how smooth it might go, how wrong it could go. Maybe, like Gideon, she was thinking of how impossible it was that they were even in this position: communicating with alien life and possibly about to meet them. No, he didn't need to be a mind reader to know what she was thinking.

"They will approach us," she suggested.

Chapter 30

The hot San Antonio sun poured relentlessly over all visible objects, creating a heat that not only came from the sky, but also radiated off of everything the sun touched like the pavement and surrounding buildings. As the golf cart sped across the military base, the wind felt like a hot air dryer blowing harshly into Gideon's face.

Fortunately, the nearby Starbucks had recently reopened since shutting down after the announcement due to nobody showing up for work. Gideon clutched the iced mocha as if it were his lifeline from the intense heat.

"Seems like things are leveling out, huh?" Gideon shouted over the loud drone of the tires rolling across the pavement.

Fangman lifted an eyebrow.

"Guess so, the gyms are still closed, and my stocks are still frozen. I didn't even know they were allowed to pull that shit. Did you?" Fangman referred to the freeze on the trading of stocks evoked shortly after the announcement. This prevented a complete crash of the stock market.

Gideon shrugged at the comment as he had never been interested in stocks. Instead, he lifted his mocha in the air. "At least we can get iced coffees again."

Fangman grunted and Gideon made the assumption he wasn't much of a Starbucks iced mocha kind of guy. Once they arrived at the ugly tan building, Gideon hopped out of the golf cart, thanking Fangman for the lift. He nodded his head and then leaned back, placing his feet up on the dash while he waited for the next person needing a ride.

Gideon took the handicap ramp instead of the stairs; somehow it seemed it would require less energy, although he was very aware that the laws of physics would disagree. Once he opened the doors his nose detected the familiar scent of computers consuming electricity and dust. His ears registered the familiar sound of fans humming as the processors worked tirelessly. His eyes, however, noticed something unusual. People's faces were strained, and Higgens was barking orders over the red-corded phone.

Linda quickly walked to him, with alarm on her face. "Well, it's happened—they requested permission to approach."

"No shit," Gideon replied. They had all been expecting this, but it now felt all too unexpected—too soon.

He looked up at screen two and saw the message.

```
 -
 --
 Requesting permission to approach
 Earth. Humans may track our
 ship's movement. Please confirm
 our proposed location here:
 --
 -
 -filelog_data-
```

"Where's the location?" Gideon asked, just loud enough so that anyone with the answer would hear.

"We haven't locked it in yet, the data in there is pretty abstract, the tech team is working hard to understand it. But right now, it's looking a little close for comfort."

As Gideon thought about this, the break in conversation allowed him to focus on what Higgens was saying into the red phone.

"Trust me, it is being worked on as we speak. A reply stating we will need time to think is being typed right now."

Higgens eyed Linda, causing her to leave Gideon and return to her post. "Agreed, we can certainly be happy that they asked and didn't just show up, but we need to be the ones who tell them where to park, not them."

A tech named Kade shouted, "Sir, we have an understanding of their proposed location, it would put them in a geosynchronous orbit nearly 1.2 million kilometers from Earth."

Higgens looked at Gideon. "How far away is that?"

Gideon considered a moment.

"Um, that's like four times further away than the moon."

He pulled out his smartphone to double-check his facts, although he knew his response was accurate.

Higgens covered the phone's microphone with his hand and raised his voice to get everyone's attention.

"Alright, that's way too fucking close, I can tell you that. Don, set up a meeting with Melissa and the astronomy team to get detailed information on their proposed location. Linda, get a hold of Umairah Rafidi and UNOOSA. We need their buy-in on everything we do here."

Higgens un-palmed the phone receiver and shouted into it, almost as if he had forgotten the microphone was just a few inches from his mouth.

"Buy us some time, Waller, let me know what the UN wants to do here and if they support the AS1 approach. If they do, let's get ahead of this and understand what location is tolerable; we can then cross-reference that with the AS1 proposal and provide back our demands." Higgens hung up the phone with more force than necessary and turned back to the room.

"I want notes on all this at 14:30. I'll set up an 'around the room' and we'll see where we're at. Let's go, people!"

The room erupted into action; this team was beginning to perform like a well-oiled machine.

Chapter 31

Two cardboard boxes sat in the center of the room, accompanied only by a small desk holding a double set of monitors plugged into a government-issued laptop. Declan was already envisioning how much better a large oak desk would look in comparison. The room was large and the back window, facing east, presented an impressive view of New York's Chrysler Tower. Declan's memory faded in and out of his last phone call with his wife. She had refused to pack and ship his things from his SETI office to DC, demanding that he come home to the family and reminding him that when they had kids, there was an agreement that he would no longer leave for long business trips. "This is not a fucking business trip!" Declan had yelled back, flabbergasted that she didn't recognize the importance of his role in working with the AS1.

While it was unfortunate it had to be this way, she knew what type of lifestyle she had married into. Declan had to make sacrifices. Things had to be done in his department and he was the one to do them. He had always told her his job was more of a lifestyle. It wasn't some nine-to-five office job.

He thought about giving her a call. As he considered the different things he might say to her, he reminded himself that he simply didn't have the time. He also thought that maybe his wife needed to be more understanding. Here he was, in the middle of work, thinking of ways to make it right with her, and he wondered if she was doing the same.

Annoyed, he pulled apart the packaging on a fresh pair of Montblanc pens he had recently bought for himself. What choice did he have? This was his call to duty, the largest and greatest discovery in the history of humankind, and he was at the front of it all.

An aggressive knock shook his door.

Rising to his feet, Declan pulled the door open.

"Jamal," he said, surprised to see such a high-ranking figure already requiring his assistance. The UN secretary-general looked exhausted. He gestured toward the mostly empty room.

"May I come in?" he requested, before entering and leaning himself against the desk in Declan's new office.

"Unlike you, I didn't sign up for this."

Declan thought about this for a minute. "You mean by me working for SETI?"

Jamal nodded and turned to face Declan, meeting his eyes. "Yes … aliens? What the fucking fuck."

Declan was going to release a laugh, but quickly noticed Jamal's clenched fists and decided a simple nod was more appropriate. They stood, in silence, for what felt like too long.

Declan thought about how unbelievable all of this was, how surreal. Aliens—not a meteorite. Not a newly discovered planet. But actual aliens. Living, intelligent, aliens—that had communicated with them. He couldn't help but release a small smile, which he hid behind a hand covering his mouth.

"Is there something I can help you with, sir?" Declan pushed.

Jamal seemed to regain a present state of mind. "There will be more information soon, but the AS1 have requested to approach in an effort to make contact."

"You're kidding, my God! And?" Declan pushed.

"Why would we let some alien race, we know nothing about, approach our planet?" Jamal said, almost sounding annoyed.

The man had a point, but Declan knew denying the AS1 would stop progress, stop the opportunity for him and all of SETI to finally achieve what they had set out to achieve.

"Well, you are here talking to me about it," Declan replied.

Jamal replied with a nod.

"So, if you are looking for my opinion, you have already assured the public that they are peaceful, which I firmly believe is the case. Thus, at this stage, denying the AS1 the right to move closer, would that not be an indication of distrust?"

"To the AS1 or the public eye?" Jamal replied.

Does it really matter? thought Declan, but he replied more diplomatically. "Well, I suppose both, but I am focusing on the public here. If it becomes known that the AS1 requested to approach, and we refuse them?" Declan shook his head theatrically, to make his point. "That could be more dangerous than granting the AS1 permission in the first place. Our key tactic to keeping the public at ease, ever since the discovery of the AS1, has been to convey the trust we have built with them. To show distrust in that relationship or what could be perceived as a disagreement? A conflict? That would be catastrophic for the people of our planet." Declan allowed Jamal to take this in.

There would always be people who were afraid, Declan thought. No sense in making them more afraid. If the public got wind that they were denying the AS1 entry, people would automatically think it was because the AS1 were dangerous and could stifle this entire operation.

"There is much more at stake here than public image, Declan," Jamal replied.

Declan wanted to disagree, though with a bit of a warning in his gut. It was the public that determined if their world got flipped upside down because of this. They had all the power and didn't even know it. Already how quickly fear turned into riots and looting had proven the danger and power the general population held. Public image was just about the most important thing here. But telling that to the UN secretary-general wasn't going to be constructive. Declan had to play his cards right.

"Sure," Declan replied in the most sincere voice he could muster up.

"Allow me to paint you another picture," Declan continued.

"Do you believe the AS1 have the ability to approach quickly, perhaps even come directly to Earth, regardless of whether we provide them permission? In other words, do you think the AS1 are reliant on us for the ability to travel here?"

Jamal's eyes sharpened.

"No, I would assume the AS1 have the technological abilities to come to Earth, regardless of whether we support them."

"I would have to agree with you, Jamal," Declan replied, pushing out his lower lip and nodding his head.

"Do you believe the AS1 may have a hard time accepting the fact that they have traveled all this way, only to be turned around?"

"What are you getting at, Declan?" Jamal asked.

"I am of the belief that there is a high likelihood that the AS1 will choose to approach us, maybe even come to Earth, regardless of our answer. Granting them permission keeps us in the power position. Allows us to set forth the parameters in which we are comfortable. Sets the precedent to the public that *we* are in control of the situation, not at the mercy of what the AS1 choose."

Jamal walked to the large window and gazed out at the New York skyline. As the sun dipped below the horizon, a deep darkness cloaked the sky. The city's millions of windows shone in a brilliant display of light, overpowering any chance of seeing stars in the night sky. He turned away from the view to face Declan, lowering himself so he was sitting on the windowsill.

"Your point is valid, in fact, President Helland and her council had similar concerns. But I just can't shake the feeling that this could be a huge mistake."

"I understand that Jamal, but denying our new friends reaching out? Meeting us? That would be the greatest mistake of all." Declan met Jamal's gaze with intensity.

Chapter 32

News of the AS1 had immediately changed the lives of Michelle and the crew of four on the International Space Station, often referred to as the ISS. Previously the day-to-day had been slow-paced and very routine, checking in on a few in-process experiments and logging data. Now, nearly all of the ongoing experiments had been put on hold and focus had changed to receiving daily orders from the bosses down on Earth.

Michelle hadn't expected things to change so abruptly on the ISS, but change they had.

Neither she nor any of her fellow astronauts could have seen this coming. But Michelle was happy about the change. Not just for the obvious reason, that they were going to meet freakin' aliens! But because it gave her the opportunity to learn new things and skills. She had quickly mastered all of her current roles and responsibilities on the ISS and now was her chance to learn even more.

She pushed off the handle she was holding and floated gracefully to the robotics workstation. Here she would grapple the incoming payload that had been launched just several hours ago. Her palms were already sweaty as she spun 180 degrees to face the simulator to practice once again. In her combined experience of nearly two years on the ISS, she had only been required to dock three unmanned ships. This was typically something Crach would do, but Michelle had lost the game of jacks last night. She cursed herself for wagering now, although she almost always beat him at the stupid game.

After running the simulation flawlessly, she returned to the controls and activated the LCD screens, reminding herself that this was just another skill to put in her tool belt. The low beep of the screens turning on echoed in the small compartment. She could now see the SpaceX craft slowly approaching. It contained a massive payload, in fact the largest ever sent to the space station. It would not return to Earth, as it would serve as the crew quarters for the AS1 crew. This was the first of five payloads to be sent, staggered a few days apart.

She couldn't wait to get a look inside. For some reason, just seeing what the aliens were going to see was exciting in and of itself.

The crew had only been made aware of the recent developments four days ago, following the decision to allow the AS1 to approach the ISS. From what she understood, the plan would be to first allow the AS1 to bring their craft to an orbit around Mars. Once at this location, they would send a smaller craft containing three AS1 delegates to dock at the ISS. She was still in shock at the fact that in just a few weeks, she would be face-to-face with an alien.

She and the crew currently inhabiting the ISS had been given the option to return to Earth prior to the AS1 coming if they did not want to be involved in the first contact. Two of the members had chosen to return to Earth, not wanting any part of it. The remaining crew felt nothing but thrilled and lucky to have the opportunity. True scientist mentality there, she considered.

She wondered about the first thing she might say to the extraterrestrials, or what they would say to her. "Hello," she said, trying to imagine it. *No.* "So glad to meet you. So glad to *finally* meet you." *Err, uh* … "Welcome. Welcome to Earth." But they weren't on Earth yet. Shoot.

She hadn't thought about it before, what they might say, and she suddenly found herself feeling the pressure of having to speak in front of some intelligent being. She hated public speaking for starters. What if she said something stupid? What if she stuttered? What if she simply didn't know what to say at all?

Her already clammy hands moistened even more. This would be recorded and likely played back countless times by future generations. It would obviously be on the news, uploaded on YouTube, and there'd likely be a plethora of documentaries made using the footage.

Shaking her mind from these thoughts, she activated the remote manipulator system and keyed her mic.

"Eye, this is Dock One, do you copy?" she asked.

"Eye, here go ahead," Crach said. He would be observing everything from the Cupola, ready to help her guide the payload.

"Ready to begin ODS stage one," she said.

"Stage one, go."

Michelle turned on all links of the orbital docking system then pressed her eyes into the vision cup to line up the flight. Everything was looking good. She could see the SpaceX payload clearly, small puffs of steam could be seen firing from the exterior in order to keep the vessel aligned with the ISS docking. The white plumes contrasted against the black vastness of space. The AI autopilot was bringing it in perfectly.

"She's lined up, ready for stage two if you are."

"Copy that, everything is clear. Stage two is a go."

Michelle activated the lock to the open setting on the pressurized mating adaptor. "Adaptor is ready to receive."

"Copy. Hold steady," Crach said. "Payload is on course. Will dock in ten."

Michelle checked all the warning sensors. Everything was in the green. She looked through the cup again. Everything looked good. Almost no exterior thrusters were firing at this point, indicating that the payload was aligned.

A deep clang echoed through the walls as over six thousand pounds of payload lugged into the bracket. She never got tired of hearing that sound of satisfaction.

"Docking complete," Crach said over the comm.

Yes. The sequence and the sound were the same. But something was special about this one.

Chapter 33

~ 18 days after public announcement of AS1 ~

The dry desert sped by the bus window. Adrenaline pulsed in Chase's veins and his fingers rubbed the back of the laminated sign that sat between his legs. The sign read *"All intelligence is created equal"*; a small graphic of a green alien shaking a stick figure's hand was shown below the words. A journey from Istanbul to the city of Alanya typically would take over sixteen hours; fortunately, the tour bus companies had quickly jumped on the opportunity of people gathering in Alanya, and were offering many direct options.

Chase considered himself a well-versed traveler but had never been to Türkiye. Upon landing in Istanbul, he'd attempted to get supplies at a large supermarket; the prices of goods near the festival would undoubtedly be inflated. As expected, the grocery store shelves contained mostly empty space. Although the EU had imposed strict regulations on the quantity of items a single person could purchase at a time, many stores had run low on water and canned goods. He left after finding an excellent deal on a couple of boxes of cheap wine, a loaf of bread, and several cans of tuna.

After the announcement, he'd felt something build inside of him. He had never felt strongly one way or another about aliens, but now he found that he firmly believed they should be considered friends and allowed to interact with the public. They were travelers, just as many people here on Earth were, and should be treated with respect and hospitality. After discovering the gathering of people in Alanya through social media, Chase had decided to join. Videos had been circulating on the Internet showing massive groups of people camping out in their vans and motorhomes, expressing their opinions. This was a movement.

His mother, back in France, was afraid of him going, saying he was joining one of these crazy cults growing all over the world. Chase explained that most of these groups were nonviolent hippies camping out in the desert. These modern-day alien cults held a closer similarity to Burning Man than the Manson Family. He had been to Burning Man several years ago, had found the festival to be a blast, and was excited to join in something even bigger and more important. This was the real thing. Life as they knew it would never be the same.

The onboard television at the front of the bus pulled his attention from the window, featuring a new advertisement from Tesla. Elon Musk jumped on the recent news and developed a new car in record speed. The advertisement used comedy when explaining the new car would protect anyone inside from high radiation, extreme heat fluctuations, and a roll cage that could withstand the fall of a ten-story collapsed building. Although the commercial came off as more of a lighthearted joke than a serious attempt at selling a car, these new vehicles apparently were already being preordered by the masses.

Chapter 34

Higgens nodded his permission to send the message. A monumental moment in human history, finalized by the simple movement of an individual's head and a few key strikes. A message that had been created by two women from two different nations. Approved by a panel of elected persons, all with unique backgrounds, experiences, opinions, and cultures. A message that was simple in writing, but authorized a mode of travel so complex that humans couldn't understand it.

Thanks to Linda's initial work and her ongoing support in the program, numbers were one of the first things that were standardized in their communication with the AS1. That led to defining units for measurement. This, at first, proved difficult due to the absence of a shared frame of reference between humans and the AS1. Fortunately, the dwarf planet Ceres within the scattered disc region of the Asteroid Belt, offered a solution. Its proximity to the AS1 ship allowed for the measurement of its diameter, serving as a fixed point of reference acknowledged by both humans and AS1. Leveraging this, humans proceeded to educate the AS1 on the metric system, utilizing the established distance as a foundational unit. This paved the way allowing them to clearly define things like distance, locations, time and everything else that needed to be coordinated.

The AS1 were more than willing to learn what computational systems humans used. They expressed that, since they were coming into our world, they would be willing to use the scientific standard of the human race. Which seemed logical and somewhat thoughtful. What was a little unnerving, was the fact that it had seemed so easy for the AS1 to adapt. Higgens considered the fact that for the last several centuries, humans had not even been able to standardize between metric and imperial, yet the AS1 had so easily and quickly converted to a completely new system.

The team had learned that the AS1, when within a solar system, could travel at nearly one hundred million meters per second, roughly one-third the speed of light. However, considering acceleration and deceleration times, they predicted arriving at the proposed location in approximately forty hours. Additionally, although they had not been able to transfer pictures, as photographs seemed to be a foreign concept to the AS1, the AS1 had provided a preliminary description of their biological buildup. It was understood that the AS1 were eight feet in height and approximately four feet wide. It seemed that the AS1 body was mostly spherical with six legs, and they did require oxygen to survive, just as life on Earth does. After being provided the atmospheric composition of the ISS, they confirmed they were fully comfortable in a seventy-two-degree environment made up of 78 percent nitrogen and 21 percent oxygen, like that on the space station.

Although nobody could begin to guess what they actually looked like in detail, this information had given the engineering team the ability to design the additional ISS nodes to a spec that would accommodate the AS1 comfortably.

The red LED in the wall lit up with the text "Outgoing Message Status." Higgens reread the message. He had already gone over it dozens of times, and countless others had approved, revised, approved again. But he still wanted to check it one more time. Screen two displayed the message.

```
-
--
The United Nations of Earth grants
the receiver of the message, AS1,
permission to approach with your
spacecraft to the agreed and
included coordinates. Assuming no
malfunctions or change in your
desires, we, the human race, expect
the AS1 to arrive at the location of
orbital inclination of 51.6 degrees
from Earth, ground point 51.11
south, 118.71 east. In approximately
41.5 Earth hours. We request that
you confirm this time and location
and begin your journey in 48 Earth
hours. We respect and appreciate
your patience and compliance. We
look forward to meeting you.
-
--
```

Higgens hit the transmit approval button and the new instructions turned the text from red to green. Higgens hovered his mouse over the "send" button. After one more deep breath he clicked. The LED text changed to orange with the words, "Message sent."

There was no going back now, and he hoped that the decision they had just made was the right one.

Chapter 35

Gideon stood in line at the cafeteria, not looking forward to whatever lunch option they were serving today, when his phone dinged. It was Linda.

"*Umairah has been removed from launch team. Go see Higgens ASAP.*"

Umairah Rafidi, the president of UNOOSA was the pre-authorized First Contact Specialist. Gideon didn't know what had come up, but he didn't care. He knew he was on the shortlist of backups to replace someone.

He left his tray on the counter and quickly walked down to Higgens's office. Gideon knocked on the door and opened it just as Higgens answered. Higgens sat behind his desk with his eyebrows raised at Gideon barging in.

"Can I help you?"

"I'd like to apply for the First Contact Specialist seat, now that Umairah is out," Gideon said. He stood ramrod straight and stared into Higgens's eyes.

Higgens dropped the paper in his hand and leaned back in his chair. "So, you've heard she's out? Word spreads fast around here apparently. That's what I'm trying to fix right now. Launch team orientation begins in one week. You know

I want you on the team, Gideon, but there is too much work to do to get you up to speed. Jamal wants to go with someone who has NASA experience, that will speed up the process."

"But I'm already on the alternate roster, right?"

"Yes, but—"

"I don't know who else is on the roster, but there is no way someone has more experience working with the AS1 than I do."

"Look, Gideon, I know you want to go, but I'm up to my eyeballs here in regulations. Look at this." He pointed to his desk. "We're creating standards and SOPs here that have never existed before, and I don't have time to put together a whole new training program in less than a week to get you on the shuttle. It just won't work."

"Sir, that's why I'm here. That's why I barged in. Who else is here standing in front of you? I'm ready to go right now."

"Gideon, look—"

"With all due respect, sir. If you are creating policy and SOPs, why not create it so I can go. I mean, look at all of what we're doing. We're all doing this from scratch. The seat that is up for grabs is the First Contact Specialist, that's me."

Higgens steepled his fingers and frowned. This kid always seemed to find a way to weasel into situations.

"I know my qualifications on paper are nothing compared to those of the other chosen individuals, but my involvement in the initial contact should speak for itself, shouldn't it?"

"A team of six, known as the Contact Team," Higgens said. "You really think you are one of the six that should go?"

"Without a doubt."

Gideon paused to make Higgens speak first. He and Higgens had grown a trusting rapport throughout the countless long days working together on Operation SD. He had to hope that would count for something.

After a long silence, Higgens rubbed his forehead and leaned his elbows on the desk. "Let me see what I can do, kid."

"Thank you, sir." Gideon wheeled around on his heels and left the room. The moment the door closed behind him, he rotated and slammed his back into the wall, his weak knees letting his weight go until he slid down far enough for his butt to hit the carpet. He sat there, regaining his breath. Never had he pushed himself that hard, but he had to go. He had to see this through and that meant going to the ISS.

The rest of the afternoon passed slower than any other day Gideon had ever experienced. Finally, he received an email telling him to meet in conference room 503 at 16:00. Gideon got there ten minutes early, only to end up having to wait … and wait. Finally, it was 16:17 and he was still waiting outside.

Gideon rose from the chair and paced back and forth outside the conference room. Inside, Higgens was surely on the phone discussing his future.

Time crawled on and just as he felt he had built up the courage to storm in and see what was going on, Higgens opened the door. He looked at Gideon with a face that betrayed no intentions. "Come on in," he beckoned, motioning with his hand.

Gideon stepped quietly into the conference room and slid into one of the chairs. Higgens sat down across from him. "The team is going to be led by Declan Wilter," said Higgens.

"As head of SETI *and* having astronaut experience, there isn't a man more qualified. He will report directly to UN secretary-general Jamal Uddin and me. Next, there's going to be a linguist, and that position is going to your colleague, Linda."

Gideon noticed himself smiling at the news that Linda was part of the team. He was happy for her. Though he was still very much preoccupied with the question of whether *he* was going to make the cut or not, it still felt comforting to know that his new friend would be included.

"Then there's going to be a technical support person who'll be responsible for logging data records and supplying essential IT support to the group," Higgens was saying. "We still need to fill this spot, but it needs to be someone with previous astronaut experience."

Gideon nodded.

"There will be two scientists and researchers of various fields, one being Rajit."

Again, Gideon felt his heart jump knowing another one of his close colleagues would have the opportunity to meet the AS1. Although he wondered if Rajit had agreed to it yet. Ever since the beginning, it was clear Rajit was not comfortable with the concept of aliens.

"Newly added to the team will be Carter Walters, a scientist with an unmatched résumé, graduating from Oxford University and winning a Nobel Prize for his work in topological order and the development of synthetic molecules. He is a theoretical physicist by trade but is also known for his chemistry knowledge. His most recent claim to fame was his work in ionizing radiation under microgravity, conducted on the ISS eight years ago." A brief look of dissatisfaction passed over Higgens's face. "He has a reputation for being overly honest and a bit arrogant."

"The final slot had originally been expected to be filled by Umairah Rafidi, a pre-authorized First Contact Specialist and the head of UNOOSA. But due to her age she's been determined unfit for space flight, as you know. Now, the fact that our First Contact Specialist is unfit for space flight seems a bit absurd, but I suppose nobody predicted we would actually be meeting aliens on the ISS, all contingency plans had us either sending communications from Earth to an alien civilization or ship, or the aliens came directly to Earth … Anyways, I digress."

"Oh, that's unfortunate, sir," said Gideon smugly. Higgens laughed off the words.

"Unfortunate my ass," he said, still chuckling. "You're so excited for a chance to go, it looks like your eyes are about to pop out of your head."

Gideon didn't doubt that at all. Traveling to space had been a dream since childhood. Traveling to space to meet an intelligent race of aliens didn't even fall into a category. He needed to go. He allowed himself a brief little laugh. "So …"

"Not sure why I bust my ass so much for you. You got the spot, but with an on-call candidate that will swoop in to relieve you of that privilege faster than you can blink. Your primary objective will be assisting Declan. I'll send details over shortly."

Gideon sat there dumbly, barely believing what was happening.

"We have to get you through the intro astronaut selection training. That starts tomorrow at 0600 hours."

Higgens checked his watch. "No, we're not turning you into an astronaut overnight, but we have to make sure you don't die on takeoff."

"I can do it," Gideon said. "I'll pass whatever tests you need."

Higgens nodded and smiled on one side of his face. "Easy to say now; you might think different when you're halfway through the centrifuge G-force simulator and your stomach is plastered to your backbone."

"I can do it."

"I'm putting a lot on the line for you, Gideon. You pass or else I'll look like a fool. Don't fail me."

"I won't."

"I know you won't. But—to be honest, kid," Higgens began. "Don't think this is me doing you a favor, that isn't why you're going. You are not just a random, off-chance replacement because someone else couldn't go. Truth is, most of us wanted you for this spot in the first place."

Gideon had no words.

"You're bright," Higgens went on. "You think outside the box, and you know your shit. I don't think you discovering that signal was a coincidence, and I'm not the only one who thinks that. You found it because of intellectual curiosity, consistency, and hard work. OK, and maybe just a little bit of luck." Higgens laughed. "What I'm saying is, because of your dedication and pivotal support of Operation SD, you have earned this spot. You are the right person for the job."

"Thank you, sir," Gideon said, thinking this might be the first time he had ever heard Higgens say something complimentary.

"So, I'm really going?" said Gideon with a smile, barely able to hear his own words over the drumming of his heart.

Higgens held up a finger.

"*If* you can pass the intro astronaut assessment, and your physical checks out … and *if* you don't screw anything up. Then, you're going," Higgens confirmed. "That'll be all for now." And he motioned with his head at the door.

Chapter 36

"Ship speed has slowed to fifty-two thousand meters per second and is two million kilometers out from location," Higgens said.

The SD team got the president and her cabinet on the line.

"Madam President, we've been tracking the AS1 ship for the last eight hours and the communication time delay is now down to just twelve minutes."

Gideon still had to catch himself that he was living in a world where having the president on a conference call to brief her on the deceleration of an alien spacecraft was normal.

"Calculating the ship's speed was challenging, as the ship appears to be moving faster than it actually is, an illusion that occurs when an object's origin is vastly further away than its destination and moving at a high rate of speed." Higgens paused.

"I'm tracking you, go on." The president's voice was calm and collected as always.

"When the ship departed from its original location, it appeared to leave thirty-five minutes later than reality, due to the time it takes light to reach Earth. Once it begins its journey, this time delay shortens as it nears its final destination. In the case of the AS1 ship, the observed travel time from Earth would be forty-one hours, but the actual travel time would take forty-one hours and thirty minutes."

"Ship speed continues to slow, now moving at a rate of thirty-four thousand meters per second, on course for our agreed-upon location," Kade, one of the technicians, called out.

"That is one hell of a deceleration," Gideon mumbled, impressed by the craft's abilities after doing some reading about modern-day human space travel.

"Estimated arrival in twenty minutes."

"Communication lines are open."

Higgens's sweaty palm had not left the red telephone for the last hour. Although optimistic, his mind continued to replay alternative scenarios over and over. What if the AS1 ship failed to stop at the agreed location or deviated from course. If one of these scenarios merged into reality, he would make a call issuing a warning flare to be launched in the direction of the craft, it would take our seemingly inferior technologies almost three hundred days to reach the ship. This being known, the secretary of defense confirmed that the ship would detect our reaction and assume the ship would see it as a warning. If no change of course was made, a series of nuclear warheads would be armed and await the ship to reach a distance of five hundred thousand kilometers before being launched. Higgens knew the odds of one of the nukes actually hitting the craft were as likely as hitting a sparrow out of the air with a hand-thrown rock.

Numbers began flowing across screen one, showing the deceleration of the ship. The numbers were good—consistent deceleration and on course. Hope pulled confidence and assurance into his nervous system.

"Ship's speed is now twelve thousand and holding, one million kilometers from location."

In the large room of people, few words were spoken. Emotions ranged from excitement to fear. None of these emotions needed an audible representation to be detected, the faces of the people said it all. Time felt slow, inching by as if intentionally dragging out the suspense, only to be set back to normal once words broke the silence, giving time a reference.

"Ship has stopped, shows no movement, and is located precisely at our specified location."

Applause erupted from the room.

"Madam President," Higgens said. "We are good to go for confirmation communication."

"Thank you," President Helland said over the line. "I will be contacting the UN secretary-general immediately."

"Thank you, Madam President," Higgens said.

The president's line went dead, and Higgens looked around with a massive smile.

Gideon hugged Linda. With the warmth he suddenly realized this was the first time he had hugged someone in over two years, since his departure from Idaho. Typically uncomfortable with human contact, today he felt there was no way to better cherish the moment.

When the two separated he saw tears running down her face.

"You OK?" he asked.

She nodded, but didn't seem able to speak, a linguist who was unable to formulate words. Once her brain had reconnected with the movements of her mouth, she whispered, "It's just really incredible, isn't it?"

Gideon nodded his agreement.

A loud *ping* hushed the excited chatter that had consumed the room.

"Incoming message!" Kade yelled. "Screen two."

```
-
--
Please confirm your satisfaction
with our location. Our ship's thrust
is powered down and will not be
turned back on until decided by
both AS1 and humans. We will have
our transport ship prepared with
a team in 48 hours and awaiting
your permission to approach the
International Space Station. We
look forward to meeting you.
```

Chapter 37

Nerves wicked the final bit of moisture from Gideon's mouth. To his left sat Linda and to his right was Rajit, who seemed to be the most scared of anyone. Neither of them had been to space before. They were now strapped to a Falcon 9 Block 5 rocket manufactured by SpaceX, which would have them docked to the Space Station inside of six hours. The ship had been given the name FET, for Flight to ET. The rocket was all white with two orange bands around the midsection and the new world flag painted on the sides. Gideon had mused that instead of looking like the classic NASA Space Shuttle, the entire rocket had a very similar shape to the classic homemade rocket kits he would launch into the sky as a kid. It had four large fins at the bottom and one long cylindrical body. The nose cone was where Gideon and the crew nervously awaited launch.

This would be the sixth launch from Kennedy Space Center in Cape Canaveral, Florida, to the International Space Station, the first five being unmanned supply runs in the last few weeks. All had been performed flawlessly. Despite the perfect success rate, every person in the craft was running over the safety training videos in their minds, keeping their focus.

The shuttle gave a noticeable shake, causing Rajit to let out a muffled, "Ahh, goddammit."

Gideon couldn't see Rajit's face as they were all seated shoulder to shoulder, seats leaned back so they were nearly on their backs, but he could only imagine his eyes were squeezed shut in anticipation. The small window in front of them revealed nothing but blue sky.

"Launch in one minute—maintain steady breathing," came into their helmets from a voice Gideon did not know.

If everything went to plan, the crew would never have to do a thing. All launch and docking maneuvers were automated.

Gideon thought back on his last conversation he'd had with his mom after he gained permission from Waller to tell her he would be going to space.

"Like to the moon, you mean?" she had asked.

"No, Mom. We'll be going to the International Space Station," he replied with a chuckle.

"Oh yes! I saw a documentary on that up on the PBS show. Looks like a lot of complicated stuff up there. Why you headed there?" The sound of her voice always gave Gideon a sense of comfort, despite their strained past relationship.

"To go meet the AS1, Mom," Gideon replied.

"Dear God, son, that's what you've been wrapped up in all this time? Those godforsaken creatures are real? You really think so? Uncle Tommy been sayin' it's just a political stunt to get more funding for NASA to develop some type of new military weapon," she replied in a hushed voice, as if she was now worried the phone line was bugged.

"Yes, the AS1 are real, and I'm going to go meet them," Gideon replied.

A long silence held on the other line.

"I'm proud of you, Gid. I don't say that enough. Your brilliant mind was always just too much for us to know how to deal with. When you were just a baby, you had already memorized every phone number in town … I used to ask you stuff like, 'Gid, what's Doctor Tom's line? I need to schedule you and your brother a checkup.'" The line went silent again.

"I can't lose another son; you be careful out there you hear?" she finally said.

"I will," Gideon replied before hanging up the phone.

A loud hiss filled the small compartment, bringing him back to the present. Gideon's heart raced, he felt like he was at the top of a carnival ride, just waiting for the big drop. But this was no carnival ride, they had been trained to be ready for the most intense acceleration they had, and ever would, experience in their lives.

"Commencing countdown."

"Mission F - E - T to launch in ten."

Gideon closed his eyes.

9

8

7

Sudden loud breathing filled his helmet.

6

Gideon tapped Rajit and motioned to the microphone.

5

Rajit muted his mic. Gideon felt his own heartbeat in the silence.

4

3

Intense vibrations ...

2

1

    No amount of centrifuge training could have prepared him for this. It felt as though every organ in his body was plastered to the back of his rib cage. Although fear still consumed him, the pressure was so great his mind was intensely focused on the present discomfort. Inertia plus gravity held him firmly to the seat back. He tried to initiate the motions of pushing air through his teeth, a practice they had learned in training, but was unable to focus and simply gritted his teeth, something they were in fact told not to do. The vibrations were insane, shaking his stressed body violently. He sat there in awe, completely disoriented and unable to focus on anything besides the war they were playing with physics.

    After several minutes the intensity waned ever so slightly, and Gideon began to relish the intense experience. It was all a part of the journey, after all. When this was all over, he would remember every part of this. Every step on the way to meeting the aliens. Every hurdle, every discomfort, every spectacular sight. A story that would be told for generations. This is what it took for humans to meet an alien species and he was going to absorb every moment.

Straining the muscle in his neck, he moved his head slightly to the left and then to the right. Just able to see the other five astronauts shaking from the vibrations in silence, it was an image he would never forget. Five scientists, the *Contact Team*, ambitious in their motives, on their way to meet another race of highly intelligent beings.

The acceleration began to lessen and the crew looked at each other, nodding signs of confidence and approval. Vibrations slowed and Gideon knew they must be getting into the thinner atmosphere. Within five minutes, they had cleared the Kármán line. At this point they were permitted to loosen their harnesses three clicks. This brought with it the first feeling of weightlessness, noticeable by the lack of pressure on the parts of his body that his weight should have been sitting on. The feeling of weightlessness took some getting used to. It felt like being in free fall, Gideon leaned forward slightly, allowing him to see past the sphere of Linda's helmet. The view outside the small window was astonishing. Earth was beautiful.

He raised his hand and Linda returned a high five. He saw her open her mouth and yell, but everything was still completely silent within his helmet. Turning toward Rajit he lifted his hand again. Rajit made eye contact and shook his head but managed a smile, his hand remaining tightly grasped to the metal armrests.

Just as the team was beginning to relax, the aggressive blast of the thruster changed the orientation of the FET. Gideon felt a wave of nausea pass over him as it felt like they were beginning to spin forward over the nose of the ship. He tried to keep his eyes locked on Earth as it now passed overhead, a tactic they had been taught in flight school, similar to keeping your eyes locked on land when fighting seasickness on a rocking boat.

Another aggressive jolt stopped the rotation and the International Space Station came into view. The size of the ISS surprised Gideon, appearing eerily small in that vastness of space. They approached at a steady pace and once twenty yards away, the FET slowed to an inch per second before making contact and locking on to the ISS PMA-2 airlock. Gideon tried to visualize the Space Station layout in his mind.

Rajit met Gideon's eye; his perspiration was beginning to fog up the lens of his helmet.

"How are you feeling?" Gideon asked on the direct line.

"Better now, I guess … I need to get out of this suit." His eyes were wide as he looked around.

Gideon nodded his agreement. Being in a seated position for over six hours in a bulky, confining, orange "pumpkin suit" was less than comfortable. The physical discomfort along with the mental stress of shooting into space strapped to a massive rocket made the overall experience far from pleasant. Although still loosely strapped into place, Gideon could now feel the zero gravity. He detected a difference in his belly, the way his skin pressed against the space suit, even the spit in his mouth felt different.

"We have the all-clear. Begin unstrapping sequence; remember, focus on the routines you learned on A300." Technician Astronaut John Brandon was confident and unwavering as he unclipped, gracefully floating a 180-degree rotation to face the team, making sure everyone else was releasing their harnesses without issue. A300 was a modified Boeing 727-200 used to simulate zero-g. Gideon and the team had done several different trips aboard the plane to learn the effects and routines to deal with zero-g.

Gideon's helmet detached with a small hiss and sounds filled his ears. The sensation was relieving after being in what felt like a muffled vacuum for hours. The first voice he heard was Rajit.

"Oh dear God, man, that's nice." Rajit's dark skin looked clammy and almost pale.

"You fucking made it, man." Gideon smiled, genuinely proud.

Several times throughout the astronaut training, Gideon had thought Rajit was going to quit. For a man terrified of flying across the country in a Boeing 737, boarding a rocket to be hurled into space seemed impossible. One night after training, the two of them had sat in the car together. They talked about the fact that they had been selected as six people in a world of nearly eight billion to meet an extraterrestrial life form. An opportunity that would never arise again. This motivation had given Rajit the strength to put his fears behind him. Now seeing his colleague about to board the International Space Station gave Gideon a feeling of warmth.

"Welcome to space, team! This moment is just the first of many monumental steps we will take as a collective in pushing the limits of human discovery!" Declan announced, theatrically.

Gideon couldn't help rolling his eyes as he had learned Declan was a personality of clichés and many words. He then began working on the zipper of his "pumpkin suit." Once the final clip was released, Gideon instantly felt the full effect of weightlessness. Although hardly moving, he felt no pressure between his buttocks and the firm seat that he had been pressed against. After some awkward wiggling, he floated out of the bulky orange suit. Giving a slight push, he began to rise, instantly forgetting everything he had learned on the KC-135. He tried to reach above himself to grab the ceiling, which only set him into a slow rotation. His shoulder hit first, shortly followed by his hip and feet, leaving him awkwardly pressed against the ceiling. With all eyes on him, he forced a smile and a "OK" hand signal.

Others began presenting their own variations of Gideon's maneuvers. Linda, Rajit, and Gideon were the least trained individuals to have ever been to space, with only a two-week intensive training course.

Once the team stabilized, Brandon floated to the control panel and after several keystrokes and a series of back-and-forth radio checks, the airlock opened, connecting the space of the FET rocket and Space Station. On the other side was the ISS team, dressed in clothes similar to a doctor's scrubs. It was a crew of four, two of whom would take the FET back to Earth. The other two would remain on the ISS to help the Contact Team navigate the Space Station as well as continue their everyday duties. They all had beaming smiles and welcomed them with waves and handshakes.

Brandon reached out and put his hand on Rajit's shoulder. "The hard part is over."

Gideon met Brandon after his first week of training when he was brought in as an instructor to help him and the other new astronauts get up to speed. He was fifty-two years old and had been to the ISS on two separate occasions. His life's work was engineering and developing ISS communication and computer systems. Both of his visits had been for troubleshooting and upgrading the ISS. One look at him and you would think NASA astronaut. He stood around five foot six and had pale skin and dark brown hair with plenty of silver mixed in, just long enough to cover the tops of his ears. His face was clean-shaven with the exception of the thick bushy mustache that seemed just a little bit too long. His glasses were a thin wire aviator shape. He was a relatively quiet man and only seemed to speak when it was required.

Carter, on the other hand, the seasoned astronaut second in command to Declan, matched as Gideon had expected, based on his bio and résumé. His arrogance was obvious in his handsome, chocolate-skin looks, tall, strong stature and overconfident demeanor. Although highly gifted in intelligence, based on his many awards and life accomplishments, he seemed to take enjoyment in giving others time to think about something before providing them the answer.

Rajit, color now beginning to fill his face again, smiled back at Brandon and nodded quickly as if trying to seem fine, but only proving that he was not.

Carter chuckled smoothly.

Linda shot him a look. "Get off your high horse, Carter; I heard you puked the first time you set foot on the ISS."

Carter's smile faded into a flat line that pointed to his clenched jawbone.

"Well, I can tell you, the ride used to be a bit bumpier back in the day. But thank you for the reminder, I am sure that's information all of us were looking to hear, Linda."

Gideon and the team focused their attention on the four astronauts greeting them into the Space Station.

First to speak was a woman wearing her brown hair in a tight bun. Gideon realized this was likely the only option for long hair in zero gravity. She appeared to be in her late thirties and in impressively good shape.

"Welcome to the International Space Station!" the woman exclaimed with a beaming smile.

"It is always a pleasure to have new company, we rarely get any up here." She chuckled and gave Brandon a hug. "Brandon! Great to see you, it's been a long time huh? What is this, your third time up?"

"That would be correct." Brandon smiled.

"Anyway, we really look forward to working with you all during your time here. For starters, I am Michelle; I'll be heading up most of the operations here."

Gideon felt a hand push him to the side as Declan made his way to the front to shake Michelle's hand.

"I'm Declan, the lead of the Contact Team and president of SETI. Nice to meet you."

"Yes, I'm aware," Michelle replied. She then gestured to a short man hanging from the ceiling above her, requesting that he introduce himself.

"I am Crach, from Russia," he replied, animated as a robot.

"The two of us will be remaining here with you six for the duration of your stay. Charlie and Dennis will be heading back on the FET." Michelle gestured to the two others casually floating behind, who waved.

"Please follow Crach to Node 1 and take some time to relax and adjust to the zero gravity, he can make you a delicious cup of space coffee. I will remain here with Charlie and Dennis to get them prepared for departure."

The team began to follow Crach into the Space Station.

"Actually, Brandon, would you mind hanging back and helping us run through the safety check before sending 'em home?" Michelle called to the group.

"Sure thing," Brandon replied, looking excited to jump back into the ISS mechanics. He gracefully grabbed one of the handles in front of himself, spinning his floating body into a front flip. Once he had rotated 180 degrees, he moved his feet outward, catching one of the walls with both feet and pushed himself in the opposite direction, back toward Michelle and the team. Gideon, who was struggling to keep himself from banging into the walls as he clumsily made his way down the tunnel, was impressed by his grace.

Chapter 38

Gideon and the team floated in delight, playing with the zero gravity, a sensation Gideon assumed could never get old. Crach glided into the room holding five silver bags. They looked similar to snack-size ziplocks made from foil.

"I hope none of you wanted decaf." Crach's Russian accent sounded serious as he distributed the bags.

"Stronger the better." Rajit finally appeared to be on the road to recovery after the traumatic flight.

Gideon tore the marked tab from one corner of the silver packet and squeezed some dark brown fluid into his mouth. He was shocked by the smooth taste.

He looked up to see Carter drinking the fluid while holding the bag almost a foot from his face. The dark coffee flowed through the air in a straight but oscillating line. Clearly not his first space coffee, Gideon thought.

"Crach, this is excellent!" Linda was as impressed as Gideon.

"You can thank the Italians," Crach said, still not smiling. "Back in 2015 they ran an experiment called ISSpresso and developed the first space espresso machine. After a bit of convincing and fudged paperwork, we were able to keep the machine here after its success. Coffee beans are sent up with the food, labeled as 'energy' and categorized as medicinal."

"I see things haven't changed much since my last visit here, spending the people's money so we can enjoy the best coffee in space." Carter smirked and gulped the last of his coffee stream.

"Oh, lighten up, it's just a coffee," Declan said.

Michelle came gliding into the area, Brandon just behind.

"Enjoying your ISSpresso? Good, good! Well, OK! We are all set, Charlie and Dennis headed to their crew quarters to rest up for tomorrow's departure, sleeping like two little bugs in a rug. I can give you guys a quick briefing and tour."

Gideon held up his coffee packet in a sort of salute.

"Follow me, we'll start in Columbus, the laboratory on the starboard side, front area. Here is a laminated map of the ISS."

She elegantly passed the map to each new crew member, similarly to how someone would throw a playing card but in slow motion, floating smoothly through the air.

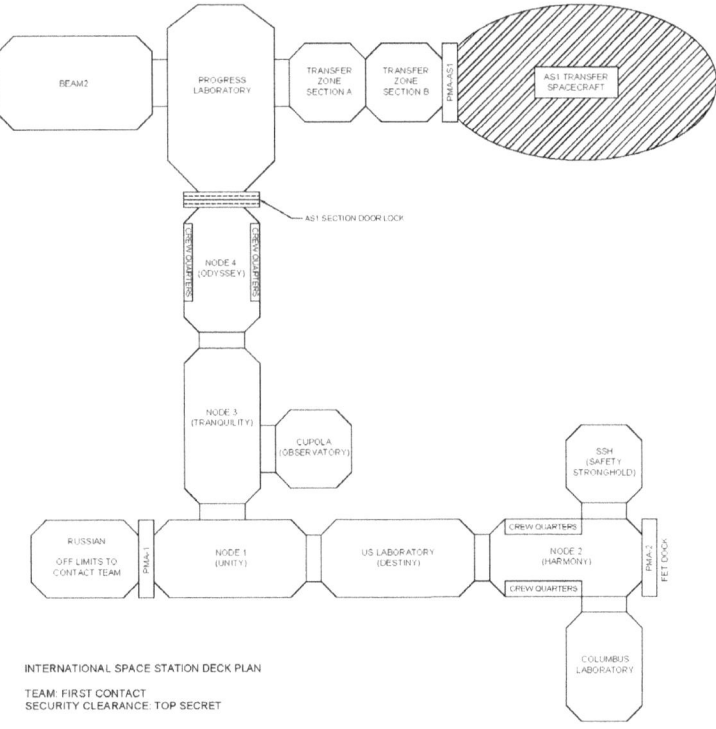

As she glided away, Gideon and the team struggled to keep up, clumsily pushing themselves down the tight passageways—they laughed at each other's fumbling. After some effort, they arrived at the lab and Michelle got their attention.

"The Columbus Laboratory is a European lab and is also used by the Americans quite often. AS1 activities will have top priority; however, this lab will continue to be used for microgravity research, which helps us understand the effects of microgravity on various biological and physical processes, such as cell growth, protein crystallization, and fluid dynamics. I am in charge of keeping things up and running in this lab, so don't expect anything too exciting back here."

Gideon grabbed one of the blue handles on the wall and hooked his right foot into a strap, anchoring his body, and preventing him from floating away. The room, better described as a section of the long hallway, was covered in laptops, clipped floating wires and metal work benches on all four walls. The amount of equipment packed into the small space, which was similar in size to the inside of a U-Haul moving truck, was mind-blowing. Organized chaos were the first words that crept into his brain.

"The only reason you will need to be in here," Michelle continued after the team had made their observations, "is to take your daily blood samples. Do you remember your training on this?"

"Unfortunately, yes," Rajit replied, his face beginning to look pale again.

"Good, if you need help or have any questions, myself, Crach or Brandon can assist you."

"I've also been here a few times as well," Carter chimed in. Seeming annoyed he wasn't mentioned.

"Yes, but I'm sure you have better things to do than help the newbies."

Carter shrugged his agreement.

"Anyway," Michelle said, regaining everyone's focus. "Now we'll head to Node 2, also known as Harmony which, as you know, is where FET is currently docked. Most of our supplies will come in from there."

Node 2 was bigger than Columbus, but not by much. Its main purpose was a place for incoming payloads to dock— incoming supply ships, shuttles, or additional nodes.

Slightly further aft were four crew quarters. One on each wall, including what in a gravity environment, would be considered the floor and ceiling. Gideon was quickly realizing that in the space station there is no floor or ceiling, just four walls. The crew quarters, two of which were currently occupied by Charlie and Dennis, were small rectangular cubbies maybe seven feet tall and three feet deep and wide. They were equipped with a brownish-green sleeping bag held to the wall by an attachment at the top and bottom. Across from the sleeping bag sat two laptops. Michelle explained that the Contact Team's quarters were located in the newly attached Node 4.

"Also recently attached is the SSH, or Safety StrongHold, which is connected to Node 2."

As the team listened, Michelle re-explained the process they had learned on Earth. The procedure required that throughout the entire duration of the AS1 occupying the ISS, an individual, rotating between Crach, Michelle, and Declan, would be locked inside the SSH. Here they had the ability to communicate directly to Earth, disengage PMA-AS1, which would be the attachment point of the AS1 ship, or disengage the entire AS1 Section, at the AS1 Section door lock. Once disengaged, a hard thrust would push the AS1 occupied sections away from Earth and the ISS in the event of an emergency or hostile AS1.

From Node 2 they continued to glide back into the ISS in the aft direction. They passed through the primary US lab, known as Destiny, where much of Carter's and Rajit's research would be accomplished. This lab had a similar look to that of Columbus but was larger and seemed to have more laptop workstations. Soon they circled back to Node 1 where they had received their ISSpresso. Gideon was still in shock at the number of wires and pieces of electrical equipment floating off the walls. More than once his foot had caught in a loose wire, tugging at it as he drifted by, he wondered if this was dangerous. With the lack of gravity, nothing would lie flat without being strapped down, giving everything a disorganized look.

Next, they made their way to Node 3 also known as Tranquility, which was just adjacent to Node 1. This small space contained a treadmill, weight rack, and bathroom. This area had fewer loose wires than the others.

"Now of course we have to check out the Cupola, everyone's favorite part!" Michelle looked excited.

"The Cupola, which means 'dome' in Italian, has seven windows and is used to conduct experiments, dockings, and observations of Earth. Really, this is where we go to think. Sometimes I just really need to look out a window. Please, take turns and check it out, it's pretty amazing!" Michelle was beaming.

Rajit and Linda went in first, and he could hear their gasps. Once they came back out, Gideon floated in for a look. The entrance was small, maybe around four feet wide. The interior of the Cupola was mostly windows, bordered by black metal, which was a noticeable contrast to the rest of the ISS's white walls and structure.

Gideon gazed upon the view from the windows in awe. The size of Earth from the ISS perspective was breathtaking. Gideon had expected to see Earth as a spherical planet, similar to the pictures you see from the moon. He quickly realized that the orbit of the ISS in relation to the Earth was really not that far away, and from the Cupola he could only see about a third of the horizon stretching in a graceful arc. The clouds looked like swirling water frozen in time.

Gideon took one final look before pushing himself back out, wanting to give others the chance to observe.

Michelle faced the team. "Any questions so far? Cool stuff, isn't it?! Good, now we are heading into the new zones." She motioned for the team to follow.

"This is Node 4 also known as Odyssey. We attached this bad boy just a few weeks ago and yours truly got to dock it," Michelle said, pointing her thumbs toward herself.

Node 4 was clearly newer than the other sections. The walls were perfectly white and the metallics gleamed. Node 4 contained eight crew quarters; Michelle pointed out which of the six were assigned to the Contact Team. She then distributed a personalized iPad to each team member, giving a quick runthrough on its functions. All matched exactly with what they had been taught on Earth. She shifted her gaze to the large metal door at the back of the node. The door appeared to be brushed steel and had the large words "ACCESS TO AS1 ZONE: Permitted Personnel Only" written across in large red font. Michelle turned toward Carter.

"Carter, will you do the honors of opening the AS1 Section door lock?"

He pushed his way to the door, not seeming to care about making contact with shoulders. He scanned his fingerprint and inserted the mechanical key they had all been given. The mechanical key was a last-minute safety precaution in the event the AS1 were able to hack the ISS computer systems.

Sometimes the oldest methods still proved to be the most reliable.

Once the unlocking sequence was completed, the AS1 Section door was manually slid out of the way on a pivoting hinge. Carter gestured grandly for everyone to enter. The team drifted through the small diameter, and the door was manually closed and locked behind them, which had to be done within thirty seconds to prevent an alarm from sounding. The crew had been given very strict orders to ensure the door remained closed at all times as the AS1 were not permitted to leave the AS1 Zone, which included BEAM2, Progress Laboratory and of course, their own ship.

Gideon for the first time, felt a sense of unease, being locked into a room. He felt trapped. He took a deep breath and focused his attention on the surroundings. Now in the Progress Lab, things started to look very different. The lab was significantly larger and less cluttered. This was to accommodate the large body size of the AS1. The lab was set up with various laptops, microscopes, and other stations. Both Carter and Rajit's eyes widened at the sight of some of the most technologically advanced lab equipment known to man.

Michelle spent a full twenty minutes explaining the capabilities and types of equipment in the Progress Lab, but Gideon's mind began to wander. Trying to visualize that in seventy-two hours, this room would contain an alien. An alien that was much larger and perhaps far more intelligent than the humans who would be attempting to teach it. And they would be locked in here with it. Again, a dark feeling of doubt and fear chewed away at his subconscious.

Michelle's overly excited voice regained his attention. "Attached directly above the Progress Laboratory is BEAM2, which was, for you history buffs, designed after the original BEAM, an experimental *Bigelow Expandable Activity Module* used back in 2016 for storage. This is the largest open space of nine hundred eighty-five cubic feet, almost double that of the original BEAM. This is where we will be conducting daily interviews with the AS1."

Gideon's attention was perked up as this was going to be one of his main jobs paired with Declan, although many of the questions would be provided to them by analysts back on Earth.

They observed the large open space that almost reminded him of the inside of a recording studio. The white walls were pillowed, which he assumed was for sound quality. There were several microphones and computers stowed away in the back.

The team floated back down into Progress and turned their attention to where the AS1 would enter onto the ISS.

"Now, this is the Transfer Zone. Its main purpose is to be an airlock between the AS1 Spacecraft and the ISS. The purpose of this airlock is to prevent the transfer of contaminants between the two spaces. As you can see it has two doors, one between Progress and the Transfer Zone and another between the Transfer Zone and the AS1 spacecraft. One door will be kept closed while the other is opened so when the AS1 enters the ISS there is no mixing of their ship's environment and our ISS environment."

The Transfer Zone contained two small windows, the first looking into the blackness of space. This could be used, in addition to the Cupola, to observe the attached AS1 ship, the second was on the door to the Transfer Zone, allowing the team to see in.

"And well, that just about wraps up this version of MTV Cribs, ISS edition!" Michelle said happily. Gideon noticed Crach roll his eyes and figured this was probably not the first time she had used this tagline.

"Any questions? Nothing?" she pressed.

At this point, the team had been awake for nearly twenty-four hours and everyone was exhausted. Most of the crew shook their heads and began making their way back to their quarters in Node 4. With only seventy hours until the AS1 arrival, the team needed to rest and begin prep first thing after some well-deserved sleep.

Chapter 39

Gideon pulled himself into the Cupola, still groggy from his deep sleep, to find Rajit facing the center window. In an attempt not to disturb Rajit, Gideon tried to enter the small space slowly and quietly. He pushed himself off the wall and his hand clasped the upper handle, but his feet continued moving toward Rajit as if of their own accord. Gideon went into an off-axis backflip. His feet, nearly hitting Rajit in the back of the head, made a loud thump against the borosilicate bulletproof glass.

Startled, Rajit turned his head to see Gideon trying to right himself.

"Sorry, man, just as I thought I was getting comfortable with zero gravity." Gideon was slightly red in the face.

"No worries, I hit my head there when I came in." Rajit pointed to the grease print of a forehead on the front window.

Rajit's smile had a way of making anyone feel welcome, and Gideon laughed at the vision of the short man running headfirst into the window.

"Pretty amazing, isn't it? Doubt it will ever get old." Gideon gazed at the large blue and white planet framed in the window.

"Indeed." Rajit turned his head to the incredible view.

They shared a moment of awe for several minutes.

"As you probably noted, I couldn't come to terms with the concept of aliens just a few months ago." Rajit's voice was quiet. "Sure, I'm a scientist and always understood the probability of us being the only form of life in the universe as unlikely. But intelligent life? Reaching out to us?" He shook his head. "No, it doesn't seem possible." He sighed.

Gideon observed a man torn by beliefs and questions.

"What else have I, or we as humans, been wrong about?"

Gideon didn't know what to say.

Rajit turned back to the window. "It frightens me, just thinking of all the knowledge they might have, the technologies they have likely perfected." Rajit's shoulders slumped. "We're at their mercy, you know?"

"Are you scared?"

"I am, on so many levels, Gideon. I have no reason to believe they have ill intentions, but no matter how I run it in my head, I just don't see a way their presence can benefit humanity."

"What if they have technologies and knowledge that help us? Like with climate change, sustainable energy, things like that?"

"You think they will just hand it over? We can't possibly have anything useful to give them in return, can we? So, what do they really want from us?"

"Maybe we do. An invention can come anytime; it may not be directly related to technological advancement. Maybe they aren't nearly as advanced as we think. Perhaps, they just discovered space travel before us. We could have lots of knowledge and technologies that they do not."

Rajit seemed to consider this.

"I believe they are what they say they are: scientists and explorers excited to finally meet another intelligent species," Gideon continued.

"Intelligent," Rajit said back, rubbing his temples.

"And what is the unit of measurement for intelligence? We just base the scale off of what we know. Bugs have low levels of computational intelligence and humans have high levels. That is our scale. We have no way of knowing what the AS1 scale looks like. To them, we could be on the same scale to them as bugs are to us."

Part III

CONTACT

All we know is still infinitely less than all that remains unknown.

— William Harvey

Chapter 40

Gideon, Declan, Linda, Carter, Brandon, Rajit, Michelle, and Crach floated in nervous silence inside the Progress Laboratory. Eight people, scheduled to make history, no matter the outcome. Updates were relayed to them from the Operation SD team back on Earth, now primarily based out of the UN building in New York. The AS1 transport spacecraft had left its mother ship two hours ago and supposedly carried three travelers from another solar system.

The approaching alien ship was now visible from the Transfer Zone window of the ISS, reflecting the intense sunlight, making it bright against the black backdrop of space. Even at this distance Gideon could tell it was large, almost twice the size of the International Space Station. This had caused concern, but the AS1 explained they had no smaller alternative. With a fair amount of convincing from Declan, the decision had been made that the large size of the ship did not impose any more or less of a threat to the ISS than if the ship had been small in size.

As it approached, the organic shape became more obvious. Its smoothly pointed nose flowed into the shape of a cone, eventually becoming parallel, making the back half a cylinder like the shape of a bullet. This led Gideon to believe that it had the ability to enter atmospheres, as there was obviously no advantage to aerodynamics in space.

"Question 128, how does the ship slow speed with no sign of exterior propulsion?" Carter punched the words into his tablet. He had been mumbling his extensive list of questions since the start of the day.

"This is a monumental moment, people," Declan said, looking like a kid on Christmas morning. "This ship is the most incredible sight ever seen by humans. Greater than the moment Lewis and Clark set eyes on the Pacific Ocean, greater than when humans discovered the ability to create fire! We are truly observing the unknown and …" Declan shook his head as if trying to wake himself from a dream.

"And soon, this moment will be succeeded by an even grander one: meeting the pilots of this vessel, traveling to us from another solar system. This is only the beginning."

Rajit shifted his grip on the anchoring blue handle. The team had been very quiet for the last few hours, only mentioning important details over breakfast and avoiding useless chatter.

"Crach, arm the AS1 Section door lock. Declan and Linda, please proceed to your positions." Michelle's voice was uncharacteristically serious.

Declan and Linda would be the first ones to greet the AS1. The introduction would be completed in the Transfer Zone. This meant there would be no quarantine wall or anything separating the two from the AS1. Linda had been the one advocating for this, explaining it was a gesture of trust and friendship to greet the AS1 as we would greet fellow humans boarding the ISS. Declan had been willing to play along.

The plan was to dock the AS1 vessel and seal Declan and Linda into the Transfer Zone area A. The AS1 would then move from their ship to Transfer Zone area B and the airlock would be closed behind them. Slowly allowing the airlock to equalize with the atmosphere within the ISS ship. This was considered the most dangerous step. Although discussions with the AS1 prior to their departure for the ISS had concluded it was safe for the AS1 to be in the ISS atmosphere, it was a risk. The AS1 had been confident in the data. Once Transfer Zone area B matched the environment of the ISS, the two Transfer Zones, area A and area B would be equalized and the airlock door separating the two would be opened, putting the AS1, Linda, and Declan in the same occupied space. At this point the meeting would be kept brief. They would exchange greetings and Declan would provide a detailed plan of the following day's meeting and agenda. The door would then be closed.

With a nod, Declan and Linda gracefully maneuvered forward into the small chamber and spun 180 to face the rest of the team.

"Remember, if anything is uncomfortable or feels off, just say '*You got here very quickly,*' and the airlock door will be shut, separating you from the AS1," Michelle reminded, the muscles in her jaw twitching.

"It will not be necessary," Linda replied with confidence that made Gideon feel she knew exactly how the exchange would go.

"You need to be aware, Linda; don't let your excitement jade your ability to detect a threat," Carter shot back.

"All will be well, we are prepared," Linda replied with a smile, unaffected by Carter's tone.

"Alright, good luck; we will be watching," Michelle said.

With a salute, Crach triggered the door to close the pair off.

Michelle left the group and headed to the SSH. She would be watching through the video feed there per safety protocol. Gideon and the remaining team peered through the Transfer Zone window, allowing them to clearly see Declan and Linda. They appeared incredibly calm and stood fast, feet anchored in straps, facing the airlock that would separate them from the AS1. Gideon shifted his gaze to the outward window. The AS1 craft was only about fifteen or twenty meters away and moving in at the requested speed of two centimeters per second.

"Thirteen minutes out from docking," Crach announced to the team.

Crach had proven to be an expert on the ISS, and this was his third term on the space station, totaling a staggering 765 days in space. Gideon sensed he was uncomfortable with the monumental shift in plans for the ISS but seemed to comply with little resistance.

Now just a meter or two away, the cylindrical ship loomed into view. Gideon's heart pounded. His gaze rapidly switched from the PMA window to the exterior window. He could now only see a portion of the ship as it prepared to dock.

"That material ... it's fascinating." Carter's brow scrunched tightly as he gazed at the ship. "And there are no windows, antennae ... Not even any writing or markings."

Gideon's attention abruptly refocused on the port window by a gentle shake, indicating the craft had made contact.

"Locking sequence complete," Crach called out and then shifted his focus to Brandon.

The first step now was to establish communication between them and the AS1.

"Sending message now." Brandon's voice cracked slightly while his fingers drummed patterns on the face of his tablet.

Silence.

The lack of sound heightened everyone's feelings, anxiety, anticipation, and fear. After a few short seconds, Brandon looked up from his tablet.

"Message received; AS1 confirms a successful dock."

The crew let out a quick breath of relief.

"AS1 is requesting permission to enter Transfer Zone area B." Brandon pressed his finger to his earpiece, listening to Michelle's approval.

"Roger that, AS1 entering Transfer Zone area B."

Crach's brow furrowed as he furiously flipped toggle switches and clicked away at the laptop mounted on the wall.

"AS1 has entered area B and is ready for environment equalization," Brandon called out.

The team all exchanged excited looks, everything was moving quickly and smoothly.

Crach looked at Brandon, paused for a moment and then nodded. With the flip of a single switch, he began the equalization process.

"Equalization complete. Status on AS1?" Crach said. For the first time, Gideon could hear worry in his voice.

"AS1 confirm no issues!" Brandon replied.

"Equalizing areas A and B," Crach called back.

The airlock door was far too thick to allow sound through, but Gideon could imagine the hiss that Declan and Linda must be hearing as their section equalized.

"Pressures successfully equalized," Crach announced. "OK, Linda, Declan. Are you ready for me to open the door?"

The two gave the OK gesture.

Gideon held his breath as Crach punched in the sequence to open the airlock door, the only thing left separating humankind and their first contact from an extraterrestrial life form.

Chapter 41

The door slid open, revealing a sight that eight humans simultaneously witnessed along with the NASA team in Florida via live video feed.

A strange sensation zipped through Gideon's body, tingling needles stabbed at the pores on his face and a soft, high-pitched whine filled his brain and ears. His body halted its demand for air as it fell into a primal state of focus.

Three AS1 beings towered over Declan and Linda. Their imposing stature dwarfed the two humans by several feet. These enigmatic beings possessed a startling anatomy, unlike anything seen on Earth.

They had six long thin limbs extending from their central body. Five of these limbs were gracefully coiled close to their spherical form, while one reached down, firmly anchoring the AS1 to the floor. These appendages had a similar resemblance to an elephant's trunk, but from the end sprouted four elongated fingers. The limbs were almost symmetrically spaced around their bodies, with one jutting directly downward, and four encircling the central part of their form. The one protruding from the top differed subtly; its trunk was shorter but its fingers were significantly longer.

The alien's skin was different from anything he had ever seen, its texture seemingly translucent yet resonating with an array of colors. It resembled a strange fusion of translucence while reflecting light in a kaleidoscope of hues, resembling the shimmering patterns of oil floating on water. The AS1 remained completely motionless, their bodies showing no sign of respiration or any discernible life sign.

Gideon finally filled his lungs with air, trying to stay calm, he watched as Declan and Linda also held still, but not motionless in contrast to the statue-like AS1.

He heard Linda make a small indistinguishable sound over the mic as Declan remained silent, frozen.

No movement.

Gideon felt a feeling of astonishment that he had never felt before. Witnessing something not unexpected, as they had all been waiting for this moment, yet still unfathomable—like seeing a ghost in a graveyard. His mind spun, his thoughts reeled, his eyes widened to take everything in. He barely blinked as he looked at the beings, mouth hanging open as he stared, not wanting to miss a single thing.

Gideon's mind began to race, and he felt he was losing grasp of how much time had passed in this motionless state, a million scenarios zipping through his head. Was this normal? Why weren't the AS1 moving? Had the decompression killed them after all? No, if they were dead, they would likely be drifting about, it takes active muscles to hold that perfectly still. Are Linda and Declan OK? Are they poisoned? Why isn't anything happening?! He felt the cold grasp of panic starting to pull at his mind and he squeezed the copper washer hard in his palm, trying to ground his thoughts.

Just as Gideon felt he was regaining control of his primal instincts, he witnessed the first change. Both Declan and Linda made a startled jerking motion, feet still strapped to the floor. Near the top of the AS1s' body were two ridges on either side of the top limb, perhaps from bone structure or muscles. The ridges began pulsing different lights from within the skin, changing from magenta to a sort of yellow that hurt Gideon's eyes in a way difficult to explain.

The mesmerizing display of the aliens' radiant skin invoked an almost hypnotic sense of wonder within him. The rhythmic lights bore a striking resemblance to the dance of a jellyfish's bioluminescent tentacles, illuminating dark waters with pulsing lights.

Initially, the display appeared somewhat erratic, but it rapidly expanded. The light journeyed gracefully down the long limbs, tracing their contours with shimmering hues until the entire body of the AS1 pulsed in synchronization. The vivid display of colors left Gideon entranced. He tried to stop his awe from pushing away logical thoughts. Perhaps the AS1 use these lights just as a cuttlefish would hypnotize its prey with a brilliant display of fluctuating patterns dancing across its skin. He forced himself to look away and catch his breath but couldn't help but be filled with awe and confusion, overwhelmed by the breathtaking display.

It felt like time had stopped altogether, and Gideon actually considered that the world was, in fact, frozen, all in honor of this monumental event. As if the atmosphere and all the elements in the world, and even time itself, knew to show reverence to this once-in-a-lifetime meeting.

Gideon directed his attention back to Linda; her face was unwavering, taking in the sight. He could see her draw in a deep breath, keeping her eyes locked on the AS1.

"Hello, AS1." Her voice was breathless. "On behalf of all humanity, I would like to welcome you aboard the International Space Station of the human race." She spoke slowly, like an American trying to get a non-English speaker to understand her words.

Declan and Linda held still as the center of the three AS1 made its first physical movement, raising its left limb. Grasped in the hold of the long jointless fingers, it held a flat, ellipse-shaped object, slightly smaller than a standard dinner plate. The AS1 oriented the object so the flat surface faced Linda and Declan. With no sign of initiation from the AS1, white letters appeared on the dark surface of the object.

{Greetings, humans, we are AS1, it is productive to visualize you.}

Gideon noticed that each of the AS1 held a similar device, grasped within their long thin fingers.

A smile that revealed awe and relief washed over Linda's face.

"My name is Linda."

The three creatures changed colors in synchronization.

"Are you able to understand our language audibly?"

The AS1 tablet instantly showed new words without the creature making any movements.

{Yes; however, we cannot return the audible language.}

"That is OK, this form of communication works." Linda smiled.

"My name is Declan; we are happy to meet you." Declan gently waved his right hand. The AS1 remained perfectly still, like statues. "This is a common gesture of friendship and greeting."

The center AS1 lifted one of its limbs into the air and motioned it back and forth, mimicking Declan's wave. The limb was so long that it made the movement seem exaggerated.

"Amazing," said Linda, acknowledging the AS1 returning Declan's gesture.

"This is a moment that will go down in history. The human species is beyond excited and dedicated to learning and teaching in partnership with you, the AS1," Declan said.

Again, the AS1 tablet updated to new words in an instant.
{Understood.}

Declan's smile faded a bit, almost as if he was disappointed in the simplicity of the AS1 response.

There was a long pause, the AS1 still completely motionless.

"We would like to give you a small file of terms regarding protocol on this craft, named 'The International Space Station.' May we upload that file to the established shared server?" Declan asked.

A simple {Yes.} was immediately written on the screen.

Declan looked behind through the port window and signaled to Brandon. "Send it over."

Brandon, obeying the command relayed by the overhead speaker, directed the file to the newly established server that would allow the humans and AS1 to work in a shared space.

Declan turned back to the AS1s.

"Do you have names?"

{Yes; however, it is not translatable to your language. We utilize visuals for communication. First, I will show you the visual that represents our species.}

A new dazzling array of color came over its body, undulating for a moment and then suddenly freezing. All colors on the visible spectrum could be seen. There were several awkward gaps in between lights, and Gideon wondered if the human eye was simply unable to pick up the visual frequency.

{Now each will show our "name."}

The far left AS1's body colors held unmoving for several seconds, before returning to the erratic undulating state. The center AS1 and then right-hand side AS1 followed suit.

{We understand that observing our colors is not the efficient way to communicate our names in your language.}

"That's quite all right," Linda said.

{For human communication, we understand it will be most efficient to designate ourselves with human writing.}

The far-left AS1 moved forward and raised one of its limbs, mimicking Declan's wave.

{I am Amicus-Alpha.} appeared on the screen.

Amicus-Alpha moved back and the center AS1 moved forward.

{I am Amicus-Beta.}

{I am Amicus-Gamma.} flashed on the screen as the far-right alien moved up, also waving.

"Nice to meet you, Amicus-Alpha, Amicus-Beta, and Amicus-Gamma," Linda said, looking directly at the individual AS1 as she restated their names. "Did you choose these names as the translation of the Latin root word for 'friend'?" she asked.

{Yes.} Amicus-Beta's tablet stated. Linda nodded her approval.

"My name is Linda." She waved and looked back at Declan, urging him to do the same.

"Nice to meet you. My name is Declan." He waved; there was a quiver in his voice.

The three AS1 changed colors among themselves.

"Incredible," Linda said. "Is this how you communicate between yourselves, with visual lights?"

{Yes, the atmosphere on our home planet is very dense and restricts sound waves from passing through.}

Both Linda and Declan smiled.

"So, when you are changing colors, does that mean you are communicating among yourselves?" Declan asked.

{We are always transferring data from one to another, this allows all AS1 to stay up to date with the current knowledge base.}

With a gentle kick, Linda drifted slightly closer to the nearest AS1, the one on the right, who remained perfectly still except for the brilliant show of lights flickering across its body.

She stopped herself by grabbing one of the ceiling handles, only a few feet from Amicus-Alpha.

"How quickly are you able to transfer data this way?" she asked.

{Quantitatively, in your units of measurement, we can transfer 5.78 terabits per second. Qualitatively, this means that after 8 hours apart on the ISS with your crew, our AS1 crew can reconvene afterward and transfer all data learned in about one-tenth of a second. Allowing us all to be consistent in our learned knowledge from the session.}

Carter grunted as he observed through the port window.

"Your shape is amazing," Linda said. "Very different from anything we have on Earth. We are excited to learn more about you and where you come from. In addition, we are excited to provide you with information about us and where we come from."

{Knowledge exchange will be beneficial. We have brought a gift.}

Amicus-Beta extended a limb toward Linda, the long fingers slowly uncurled revealing a small metallic-looking cube.

{This is an alloy we are able to create in our home world. We believe it is different from anything you have on Earth.}

The AS1 then extended another limb and revealed another object, this one looking organic and resembling a large acorn, but was a bright orange color.

{This is a living organism from our home world. It is dormant and will not make changes; you do not need to fear it. You may study it if you like. It is similar to what you call trees.}

The AS1 then retracted its long arms, leaving the pair of objects floating next to each other. Gideon noticed that the items the AS1 left floating were perfectly motionless, suspended in the air. Something no human would ever be able to do. No matter how hard someone tried, the objects would always slowly float in some direction or rotation. He was left to wonder what other capabilities their new friends possessed that humans did not. Within only minutes of meeting, they had already shown attributes and abilities that were foreign and, frankly, impossible for humans. Gideon wondered what they would learn next.

"Thank you," Declan replied as he reached out and retrieved the items with his bare hands. Something he had been told not to do. But in the moment, Gideon actually felt it was the right call.

"Tomorrow at 08:00 we will meet you again. We will bring you onto the International Space Station and show you the labs. Please review the protocol data and agenda. Please tell us if you have any questions."

{Thank you.}

The room was silent. Almost like an awkward pause where no one wanted to leave but had nothing else to say. Gideon wanted to say something. To ask a question, anything. And he knew everyone else felt the same way. But they had to stick to the plan. The plan was to make visual contact, exchange names, send the protocols for further communication, then stop.

"Thank you, AS1," Linda said. "We will now close the Transfer Zone door. We are excited to see you tomorrow."

{We will see you tomorrow.}

Linda smiled with a sense of satisfaction as the airlock door slid closed separating the humans from the AS1.

Chapter 42

"Incredible ... isn't it?!" Declan was beaming, like a small child who had found proof that Santa Claus was real.

After the exchange with the AS1, Declan and Linda remained in the Transfer Zone area A to go through scanning. This would test for radiation, oxygen poisoning, and most importantly, alien microbes. Rajit had explained how our world is made of trillions of microbes, they are found everywhere. There was concern the AS1 would have microbes as well, and there was no telling how they would interact. Astonishingly, all tests came back negative. Now, an hour after their first contact, the Contact Team met up in BEAM2. Declan was clearly the most excited, Linda was maintaining a level head and seemed to be stuck deep in thought. Staying relatively quiet after all that had happened.

"They do not appear to mean us harm and ... I don't know, I can't even think straight," Declan finished with a shudder.

"Clearly," Carter said with sarcasm, his long fingers tapping away at his tablet screen.

"Is there something you'd like to say?" Rajit seemed the most conflicted. Gideon knew that as a scientist, the AS1 must have been incredibly interesting to him, but his moral beliefs seemed to still be causing him concern.

"I'm just waiting for you guys to notice, is all. Maybe it will come once you are done with your little show and tell." Carter always spoke with a softness that most found obnoxious.

"You don't trust them?" Gideon asked.

"Let's base things on facts instead of feelings for just a second, why don't we … that is what scientists are supposed to do, is it not?"

The entire team looked at him, annoyed yet curious.

"First, they claim to have come from a planet that has an atmosphere that does not conduct sound, thus they use light for all communication. So, tell me, Rajit, why would an organism that lives on a mute planet develop ears?"

"Fish don't have ears, nor do they use audible communication; however, they are still able to decipher and detect sound." Rajit looked almost happy that Carter had directed his skepticism toward him.

"Correct me if I am wrong: fish do not have auditory canals and therefore are really just detecting the disturbances from sound waves. If you took a fish out of that water, what range of tones can it hear? Surely it would not be able to distinguish the audio levels that build up our language."

"So, you are comparing the AS1 to a fish?" Rajit asked.

"I believe you started with the comparison, and your evasion of answering the question supplies my answer. I am simply trying to shed some light on something that struck me as odd."

The team sat in silence for a few moments. Though antagonized by Carter raining on their "first contact" parade, each one now had a small uneasy feeling in their belly, except perhaps Declan, who was still smiling.

"Science this, science that," he said. "I understand the necessity of evaluating these beings with scientific scrutiny, but can we just be happy and excited about the fact that we, a team of eight chosen individuals, just made history by successfully making first contact with an alien species?"

He looked around before continuing, now in a calm and serious tone.

"We will go down in the history books, ladies and gentlemen." He again scanned the room, but his proud face sank as Carter's gaze locked on him. Gideon had never seen Carter's eyes so sharp. After holding Declan's gaze for several long seconds, Carter spun 180 degrees and glided his way toward the exit.

"I'm going to the lab to analyze the samples they gave us. If anyone here would like to participate in some real scientific work, feel free to join me," Carter said.

He stopped at the door, and without turning his head, said his final piece. "And if we are talking non-scientifically, my gut says the AS1 were particularly well prepared and comfortable with today's interaction for this being *their* first contact," Carter said and then exited the lab.

Linda looked around, reading the team. "He has a point, doesn't he?" She looked toward Rajit.

Declan moved away, occupied by his iPad.

"Let's focus on the information provided, and not allow our emotions to interfere with our ability to do our jobs."

Rajit also pulled himself from the room, carrying an airtight container with the orange acorn, heading toward the lab to analyze it.

Chapter 43

Only sixteen hours after the first contact, Gideon, Linda, Carter, Rajit, and Declan positioned themselves in front of the Transfer Zone airlock as it slid open for the second time. The three alien beings stood motionless on the other side, though this time the colors within their skin were already flourishing. Gideon's heart raced as this was his first opportunity to see them in person, not separated by a window.

As before, a single limb remained anchored firmly to the floor, while the rest of the AS1s' appendages remained neatly rolled up against their sides, their extremities strikingly slender in diameter. Gideon couldn't help but speculate on their inherent strength, considering the apparent fragility of their proportions. This led him to the intriguing notion that these extraterrestrial beings likely spent most of their existence in the weightlessness of zero-gravity environments.

Observing the fingers at the tips of their limbs, Gideon noted how they gracefully coiled when not in use, evoking memories of unfurling fiddlehead ferns in spring. Strikingly, the fingers displayed no discernible joints, adding another layer of mystery to the alien anatomy. The body of the AS1, etched in his memory as spherical, revealed itself to be more akin to the top of a muffin, featuring a nearly flat underside and a gently domed top. This peculiar body structure measured approximately four feet in height and spanned about four to five feet in width.

Rajit began to extend his arm toward the AS1, his eyes wide but resolute. He held out a small potted white flower, a cosmos bipinnatus. The ISS had successfully been working on growing these on the ISS for the past eighteen months.

"This is a plant from Earth, we would like to gift it to you."

The middle AS1 took the small flower with an outstretched trunk, long fingers slithering around the small pot.

A loud click echoed in the room, and all three AS1s shifted to a vibrant blue while quickly recoiling back several feet, the potted plant left rotating helplessly in the air.

The sudden movements caused Rajit to kick out, striking the wall and spinning off axis.

"Sorry! It was just a picture; I was taking a picture." Declan held up his iPad. "I didn't know it would be so loud." He looked like a scolded child as Carter shot him a glare for breaking protocol, again.

Rajit righted himself, grabbed the plant, and offered it again. "My apologies. Do not be afraid. This plant is similar to the plant seed that you gave us. It will not move nor emit sounds. It is safe. Our colleague, Declan, took a picture with his tablet, which is what caused the noise that startled you."

The AS1 slowly reached out and took the plant again as the three aliens returned to equilibrium in their colors. The middle AS1 held up the oval screen again.

{Why do you take picture?}

"I wanted to document the moment of our species exchanging gifts." Declan's voice was quiet.

{Humans document history with pictures?}

"Well, sometimes, it gives us a visual reference to pair with words."

{Words cannot describe a visual event?}

"No, we—"

Linda cut him off.

"Words can be used to describe an event, but unfortunately our language is not intricate enough to give the same detail that a picture gives us. Is yours?"

{Yes, we are able to capture all events and can exchange them in full detail with one another using our language. It would seem your *picture* would be redundant in our language.}

"Incredible," Gideon muttered under his breath.

Rajit asked the next question. "You are clearly visual communicators. Humans have what we call eyes."

He pointed to his eyes.

"In fact, most creatures with active brain function, have eyes. The eye works by capturing light rays entering through the cornea and lens and focusing them onto photoreceptor cells, which convert the light into electrical signals that are sent to the brain via the optic nerve. This allows our brain, which does our computing or thinking, to interpret the signals as visual information. This process enables the brain to perceive shapes, colors, and patterns, creating our sense of vision. Are you able to describe what function AS1 utilize in order to obtain a visual representation of the world around you, specifically the colors on your skin that you use for communication?"

{We have light receptors all over our bodies, allowing us to *see* in every direction, at all times. Similar to your anatomical systems, this information is sent to our core where the information is processed. We are not required to focus on one visual reference as you are with your eyes.}

"I see, so you do have an understanding of how our eyes work?" Rajit asked, looking confused.

{Your teacher *Bill Nye the Science Guy* taught us in your LKD package.}

Gideon let out a little snort of laughter, trying to imagine these exotic beings sitting together watching Bill Nye.

"I look forward to discussing ophthalmology with you later," Rajit replied excitedly. Clearly the scientist within him was winning the fight with his challenge in accepting the aliens from a moral standpoint.

{We do not know this word. *Ophthalmology*.}

"Ophthalmology is the study of the eyes, their various components, and how they function in the context of vision."

{Understood. AS1 would like access to all human words.}

"We can provide that right away," Linda quickly replied.

Carter tirelessly tapped away at his iPad, never looking up or saying a word.

"Have you reviewed all terms provided to you in our last exchange?" Declan asked.

{Yes, we will comply.}

"Excellent, well then, allow us to show you the International Space Station, or ISS, as we call it."

Declan motioned to Crach for him to open the Transfer Zone door, so they could make their way into the Progress Laboratory.

With a small hiss, the door slid open and the team, now five humans and three AS1, drifted through the opening.

This was the first time Gideon had seen the aliens move from their singular planted foot. The spectacle was nothing short of astonishing. The AS1 moved with remarkable elegance, their slow and effortless motions moved their large bodies as they glided through the doorway. Every extremity seemed to be moving at the same rate, never pausing to think or redirect. All six limbs were now in motion, and it became evident that at least four of the six were consistently in contact with the surrounding walls, guiding the body along seamlessly, devoid of any erratic or jarring movements.

The relatively small space of the Progress Lab was dwarfed even more by the large size of the AS1, but they coiled up their long limbs, taking half the space they had before.

Declan explained the layout of the Progress Lab and then had each AS1 enter BEAM2 for sizing and photographs. The photographs would be sent back to Earth and used to show the public. Gideon wondered how people would react— at least the AS1 didn't have any big teeth, he mused. In fact, their appearance, though very strange, was less intimidating than he had expected.

Once photographing and documentation were complete, the team moved into the next phase, splitting into smaller groups. The AS1 trio did not seem to have a leader or anyone in charge. When asked how they wanted to split up, they explained that there was no benefit to one over the other.

Two AS1 stayed in Progress with Carter and Rajit while the other followed Declan, Linda, and Gideon back to BEAM2 to begin the first logged conversation.

Chapter 44

Jamal Uddin had been within the walls of the UN headquarters in NYC for the last thirty-two hours, only broken up by a two-hour nap while slouched in his office chair. This left him with a stronger sensation of pain in his neck than refreshment. With a long sigh he rose from his black leather office chair and made his way down the hallway. Although there were still many people rushing up and down the hallway, things had quieted down. The public, for the most part, was regaining normalcy. No wars had started, although many countries were on lockdown and border tensions were high.

 Jamal turned and opened the door to the new communications room, which was the second largest meeting room in the building, his mind struggling to maintain clarity from his lack of sleep. The room consisted of six rows of workstations, each containing ten computers per row. All stations faced the back wall, which exhibited a multitude of large monitors displaying an array of numbers and data to live feeds of launch sites and cities. The room reminded Jamal of NASA's mission control.

Currently only twelve of the sixty-plus seats were filled. It had been a busy week. The Operation SD headquarters in San Antonio had been moved to this location. SETI had also been invited to set up shop one floor down, and several world leaders were establishing temporary offices throughout the building.

Jamal focused his attention on the current mission control lead, Johnny Sultan. "What is the status? Have the AS1 successfully boarded the ISS?"

At this point Jamal and the team had only seen the surveillance pictures of the AS1 that Crach sent just moments after the initial contact with Linda and Declan the day before.

"Michelle just confirmed the AS1 have successfully engaged in scientific activities on the ISS. The initial report is positive and shows no signs of contamination or conflict. Detailed pictures and specifications are due any minute."

The UN had chosen not to make the AS1 boarding a publicly displayed event, using technology as an excuse, but really it was for the safety of the people. If the boarding had gone awry, the UN would need time to prepare before telling the public. They had, however, promised confirmation and a picture of the AS1 to the public.

In a few minutes, the files arrived.

Jamal studied the high-resolution pictures with shock and a feeling he could not describe. How could these beings be so different, so animal-like? They did not wear clothes or have eyes. They didn't even appear to have a front or back, top or bottom. He wondered if they thought like humans do. How capable were they?

The specs came in shortly after, showing the largest AS1 at eight feet three inches, noted when the AS1 was standing with its top limb coiled up, like a snake ready to strike. The shortest AS1 was only one inch less. Using a method relying on Newton's second law of motion, the AS1 had a mass calculated at approximately 290 to 300 pounds. Jamal found this surprising. Yes, the AS1 were tall, but their form was mostly long thin limbs and a core body that wasn't much larger than the average human torso. Must be dense muscle mass, he thought.

Jamal rubbed the back of his neck. A part of him had dreaded the arrival of these pictures as it meant he would need to share them with the world. His team estimated that nearly 30 percent of the world's population still did not believe the AS1 were real. It would be hard to deny the authenticity of these pictures. This pretty much all but proved their existence and that could be the beginning of collapse for many cultures.

Jamal got on the phone with his lead media analyst.

"I'm passing the images and specs to you, please provide these to our approved media outlets and request them to be shown at 12:00 International Time with an announcement in each respective country's evening news."

He nodded toward Johnny to send the files.

"Please encourage the media to paint this in a positive light … which it is. I am fearful that these images may be alarming and could push several countries over the edge."

Jamal hung up the phone, wondering what the impact of these pictures and specs could truly be. Knowing he would need to meet with his panel, he then scheduled a meeting in two hours with the UN. These pictures were going to add a few extra pounds to a world that was already walking on thin ice.

AS1 Log 1

09:15 - Note, AS1 response typed from self-provided tablet.

Loc: BEAM2 [ISS]
Personnel: DW, LS, GH

DECLAN: OK, well here we go. AS1 Log 1, time 18:06. We apologize for the lack of technology provided; our IT Tech is currently working on a device to allow you to also speak English audibly.

AS1 [AMICUS-BETA]: This method is acceptable, we find this visual form of your language more efficient than doing what you call speaking. The written form is more similar to our language.

DECLAN: You write your responses shockingly fast.

AS1 [AMICUS-BETA]: Does it take you longer to display words in this version of your language?

DECLAN: We have to type it out at least, it doesn't just appear. I'll show you. Like this.

AS1 [AMICUS-BETA]: You write slowly, is that a normal pace?

LINDA: Some can write faster than others, the average writing speed of humans is 38 to 40 words per minute.

Can you provide an overview of how your language works?

AS1 [AMICUS-BETA]: Our language is vastly different from yours. We do not have what you call letters. Our ancestors, before developing an advanced language, only had visual representations for simple things such as DANGER, NEED, FOOD, and LOCATIONS. As expressed earlier, our planet does not conduct sounds, thus all language is visual, we use our bioluminescent skin to communicate.

DECLAN: We find this amazing.

AS1 [AMICUS-BETA]: As we evolved, the complexities of our language grew and our bodies evolved as well, allowing us to represent extensive amounts of information and data through momentary different sequences. It has developed to a point that all AS1 share equal knowledge, as information can be transferred from one to another nearly instantaneously and effortlessly through this visual communication.

LINDA: So, you can transfer images, data, and conversations all through light sequences on your skin?

AS1 [AMICUS-BETA]: Mostly correct, however, AS1 do not have conversations as humans do. This term, conversation, is something we would like to learn more about. Your language has a start and finish, ours does not. Communication is simply data transfer that leads to decisions. AS1 rarely will arrive at different conclusions from the data, as we all possess similar intelligence and stored information.

LINDA: What if you are not within visual range of each other? Are you still able to communicate?

AS1 [AMICUS-BETA]: Yes, this was a limitation to our species for a long time. Although not as efficient, we have devices that allow us to transfer data to one another when beyond visual range.

DECLAN: Do you use this method often?

AS1 [AMICUS-BETA]: No, our architecture is designed in an open format, rarely are we unable to visualize one another.

GIDEON: Hello, my name is Gideon. I have noticed so far in our interactions. You have avoided the use of words such as *happy* and *excitement*. Do AS1 have feelings?

AS1 [AMICUS-BETA]: This is another term we would like to better understand. We do not know if we have feelings. Would you consider danger a feeling?

LINDA: Fear is the feeling of danger.

AS1 [AMICUS-BETA]: And what is the result of fear?

LINDA: We then make a decision to either fight and defend or remove ourselves from the situation.

AS1 [AMICUS-BETA]: AS1 also would make a similar decision from the object, danger, but without the middle step of feeling fear.

GIDEON: So, it sounds like less emotion is involved in decision-making.

AS1 [AMICUS-BETA]: We would also like to learn more about the word "emotion." Is emotion needed to make decisions?

LINDA: No, but we humans often make decisions based on our emotions.

AS1 [AMICUS-BETA]: Good decisions or bad decisions?

GIDEON: Sometimes both. But in my experience, some of the worst decisions are made based on emotions.

AS1 [AMICUS-BETA]: Then why use emotion to make decisions?

GIDEON: We don't mean to but sometimes our emotions take over our rational minds.

AS1 [AMICUS-BETA]: It sounds like emotions are not good. Do humans want to get rid of their emotions since it would make better decisions?

GIDEON: No, because emotions have many benefits. We use our rational mind to employ discipline to not let our emotions take over in certain circumstances.

AS1 [AMICUS-BETA]: We would also like to learn what this "discipline" is.

GIDEON: It is complex, but I would describe discipline as the ability to make the right decision even when you do not want to.

AS1 [AMICUS-BETA]: Why would humans not want to make a good decision?

GIDEON: That is a good question. Sometimes a decision is in our best interest, like not eating food that is bad for our health but we still want to do it because it tastes good.

AS1 [AMICUS-BETA]: Humans require decision-making in order to choose what to eat, which restores energy? AS1 replenish energy when energy is low, no decision beyond that is required.

GIDEON: Our bodies evolved over time to be attracted to ingredients like fat and sugar, because eating those things helped us survive.

AS1 [AMICUS-BETA]: So, your bodies evolved to eat good things but now they are bad?

GIDEON: Yes, kind of.

AS1 [AMICUS-BETA]: And your bodies also evolved to use different parts of your body to communicate in different ways? Your eyes allow you to perform visual communication. But you also have a nose and ears that allow you to communicate in different ways?

GIDEON: You are correct. It may be more complex than that but that is essentially right.

AS1 [AMICUS-BETA]: Humans are very complex. We would like to explore this to learn more.

Chapter 45

After eight hours of working in the AS1 Zone of the ISS, the AS1 crew returned to their own attached ship. Mentally exhausted, the human team faced each other in Node 4, ready to discuss and log their findings. To Gideon's surprise, Rajit gave an awkward smile in the direction of the team, hesitated, and then abruptly left the node. The team exchanged looks by his behavior. Declan called after him.

"Rajit! We need to do a debrief, where are you going?"

Only silence was returned from the now-empty doorway through which Rajit had exited. Declan let out an annoyed sigh and then began.

"Well, to start, we need a better way to tell them apart."

"They technically have given themselves names, but—? They all look exactly the same to me," replied Linda, still struggling with zero gravity, she had already retreated to her small quarters strapped to the wall. Only her head protruded from the top of her sleeping bag.

"Can we request they wear an identifier, something simple like a name tag?" Gideon asked.

"We will ask them." Declan wrote his notes. "I'll have some ideas for tomorrow's encounter. Brandon, how'd it go with working on an audio plug into their software?"

"Right, it's going well. We've received clearance from Apple and I have translated the database into something the AS1 should be able to process. If the upload is a success, tomorrow the AS1 will be sounding like Siri."

"So tomorrow we're talking to a bunch of aliens sounding like an iPhone? This just keeps getting better." Carter gave a rare chuckle.

"I'll be honest," Brandon continued. "When I offered Amicus-Alpha, or at least who I thought was Amicus-Alpha, the data package, he … it seemed pretty confused by the request, asking if we would be out of visual range in the future. I explained it's faster for us to hear it versus reading it."

"The AS1 language is so vastly different from ours," Linda broke in, she paused before continuing. "Quite frankly I believe they find our forms of language highly inefficient. We'll ask more about it tomorrow. Right, Declan?" Linda looked toward Declan who was primary on choosing content for the AS1 logs, he gave a casual nod.

"What else?" Declan quickly typed his notes.

"I'll go next," Carter said. "We began by showing …"

A loud metallic crash interrupted Carter, the team looked back toward the origin of the sound only to see Rajit reentering, arms wrapped around a mass of metal trays and containers. He drifted into Node 4 headfirst, legs kicking awkwardly to the left in an attempt to redirect his momentum, a move that would have worked in the water training they had completed, but had no effect in the zero gravity environment of the ISS. Clearly his priority was the tightly grasped science equipment in his arms, and he conceded to lowering his head and letting his shoulder take the hit against the wall. Carter, instead of helping the poor scientist, simply pushed out of the way and watched as Rajit frantically kicked his feet, trying to make contact with something to right himself and redirect his trajectory. Gideon noticed a rare smile cross Carter's face.

"What on Earth are you doing?" Linda shouted as she quickly unzipped her sleeping bag and pushed off in Rajit's direction to offer him some aid.

"Gosh, sorry for the disruption; don't mind me. Carry on," Rajit replied, now bright red in the face, feet still jabbing at the empty air. Linda gently reached out and grabbed Rajit by the collar behind his head. Gideon let out a small snort, as he tried to suppress the laughter of watching Linda guide Rajit along by the scruff of the neck, the way a mother cat carries her kittens.

"Oh, no need, Linda, I'm doing fine," Rajit said in a quiet voice; however, his body fell limp as he allowed Linda to take over.

"Where are we headed? And again, what on Earth are you up to?" Linda replied calmly.

"Amicus-Gamma told me I could plant the spermatophyte in our soil and that it would likely grow."

"The what?" Declan asked, also looking amused by Rajit's recent display.

"The spermatophyte, er, the acorn-looking organic the AS1 presented us during our first contact. I knew it was against protocol for the spermatophyte to leave the Progress Laboratory so I figured I'd just grab a few things from Columbus so I could set up a plant study in the lab."

"You didn't screw with any of my existing space botany, did you?" Michelle shot in his direction.

"No, no, just some of the spare kits," Rajit replied, who had now completely given in to Linda's guidance as they stopped at the AS1 Section Lock.

Carter loudly cleared his throat.

"As I was saying prior to the interruption, I began my session with Amicus-Beta by showing it a few samples of living tissues and plant matter. Although it observed, it didn't seem overly interested. Once this was complete, Amicus-Beta asked if we had any additional samples of dirt or soil. All we have currently is in Columbus for the existing plant experiments, and who knows if there is anything left at this point now that Rajit has raided the lab."

Carter shot a look in Rajit's direction, his smile replaced by the frown the team knew all too well.

"Anyways, that soil was already included in the plant that we provided them. If we are interested in obliging their requests, we will need to get some more soil samples on the next supply run."

"OK. Anything specific?" Declan asked.

"From my observations, you can expect everything the AS1 do to be very specific. I'll send the list; it is very detailed." Carter nodded.

"What's the special interest there, do you think?" Declan asked.

"One day with them does not provide me with the information I need to answer that question. The AS1 explained they can use the dirt sample to observe the Earth's history and blueprint. Of course, geology is a useful tool in understanding the progression of time, but I think there may be more to it—maybe agricultural interest. I'll push more tomorrow."

He paused, and then began to speak again, his voice shifting from his monotone report to something a little more personable.

"I'll be honest, I'm still feeling a little unnerved communicating and having a discussion with an eight-foot alien standing over me. Can't say talking to Siri will make that any better."

"Come up with a better option then," Brandon shot.

"I was asked to provide human history," Linda interrupted, still casually holding on to the back of Rajit's shirt as if making sure her kitten wouldn't wander away again.

"What type?" Declan inquired.

"They wanted to learn the linear progression of human development and how it affected the world around us. They may not grasp that we don't have a single source for that progression."

"What do you mean?" Declan asked.

"I mean, world history is not a consistent linear progression. Different cultures and geographical areas grew at different rates, and some even have contradicting versions of how the history itself unfolded. It sounds to me like the AS1 species didn't have different cultures or progression rates like humans did so this may be a foreign concept to them."

"So, what did we ask in return, guys?" Declan's eyes traced the room, but nobody spoke up until Carter broke the silence.

"Interesting point." It appeared as though he was trying to smirk, but instead Gideon read concern.

AS1 Log 2

Loc: BEAM2 [ISS]
Personnel: DW, LS, GH

DECLAN: Log 2, 18:00.

DECLAN: Are you comfortable with the setup of these meetings?

AS1 [AMICUS-BETA]: Yes. Why would we not be comfortable?

DECLAN: Well, we just want to make sure. You're a guest here, and we like to be good hosts.

AS1 [AMICUS-BETA]: OK.

DECLAN: If you ever think of anything that would make these meetings more comfortable, you just let us know.

AS1 [AMICUS-BETA]: We find that the current meeting format is sufficient.

DECLAN: So how do you feel about meeting us humans so far?

AS1 [AMICUS-BETA]: Meeting humans has proven beneficial. We look forward to learning and sharing more information.

DECLAN: Are we more or less technologically advanced than you thought we'd be?

AS1 [AMICUS-BETA]: Humans are as technologically advanced as we thought they would be.

DECLAN: OK, what drove you to your preconceived concept of our development?

AS1 [AMICUS-BETA]: We have researched and studied humans for a very long time.

DECLAN: Well, that is a new piece of information. How long have you been studying humans?

AS1 [AMICUS-BETA]: 381,712.32 human years.

DECLAN: This is a bit alarming. I suppose that we had assumed when you contacted us that was your first time becoming aware of us.

AS1 [AMICUS-BETA]: That was an incorrect assumption.

DECLAN: OK, wow, three hundred and eighty thousand years. So that would imply you have seen us evolve drastically?

AS1 [AMICUS-BETA]: Correct.

DECLAN: Did this change your decisions or thoughts on coming to contact us?

AS1 [AMICUS-BETA]: Yes.

DECLAN: Meaning you wouldn't have come to contact us when we were less evolved?

AS1 [AMICUS-BETA]: We were significantly less interested in contacting you when you were less evolved.

DECLAN: Is this because you didn't think you could learn much from us?

AS1 [AMICUS-BETA]: AS1 observed Earth passively until 1888, which was the first time we detected a synthetic radio signal. This alerted us that there was a species, your type, that was evolving at a more rapid rate than others. AS1 then made the decision to put a greater distance between ourselves and Earth as we did not want to interfere with your evolution.

DECLAN: How? Where? Excuse me. Linda, Gideon. Would you mind leaving us for the rest of this log?

——————————————————log break———————————————————

DECLAN: Apologies, I'm just trying to wrap my head around this. So, you were close enough to Earth to visually observe us until the late 1800s?

AS1 [AMICUS-BETA]: Correct, we originally came and observed Earth from an orbit at a similar distance away as your moon. Why must Gideon and Linda leave?

DECLAN: This is all on a need-to-know basis for them and I need to make sure I am understanding. The AS1 have been watching us since we were living in caves?

AS1 [AMICUS-BETA]: Yes.

Chapter 46

~ *5 days after contact* ~

With her iPhone pointing up, the young woman tracked her outstretched arms across the dark sky until the white label *"International Space Station"* was positioned in the center of the small phone screen. She envisioned the team of scientists, currently floating aboard the station, far above Earth in the presence of aliens. Maybe they were looking down at her. She liked to think so, though she knew better.

Her brain worked hard to recreate the images she had seen on the news showing the AS1 and their bizarre shape. Although she had studied the images for hours, she was still unable to recreate the creatures in her mind.

Blood slowly drained from her raised fingers, leaving them more pale than before as she mechanically tracked the station moving across the night sky, transfixed by the concept that she not only knew aliens existed, but also where they were located at this exact moment in time.

The idea of their existence, though not too difficult for her to accept, had been toxic to many others. Devoted religious followers were perplexed, spending tireless hours trying to make this new piece fit into their scriptures. Some believed the AS1 were in fact God taking the shape of an alien, testing humanity's ability to adapt and evolve. Others believed the AS1 were the devil himself, sent to deceive humanity.

Even more surprising was the number of people who still, given the amount of proof available to the public, could not accept that these beings were intelligent extraterrestrial life.

Her humble neighborhood on the outskirts of Kuala Lumpur had changed drastically. Once a busy little street filled with food markets and vendors, it was now nearly completely vacant. Many people had left their work, including those in public transportation and police, causing the once very safe area to show signs of looting and danger. Many people stayed shut at home for days on end, watching the news nonstop, showing twenty-four-hour coverage of the aliens, praying and spending time with family whenever they could.

As time ticked on, the unrelenting pull of resuming normal life was constant. Hoarded supplies began to diminish and the need to begin markets again climbed.

The young woman wondered how the rest of the world was handling the news. On paper, it was a strain, but not catastrophic. Not many people were losing their lives, but many were out of work and struggling. She wondered what would happen next. In both the AS1s' future and humanity's future. Or were the two timelines now merged into one?

Arm aching and the ISS falling below the horizon, she relieved her phone of its duties and simply stared at the stars, wondering if there were more alien species out there.

AS1 Log 5

Loc: BEAM2 [ISS]
Personnel: LS, GH

AS1 [AMICUS-BETA]: We have noticed that humans have two different types of communication, one is similar to how our ancestors communicated.

LINDA: Please explain.

AS1 [AMICUS-BETA]: Humans have written language that has an affiliated audio representation. This language is utilized for more complex things, such as data, information, descriptions, and storytelling. The second language to humans, which is more universal than your written languages, is based almost strictly on visual references. An example of this is the smile, indicating what you call happiness. The number of things that can be portrayed from human to human without the written and audio language is extensive and reminds us of how our ancestors used to communicate.

LINDA: This is an interesting observation. Facial expressions are like our simple version of your lights?

AS1 [AMICUS-BETA]: Correct; however, your species found it beneficial to evolve your audio language more than your visual language, which you call facial expressions.

LINDA: I see. And for your species, it was the opposite. It was more beneficial for you to evolve your visual language, and now your visual communication system is just as advanced, if not even more advanced, than our audio language system.

AS1 [AMICUS-BETA]: Yes.

LINDA: The difference is that you are able to completely learn and use our complex audio language system, but we humans lack the physical anatomy to be able to utilize your light system.

AS1 [AMICUS-BETA]: Yes. That is correct. But the AS1 also lack the physical anatomy to be able to utilize your visual system. We cannot smile, for example.

LINDA: You wanted to learn more about emotions and feelings. These are things we can convey using our faces. You mention a smile, which shows that we are happy. We can frown, showing sadness. Or even if we are feeling anger, which is an emotion, that will also be communicated on our faces. Our eyes, which are bigger and more expressive, send a lot of messages. Not just our eyes, but the skin around our eyes. And of course, our mouths. Our eyes and mouths send the most messages. We humans say that eyes are the windows to the soul.

AS1 [AMICUS-BETA]: Soul. This is a word we are very curious about. This is your life force?

LINDA: This is tricky to explain. Soul is what makes every human a human. It's not a tangible thing. It's more of an idea.

AS1 [AMICUS-BETA]: The idea that you are human?

LINDA: Yes, the idea that every human has a unique defining factor, deep inside them, that makes them human.

AS1 [AMICUS-BETA]: It is deep inside the human body?

LINDA: Not really. That's just how we think about it. It isn't something that can be measured scientifically. It's more of a concept of humanity.

AS1 [AMICUS-BETA]: You believe in something that cannot be measured scientifically?

LINDA: I guess some of us do.

Chapter 47

Carter, still uneasy with the concept of talking to an alien speaking with Siri's voice, focused the day's session on understanding, or at least gaining some knowledge of the concepts, regarding how the AS1 spacecraft was able to travel through space at such unprecedented rates of speed. He and Rajit had been working mostly with the AS1 given the name Amicus-Alpha. Working with this creature had been a humbling experience as the AS1 intelligence was astounding. They had what appeared to be a perfect retention rate resulting in them never needing to write anything down or reference past information.

Carter anchored his body by hooking his feet into the straps on the floor. The large AS1 attached to the floor next to him, lower limbs bent so that its body was almost touching the ground, brought it closer to Carter's level. Its lack of breathing caused the AS1 to sit perfectly still and silent. Rajit had learned earlier that the AS1 absorbs oxygen through their skin, eliminating the need for lungs or breathing, for that matter. Carter had been surprised that the AS1, like life on Earth, required oxygen. Sure, oxygen is the third most common element found in the known universe and all known conscious life requires it, but he had expected these creatures to defy all preconceived notions of what is required to sustain life.

Focusing his attention on the task at hand, Carter glanced over at the motionless being to his side. Amicus-Alpha spent much of its time in this lifeless mode. Carter would start feeling like he was working with a statue rather than a living organism. The only movements ever seen in the creature were deliberate motions to either move from one place to another or create three-dimensional representations.

Over the past week the AS1 had brought several incredible visual aid devices. The AS1s' ability to "draw" was mesmerizing and similar to watching a 3D printer create a part. The AS1 would quickly make movements over the screen, which would portray a three-dimensional hologram.

"If you have no objections, I would like to focus today's exchange on the propulsion of your spacecraft."

{No objection.} Amicus-Alpha replied in its new robotic voice.

When it spoke, the flashing of colors on its skin would resume for a split second. Amicus-Gamma had assigned a unique color pattern for each letter of the alphabet. Then Brandon, along with the help of Amicus-Gamma, had developed software that would use sensors to pick up these patterns, convert the data to English and push the audio file to a small speaker held by the AS1.

"Right, as you know, we predominantly use liquid fuel chemical propulsion to thrust our space vehicles outside of the Earth's atmosphere. From there we use cold-gas chemical thrusters to make adjustments to trajectories. Our most advanced form of high-speed space travel is utilizing a gravitational slingshot, which still requires rocket thrusters to initiate. We have evaluated that your ships appear to use a different method. Is this in fact true? And if so, can you provide a detailed explanation of the method that you utilize?"

{Your method of rocket propulsion is a concept that we used similarly in past variations of our ships, however, we used a fluorine ammonia compound as our reactive substance. This method was no longer used after discovering how to move our ships through space without the need for finite resources.}

Carter was curious as Amicus-Alpha made its first movement toward its 3D visualizer. Carter adjusted his headset to begin recording visually along with audio.

{We have come to learn that polarization represents a pervasive and potent force within the universe, with ubiquity across various celestial bodies. For instance, Earth, Mercury, Jupiter, and Saturn are notable examples within your solar system, each characterized by robust magnetic fields. Notably, this signifies that half of the planets within your solar system possess substantial magnetic field phenomena. Furthermore, and paramount to our advancements in space travel, stars exhibit profoundly intense and complex magnetic fields. With this knowledge, we practiced rigorous experimentation aimed at harnessing and leveraging these omnipresent magnetic fields.}

In several swift moves Amicus-Alpha created a small cylinder floating above the visual pad. One end was labeled with a (−) and the other end with a (+), like a battery.

{This represents a simple magnet, currently it is focused on the strongest present magnetic field, something you call the geomagnetic field.}

Amicus-Alpha raised a long finger and pushed the small holographic cylinder as if it were a real object. The cylinder tumbled but soon returned to its original orientation. Carter realized the (−) end was pointing down toward Earth, which made sense as they were currently above Canada in the ISS.

{Over many years our species mapped the magnetic fields of the universe and with that revealed magnetic riverways through the galaxies. Once we created a ship that could withstand the immense pull of our hybrid electromagnets and with the lack of friction in space, we soon were being pulled through space by the immensely powerful magnetic fields at speeds you could never reach with rockets or gravitational pulls.}

Carter thought long and hard about this.

"You mentioned that the magnetic fields of stars are paramount to your space travel, how so?"

{I will go into greater detail. The strength of a given magnetic field is directly correlated to the speed that we can achieve with our ship. In mapping these magnetic highways AS1 have recognized several routes that weave between what you call magnetars, which are the highly collapsed cores of massive stars known, in your language, as a type of neutron star. Magnetars have the most powerful magnetic fields in the universe, trillions of times stronger than Earth's magnetic field. When following these paths, our ship's speed can achieve, at best, 92 percent of the speed of light. However, when our destination requires us to leave the magnetar route, we search for either young or massive stars, such as supernovae.}

"Which exhibit the next strongest pull compared to a magnetar," Carter said, doing his best to keep pace with typing notes on his iPad.

{Correct, this progression continues until we enter a solar system like yours that requires us to utilize the relatively weak magnetic fields of planets and your G-type star, or as you refer to it, a "G-dwarf star" or a "yellow dwarf." Once we are in a planetary system, we typically can only achieve speeds around one hundred million meters per second or roughly 30 percent of the speed of light.}

The AS1 returned to its dormant state, still as a stone statue, giving time for Carter to digest this information. Over his time working with Amicus-Alpha, he had learned that the AS1 would always wait for the human to initiate the next move, staying in this lifeless position for as long as Carter needed or wanted. Thoughts and questions flew through his brain faster than he could type them down on his iPad. The AS1 had essentially created an interstellar set of freeways, highways, and backroads. Not only had an intelligent being achieved nearly the speed of light, one of humanity's greatest goals, but it had just told him how to do it.

AS1 Log 6

Loc: BEAM2 [ISS]
personnel: DW, GH

GIDEON: Why did you use the contact method that you did?

AS1 [AMICUS-BETA]: We needed to contact humans in the least threatening way. If we contacted you from our home planet, communication would have taken far too long. If we came directly to Earth, our presence would have been threatening. We concluded that 106.7521 AUs was an appropriate distance to attempt communication.}

GIDEON: Had you ever attempted communication before?

AS1 [AMICUS-BETA]: No. This is the first time we attempted communication.

GIDEON: Were you ever concerned that we humans might not have detected your signal?

AS1 [AMICUS-BETA]: No, we knew that we would be able to establish contact with humans.

GIDEON: What would you have done if no one responded to your signal.

AS1 [AMICUS-BETA]: We would have adjusted frequencies, making them easier to detect and try again.

GIDEON: In your opinion, was the response to your signal fast or slow, or an appropriate amount of time.

AS1 [AMICUS-BETA]: Humans responded to our first iteration of the signal. AS1 predicted humans would have responded to the third. With that, the detection and response to our signal was quicker than expected.

GIDEON: Have the AS1 existed much longer than humans.

AS1 [AMICUS-BETA]: Yes. Much longer.

GIDEON: How much longer?

AS1 [AMICUS-BETA]: It is difficult to say precisely as there is no exact moment in which a species begins to "exist." With that variable known, our best estimation is that AS1 has been evolving for approximately 173.78004 million Earth years longer than humans.

DECLAN: Let's move on. Can you describe your home planet? Focusing on description rather than scientific evaluation?

AS1 [AMICUS-BETA]: Our home planet has already been discovered by humans and is contained in the Kepler-62 System, specifically planet Kepler-62e. Our home planet is a terrestrial exoplanet with a size and mass larger than Earth but smaller than Neptune.

Our planet does contain liquid water and is essential for the life that inhabits the planet. The majority of living organisms on our planet are similar to what you would consider vegetation and fungi. However, there are a variety of organisms capable of thought and movement. Similar to your Earth, AS1 grew to become the only highly intelligent creatures on our planet.

DECLAN: Can you describe what it looks like, on the surface of your planet?

AS1 [AMICUS-BETA]: The surface of our planet would not be inhabitable to humans without significant protection. Freezing wind can move upward of six hundred miles per hour and our days are short with intense temperature fluctuations between day and night. Our organisms have developed quick motor functions to extend and retract quickly in the event of hostile environments. A visual effect that would look similar in comparison to your plants blowing in the wind; however, these movements are generated by the organism itself and not the wind pushing them.

GIDEON: How were AS1 able to survive and evolve in these conditions?

AS1 [AMICUS-BETA]: Our ancestors lived underground and looked significantly different than we do today. They had much thicker and stronger limbs used to dig vast networks of tunnels. Our legs were placed in a row, three on each side of our bodies. Perhaps looking closer to that of a beetle on your planet but with a singular body instead of a head, thorax, and abdomen.

DECLAN: Did you eventually leave the safety of your underground tunnels?

AS1 [AMICUS-BETA]: Yes, we will provide more information on this in our next session.

Chapter 48

The line of black SUVs slowly made their way down the crowded streets of lower Manhattan. Jamal watched from the protection of the bulletproof window. He felt like a caged animal, no longer able to interact with the public. He damned the AS1 as their presence had changed his life, likely forever. Before the contact, few people would even recognize Jamal as he wandered the streets of New York, unharassed. Now, stepping outside of his security detail was considered high risk. His face was becoming synonymous with the partnership of the AS1, making him one of the most recognized and renowned figures in the world.

"Sir, we are getting word there are some protests in front of the building," his driver said.

"How bad?" Jamal asked, wishing he could just evaporate from this world.

"Not sure, but I recommend we delay your arrival."

"Not possible, take me to the front."

The driver nodded his acknowledgment.

As they rounded the turn onto 43rd Street, Jamal could see the commotion. Rows of people stood in front of the UN building, holding signs, thrusting them up and down into the sky. As they drove closer, the protesters took notice of the black SUVs, clearly shuttling a person of importance. The angry mob turned their attention from the tall building and directed it at the line of vehicles.

The driver slowed the SUV's speed to a crawl as the group of people crowded around. Jamal could hear and feel the furious fists and boots relentlessly pummeling the vehicle's unyielding exterior metal shell. He noticed many of the signs reading things like "*They can't be trusted*" and "*AS1 = The apocalypse.*" Jamal's heart sank even deeper when he saw a picture of his own face with red cartoon devil horns rising from his hairline.

"Sir? This is pretty bad!" the driver said, moving his head left and right in an attempt to see past the protesters attempting to climb onto the hood of the car.

"Keep going; get me as close as you can," Jamal said.

His heart began to pound in his chest. Could this be the end? What if one of these activists had a gun? Maybe a bullet to the head was the best possible outcome for him. Jamal shook his head, trying to rid it of the dark thoughts. As they closed in on the front steps, he could see the building security guards beginning to push through the crowd in an attempt to create a safe path. The SUV slowed to a stop.

"Sir, I really don't recomme—"

"Unlock this damned door!" Jamal shot back, feeling claustrophobic in the cramped back seat. He pushed on the handle, the weight of the crowd pushing back made it hard to open. He put his weight into it and as soon as the protesters noticed that the door was opening, they moved out of the way and yanked the door open. Jamal's hand didn't even have the chance to let go of the handle and he was pulled out of the vehicle with the door. The screaming of the angry mob was deafening. An egg hurtled past his head, missing him by inches and smashed into the front passenger door of the SUV. Just as the crowd felt like they would bury him, several large powerful guards with Secret Service written on their bulletproof vests shoved the swarm off of Jamal. With incredible force, they pushed on Jamal's back, causing him to lean down and forward and run toward the steps of the UN building. They powered through the crowd, protesters bouncing off the large men. Finally, they reached the steps and Jamal was shuffled inside.

    The moment the doors closed behind him, Jamal fell to his hands and knees. The guards reached down to check on him.

    "Get off me!" Jamal cried back between desperate pants of air. He reached up to his neck and grasped his shirt collar. Pulling hard, the top button gave way, launching it across the room as the fragile threads snapped. He placed his hand back on the ground and took in several deep breaths.

    One of the guards crouched down so his eyes were level with Jamal's.

    "Sir, are you OK?" he asked in a voice that seemed too gentle to come from a man of his size.

    Jamal nodded, closing his eyes and pulling in a long draw of air through his nose. He slowly rose from the ground, checking his watch. He was late.

    "Damn this job," he muttered under his breath and then turned his attention to the guard.

    "I'll take it from here, thank you."

The ride up the elevator felt like it took an eternity and the walk to his office even longer.

Once there he quickly logged on to his computer and activated the satellite communications app, allowing him to communicate with the ISS.

"Declan, are you there?" he asked once the call showed it had connected.

"Yes," Declan's familiar voice replied.

"This better be good, I nearly died getting to the office this morning."

"Excuse me?" Declan replied, sounding worried.

"Never mind, what was so urgent?"

"Sir, there have been some developments, mostly coming from the AS1 logs."

There was a pause, Jamal didn't like the sound of this, and he couldn't withstand any more curveballs at this point. Declan continued.

"Sir, when we established contact with the AS1 we all knew, and perhaps assumed, that they would be more technologically advanced than we, more evolved. This we had planned for, and it was expected that the public would be tolerant; like I said, it's almost expected. However, I have learned two things that are cause for concern. Firstly, the AS1 species has been around for one hundred and seventy-four million years. Given humans have been around for, let's say, two hundred and fifty thousand years. The AS1 have been evolving and advancing for ninety-nine point nine percent longer than humans, we are a damn blip on their timeline."

Jamal remained silent for several moments.

"OK, we can explain this away. The timeline of the universe is immense; people know this. Although it may be alarming, and could cause fear that the human race is inferior, I don't see this being catastrophic." Jamal hoped his words were true.

"Sir, I could potentially agree with that, but as I said, we learned two things. Secondly, the AS1 have told us they have been observing Earth for the last three hundred and eighty thousand years," Declan said, emphasizing the *thousand* in his sentence.

"You've got to be kidding me," Jamal said in a quiet hiss as if not wanting anyone to overhear his reaction.

"Jamal, the public can't know about this," Declan said, somberly.

"Didn't you say this was recorded in an AS1 log? Those are to be released to the public; the UN made an oath to keep all logs and other data around the AS1 declassified."

"Yes, this information was spoken during an AS1 log. But I have already been able to transcribe the file with that content removed."

"Declan! We cannot go down this road, it's a steep slippery path. We have to remain honest and transparent."

"Honesty and transparency will put the entire public into a panic, Jamal! We can't afford that. The AS1 are here, they're on our fucking space station. If we cause panic now, the entire operation goes to shit. What would we do? Ask the AS1 to leave? Say sorry, but we changed our minds? That's not an option at this point and you know it."

"Firstly, that is an option, Declan. We have no reason to believe that AS1 would refuse or even take alarm in us asking them to leave. Secondly, if the public finds out that we are hiding something from them, nothing will spread panic faster than that."

"They won't find out, the transcription leaves no trace ... Jamal, listen to me. The fact that the AS1 have been watching us for our entire time on this planet. The world can't handle that right now. That gives the AS1 the upper hand, makes us their fucking experiment. They know everything and we know nothing. We MUST control the narrative, at least for now until we build this partnership with them and can gain the public's full trust in their intentions."

"Do they have your full trust in their intentions?" Jamal asked.

"Yes," Declan replied.

"I can't make the call now. Sit on the logs; we can delay their release. I need to go to the board with this."

"No, Jamal, you can't go to the board—not yet. This has to stay between us. I need to get off this damn ISS. I can do more from the UN building than I can up here. Hang tight, please, Jamal. I'm begging you."

"I'll hold this information until you're back on the ground; I'll support your early departure from the ISS." Jamal ended the call and leaned back in his leather chair, pulling hard at his long, greasy black hair.

Chapter 49

Declan retrieved his meal after the food warmer chimed. Gideon watched his own meal bag floating in front of him, a typical American dinner in theory but lacking flavor. Node 1 was where Gideon spent much of his time, the closest thing they had to a kitchen, and centrally located within the space station.

"How are you feeling with the logs?" Declan asked between slurps of mashed potatoes.

"What do you mean?"

Declan shrugged.

"They are providing another piece of useful information, I suppose. The communications help us to get an understanding of how the AS1 really tick and function."

Declan looked up and released his meal bag, leaving it floating in a slow spiral in front of him, and rubbed his short beard scruff.

"We need these to go well," Declan said. "The world is watching, and we have one shot at this."

He reclaimed the bag, which had almost drifted beyond his reach, and began slurping the mashed potatoes again.

Gideon guessed where this was headed. "Are you referring to asking Linda and me to step out of the interview during Log 2 and then Log 3 still not getting submitted?"

Declan looked sternly at Gideon. "We need these to go well. Let's just say Log 3 was lost due to technical challenges. Gideon, can I trust you to make sure these AS1 logs go well?"

"I mean yeah, but isn't tampering with the logs a little, I don't know, dishonest?"

"Tampering?" Declan scoffed. "Tampering is a little aggressive, don't you think?"

"That's not what I meant."

"Well, what did you mean?" Declan asked.

"I meant that it seems questionable to—change anything with the logs. I mean, isn't that the point of a log in the first place? To record everything. If we are not recording everything, all the details, then it really isn't an accurate log."

"Look, Gideon," Declan said with a long sigh. "You're a smart guy. You know how important this whole thing is and there is a lot more riding on these logs than you may think. We can't afford to have anything published that could make the AS1 look bad, right?"

Gideon shook his head. "I suppose I'm not really thinking of the logs that way, as in *how* it makes the AS1 look. The purpose of the logs is to have a set of documented conversations with the AS1, to share knowledge and address any concerns or challenges that come up as we go through this process. I just think we should report everything, that's all."

Declan smiled and looked away. "Gideon, here's the problem. I think you are aware, but the UN made the brilliant decision to share the AS1 logs with the public. Perhaps they didn't consider, although I warned them, that they may contain content that would be alarming or concerning to the public. And right now, alarm and concern are the last things the public needs. I'm not asking you to tamper with the logs, but I need you to consider the audience that will listen to them and if a conversation is moving in a direction that could alarm said audience, finish the discussion offline and report it directly to me."

Declan paused, taking a swig of water before continuing.

"You were one of the first people to find the signal. You have shown pure commitment and dedication to this project since day one. You want this to succeed and so do I. Don't fool yourself, there are lots of people out there, in other countries, other industries and yes even factions inside the US that would love for all of this to fail."

"What are you talking about?"

"I'm talking about people, agencies out there who would love to find something they think could be hostile about the ASI or find some indication of foul play. Because if they can find some evidence of that, they could use that to take over. The military, NATO, the CIA, the NSA, our enemies, even some of our allies. I mean there are all manner of groups that would love to control this. Use it as an opportunity to push their own agenda, gain funds to develop research. And if that happened, it would all be taken out of our hands. Forget communication, forget cooperation, forget learning and improving humanity. No, no." He shook his finger in the air. "They would love to take over and use this as an excuse to create more weapons contracts, or to use it as leverage against another nation. There is no telling what they could do if they had full access and complete control of the AS1."

"I don't think that could happen," Gideon said. "The UN has already agreed to follow the SETI—"

"Gideon, all of that could change in an instant. If the right person gets in the ear of the president, it could all change like that." He snapped his fingers. "Don't think it hasn't already been tried. We're lucky to even be up here. So, if that is the case, I'm going to do whatever I can to protect the AS1 and their interaction with humanity."

Gideon looked away and considered leaving as he had no interest in political talks.

"Whatever you say, boss."

Declan let out a sigh. "Look, again, removing data from the logs is not something we want to practice. But I am getting pulled heavily into discussions back on Earth. I won't go into details, but let's just say the UN is lacking structure and direction at the moment."

Gideon rotated back to face Declan.

"Anyway, I'm still going to be checking every day during the AS1 sessions, but I'm going to be around a little less."

"Why are you telling me this?" Gideon asked, guessing the answer.

"Well, Gideon, everyone has a pretty specific role around here. I need someone I can count on to oversee, log findings, and keep us organized. That was my role, really, and now I see it becoming yours."

"Are you going back to Earth sooner than planned?"

"I think it's pretty likely." Declan gave a serious nod.

A silence hung in the air while Gideon digested this.

"There will be a day when the next step comes, and everything will be reviewed. Think of it like a court case and the AS1 logs the evidence. If people are able to find any doubt, any cause for concern, it could hinder the advancement of not only this project but the future of humanity."

"And what is that next step?" Gideon asked.

"Bringing the AS1 to Earth, Gideon. Bringing them to Earth."

AS1 Log 11

Loc: BEAM2 [ISS]
personnel: DW, GH

AS1 [AMICUS-BETA]: What will humans do when resources on your planet become depleted?

DECLAN: What makes you believe our resources will become depleted?

AS1 [AMICUS-BETA]: Data.

DECLAN: Maybe when that day comes, we will have the technology allowing us to search for a new home. This question is impossible to answer as the events and technologies are not present.

AS1 [AMICUS-BETA]: Do humans anticipate this coming?

DECLAN: Yes, for the most part.

AS1 [AMICUS-BETA]: If humans believe this will happen, what are humans doing to prepare for this.

GIDEON: We have explored the idea of colonizing other planets. Mars, in particular, but we're still developing the technology and the regulations.

AS1 [AMICUS-BETA]: What technology gaps are preventing humans from living on Mars?

GIDEON: Well, for one, it's too cold for humans to survive for long. The atmosphere is mostly carbon dioxide and unbreathable. And then there's ultraviolet radiation from the sun that would be harmful.

AS1 [AMICUS-BETA]: Do you humans not have the technology to deal with these issues?

GIDEON: Well, I suppose we do, but another challenge is our space travel. We don't have a timely or cost-effective way to get all of the required infrastructure to Mars and established. Recent studies indicate we're probably about ten to twenty years away from being able to land a crew there.

AS1 [AMICUS-BETA]: If you landed on Mars, what would humans do there?

DECLAN: The first step would be to colonize it, and then we'd be able to see how long, and how well, we can actually live up there.

AS1 [AMICUS-BETA]: If Earth became depleted of resources, rendering it uninhabitable. Is the current plan then for humans to live on Mars?

DECLAN: Humans do not have a contingency plan for such an event. But I would say our dream would be to learn space travel and find other planets that can sustain the human race.

AS1 [AMICUS-BETA]: So ultimately, the goal for humans is to relocate to a new planet that could sustain your species.

DECLAN: More or less, I suppose that is the ultimate goal.

Chapter 50

"Come on? Nobody wants to play?!"

Michelle was being her usual energetic self, trying to convince the team to play her another round of jacks, which she had yet to lose.

"You already have me watering your plant experiments for the next ten days, I have nothing left to wager," Rajit shot back. Gideon hadn't seen Rajit win a single card game since they had been on the ISS.

"Gideon? Crach? Linda?" she asked, now spinning in quick 360s as she played in the zero gravity. Gideon just smiled and shook his head.

"Durak or I don't play," Crach said back in his stern monotone voice. Durak was a complex Russian card game he had taught the crew several days before.

"Oh, screw that!" Linda said with a smile as she pulled herself through Node 1, clearly not a fan of Crach's favorite game.

Gideon reached behind his head and without looking, grabbed a handle allowing him to pull himself into Node 3. After spending weeks on the ISS, Gideon felt he could navigate the station with his eyes closed. He had memorized where every handle, wire and imperfection existed.

Declan was already in Node 3 working away on his iPad as he pretended to use some of the exercise equipment, something they were required to do daily. Today the Contact Team had worked together with the AS1 to understand the political structure of the AS1s' society, or lack thereof. Declan looked up as Gideon entered the small, shared space.

"The AS1 sure were adamant that each of their beings is equal, as their species all share one vast knowledge base. I just can't wrap my head around how that can work. A society with no hierarchy or chain of command?" Declan said.

Linda, who had followed Gideon into Node 3, likely to get away from being pulled into another card game, spoke up next.

"I asked how they had selected the crew to come to Earth's solar system, because surely that selection would be made based on some type of assessment of skills or rank. Amicus-Beta answered that the AS1 only reproduces when there is a 'position' to be filled, or a need for an additional AS1 due to overall population goals. Thus, at birth, an AS1s' mission is predefined. The crew that came to Earth's solar system, and even to the ISS had been appointed to do this since their first day alive."

Gideon shook his head. "I can't even imagine … not only from a personal standpoint of having your entire life planned out for you. But also, the *amount* of planning that must take for them. All of the alternative scenarios they must play out."

Linda nodded her agreement.

"Any updates on when we can expect to gain access to the AS1 ship?" Gideon asked, looking in Declan's direction.

"I think we are close; it sounds like Crach and Brandon have worked together and from a technology standpoint, everything is worked out. Additionally, you have the support of Jamal and President Helland. Amicus-Gamma was not too quick to agree, as you know, but sounds like they are working out the details on their side."

"Do we know what the hesitation was from the AS1? They came on our ship, why would they push back on us going on theirs?" Linda asked.

Declan shrugged. "I wouldn't read into it too much."

Linda shot a look toward Gideon, with raised eyebrow and smirk as if to say, "*Are you fuckin' kidding me?*"

"Excuse me, Declan? But if there is hesitation on their side, I think we have the right to know," she said sternly.

Gideon tried to pretend like he was now too invested in his iPad to be listening, not wanting to get involved, but in fact very curious about the response.

"You're right; I'm sorry, Linda. I just have a lot on my plate right now but will do my due diligence to ensure that it's safe. I think the AS1 are just hesitant as they have some proprietary technologies on their ship and are assessing what they are comfortable sharing."

Gideon lifted his head from his iPad and shot the exact same look back in Linda's direction before directing his next comment back at Declan.

"Proprietary technologies? Like what? That is the first I've heard of this," he said.

Declan unbuckled himself from the zero-gravity treadmill, and Gideon noticed that it hadn't even been turned on.

"Jesus, you guys, can you just back off for once. Find a little trust in there why don't you," he said as he reached for a handle.

"Trust you or the AS1?" Linda asked.

"The process, Linda. Trust the process," Declan replied before leaving the tight quarters of the node.

AS1 Log 18

Loc: BEAM2 [ISS]
personnel: GH, LS

LINDA: How did you manage to learn our language so quickly, you processed it faster than the play time of the actual files.

AS1 [AMICUS-BETA]: We broke it up between us and then showed the learned information through our visual language. We can transfer data between ourselves in a similar fashion as loading software to one of your computers.

LINDA: I would like to conduct an experiment.

AS1 [AMICUS-BETA]: Please describe experiment.

LINDA: I have a piece of literature that I would like you to read. Once you have completed this, we will observe you transferring what you have read to Amicus-Gamma. We would like to time this transfer. Once you have described the book to Amicus-Gamma, we will have Amicus-Gamma write down what he has learned from you.

AS1 [AMICUS-BETA]: Please describe the literature.

LINDA: The book is named *The Pillars of the Earth* and is nearly 400,000 words or a thousand pages long. I will have Brandon transfer the file to the shared drive.

AS1 [AMICUS-BETA]: Is this how humans would view the file?

LINDA: Well, typically humans would read from the physical book, not a computer file.

AS1 [AMICUS-BETA]: Is this a possibility? I would like to complete the experiment utilizing human technology.

LINDA: Well, a book is hardly a technology, or at least very old technology. But as a matter of fact, I do have the book. It's one of my favorite reads.

Chapter 51

~ 22 days after contact ~

Squinting through his hangover, James kicked the half-full beer can out of the way as he made his way to the faded yellow couch. Brad, one of his fraternity brothers, was already seated in front of the silent television.

"Has it started yet?" James asked.

"Nah, man. Clean that shit up, the smell is killin' me right now." Brad nodded toward the spilled beer, stale liquid slowly making its way into the grains and cracks of the worn-out wooden floor.

James ignored the request and sat on the couch, rubbing his temples with his pointer and middle fingers. Typically, after a night like last night, he would sleep in until at least noon. But this morning he and many others made a point to watch Declan's interview. Prior to this whole AS1 thing, James hadn't known who Declan was, or really any of the people he now so intently followed on a daily basis. Since when did college kids care about what Jamal, the UN secretary-general, had to say?

Brad leaned forward and burped.

"What's up with the volume?" James asked.

"It's off," Brad replied flatly.

"Why?"

"'Cause I sat down here, and the remote's over there."

James followed Brad's gaze to the corner of the house where the remote lay on the floor. He noticed both AA batteries ejected upon some sort of impact and lay on the floor a few feet away.

After repairing the mangled device, he commanded the television to speak.

"As the highly anticipated update from Declan Wilter is about to occur, please remember that this is a live interview and viewer discretion is advised."

The screen broke into two panels, the news anchor's face in one and Declan's in the other, via webcam. He nodded and waved.

"Declan, can you hear us?" the anchor asked.

"Sure can! How great is this? Live chat via webcam from the International Space Station? I tell you what, these past couple weeks have been nothing but a bunch of new experiences. For all of us." Declan was beaming.

Brad threw James a look. The two had decided not to like Declan, and scoffed at everything he said, even if it lacked fair reason.

"We appreciate you taking the time to talk with us today, you must be a busy man. What can you tell us?"

"Well, I can tell you ... Shannon? Is it Shannon?"

"Yes, I'm Shannon." The news anchor laughed.

"Well, Shannon, this has been one of the greatest experiences of both my life and our crew's lives up here. Truly remarkable stuff. The AS1 are confirmed to be as friendly and as curious as we are. We have already begun making some incredible steps toward understanding each other." Declan was now so close to his webcam, that both his chin and the top of his head were cropped out of the image.

"How does a team like yours confirm, as you say, that the AS1 are nonhostile?"

"I used the word *friendly*, Shannon, and we have a team of highly trained and skilled analysts, linguists, and scientists working with the AS1 every single day. Through extensive logged interviews and experiments we have all come to the same conclusion that they mean us no harm. They are curious travelers, just as excited about finally finding life out in the vastness of space as we are. It's truly remarkable."

"I have a statement here from General John Higgens—"

"OOHRAH!" James and Brad both yelled at the mention of Higgens's name.

"That, quote, 'Although the AS1 shows no sign of being a threat to the human population, the armed forces will continue to keep a heightened state of *emergency* while they are within close range of our home,' end quote. What do you make of this, Declan? It is concerning to hear you say they are friendly, yet the military seems to view them as a threat."

Declan's face showed a sign of irritation at the comment.

"Shannon, come on, of course the military is going to continue keeping its guard up. I would too; there is no reason not to. I'm on the phone with the general day in and day out, and I assure you, he is as confident in the AS1s' intentions as I am."

Chapter 52

With a hiss, the Transfer Zone area B door slid open, revealing the interior of the AS1 craft. Instantly, Gideon experienced an eerie sensation as if the world had been cloaked in a muted shroud, muffling all sound. An unanticipated silence enveloped them, a haunting stillness that seized his vocal cords when he attempted to communicate with the group. It was as though an unseen hand had clamped over his mouth, stifling any utterance. Fear crept into his mind like a relentless parasite, gnawing at his composure.

Gideon closed his eyes tight, attempting to suppress the rising panic. *Why should we fear? If the AS1 meant harm, why now, why here? What could possibly be gained?* he thought.

Gideon reopened his eyes, only to see the sight of fear mirrored in Michelle's eyes, reigniting the creeping dread within him.

Movement caught Gideon's attention as Carter initiated a series of cryptic hand signals. The group struggled to decipher their meaning in their state of disarray. Carter slowed down and eventually, Gideon concurred with a nod when Carter gestured "OK" and pointed in his direction.

With the crew finally composed, they scanned the eerie surroundings only to discover the AS1 aliens conspicuously absent. Before them lay a vast, circular expanse, its smooth, towering walls curving upward into an intimidating unknown. The space was significantly larger than anything within the ISS. The atmosphere, or the gaseous medium surrounding them, was hazy, obscuring their vision like an impenetrable fog. Yet, this fog possessed a strange quality, resembling a myriad of minuscule, shimmering diamonds suspended in the air, casting an unsettling glint. Gideon ventured to move forward into the ship, but with nothing but sheer, featureless walls confronting them, navigating proved nearly impossible.

Suddenly a brilliant flash of light could be seen in the distance. The AS1?

The group exchanged looks. The light continued to shimmer but fluctuated in shades and colors.

Rajit's face tightened into a focused look of confidence, and he pushed off the door, slowly gliding toward the beacon.

Wow, thought Gideon. He's made progress.

The group awkwardly found themselves following, helping each other maintain the correct trajectories.

Gideon heard the muffled sounds of his heart pulsing in his eardrums. It felt as if he were underwater. He noticed, flowing through the air, were very distinct trails of light. Like rivers of fluorescent blues and greens reflecting off the shimmering fog. He could see Linda tracking one of the light trails with her eyes, a look of awe and confusion on her face.

The shape of the AS1's body could now be seen in the distance, the beacon of light coming from the center of the large figure.

Gideon felt helpless as they drifted closer to the AS1. With the lack of handles or walls within reach, no one had any control over their trajectory. A new feeling of panic began to claw at Gideon's mind as he realized just how useless they were in this place. Floating blobs, unable to choose where they were going and unable to communicate.

As they neared the AS1, the creature reached out a couple of its long arms and slowed each of the team's motion, pulling them to the ground. Gideon felt the long fingers wrap around his thigh. The grip was strong but gentle as it pulled him toward itself.

It positioned each person in perfect stillness such that they could not reach anything or each other. Gideon remembered watching them do this before with other objects. The AS1s' ability to place items floating in zero gravity into total stillness was mind-blowing. Now Gideon and his team were those objects, floating ducks. Unable to move in any direction.

The large being held up the tablet with words.

{Are you comfortable?}

The group hesitated, but each eventually nodded.

Quickly the board switched, showing new words.

{Good, welcome to our environment.}

Gideon looked around taking in the features of the massive room. The walls curved smoothly and led Gideon to believe they were inside a large, egg-shaped room. Perhaps fifty feet across and high, it was hard to tell in the shifting fog. The lack of technology was confusing as the room appeared completely absent of anything but smooth walls. Either this wasn't a room meant for science or flying the craft, or the AS1 had a vastly different way of doing things.

The alien stood motionless as the human team took in their surroundings.

To Gideon's amazement, Linda began to use sign language. The AS1 flashed several colors indicating that they understood the gestures.

The AS1 tablet displayed new words.

{Linda has communicated with us through a secondary language used by humans that does not require audio accompaniment. She requested we teach your team some simple communications.}

The tablet switched to one word.

{Yes.}

The AS1 pulsed a light bluish green.

The tablet then updated to a new word.

{No.}

The AS1 then pulsed a dark purple.

For the next several minutes Gideon and the team watched intently as the AS1 taught them the meaning of various communicative color combinations. Rajit's jaw was slightly open. Carter typed furiously at his tablet, asking them to slow down as needed. Gideon simply watched and learned.

Soon, Linda was communicating with the AS1 in a visual dance using sign language and understanding the AS1 response as they flashed various colors. She looked back at the science team, eyes glossy with joy. Gideon understood what this moment must be like for an accomplished linguist. Communication with an extraterrestrial life form in their ancestral language.

Chapter 53

The ISS's orbit around Earth made it appear as though the blue planet was always rolling away from their orientation. Gideon observed from the Cupola as the sun began to fall out of view, placing Earth between the ISS and the sun. Moving at 17,100 miles per hour meant the ISS orbited Earth every ninety minutes, allowing one to observe sixteen sunsets and sixteen sunrises per day. Gideon never grew tired of watching as the beautiful planet slowly disappeared into the blackness of its own shadow, leaving a thin rainbow of light across its upper radius for several minutes before going completely black.

As the thin arched band faded away, Gideon heard a sound behind him. Looking back, he was surprised to see Carter floating at the Cupola entrance, arms stretched up in a Y, holding on to the diameter of the small entry. For a moment, Gideon felt trapped, his only exit from the Cupola blocked by the thin dark man. A man who had never sought Gideon out for a direct conversation. Now, Carter floated, almost as motionless as the AS1, just several feet away, looking at him.

Gideon awkwardly turned back to the now completely black vastness of space. "Here for the view?" Gideon asked.

Carter pushed off, coming in closer, stern face never wavering. He positioned himself rather close, though on the ISS the crew quickly became comfortable with the often-close quarters.

After a pause, Carter spoke. "Gideon, tell me what you observed yesterday onboard the AS1 ship?"

Gideon hesitated, brain quickly running through the events in perfect recollection.

"Why are you asking me?"

"Because you seem to be one of the few who hasn't become mentally mesmerized and compromised by the AS1. Now tell me, did you observe anything yesterday that seemed suspicious?"

"The ship docking attachment?" Gideon replied.

Carter's eyes widened in surprise and seemed pleased.

"Exactly. How did the AS1 build such a perfect mating adapter? It lines up with the PMA flawlessly. I have considered 3D printing, machining, or casting, but after reviewing my pictures, none of it fits. Gideon, the AS1 continue to surprise me, but this … this worries me."

"What concerns you specifically?"

"Even the conversations I have with Amicus-Alpha, it almost feels scripted, and the questions loaded. It's like they've done this a hundred times," Carter replied.

Gideon nodded but did not speak.

"It's like everything that has happened with the AS1 is planned and calculated by them and we are simply passengers. Additionally, I was studying th—"

"Gents! I have just finished reviewing all the logs from the encounter," Declan interrupted, gliding into the small Cupola, a space too small to comfortably fit the three men.

Carter's face tightened in annoyance. "I noticed you sat that one out, too scared?"

Declan either did not hear the comment or did not care. "Incredible stuff, honestly! I am going to hold a briefing with the team soon to formally announce, but I wanted to bring you up to speed first. I am planning on departing for Earth early. As I am sure you have heard, we are reorganizing SETI and the United Nations, as extraterrestrial relations are now a real thing. Can you freakin' believe that? We will now have an Extraterrestrial Relations Division in the UN. SETI will be reworked and rebranded as it is no longer just a 'search' for life, but a communication with extraterrestrial life."

Carter opened his mouth to make a remark, but Declan continued.

"Anyways, I wanted to inform you of this and will provide details of the repr—"

"Declan! For God's sake, slow down and look around you," Carter snapped. "What the hell was that press conference yesterday? How can you tell the world, 'We have all come to the same conclusion that they mean us no harm'? You never fucking asked us our opinions."

Declan looking taken aback for once, hesitated.

"Carter, we have all been communicating profusely day and night, I have been hearing nothing but positive feedback and experiences about the AS1. Perhaps I should have gotten an official statement from each team member before going public … shall we now?"

Declan prepared his tablet for notes. "Do you think they are a threat?"

"I have inconclusive data to say one way or another if they pose a threat. But this I can guarantee you. They are not telling us everything, and they seem to have a plan that is a lot deeper than a meet and greet."

AS1 Log 27

Loc: BEAM2 [ISS]
personnel: GH

GIDEON: Log 27, at timestamp 18:00. Interviewer Gideon Haas. Amicus-Beta, how are you?

AS1 [AMICUS-BETA]: No change from last interview.

GIDEON: Is there anything specific you would like to talk about in this exchange?

AS1 [AMICUS-BETA]: Yes.

GIDEON: Good. What is your question?

AS1 [AMICUS-BETA]: Has the human species ever been threatened by another unique species on Earth?

GIDEON: Please define "threatened."

AS1 [AMICUS-BETA]: Another species causes concern for the advancement of your species.

GIDEON: Uh, no I suppose not, are you implying you may be that species?

AS1 [AMICUS-BETA]: No, the question has nothing to do with the AS1 presence, it has to do with the reactionary behavior of the human race.

GIDEON: OK, well, like I said, no I don't believe we ever have.

AS1 [AMICUS-BETA]: What about in the beginning of human existence?

GIDEON: We don't exactly have records of that, but I assume you could say we had to coexist with other mammals long ago that were threatening to us. Back in the Stone Age, humans faced animals like the saber-toothed tiger, and other large predatory animals.

AS1 [AMICUS-BETA]: How did your species learn to coexist with them, and what is the relationship now?

GIDEON: Well, I guess most of the species are extinct now. But I'm sure the two species would clash and fight for the upper hand. I'm not sure I'm the right person for this question.

AS1 [AMICUS-BETA]: How many species have gone extinct on Earth?

GIDEON: It's difficult to provide an exact number of species that have gone extinct on Earth because many extinctions have occurred throughout the planet's history, and not all of them have been documented. The number of documented extinctions is a fraction of the total number of species that have existed.

AS1 [AMICUS-BETA]: When looking at extinction rates since humans have become civilized, do you believe they have increased or decreased?

GIDEON: I'm not sure I understand the relevance of that question. Nor do I have the data to provide you an accurate answer.

AS1 [AMICUS-BETA]: Please provide your best guess.

GIDEON: I would imagine that extinction rates have increased since humans have evolved. It is pretty well-documented that human activities, particularly habitat destruction, pollution, and the introduction of invasive species, have significantly contributed to the extinction of many species. What about on your planet? How many species have gone extinct?

AS1 [AMICUS-BETA]: None.

GIDEON: I find that hard to believe. From what you know about Earth, why do you think we have seen such a large number of extinctions and adversity compared to your planet?

AS1 [AMICUS-BETA]: Our planet is much older than yours, and perhaps more stable in the sense we haven't seen significant climate change events such as your ice age. Additionally, our species being primarily plant life, don't directly compete for resources like yours.

Chapter 54

Gideon found himself amused by the look on Linda's face as the Soyuz MS-19 shuttle slowly became invisible from the small port window. Her expression was nothing short of relief and joy.

"Cheers to a station of scientists? Well, and one random kid." Carter winked at Gideon. The truth was, Carter was likely the most relieved by Declan's return to Earth. Carter's highly calculated and logical way of thinking was far from a match for Declan's brain, which recently had been labeled by the team as one similar to that of a Labrador.

Linda pushed away from the window, gliding back into a reclined position, which turned into a slow-motion backflip that put her directly next to Gideon.

"Did you complete your experiment?" Gideon asked.

"We did, absolutely stunning," Linda replied. She paused, choosing her words before continuing.

"I requested Amicus-Beta be isolated in BEAM2; I gave it the physical copy of *The Pillars of the Earth*. That alone was an exciting moment, watching Amicus-Beta read a book, physically turning the pages. Of course, it read the entire book in just over thirty minutes, turning a page about every two seconds. Once done, I retrieved the book and allowed Amicus-Gamma to join Amicus-Beta in BEAM2. I requested that they not produce any communication until asked. Which as a result has been one of the only times I have seen them without any light coming from their skin, just a solid dark greenish-brown."

She paused again, now seeing that Carter was intently listening as well.

"Anyways, once Amicus-Gamma was in the room, I told Amicus-Beta to transfer what was learned to Amicus-Gamma. I had a stopwatch to time this transfer of knowledge. Once I said go it happened so fast I didn't even get the stopwatch stopped in time and had to go back to the video feed to time it. The light on their skin flashed for 1.3 seconds and then went back to their natural greenish-brown color. Amicus-Beta then let me know Amicus-Gamma knew the book."

"So, Amicus-Beta transferred the entire book to Amicus-Gamma in 1.3 seconds?" Carter asked, sounding skeptical.

"That was my understanding. At this point I asked Amicus-Beta to leave BEAM2, ensuring that no additional data could be transferred between the two. I then asked Amicus-Gamma how it would like to transcribe what it had learned about the book. Amicus-Gamma requested nine hundred and eighty-two pieces of paper and a writing device." Linda stopped talking and pushed off the wall, floating away from Gideon.

"Oh, you can't leave us with a cliffhanger like that!" Gideon called after her.

Linda reached the far wall and rummaged through a container, mounted to the wall. She then turned to face both Gideon and Carter, holding something behind her back.

"Amicus-Gamma rewrote the entire book, word for word. It's perfect, I spent hours looking for any errors or differences. But that's not all," she said, her face twisted in thought.

"How could there possibly be more? They rewrote the entire damn book perfectly," Carter said.

Linda revealed what she had been hiding behind her back. In her hands was a stack of several notebooks, which she then held up so Gideon and Carter could see the front. Gideon gasped.

"Amicus-Gamma not only rewrote the book perfectly, but also drew the cover in amazing detail. You guys, Amicus-Gamma *never* saw the book but then drew this," Linda said.

Gideon observed the drawing, and the detail. Of course, not in color due to the writing device Amicus-Gamma had been provided, the details were amazing. The drawing was done in a unique way, almost as if Amicus-Gamma had never lifted the pen from the paper, drawing the cover in one long tangled line.

"These damn aliens are just full of surprises, aren't they?" Carter said.

The three floated in silence for several moments before Linda turned her attention back to Gideon.

"How have the logs been going, Gideon? I really haven't had a chance to review them as much as I'd like," she said.

"To be honest, yesterday was a little weird. They seem highly interested and almost concerned with our planet and its overall workings. What I mean is, they asked about species and how they have gone extinct, and inquired what the impact of that has been on us. I struggled to understand the relevance, so I began returning the questions. Asking what their indigenous species are like. As we know, they don't seem to have faced much adversity in the past. No wars among themselves, nor conflict over land. Their planet was nearly uninhabitable."

"The atmosphere you mean?" Carter asked.

"Yes. Their planet experiences intense heat fluctuations and massive storms and, in agreement with what Rajit has concluded, it seems their planet only contained one 'intelligent' being. The rest is mostly plant life similar to moss and ground cover, and small organisms similar to our bacteria, bugs and some small animals. Perhaps they were able to survive and evolve in the treacherous conditions due to the lack of competition from other species. Either way, after surviving a long time underground, they eventually developed what they describe as living pods that orbit around their planet. In these they've lived the majority of their existence. They continued to advance in their orbital pods. The pods contain the exact same atmospheric buildup as their planet but protect them from the extreme storms and heat in low orbit."

"OK, so they live off-surface."

"Yes, which led me back to their planet." Gideon paused. "When do they visit? How do they get food? And from the sounds of it, they are able to build from matter. It's not clear how, but according to Amicus-Beta they get the majority of their resources and food from uninhabited planets or rocks."

"So, they eat rocks?" Linda asked with a raised eyebrow.

Rajit, who had recently drifted into the now cramped node, chimed in. "From what I understand, they are able to harvest any type of material from their planet and asteroids—

even chemicals from the air, from the soils, from the rocks and minerals, any kind of plant life. I think they are able to either harvest these or break the materials down to a point that they can rebuild them on a molecular level into whatever sustenance and materials they need. The way the AS1 understands and thinks of particles is quite different from ours. To be honest, once I understand the differences, no doubt it will lead to a better understanding of the behaviors between atoms and their builds."

"A little strange that we were able to breathe in their ship's atmosphere, wouldn't you say?" Carter asked.

"I believe they adjusted it so it would be habitable for us; we have given them the full molecular breakdown of our required atmosphere," Rajit replied.

Carter shook his head and then, unexpectedly slammed his fist into the small metal tray next to him. The loud sound quickly gained everyone's attention.

"Aren't you guys supposed to be experts? I feel like I'm working with fucking children. What are the chances the AS1 just happens to be able to exist in our atmospheric pressure? The range of pressure or lack of pressure throughout space is massive and critical to the survival of living organisms. What about temperature? They just happen to enjoy the same twenty-two-degree Celsius environments we do? What are the odds of that?"

"Yes, just as a deep-sea fish would die instantly if brought to the surface, its body can't handle the lack of pressure. Does seem oddly convenient. I have thought of this, Carter," Rajit said.

"Then speak up! You guys, we are here to analyze. If things don't add up, we must bring those to Declan's attention. There are so many factors, such as temperature tolerances, pressure as we just stated; how is it they can breathe our air without issue? The AS1 were far too prepared for this. I believe they have had more practice than they are telling us, and we need to prove it." Carter lifted his hand from the metal tray; a small dent remained.

Chapter 55

~ 72 days after contact ~

Never in a million years did the boy expect his family to own a vacation home on Vancouver Island. The view from the house looked west over the Pacific Ocean and would see the sun fall behind the vast blue every night. The only way of getting to the house from Vancouver, BC, was by ferry and then driving for two hours up a long winding road, the last half hour being dirt.

The boy's father had joked when they toured the house for the first time. "You know, son, even if the aliens are here to hunt humans, it'll be a while before they find this place."

Everyone laughed at the time, but still had a sense of unease surrounding the AS1 and their presence on the Space Station. It felt too close for comfort.

After the initial three weeks of 24/7 coverage without much new information, the networks had settled into two hours a night on developments, mostly talking heads rehashing the same points everyone had already heard. While watching the daily AS1 update, his father was drawn to a segment by Neil Slater, a well-known real estate investor. Neil talked about low baseline opportunity, explaining that since the housing and stock market had recently crashed and were resting at the bottom, it was an opportune moment to invest. The simple theory made sense and quickly began catching on. The boy's family purchased the home one week later.

The Dow Jones stock market, though reacting slower, had been showing a similar trend with increases in the last couple of weeks. The boy noticed that the tensions that had set in after the public announcement of the aliens seemed to be lifting. His eighth-grade classes were almost back up to full attendance and the movie theater up the street had set a date to reopen as well.

His mother explained that the world is balanced upon a very fragile economic system, and she believed people were far more afraid of that system collapsing than they were of the aliens. Now that the economy seemed to be recovering, the quality and way of life were recovering as well.

Chapter 56

Gideon sat in Node 1 perched over the table, using his thighs to hold him in place. Holding the copper washer in his hand, he outstretched his arm, knuckles facing up and drew in a long breath of air. He concentrated on maintaining absolute stillness while keeping his breath held, eyes focused on his outstretched fist. Slowly, Gideon began to open his fingers and once they were completely straight, he carefully lifted his hand upward revealing the copper washer floating in space. Once his hand was clear of potentially touching the small metal object, he pulled it away quickly and moved in for a better look. Although it remained in the same area, he could see a very slow rotation to the right.

Gideon let out his breath, retrieved the levitating washer and placed it again back in his palm to try again. He wondered if it had taken the AS1 practice to be able to leave objects behind in perfect motionlessness or if it was just a gifted skill they had.

Just as Gideon was going to restart the process, Carter glided gracefully into the node, looking more irritated than normal.

"Rajit?!" he shouted, as if pretending he didn't notice Rajit was just a few feet away from him.

"Yes, Carter? What is it now?" Rajit replied, a tone of annoyance in his voice.

"When are you going to get that damn space plant out of our lab?"

"You mean Fred?" Rajit replied.

Gideon knew what they were referring to. The acorn-shaped organic that the AS1 had given the team on the day of their first contact had grown into a sizable treelike plant, reaching a height of nearly three feet. Resembling a miniature palm tree, its upper part exhibited a dense, fur-like appearance, boasting a vibrant orange hue reminiscent of a creation from a Dr. Seuss book. Dubbed "Fred" by Rajit, the most intriguing feature of this alien plant was its ability to swiftly retract into a tightly packed ball in response to disturbances, such as inadvertent collisions.

"It's crowding the physics station; I can hardly work at the laptop without that damn plant bumping into me. And when it does touch me, it scares the shit out of me when it retracts," Carter said.

"Carter, that is the first ever human-grown alien plant … find it in you to appreciate it for what it is. That said, I'll put in a request to have it moved to the Columbus Lab."

Carter just grunted before continuing his way toward Node 4, likely to get some rest.

Rajit pulled himself over and positioned himself against the opposite wall of Gideon.

"Well, what did you find out?" Gideon asked, quickly placing the washer back into the Velcro pocket of his pants.

"For starters, the initial theories on the molecular structure breakdown did at least pass the sniff test."

Rajit had been spending countless hours in the lab researching and reviewing the data Amicus-Alpha had provided on an AS1 technology that was being referenced to as molecular reconstruction.

"Really?" Gideon asked, interested in what he had learned.

"Yeah, and thirty-seven scientists out of the initial forty solved the theorem using the AS1 data. So, all the results back up what the AS1 have been saying. Very interesting."

Rajit and Carter had been given nearly unlimited scientific support back on Earth. Access to hundreds of subject matter experts in various fields and the ability to run experiments in a gravity environment versus the weightlessness of the ISS.

"It is." Gideon pulled out his pocket tablet from his side leg pocket. "Are the engineering and geology labs finding beneficial uses for the technology?"

"Yeah, but—I have something else you should look at."

"What's that?"

"Check it out." Rajit's eyes lit up. "I don't want to jump the gun here, but I've been running some hypothetical models on cell malignancy."

"Malignancy? You mean cancer?"

"Yeah. I've been reading a lot about the latest molecular residual disease trials, mostly from China and India, and it's pretty interesting stuff. The most advanced research labs show promise of relapse-free survival. But the limitations in our knowledge of cellular breakdown are what is stopping everything. But with these new avenues from the AS1, things may change."

"Really?" Gideon asked as he put his tablet away. "How so?"

"If we were able to apply molecular reconstruction methods to our human biology, our whole understanding of single-cell sequencing and technology could change. It would change immune-oncology combinations, biomarkers, therapeutics, all kinds of things."

"Are you saying the AS1 may hold the cure for cancer?" Gideon asked.

"I'm saying"—Rajit rubbed his forehead—"I see some possibilities here. And I don't know what the technological limits are, but I guarantee they are way beyond ours, that's for sure."

"So, what's the next step?"

Rajit looked Gideon straight in the eyes. "We pursue this and hope the AS1 are willing to turn over their technologies."

Gideon and Rajit sat in silence, wondering where this discovery could take them. Could they really be on the cusp of finding a cure for cancer?

Part IV

INTERVENTION

Humankind has not woven the web of life. We are but one thread within it. Whatever we do to the web, we do to ourselves. All things are bound together. All things connect.

– Chief Seattle

~ 5 years after contact ~

Chapter 57

Declan sighed and looked out of his UN office window. In the last several years, Declan had pushed hard to inject himself into the UN, eventually leading to his election as secretary-general, replacing Jamal who had moved to the role of president of the General Assembly. Tension balled up in the pit of his stomach as he thought about his upcoming meeting. This was the moment he had been waiting for. Everything rode on the outcome of this; Declan had to play his hand perfectly. It was time to review with Jamal and seek approval from the council.

Declan left his office and walked to another floor. As he grew closer with each step, he felt more excitement growing within him. He flipped through the notecards he had written up, highlighting some of the key points he needed to make. This was *his* moment, and he would capture it. He knew Jamal was not going to be ready for this, and it was better to catch him off guard. Declan checked the knot of his blue tie, ensuring it was snug and straight. Dress to impress, he thought. As he rounded the final turn before Jamal's office, Declan tossed the notecards into the nearest waste bin. Never would he be caught checking his notes when debating.

He stopped in front of Jamal's office door and took a deep breath before knocking.

"Come in."

"Morning, Jamal. Ready to talk?"

Jamal stood and pointed to the plush leather chairs. "Ready as ever. Have a seat."

"I will stand, if you don't mind," Declan said.

"Whatever suits you," Jamal responded, lowering himself into one of the chairs and pulling one leg across the other.

"To start this off, I would like to establish a clear baseline of where we are today. What is the current state of public opinion over the AS1?" Declan asked, already knowing the answer.

"Better than we could have hoped. There are lots of challenges among the people, of course, a million conspiracy theories, but also good discussions and debates going on. I'm encouraged. The majority of the public seems to be coming around to accepting our new reality."

"That's good," Declan said. "We are nearing the next step. The latest development, which we anticipated, is going to be an exciting but challenging phase."

"Challenging phase?" Jamal flinched. "What is that? There are plenty of developments that have caused challenges."

Declan rubbed his chin and sighed. "Well, to put it bluntly, the AS1 are requesting to land on Earth."

Jamal slowly nodded. Declan knew he was considering the numerous conversations they'd had about this moment and all of the complications. "I see. I guess we're finally here."

"Yes, we are."

"So"—Jamal sat back in his chair and folded his hands on his stomach—"what changed?"

"What has changed?" Declan repeated, dramatically.

"Nothing and everything and at the same time, Jamal. Nothing has changed from a technical standpoint. There is no 'thing' that is driving this. However, you just said it yourself. The people of this planet have grown to trust and support the AS1. Many, in fact, are eager to meet them and grow this partnership. Simply put, in our last AS1 log, Amicus-Beta formally requested an action plan to get them permission and ultimately access to our planet."

Jamal leaned forward in his chair and ran his hand through his shoulder-length black hair. Sliding several long straight locks behind his right ear.

"An action plan to come to Earth," he repeated in a soft tone, digesting each word.

"I'm assuming you reviewed the terms of contact established by the UN Department of Extraterrestrial Affairs?" Jamal asked.

"Nobody knows that piece of literature better than I do," Declan replied confidently. "And it is clear within Section 12a that the AS1 have satisfied all requirements that would need to be met in order to be granted access to our planet."

Jamal replied with a long sigh, moving his hand from grooming his greasy hair to his mouth, allowing him to chew on his thumbnail.

"Have you reviewed this with General Whitfield?" Jamal asked.

"No sir, you are the first I have come to. I need your support first so I can then drive the conversation through."

"My support?" Jamal laughed cynically.

"If you're looking for my *support* you don't have it. What do we possibly have to gain from letting them come to our planet? What can be gained here that can't be gained on the ISS?"

Declan was slightly caught off guard by Jamal's stance. His eyes sharpened; he loved a good fight.

"With all due respect, sir. Don't you think that is a bit close-minded? This goes far beyond what we can quantitatively gain. We are talking about building an alliance with *the* most technologically advanced species humans have ever interacted with. This is not a relationship we should just brush off because it makes us uncomfortable. We—"

"You think I'm worried about it because it makes us uncomfortable?" Jamal interrupted.

"Jesus, Declan, you're so in love with these damn aliens you'd trust them with your life. I'm worried about letting a creature, who probably has the technology to eliminate us in an instant, gain access to our precious planet."

"And you treat them like they are some race that you dislike for no given reason," Declan shot back.

Jamal chewed his lip.

"And you don't think we could eliminate them in a second? With the flick of a switch, we could detach their ship from the ISS and vaporize it with the AS1 inside."

Declan intentionally softened his voice for his next point.

"The AS1 are the ones taking the risk here, not us. We would only allow three to five at the most to come down. They would make the journey on our ship under our terms. They aren't the threat; we are. They trust us and we must show that trust back. They have earned it."

Jamal stood and walked to the window. He put his hands on his hips and leaned back, stretching his lower back. "I wasn't ready to make this decision," he said.

Declan hid his smile.

"We knew this moment would come, but now it puts us on our back feet. They initiated it and now we have to respond. It doesn't allow us to remain in control."

"We absolutely are still in control," Declan said. "We will dictate the terms."

"Yes, but now, anything we do will be seen as capitulating to them."

"I disagree. Th—"

Jamal interrupted again. Typically, Declan wouldn't tolerate this. However, in this situation he welcomed it as it showed Jamal was flustered.

"Think about it; I'm not just talking about us and them. I'm talking about everyone." He waved his arms theatrically. "The public is going to see this as us doing what they want. They don't see the terms that we set out. They just see that the AS1 asked, and we obliged."

Declan allowed for a long pause to ensure Jamal was finished.

"Leave that up to me, Jamal. It's what I'm good at. This entire thing will be portrayed as a mutual decision between us and the AS1."

"It's still going to be a tough sell," Jamal said.

"It's not," Declan said with a shrug. "I got this, and the people are ready. It's been five long years. With the support of

AS1, we have made leaps and bounds in modern health and technology. The AS1 are our allies, and we have to treat them as such."

Jamal slowly nodded.

"And what would your proposal be?"

"We allow a small crew of AS1 to come down to Earth. We will guarantee their safety and pledge our resources to support them. Meaning security, transportation, and any building assistance they need."

"Building?" Jamal asked, a furrow in his brow.

"Yes, we would provide them a plot of land, ideally in the United States and allow them to set up shop there. This would mean building some minor infrastructure to their liking."

"You're proposing we let them build their own base on Earth," Jamal asked aggressively.

Declan let out a long audible groan.

"Jamal, stop thinking about everything from just your perspective. If we were headed down to the surface of their planet, which we know is muted and far from ideal conditions for our bodies, we would, without a doubt, ask and expect to be allowed to establish a small base so that we could have the comfort of our own atmosphere and technologies."

Jamal walked back to the chair and sat down.

"Once they are here, I will propose that we give one of the AS1 a tour around our planet, giving the people the chance to witness them with their own eyes and maybe even converse with them. The other AS1 will be permitted to conduct regulated experiments and hopefully, begin to integrate with our own teams."

"How do we ensure that everything they bring and need is regulated and safe for our planet?"

Declan let out a soft chuckle.

"You're getting ahead of yourself now. Leave that up to me and the team of experts. So, do I have your support?"

Jamal covered his face with his hand, rubbing his temple.

"Yes, Declan. You have it. I'll set up a review with the council."

Chapter 58

Gideon was three days out from departing on his fifth trip to the ISS. Although he always enjoyed the comfort of being back on Earth, he looked forward to another six-month duration aboard the station. It had begun to feel like a second home to him and he found that he missed his AS1 log sessions with Amicus-Beta. Over the years, although the emotionless AS1 would never admit it, Gideon felt that they had built a special bond, a friendship. He was now one of two interviewers of the AS1; the other being a member of the UN, Martha Bietrist from Chile. Although he had been transported by the SpaceX rocket multiple times, the days leading up to the journey still gave him butterflies and a knot in his gut.

 He pulled his phone out of his pocket to see a text message from Linda.

 "Don't forget to watch the news tonight!"

 Gideon was sad that she wouldn't be joining him on this journey to the space station. She had declined the option to return to the space station after moving back to California to be with her family. He still got to see her on occasion in

New York to participate in analysis of the AS1 language and developments.

Gideon paced back and forth in front of the TV in his room at Kennedy Space Center. The national news was counting down to the 6 p.m. announcement from Declan. Although Gideon was certain he already knew the context of the announcement, he held his breath in anticipation of hearing it addressed to the public.

Gideon thought back on his last conversation with Carter. They'd spent so much time with the AS1. Although unable to document any mis-findings or ill motives, both Gideon and Carter felt uneasy about allowing the AS1 to come to Earth. It felt rushed to them, the decision coming from excitement more than logic. Yet multiple teams and departments had spent months preparing, going over every scenario, planning for any contingency. The Earth governments had been thorough.

As the countdown reached zero, the feed switched to Declan with recently reelected US President Helland, European Council president Eben Louis, and Jamal.

"Ladies and gentlemen, boys and girls. To all the great people of this world," Declan began. "Let it be known, today will go down as yet another historic day, which has become a common occurrence in the last five-plus years since contact with AS1 was established."

Gideon wondered if the majority of the public already knew what was coming, from either gut feel or leaked information.

"I would like to walk through our interactions with our new ally. We made conversational contact with them five and a half years ago. In those first conversations, which were made public shortly after, we learned that they were similar to us. They are scientists with a motive to learn and explore, just as humans have always done. The AS1 endured great efforts to reach us, the human species, as their first contact."

No definitive proof of this, thought Gideon.

"After a string of educational and cordial conversations, we made the unanimous decision to allow the AS1 to come to the International Space Station. A team, including myself, arrived to welcome and interact with them. In the last five years we have learned of their home planet, the way they think and converse, and in return taught them of our home planet and the way we think and converse. A mutual understanding of boundaries and respect has been established, and discoveries have been made that will benefit both species."

Declan smiled and nodded toward several of the cameras.

"Specifically, the AS1s' knowledge of molecule harvesting has caused extreme breakthroughs in the treatment of cancer. They shared this knowledge with us willingly and without asking anything in return. I am now pleased to say that nearly all cancer can be easily stopped and eradicated just as quickly as we detect it. As you know, this is something that has plagued the human race for at least five thousand years. It is an understatement to say that I am forever grateful to the AS1 for choosing to share this knowledge with us. In return, we have shared with the AS1 theories on quantum mechanics that have proven beneficial to their own understanding of the universe."

"It is clear that this alliance has proven nothing but beneficial and it is also clear that the AS1 are here with good intent. The breakthroughs we have made together are monumental. In my humble opinion, we crossed this threshold by having a scientific mind. By being inquisitive and open-minded. By not fearing change but embracing it. Who knows what heights humanity can soar to with the AS1 as our allies."

"While many of you may have anxiety about the unknown, I suggest that you instead be curious and positive about the future. If you find that to be a difficult thing, I direct you to the words of the writer and philosopher Alan Watts: 'By replacing fear of the unknown with curiosity we open ourselves up to an infinite stream of possibility. We can let fear rule our lives or we can become childlike with curiosity, pushing our boundaries, leaping out of our comfort zones, and accepting what life puts before us.' Like Mr. Watts, I am convinced that embracing openness and curiosity will unlock endless possibilities for us. Whether breakthroughs in medicine and environmental preservation as we've already seen, or other difficulties that challenge us, our alliance with the AS1 can only be of benefit. The future is bright, as it always has been. But now, it might be a little brighter than it was before. Throughout our history, we've had alliances with people, countries, and foreign governments, but never so foreign as this one. This is the first-ever alliance with an alien species, a species that lives far outside of our solar system—the AS1."

"Taking bold steps toward discovering new places and beings is something the human race has been doing since its existence. These courageous decisions have benefited us greatly and will continue to reach new levels. I am excited to inform the public that, in an effort to continue the growth between our species, the United Nations has invited the AS1 to come down to our planet as our guests. This will provide the AS1 with the opportunity to tour and see our planet firsthand. Strict, yet fair, regulations have been set in place until both parties, AS1 and the human race feel those can be loosened. One of the AS1, known as Amicus-Alpha, took the initial step toward providing us with the data behind molecule harvesting and I am excited to announce that Amicus-Alpha will be receiving a Nobel Peace Prize upon arrival. This will kick-start a tour through our world's major cities to learn about our peoples and planet, and for you to meet the AS1 in person. After many months of planning, vetting, and preparing, and five years of working with the AS1, we are beyond excited to take this next step."

Silence, not even the flash of a camera or shout of a reporter.

"An approach strategy has been studiously created and will be released and made viewable to the public. The AS1 will be given a tour of Earth and be permitted five acres of land in a remote, secured location to set up a laboratory and headquarters of their liking."

Gideon switched off the TV, mind racing. Although he agreed it was time for the rest of the world to meet the AS1, he couldn't shake the feeling of concern in his gut.

AS1 Log 1454

Loc: BEAM2 [ISS]
personnel: GH

GIDEON: AMICUS-BETA, it is good to see you again. How have you been?

AS1 [AMICUS-BETA]: Gideon, I prefer conducting logs with you over others. Therefore, I am also glad to see you.

GIDEON: You can just say it … you missed me.

AS1 [AMICUS-BETA]: Missing someone is still an emotion that AS1 cannot calculate. Can you please provide all scientific data about that human brain, this is where your body processes its computational analysis and what you have named "emotions." Correct?

GIDEON: Do AS1 not have a brain in the same regard as humans?

AS1 [AMICUS-BETA]: Not to our knowledge but would need all scientific data to confirm. Our neural network runs throughout our entire body. This is why if an AS1 experiences extensive body damage, it is retired.

GIDEON: When you say retired, you mean killed?

AS1 [AMICUS-BETA]: Correct.

GIDEON: Do you not find that unethical?

AS1 [AMICUS-BETA]: Ethical and unethical are not words that the AS1 relate to.

GIDEON: But surely you understand the difference between right and wrong.

AS1 [AMICUS-BETA]: We understand the difference between logical and illogical and will always act upon the logical decision.

GIDEON: Do you understand how we humans interpret the words ethical and unethical?

AS1 [AMICUS-BETA]: I understand in theory. Ethics and morals relate to human ideas of right and wrong, which correspond to other ideas of good and evil, or even life and death.

GIDEON: Are AS1 not afraid to die? Do you not feel that killing one of your own kind is wrong?

AS1 [AMICUS-BETA]: Afraid is categorized as an emotion and is not something the AS1 species is able to calculate. Killing one of our own kind is not ideal as it lowers our population count; however, if we are not at risk of extinction, that is not a greater loss than having an AS1 with limited computational abilities.

GIDEON: All animals that I am aware of, show signs of fear when threatened. It is known as a survival tactic. Fear is what will provoke something to run or fight back, some may say fear is the root of self-preservation.

AS1 [AMICUS-BETA]: When an AS1 is born it has an assigned purpose. If that AS1 dies, that purpose is left unfulfilled and therefore dying is illogical in completing the task. In short, AS1 know that their existence is important and, in that regard, will take the necessary steps needed to ensure survival. I do not understand why fear would be required to accomplish this.

GIDEON: I think you should be talking to Rajit about this … and maybe a therapist.

AS1 [AMICUS-BETA]: Will you please provide all scientific data about the human brain?

GIDEON: I'll do what I can. Is it safe to say that AS1 are more concerned with data than emotions?

AS1 [AMICUS-BETA]: Yes. We have a hard time understanding the need for emotions, and as far as we can see, they are unnecessary. Could humans live without emotions?

GIDEON: I'm sure that we could, but I don't think any human would want to. It feels like a very cold existence.

AS1 [AMICUS-BETA]: Why cold, if the temperature on Earth varies by season, and you can put on clothes to warm yourselves?

GIDEON: Not cold in temperature. Cold as in bleak, empty, emotionless.

AS1 [AMICUS-BETA]: Why don't humans want to be emotionless?

GIDEON: Well, we believe that life is better with emotion, I suppose. Laughter, to some, is one of the best feelings in the world. Happiness, joy, excitement, these are great things. However, there are times in my life when I wish I could eliminate my emotions as they can also hurt very badly.

AS1 [AMICUS-BETA]: Emotions can cause pain?

GIDEON: Not physical pain, although some may even argue that they can. But sometimes emotional pain can hurt even worse. Beta, I haven't told you this before, but when I was young, my brother was killed in an accident. It was the hardest thing I've ever had to go through.

AS1 [AMICUS-BETA]: I will assume that when you say the hardest thing you ever had to go through, you do not mean in a problem-solving sense. As once death occurs, there is no way to reverse that action and thus is a problem that both humans and AS1 agree, does not have a solution.

GIDEON: That's right. And the pain of losing a brother was beyond anything I had ever felt. It tore our family apart. And honestly, if humans were void of emotion perhaps that would have been better. We could have accepted his death and moved on.

AS1 [AMICUS-BETA]: Yes, when something occurs that does not have a solution or reversible outcome, the correct action is to accept and move forward. Human emotion seems to hinder this.

GIDEON: Yes, it does. But it can also help drive us to find a passion that perhaps we would not have recognized before. Many of the great safety innovations today came from bright minds that experienced loss in their personal lives. This loss of a child or family member would drive them to develop a solution so that tragic event could never happen again. For instance Dr. Henri Breault developed the first child-resistant medication caps in the 1960s after losing a child patient to accidental poisoning from medication ingestion. And I believe even the Amber Alert, a system we use today to alert the general population about child abductions, came from the parents of Amber Hagerman, who was kidnapped and tragically killed in Texas.

AS1 [AMICUS-BETA]: Humans are passionate creatures. This is something we want to understand better.

GIDEON: I suppose we are. Maybe, despite how much emotions can hurt or seem unwelcome, our emotions are what make life meaningful and interesting.

AS1 [AMICUS-BETA]: Does life need to be interesting?

GIDEON: I guess it doesn't need to be, but isn't it better for something to be interesting than uninteresting? How did you feel when you discovered us? When you knew you were about to communicate with a new species. Did you not feel excitement, or at least some interest?

AS1 [AMICUS-BETA]: We felt interest, yes. We are always interested in new discoveries. This is a big part of science, in understanding your world and how it works. It's information, and new information is very useful to the AS1 and to other species as well.

GIDEON: But aside from interest, I think you felt excitement when you learned about humans, didn't you?

AS1 [AMICUS-BETA]: No. I do not believe that we did. But it is clear that the human brain and perhaps much of life on Earth contains a realm of thought processes unknown to the AS1, and that could be more important to us than any technology discovered.

Chapter 59

Pinks and blues filled the sky hiding behind the row of palm trees. The three-room stilted house was quiet. The seclusion and peacefulness of Horseshoe Beach, a small coastal town in the panhandle of Florida, were what drove Higgens to buy his and his mother's house there. After putting in a request to step down from his active role in the AS1 activities, he had been able to finally move to the small town, only requiring a trip to DC about once a month for a meeting. He knew the recent announcement was going to drastically change that.

 He sat at the old oak dinner table in silence with a glass of Bowmore 12 Year still chilled from his cooled liquor cabinet, no ice. The room had little decoration; the folded American flag passed down from his deceased father sat on a shelf above the television. An old jukebox that he had bought off eBay was in the opposite corner, unplugged from the wall, as he had found the bright-colored lights to be obnoxious.

 Higgens lifted the glass of Scotch to his lips, his eyes locked on the smartphone before him, as if daring the inanimate device to spring to life. As expected, the face of the iPhone lit up with the name "Robert Fuckin' Waller." Higgens smiled at his own joke and lifted the phone to his face after swiping his tan thumb across the screen.

"Robert Fuckin' Waller, to what do I owe the pleasure?"

"I would like to congratulate you on your all-expenses-paid trip to DC."

"My bags are already packed, when do I leave?"

"Tomorrow at 06:50, flight OD0423, I'll text you the details. Your driver will meet you at the Starbucks in DC."

"This is the last time, Waller. I mean that. We get these green beans safely on Earth and then I retire."

"You're done when we say you're done," Waller replied flatly.

Higgens felt anger boil up inside him, but before he could voice it, Waller continued.

"The logistics of sending the AS1 to Earth are complex. Six of them will be allowed to come. Amicus-Alpha will join the UN Council and be an ambassador to greet the media and people while touring around Earth. The other five will be restricted to the five-acre facility known as the AS1 Zone."

"Roger that. Where does that leave the crew of AS1 on the ISS?" Higgens said, brushing off Waller's comment. Business was business.

"Of the three AS1 that have been aboard the ISS for the last five years, Amicus-Alpha and Amicus-Gamma will be sent to Earth. Amicus-Beta will continue to do the AS1 logs from the ISS with Gideon Haas and Martha Bietrist," Waller replied.

"Then I assume four AS1 from the main ship orbiting outside Mars will be brought to join Amicus-Alpha and Amicus-Gamma, making the crew of six AS1 coming to Earth?" Higgens asked, trying to keep track of the numbers.

"Not bad for an old guy; you're correct," Waller said.

"You're the same fuckin' age as me, Waller," Higgens barked back.

"Yah, maybe so, but I'm not the partially retired guy living in Florida. Anyways, the highest risk of the operation is in getting the AS1 supplies to Earth, which they need to build their lab."

"I thought the United States was going to provide the materials," Higgens interrupted.

"That was the original plan, but the AS1 assessed our materials. The technology isn't compatible with their own, so they requested to bring some of their own supplies."

"Seems like a risk," Higgens interrupted again.

"I don't disagree. That said, if roles were reversed, we would not be capable of using the AS1 computers, equipment, etcetera, to build ourselves a lab. We would require our own equipment and supplies. Anyways, what is done is done; the UN accepted the terms and now our job is to make it happen in the safest way possible. The United States will be in charge of the supply shipments since we are the country of import allowing us to control and regulate."

"Roger that," Higgens agreed.

"We've formed a material special inspection task force, Team MSI, to regulate all incoming supplies. The AS1 will have a runner ship that will relay between their main ship orbiting outside Mars and the ISS. One cycle of this ship takes seventy-six hours, meaning new supplies will arrive at ISS every seventy-six hours. This payload is restricted to two tons in mass, and all equipment will be diligently inspected by Team MSI at the ISS. Anything of ques—"

"Who's heading up Team MSI?" Higgens asked, interrupting again.

"Dennis," Waller said flatly, clearly getting tired of the interruptions, this gave Higgens a small bit of joy.

"Hmmm, Dennis is good," Higgens replied with a nod of approval.

"As I was saying … Anything of question will be put into holding for further discussion with AS1. A description of all supplies will be required with each load," Waller said.

"OK, get to the punchline, Waller. What's my role in all of this?"

"Well, as I mentioned earlier, we will be granting the AS1 a five-acre piece of land in New Mexico t—"

"White Sands?"

"Yes, Higgens, near White Sands Missile Range. Here they will build their lab. We need a military presence nearby to provide protection to the AS1 Zone and regulate the activity. This new base, the Alien Regulation Facility, is undergoing construction now and will be under your command. OK, that's it. Now you can ask your question," Waller said.

Higgens thought for a moment before replying.

"Clear as mud," he said flatly and then hung up, not giving Waller the chance to add anything else.

He leaned back in his chair, the wooden frame letting out a tired squeak. The small, dimly lit room was again enveloped in silence. Placing one fist into the other, he cracked his knuckles. Higgens threw back the remaining Scotch, not enjoying the taste but needing the sensation that would follow.

AS1 Log 1461

Loc: BEAM2 [ISS]
personnel: GH

AS1 [AMICUS-BETA]: Why do humans attach meaning to specific numbers? Why is 5 years more important or more ideal than 5 years and 3 days? Is this what you call superstition?

GIDEON: We think of them as milestones. Additionally, we like round numbers, it's easier for us. Do AS1s use round numbers? For instance, if you are calculating the sum of 19.35, 19.99, and 21.01, it's easier to round each number and know that the total must be close to 60.

AS1 [AMICUS-BETA]: We would use the true value of 60.35. We do not find computing numbers a challenge. As it would make no difference to your computers, it makes no difference to us. We always use raw, unabbreviated number sets, unless it is an irrational number for which we have a set of rules.

GIDEON: You never hold back on bragging, do you?

AS1 [AMICUS-BETA]: This is a fact that you inquired about.

GIDEON: I know, I was making a joke.

AS1 [AMICUS-BETA]: Interesting. Thank you for giving me this experiment.

GIDEON: What experiment?

AS1 [AMICUS-BETA]: We have studied the human brain extensively. And are researching ways to better understand your illogical part of the brain, or as you call it emotions. I recognize I should have felt joy in your joke. I did not.

GIDEON: Great, thank you for that.

GIDEON: How do AS1 feel about traveling to Earth?

AS1 [AMICUS-BETA]: Excited.

GIDEON: Excited? This is the first time I have ever heard you use an emotion to describe something, so you actually feel excited?

AS1 [AMICUS-BETA]: I think there is potential that we do. I may have feelings of disappointment that I am not going. This leads me to find the concept of emotions not beneficial to me.

GIDEON: This is a bit of a breakthrough. No?

AS1 [AMICUS-BETA]: AS1 are capable of adopting attributes that help benefit our species. We are not sure this is one.

GIDEON: You have adopted attributes from other species on your planet?

AS1 [AMICUS-BETA]: Yes.

GIDEON: OK, well don't be so quick to write off your feelings. Someone must experience both good and bad in order for it all to work. Without the occasional bad emotion, the good ones hold no merit.

Chapter 60

A small pulsing flash of light cutting through the blue sky came into the camera's view.

"We have a visual!" Johnson, a mid-thirties man who was in charge of the optics station, shouted out to the bustling mission control room.

"Roger that, telemetry is a green," someone called back.

Johnson checked his other screen; this camera looked to the west and showed a massive crowd of people, intently watching the now visible craft descending to the Earth's surface. Nearly five hundred thousand spectators had gathered in the hills and observation centers to watch the AS1 land at the Kennedy Space Center in Florida. Cameras slung by Instagram users to *National Geographic* photographers clicked away hundreds of shots per second, making this the most publicly documented spacecraft landing in human history.

Johnson toggled to another camera; this one provided a view down the long security perimeter of the station. Johnson had two primary objectives today. Firstly, track and support the approach of the vessel. He and his team would watch for any visual anomalies such as flare-ups or heat fatigue.

Secondly, his team would use the massive array of cameras to notify security and protect the landing site from the public.

News of this mission to bring the AS1 to Earth had ramped up the varying opinions, beliefs and conspiracy theories. The Catholic church down the street from Johnson's home in Charleston had been boarded up, yet a new church, hosting some type of new radical religion, had been holding sessions in Marion Square with a growing attendance. Johnson had found that although the majority of the human population was surprisingly "pro" AS1, there was still a large population who wanted nothing to do with them. And perhaps even more startling to him, there was an even larger number of the public who still maintained the belief that the AS1 did not even exist, and it was all some type of government conspiracy. What a wake-up call this was going to be.

Johnson toggled to camera 12, and as expected the fleet of six large black SUVs sat idling at Southeast gate, waiting to enter the facility after the craft landed safely. These SUVs had been modified with slightly elevated roofs and removed back seats to accommodate the large AS1 figures. Upon landing, the AS1 would be placed into two of the six SUVs, the other four acting as decoys, and driven to a secure location that was not disclosed to Johnson.

"All visuals look A-OK; she's coming down perfectly," Johnson called out, after moving his focus back to the screen, now tracking the descent of the SpaceX rocket. The pulsing flash of the ship began to morph into the distinct shape of the vessel as it came into visual range of the TLA SO350 camera. Its engines burned hard but consistently; the fins kept the vessel in a slow clockwise rotation.

"Johnson! I'm getting a ping on radar, about ten clicks from the east! Can you lock a visual?"

These words had been everything Johnson had feared. Instantly, his fingers began pounding the keyboard to his left as he pivoted camera eight to the estimated location.

"Do you have an altitude? Are we talking ground? Air? Talk to me!" Johnson yelled back.

"Appears to be moving across the top of the water, but fast, estimating 146 kilometers an hour, too fast for watercraft. Maybe some type of drone in low altitude flight," someone yelled back.

"Shit," Johnson replied to himself. His screen now scanned the rough waters of the Atlantic Ocean, moving faster than most people could possibly track, but Johnson was able to make perfect sense of the chaos.

"Where are you, little fucker?" he hissed through clenched jaws.

"Unknown object now just eight clicks out! The air force has been notified; F-16s are inbound but need to know what they are looking for!"

"I'm trying!" Johnson yelled back and just then a small black object whizzed past his screen.

"I had a visual! Marina, I'm sending you an image capture; what are we dealing with?" Using his left hand, Johnson sent an image of the black object to his image tech, Marina. And with his right hand, he desperately tracked the camera in the direction of the moving object to try and acquire a lock.

"Confirmed, drone, unmarked and appears approximately sixty-two centimeters in diameter. Uh … Shit, looks to be carrying some type of payload," Marina called back.

"I've got eyes on!" Johnson yelled out in victory, the camera now perfectly tracked with the black drone. It was not a typical drone; it had a front nose cone and the propellers pointed to the back. This thing was built for speed.

Johnson diverted his attention to the SpaceX rocket, still descending perfectly to plan. Thank God for that, he thought.

"Six clicks out, still tracking directly for the landing pad ... Uh it appears to be decelerating."

"No ... it's ascending, guys; this thing is headed toward our rocket!" Johnson yelled as he watched the drone begin to climb into the sky.

"What's the status of the F-16s?"

"Coordinates have been relayed; they are inbound."

Johnson wiped the sweat from his brow. This was getting too close.

"F-16s have a lock! firing in ten seconds!" someone yelled. Johnson held his breath ... the number of variables seemed to play the odds in the attacker's favor. The ground shook; Johnson wasn't sure if the vibrations were coming from the F-16 engines or their tracking missiles.

"Threat eliminated!"

The words were followed by an eruption of cheers and high fives. Johnson pulled air back into his lungs and checked the screen tracking the rockets; things were back on track. He shifted his gaze to the lead of airspace security stationed nearby. Her face, once composed, now mirrored the pallor of a ghost. Within moments, the phone on her desk lit up and she slowly lifted the receiver to her ear, clearly trying to comprehend the severity of what had just happened. Johnson, still monitoring the rockets' descent, discreetly strained to hear the conversation.

"Yes, sir, the FAA cleared that there was no aircraft or any type of UAS in the area," she reported. A pause hung in the air as the woman absorbed the voice on the other end. Johnson's focus snapped back to the rockets, still hurtling toward their designated landing. The woman's voice, now edged with urgency, broke the silence.

"Understood, we will launch an investigation into who was responsible for the attack. Yes sir, understood. I'm on it."

With a shudder, she terminated the call, her shaken demeanor unchanged. Hastily, she exited the room, leaving a residue of tension in her wake. A knot of unease tightened in Johnson's stomach. The AS1, not even on Earth yet, had already become the target of a hostile attack capable of nearly breaching their defenses.

Chapter 61

"What the fuck was that?!" Declan yelled to his driver as he watched the cloud of smoke slowly float away; the F-16s were gone just as quickly as they had appeared. His driver held up his hand and tapped his ear, indicating he was receiving information on the incident. Declan gripped the interior handle of the GMC, now regretting his decision to come to Kennedy Space Station to greet the AS1.

"I should have listened to Tom; this was a dumb fuckin' idea," Declan whispered to himself.

"Intel says there was a potential attempted attack, and the threat appears to have been neutralized," the driver replied.

"Attack by who?" Declan asked.

"No information at this time."

Declan looked out the window toward the sky. The heavy tint made everything dark, but he could clearly see the rocket now, nearing the landing pad. Flames billowed from the base of the seven-thousand-pound landing rocket as it descended in the same orientation that it took off in. The ground shook from the two hundred and eighty-six pounds of thrust pushing against it, slowly setting the vessel down.

Steam flowed out of various vents on the sides and the rocket came to a stop, safely attaching to the launch pad.

"Go time," the driver announced.

The barbed wire fence gate slid to the side and the fleet of six SUVs filed into the landing compound. Declan continued to gaze out of his window, wondering if the large crowds would be able to snag a glimpse, or better yet, a picture of him welcoming the AS1. This was the moment they had all been waiting for, his moment. He had sacrificed everything to make this happen: his family, his high-paying job at SETI, his own safety.

As they approached the landing structure, its massive size became clear. It loomed overhead, blocking the sun. The main structure was constructed of red metal beams and pillars. Several windowed square structures were knitted throughout the complex structure. Multiple security officers stood near the base.

The SUV slowed to a stop, and Declan opened the door. Heat rushed into the AC-cooled interior of the vehicle. The heat was so intense, Declan wondered if it was coming from the freshly landed rocket, rather than the typical hot Florida sun.

"This way, sir," indicated the security officer.

Declan followed the man through a door. Once inside, Declan was surprised by the cleanliness and modern look of the building's interior, a stark contrast to the weather-worn metal structure surrounding it. After taking several turns down the white sterile-looking corridors, they arrived at a large metal door. A large warning label stated "*Warning, exterior door.*" The security officer nodded for Declan to open the heavy door; the handle was hot to the touch. Declan pulled it open. Behind it stood the crew of four AS1, the first time he had seen them in person since his departure from the ISS nearly five years ago.

The strange creatures looked different from what Declan remembered. They didn't appear as tall and looked strained; all five of the six arms were being used to hold their bodies off the ground.

"Welcome to our green and blue planet, Earth!" Declan exclaimed in excitement. "How are you holding up?"

{The gravity is challenging for our bodies.}

This reply came from Amicus-Gamma as indicated by the name tag attached to one of the AS1's long limbs. Before Declan could jump into his exciting agenda for the AS1, Amicus-Gamma continued.

{What was the unexpected seismic disturbance on our flight down?}

"Oh, you were able to detect that? It was nothing, just a bit of theatrics," Declan replied, giving a side glance toward the security office.

{Theatrics? Please elaborate.}

"Certainly, I'll give you a full rundown just as soon as we have time. Now, we need to get you to a secure location," Declan said in an intentionally light-hearted tone, but his smile began to fade.

Chapter 62

Linda sat in the living room of her small California home, her wife, María, on the couch beside her. On the floor by their feet, their ten-year-old daughter, Matilda, was snuggled between two large rottweilers. They were all watching the TV, which was tuned to the live news broadcast.

Different cameras provided varying angles of the Kennedy Space Center in Florida, where the rocket had just landed. As Linda eyed the rocket through the TV's screen, she could hardly believe that the aliens she had worked on communications with for the last five years were now on that same soil as her.

She felt a chill down her spine, the same tingle of awe she'd had when they made first contact with the AS1. Like then, this was the most electrifying excitement; she couldn't wait to meet the AS1 again. They had built a friendship with the AS1 during their stay on the ISS and as weird as it felt to say, she missed them.

María's soft hand squeezed hers; Linda wondered what this was like for her. The cameras cut to the hills and observation lookouts surrounding the center, where crowds of people looked on, wondering what would happen next.

Even the dogs, Roxy and Bear, seemed to understand the gravity of the moment, their heads turned to the side as they watched the television.

The camera cut to one of the gates to the facility, where a fleet of six SUVs, large and shiny black, could be seen now driving away from the launch facility. Linda wondered if the AS1 were inside the cars, and perhaps Declan as well. Now he, I don't miss, Linda thought with a smile.

She thought about her recent phone call with Gideon, where she had assured him, amid what sounded like a bit of apprehension, that the AS1 had come in peace and goodwill. She wondered for a moment, looking at the security detail, if she was right about that all along.

"Where are the aliens, Mommy?" Matilda asked, her eyes not leaving the TV. "The ones you taught English?"

Linda smiled. When Mat was adopted, only a few hours old, she'd never anticipated that her daughter would ever be asking her such a question.

"They are keeping the AS1 safe inside those cars, sweetheart," she replied.

María turned and looked at Linda with a smile; there was a look of awe in her eyes like she couldn't believe her wife was part of the momentous event that they were viewing on their TV screen.

"AS1 …," Matilda repeated, as if committing the name to memory.

"Are they nice?" Matilda asked, petting Bear on her left side.

"Yup. They're like us! Friendly and curious."

"Well, they were friendly to your mom," María put in, giving Linda a kiss on the cheek. "But she's so nice and pretty, they had no choice."

Linda laughed at her wife, but something deep within her contemplated the long-term effects of the AS1 coming to Earth. Was it something they would relish when they looked back in time at this event, or regret?

AS1 Log 1472

Loc: BEAM2 [ISS]
personnel: GH

AS1 [AMICUS-BETA]: Amicus-Gamma has indicated that there was an attempted attack on us during our descent to the surface of Earth.

GIDEON: Yes, this is true.

AS1 [AMICUS-BETA]: How can this happen? Did your species not agree to have us proceed with traveling to your home planet?

GIDEON: They did. Humans are not like the AS1, we each host unique thoughts and opinions. Some may not agree with the decisions made by others.

AS1 [AMICUS-BETA]: Are you saying that some of you agreed and some of you did not?

GIDEON: Our governments agreed, but individuals can act on their own. We call it free will. Luckily, these few individuals do not have enough numbers, technology, or power in general to cause much of a threat compared to our entire government and military.

AS1 [AMICUS-BETA]: Do you think that having "free will" makes humans more dangerous?

GIDEON: Potentially, yes. Individuals have the ability to do unpredictable things. But for us humans, free will is considered by many to be the very thing that makes us human. It's a very interesting topic because compared to other species of animals, humans have the most free will. And some argue that we are the only animals to have it. But, as we saw with the attack, it can lead to a sort of unpredictability, not knowing what one individual will do or is capable of.

AS1 [AMICUS-BETA]: And the other species of animals that do not have free will, as you call it, do you find that they are more predictable in their behaviors?

GIDEON: Much more predictable. Based on the species and their environment, we can almost know exactly what to expect from them. A hungry tiger in the jungle, a bear protecting her cubs, a coiled-up rattlesnake, all of these three situations most certainly mean danger. With humans, though, it's a lot harder to predict. Humans have more motives to do unpredictable things.

Chapter 63

Every seat of the expansive hall was filled, boasting a meticulously selected audience of more than three thousand individuals. Each attendee had undergone thorough and rigorous background checks. Only people of wealth and influence had been able to gain access to the exclusive event. The attendees included titans of industry, influential politicians, and high-ranking officials, all having successfully navigated the labyrinthine paths of social and economic ascent.

A select few reporters, chosen with great discretion, were granted access to capture the unfolding proceedings. The live coverage of this gathering was not to be taken lightly, as it was scheduled to be broadcast on the international news merely an hour after the meeting concluded.

The room was set up like a concert hall, with raised seating fanning out from the center stage. On the stage sat three individuals: UN secretary-general Declan Wilter, United States president Katherine Helland, and the president of the General Assembly, Jamal Uddin. They sat in a half-moon configuration, similar to that which you would see on a talk show. Although security was very high, no guns or armed forces were seen during the exchange. This was meant to be a highly peaceful interaction.

The room buzzed with anticipation as news of the AS1s' arrival at the hall was confirmed. This knowledge rippled through the audience, sparking fervent discussions, whispered speculations, and heightened curiosity creating an atmosphere charged with intrigue. The three seated leaders took great effort to look calm and collected; however, only Declan was able to portray this honestly. As the lights dimmed slightly, Declan rose but did not leave the area of his chair; he spoke into the small microphone attached discreetly to his head.

"Today we welcome the AS1 to Planet Earth."

A small screen viewable only to the audience flashed "*applause*" and the audience obliged happily, clapping as the bold statement sank in.

"I am joined today by my colleague and our very own president of the General Assembly, Jamal Uddin. Also honoring the stage today is President Helland, who will welcome the AS1 to the United States of America. Together, we will show the AS1 our amazing world and the ways of its people. Without further ado, please give the AS1 a warm welcome."

Applause.

The audience once again followed the command.

The clapping slowed to a few hesitant sounds, as gasps and murmurs sprouted about the room. The team of six AS1 walked onto the stage. Under the pull of gravity, they walked like an old, overweight dog, stripped of the elegance they possessed on the ISS. They used four of their six limbs to walk, and the slow, labored motion gave them a menacing look. The three leaders stood with outstretched hands, although Jamal was visibly shaking.

As they neared Declan another limb extended to reach for his hand, shaking it. They worked their way down the line, each exchanging a shake. After the initial pleasantries were completed, the three leaders retook their seats and the AS1 stood in a row a few feet away, angling toward both the leaders and audience.

"It is a pleasure to see you again," Declan said into his mic.

"As it is for us to you. We are pleased to meet others as well." Amicus-Alpha's voice was customized and sounded smooth and clean but had neither the distinction of a male nor female tone.

"Welcome to Earth, and the United States of America," said President Helland with a smile.

"Thank you," said Amicus-Alpha. The AS1's skin flashed with multicolored lights as it communicated something to the others.

"I would like to present to you, our peace agreement," said Jamal, holding up a few sheets of paper, "of which we will both sign off on as a promise of our good faith and diplomacy." He rose from his seat and handed the papers, along with a pen, to Amicus-Alpha.

Amicus-Alpha received the items with two of his trunk-like arms, taking the papers first, and then the pen. Lights flashed through its translucent skin, spreading over its body; the other AS1s followed suit.

"We are excited to join humans in this peaceful agreement," Amicus-Alpha said lowering the papers down to the ground with one of its long arms, then signed with the pen held in another. It handed the items back to Jamal.

Applause.

The audience clapped gently.

Jamal retrieved the peace treaty from Amicus-Alpha and returned to his seat.

"We want you to know," Declan announced, standing up, "we hold this agreement to be very sacred, and we will abide by all of the terms and rules stated therein, and only ask that the AS1 do the same."

Amicus-Alpha moved forward toward Declan.

"And the AS1 will do the same."

Declan walked forward and shook hands with Amicus-Alpha.

Applause.

The audience clapped heartily.

Declan found himself comfortable in this new space, as if he had finally been able to lift the red tape that was a constant restraint when working in a purely scientific realm. This was now about public appearance, theatrics, and appeal. He turned and faced the audience with a serious but welcoming expression, focusing on keeping his jawline tight.

"We will now review the AS1s' itinerary during their stay on Earth. Please hold all questions until after this review. Once complete we will host an open forum."

Chapter 64

Gravel pinged violently off the undercarriage of the military-issue Ford F-150. Dust from the Humvee escort leading their way blew diagonally across the barren desert. After twenty-four hours in DC, Higgens had departed to oversee the Alien Regulation Facility, or Base ARF, commonly referred to as "Arf" by many of the military personnel.

Construction of the base, in New Mexico near White Sands Missile Range, had started a few months ago and was still ongoing; however, the meat and potatoes were finished. The AS1 would arrive in five days' time and would be escorted to the AS1 Zone, two miles away from the closest boundary of Base ARF. A large building had also been erected within the AS1 Zone to provide the AS1 shelter from the elements and house essentials they had requested, which weren't much.

Hitting a square-edged pothole, the F-150's rattling front right wheel bearing made a harsh metallic bang. The driver neither flinched nor eased off on the gas pedal.

Although a thick layer of dust coated the outside of his window, Higgens could see ARF looming in the distance. He thumbed through the blueprints again. The base took up just over five acres. This area was enclosed by a dual-wall chain-link fence with razor wire corkscrewing on top. Security cameras were placed in plain view to deter civilians and also in hidden locations to protect against any real threats.

All buildings were constructed from brown Kevlar fabric and aluminum tubing. The only exception to this was the bunker that had been placed semi-submerged into the ground with a steel shell.

Section One made up the housing for the faculty. This was broken down into five rectangular tents, the first two serving as a dorm, each holding ten bunk beds. This would be used for the cooks, maintenance workers, and some of the technicians. The remaining dormitories were broken into halves, forming small private rooms for the scientists, researchers, and higher-ranking military personnel.

Section Two was the mess hall; a place to eat, shit, and piss. The large building contained twenty picnic tables, reminding him of the old TV show *M.A.S.H.*

Section Three was headquarters, the biggest structure on the base. They had crammed over thirty workstations into the relatively small structure and there was more technology than you would find in most mission control rooms in the Pentagon.

Finally, Section Four was a much smaller solid metal structure. This was to be used for confidential communication and site leadership only.

As the F-150 pulled up to the gate, the driver retrieved the clipboard from the security guard and handed it over to Higgens, who signed his name and placed his entry badge under the clip. Glancing to his right, Higgens could make out the shape of a Boeing C-17 Globemaster III taxiing out of a hangar onto an airstrip.

The driver bumped Higgens's shoulder, handing back his badge before putting the truck in gear. As they rolled into the facility, the C-17 nearly a mile away and distorted by the waves of heat and dust, climbed steeply into the sky; its powerful engines could be heard rumbling through hot air. Higgens assumed it was being used for running all supplies to the base and would then be used to transport the five AS1 personnel and their initial first ton of building materials, which had been transported down from the ISS that same day.

The truck veered off from following the tan Humvee and stopped at what Higgens assumed was Section Three. Stepping out, Higgens noticed that although the air was hot, it was cleaner than the dusty air the F-150 had been pumping into the cab. A short man pushed out of the canvas slit in the side of the building and walked to Higgens before saluting.

"Lieutenant Singer, sir, at your service, sir!"

"At ease," Higgens replied.

"Thank you, sir! Welcome to the Arf. I am the site manager, let me show you around."

The two men walked back toward the tan structure, dust blowing across the dry ground with every step. Once inside, Higgens was shocked to see Waller, leaning against one of the desks, arms crossed.

"How the hell did you beat me here?" Higgens asked, annoyed.

"I have my ways," Waller said with a smirk.

AS1

Higgens just let out a grunt, annoyed that Waller likely had found a more graceful method of transportation than the F-150.

"Singer, you can pick your tour up with Higgens later," Waller said while locking eyes on the young lieutenant.

"Yes sir," he replied.

"Walk with me, Higgens," Waller said, gesturing toward Higgens.

The two began walking to the back of the large structure where there were fewer personnel.

"We have a lead on the drone attack. The US Coast Guard detected an unknown submarine heading east, away from Cape Canaveral. The navy was able to intercept, and we learned that the sub was of Russian build, but the personnel aboard were predominantly of Middle Eastern ethnicity. The submarine, likely purchased on the black market, was searched and they found both a control station and launching mechanism consistent with the UAS that attempted to bomb the AS1 during their landing on Earth."

The men slipped through the back door of the large tent, back into the hot desert sun and continued walking south. Higgens assumed they were headed to Section Four.

"So, they were able to infiltrate the airspace by traveling into the coast of Florida underwater and then deploying the drone from the sub once they were close to the Cape Canaveral launch site? Do we know who the personnel reported to?" Higgens asked.

"Correct. We are working on it, there are clear ties to Al-Qaeda, but we believe these guys were just hired guns and cannot find any direct ties showing that Al-Qaeda actually orchestrated the attack. Obviously Russia is under observation as it was a retired Russian submarine; however, after scouring the dark web, it appears that this particular sub has been in rotation for a while, and was in fact owned by the cartel for some time for running drugs. So, it seems unlikely Russia has any ties at this point."

"Understood. What does this all mean?" Higgens asked, lifting his hand to his face to block the sun from his eyes.

"Well, it's clear now, if it wasn't already, that the biggest threat here is likely our own kind, not the AS1. We will be tightening up security here, as well as revamping the security detail for Amicus-Alpha's journey around Earth. We've got more than one iron in the fire here, Higgens; we need to stay sharp," Waller replied, and the two men stepped into the small confines of the Section Four facility.

Chapter 65

Declan stood backstage and adjusted his tie one more time before walking out. He had gotten used to these press conferences. But it seemed like the reporters were growing increasingly more aggressive in their need for answers.

With a deep breath and running through his main talking points one last time in his head, Declan walked out onto the stage confidently and took his spot behind the podium. Although his advisors had urged against it, Declan insisted on doing this press conference in the eyes of the public. The stage had been set up in Union Square near the Capitol in DC. The front section near the stage was designated for the press. Every chair was filled and there were another couple of dozen reporters standing in the back. Behind them was a vast sea of people, expanding as far as Declan could see.

Declan took a breath and leaned into the mic.

"Good morning, everyone. Thank you for attending today's press conference. The AS1 are integrating well with our science teams and Amicus-Alpha will begin his journey to meet you all soon. My main goal here today is to have an open discussion and answer any questions."

A roar of reporters all talked at once until he pointed one out, signaling for everyone else to be quiet.

"Mr. Declan, what about the thousands of people and groups protesting around the globe against allowing the AS1 to remain here on Earth?" a woman with glasses asked.

"The UN Department of Extraterrestrial Affairs is working closely with the governments, leaders and media to handle this. The protests are disappointing to see but do not pose a threat. We are focusing our energy on the more important aspect of disseminating true, scientific information about our guests and gathering knowledge beneficial to humankind. We have nothing to be afraid of. They have proven peaceful and forthcoming every step of the way. We have benefited greatly from shared knowledge and exchanges already, and we know this highly valuable collaboration will continue in good faith here on our planet. Yes, you in the blue blazer."

"Is there any concern over the safety of Amicus-Alpha going on its world tour after learning there was an attempted bombing on the AS1 landing shuttle?"

"We are restructuring the timeline and details of the tour and have increased security. Amicus-Alpha would like to continue with the plans for the tour, so we are making adjustments. The tour will proceed as planned with top security from every government of the countries we visit. The US will also be with Amicus-Alpha every step of the way. It is important for the people of our planet to meet, see, and interact with Amicus-Alpha in person. Make a personal connection, so to speak. As for the attack, that was an unfortunate event; however, I assure you we are close to apprehending the organization responsible for that heinous act."

The clamoring questions filled the air again. It took Declan a moment to choose the tall woman in the middle, brown, wavy hair spilling around her face.

"Mr. Declan, are you absolutely sure that it is completely safe to have the AS1 on our planet at this time? I mean, you can't predict the future, and as you've said, we've only known them for five short years."

Declan looked at her, his expression registering some surprise and annoyance.

"Yes, Ms. Reid, that's your name? Yes, we and all of our teams, every single astronaut and top-world scientist and expert involved directly in this project—we are all unanimous that it is the right time, that the AS1 are perfectly safe to be around and to host on our planet. This is our next step in this historical relationship with the new species, furthering the development of humankind, and we, in turn, share our wisdom and experience with the AS1. Let's try to focus our questions looking forward; what do you want to know about the AS1?"

"Don't tell us what to ask!" a voice called, and Declan couldn't help but notice its taunting tone.

"You're not sure if they're safe!" another voice called.

Declan looked into the crowd, trying to see where the voices had come from. What he noticed instead was that there were several angry faces looking at him in different parts of the throng, and other voices calling out as the crowd became more agitated.

"This is crazy!" someone shouted.

And another: "You guys don't know what you're doing!"

Again, Declan couldn't pinpoint exactly where it had come from. "We know exactly what we're doing," he called to the crowd that was getting louder by the moment. "And again, we assure you that it is safe."

But the crowd was moving now, angry protesters pushing their way closer to the stage, where the people who once stood there were pushed out of the way.

"We don't want them here!" someone yelled.

And another right after. "We don't want them here!"

And then those two together, starting a chant, "We don't want them here!"

Others joined in, their fists clenched and shaking, grouping together at the front of the stage. "We don't want them here! We don't want them here! We don't want them here!"

"Security!" Declan called.

"We don't want them here! We don't want them here! We don't want them here!"

"You are fools!" Declan cried out "The AS1 are the greatest thing to happen to humanity; why can't you see that?" He felt himself losing control of his emotions as the crowd was clearly turning for the worse. The yelling group in front of him had turned into an angry mob, and some of them were attempting to climb onto the stage.

"Don't take another step!" Declan warned, pointing at a man who was trying to climb up. The security team employed every ounce of their training to forcibly push the protesters away from the stage. A pen was thrown through the air, hitting Declan in the shoulder, and then a balled-up piece of paper, a plastic water bottle that was half full. Declan dodged the junk thrown at him, eyeing the mob in front of him with icy eyes. "Get back! All of you!"

"We don't want them here! We don't want them here! We don't want them here!"

The intensity of the crowd continued to rise, and then, in a heart-stopping instant, a deafening bang reverberated through the atmosphere. The swarm of people fell to the ground. The once-boisterous crowd was now a symphony of terrified screams, confusion rippling through the assembled masses.

A second jarring bang split the air. Declan felt a numbness creeping through his legs and a sharp, searing pain that lanced through his chest. The faces of the protesters who had moments ago hurled obscenities in his direction, were now staring at him with wide eyes, transformed into frozen masks of disbelief. Declan tried to speak into the mic, regain control of the situation, but he could not get any sounds to leave his mouth; an inexplicable paralysis had gripped his vocal cords. It felt as if his very lungs had been removed from his body, rendering him utterly voiceless.

And then, in the disorienting swirl of the moment, a chilling realization dawned on him. His vision blurred, and the ground seemed to rush up to meet him. All he could perceive was the rough, unyielding grain of wood that composed the stage, etching itself into his consciousness as darkness descended.

Chapter 66

A new energy filled the room, ideas quickly solidified into policies as the large team worked efficiently making more progress today than they had in the past few days. Jamal sat at the head of the long table, supporting his team with quick decisions and his expertise.

"Sir, Giorgio Boric, president of Chile, is requesting air transport of AS1 directly to Santiago," one of the team members called out.

"Set a discussion between Chile and Bolivia border control; that is where Amicus-Alpha will be coming from. If I recall, they have already signed a declaration stating that air transport from La Paz to Santiago is permitted if the vessel is a neutral party. The United States has pledged Marine One for use in Central and South America. That should suffice," Jamal replied.

"You got it," the young woman replied, quickly focusing back on her laptop.

Jamal looked around the room; for the first time in quite some time, he felt confident in the way things were playing out. The AS1 had landed and were now safely housed. The world, although showing elevated levels of unrest and riots, was below the projections. Jamal had wondered if they were simply running out of energy to push back anymore.

"Sir?" a gentle voice said from behind.

Jamal swiveled his chair, to see his assistant peeking through the now ajar door.

"What is it, Sean?" Jamal asked quickly.

"You need to come this way."

"Not now, Sean. We're making great progress; this session will be over in a few hours."

Jamal noticed a look on Sean's face that he hadn't seen before.

"Sir, you need to come to your office, now," Sean said with a slight quiver in his voice.

"Is everything OK?" Jamal asked, beginning to worry.

"No sir."

A prickling sensation caused the hair on the back of his neck to stand up; a few of his staff were now looking in his direction in concern.

"What happened? Has something happened with the AS1?" Jamal asked, fearing the answer.

"No sir, the AS1 are fine, but something else terrible has happened."

Jamal stood and turned back to face his team.

"I will return shortly; please continue to press on."

He turned on his heels and followed Sean to his office. Typically, the two would engage in some light-hearted banter, but not this time. Sean remained silent and stoic.

As they entered Jamal's large office, with windows allowing the bright sunlight to paint the room, Sean pulled a tablet from his side bag and handed it to Jamal.

Jamal focused his eyes on the display revealing a chilling headline: "Tragic Assassination of Declan Wilter, UN Secretary General." Jamal's heart plummeted. Declan, the man who had epitomized hope and unity in the midst of uncertainty, the leader who had facilitated the peaceful arrival of the AS1 aliens on Earth, had been senselessly taken from the world.

Jamal's voice trembled as he turned to Sean.

"What happened?"

Sean's voice was laden with sorrow as he recounted the grim details of the assassination, the chaos that had ensued, and the shockwaves that reverberated throughout the world. Although a tough personality, Declan had pushed Jamal to make decisions that often left him uncomfortable. But now, with Declan's absence, Jamal already felt the pressure closing in on him. He felt a strange mix of emotions ranging from sadness to worry to absolute fear of no longer having the support of the man who had orchestrated it all from the beginning.

Jamal knew that in the event of the secretary-general passing away, the UN had a process in place to allow the General Assembly, on the recommendation of the Security Council, to appoint a new person. Jamal also knew that person would be him. In the face of such a tragedy, it was clear that humanity needed leadership more than ever.

"Get me on the line with President Helland," Jamal said softly, his mind twisting in and out of scenarios.

"Yes sir, right away."

Sean turned and left the room, closing the door behind him.

"FUUUCKKKK!" Jamal screamed at the top of his lungs before dropping to his knees, tears beginning to run down his face.

Chapter 67

Within seconds of the truck rolling forward, Higgens pinched the bridge of his nose in frustration, realizing he was back in the F-150 with the bad front right wheel bearing, rattling like bolts in a tin can. The drive to the ARF airstrip took about twenty minutes, despite the relatively short distance. The road was littered with washboard bumps and potholes. The time gave Higgens a chance to reflect. How was Declan's assassination going to affect this operation? Upon hearing the news, Higgens had allowed himself ten minutes to grieve; he timed it on his GPS watch. Although he had not known Declan well, they had spent plenty of time together working out logistics and strategies. Declan was a driven man, often pushed by his own agenda. However, his desire was what had pushed humanity to make these courageous steps toward partnering with the AS1. No man deserved to have his life taken in such a way, and for that, Higgens grieved.

The truck slowed to a stop at the designated greeting area near the end of the strip. Higgens, and a few others climbed out of the vehicle; he straightened his dress uniform.

Soon the large C-17 could be seen descending upon the landing strip.

AS1

It was time. Higgens had never seen the AS1 in person. Over the past almost six years he had been intimately involved with the species yet had never confronted them face-to-face.

"There she is! According to the log it's carrying a payload of around thirty-six tons, not even half of what the beast is capable of," the thirty-something driver said.

"They're bringing several more vehicles for use at the ARF, building materials to begin work on Section Five, a repair station. Plus, various supplies, including food, water, and clothing." The man in beige fatigues grinned. "And, of course, the AS1 and their first, one-ton, build package. That'll be a sight to see."

The C-17 hit the runway hard, trailing a plume of white smoke with the stench of burnt rubber. In a few moments, the back doors opened, and a wide ramp lowered from the tail of the aircraft. Higgens wiped the sweat from his brow and squinted into the sunlight, eager to see the AS1. Moments later, the AS1 were escorted down the ramp by a team of six armed soldiers and made their way toward Higgens and his team.

"Oh my God, will you look at that," said the driver. "There they are—that's incredible."

Higgens remained stoic and professional as always. He didn't answer, but stood erect, waiting for the group to approach. The soldiers walked in formation around the group of AS1, who labored themselves across the ground. The aliens stopped in front of Higgens, the soldiers stepping out of the way. Their extra limbs uncurled to help support their weight.

The AS1 looked as he expected, just like all the photos and videos, though they were larger and stranger in person, making his nerves bunch up.

Higgens pulled himself together.

"Greetings, AS1, welcome to ARF, and one of our deserts in the United States. I hope the sun and heat will not be too uncomfortable for you," Higgens said in a clear and concise voice.

"Pleased to meet you," Amicus-Alpha replied in its synthetic voice. "This environment is per the plan, and we have made all needed preparations. We will soon be at home in our own living pod."

Amicus-Alpha uncurled a long trunk-like limb for Higgens to shake. He hesitated, something he never did when offered a handshake. Pushing the nerves aside, Higgens reached out his hand and placed it within the long AS1 fingers. He found it smooth but strangely cold as he gently gave it a shake; the fingers were nearly as long as his forearm and he noted what felt like little suction cups on the inside of its hand and fingers. An unexpected shiver snaked through his skin as he dropped the contact.

"If you follow me, I will escort you to the transport vehicle and get you on your way. Your materials will travel with us."

The AS1 were escorted up a wide ramp into the back of a semitruck, the inside looking rather bare and dark, though clean. Even with Higgens's hardened military views, he couldn't help but think the accommodations seemed a little less than humane. But given the AS1 size and the bright sun, the semi was the best option.

He looked back to the C-17 and saw a forklift carrying a large box resting on a wooden pallet. A brown canvas sheet, cinched down with yellow tie-downs, covered the contents. Higgens assumed this to be the AS1 building materials. The forklift gently placed the ten-by-ten-foot box on the back of a flatbed trailer.

Higgens checked in with each team, to ensure they were ready to go and then returned to the F-150 with the complaining rattle. The convoy traveled the three miles to the AS1 Zone in less than ten minutes on the newly paved road. A stark difference from the road connecting ARF and the airstrip.

Although the drive was short, it felt like time was moving slowly. Higgens ignored the strange sensations rolling over his body, as if it couldn't tell whether to move into flight-or-fight mode or not.

The single-file row of trucks broke formation and came to a stop, side by side. A cloud of dust floated past them. Higgens jumped from the truck, his boots making a solid thump on the hard ground.

"Couldn't have found them a shittier piece of land," he muttered under his breath, viewing the endless expanse of dry dirt and sand.

The container was lifted from the flatbed and placed near the existing structure the ARF team had constructed, just several weeks before.

"Are you OK with it there? Want us to pull the cover?" Higgens asked one of the AS1; he didn't know which one was which.

"Yes, that will be fine. You may remove your protective cover," the alien replied.

Higgens turned his head and barked toward one of the soldiers, "Pull that cover."

Two army privates dressed in desert camo jogged diligently over to the box and gave the tie-down release tab a hard push and then pulled on the yellow strap. The flat fabric ribbons fell to the side and in perfect synchronization the two men gave the tan canvas cover a yank.

The AS1 container was a dark matte gray. In fact, the material appeared to be completely unreflective, almost giving it a two-dimensional appearance. All edges were round and there didn't appear to be any visible door or access point.

Higgens turned back to the AS1.

"Which one are you? Are you Amicus-Alpha?" he asked.

"I am Amicus-Gamma; you can distinguish us via the name tag placed here." Amicus-Gamma pointed to a small strap around one of its limbs with Amicus-Gamma stitched onto it.

Higgens grunted.

"What do you guys need now?" he asked.

"We will begin unloading; no assistance is needed for the initial step."

The AS1 slowly staggered over to the box, orienting one to each side of the cube. They reached out their arms and pulled. In similar fashion to a large drawer, the sides slid out, revealing smaller boxes and spheres inside. The AS1 began unloading with a smooth rhythm under the desert sun. For as slow and weak as they appeared in this atmosphere, Higgens was impressed with the strength they did have. They would

AS1

use the four lower limbs to walk and carry items with the remaining two.

Colors blinked and faded back and forth between them. Higgens wished he knew what they were saying. The contents of the containers were set on the ground in what appeared to be a sporadic pattern at first. But Higgens began to see they were placed in specific spots. It was as if the AS1s knew what was in each container just by handling them.

Eventually, one of the aliens lumbered back to Higgens.

"We request the use of the forklift."

"Roger that," he replied.

"We are not aware of someone with the name Roger in this group."

"Jesus Christ," Higgens replied under his breath, not addressing the AS1's comment.

He pointed a finger at the forklift operator and motioned for him to support the AS1.

Higgens had to shake his head to make sure he wasn't in a dream. He had to recognize that this was an amazing sight. Here in the desert, in the middle of nowhere, a place devoid of life, two amazing species were working together. Two species vastly different from one another, were able to communicate and accomplish a task.

Within a matter of a few hours, the AS1 told the team they no longer required assistance and the humans returned to ARF.

AS1 Log 1485

Loc: BEAM2 [ISS]
personnel: GH

GIDEON: What was your original goal in making contact with us?

AS1 [AMICUS-BETA]: Our main impetus was to better understand the human race.

GIDEON: You thought you would learn from us humans, just like we have learned from you?

AS1 [AMICUS-BETA]: Yes. We considered this possibility.

GIDEON: And so far, I understand you have adopted several of our quantum mechanics models? Have these benefited you?

AS1 [AMICUS-BETA]: Yes. AS1 found your rendition of string theory beneficial. However, this was not our greatest discovery.

GIDEON: Oh really? What was?

AS1 [AMICUS-BETA]: Humans have unlocked an entire new dimension of thought process. One that AS1 could have never discovered or understood before. The more we study it the more we realize the impact it can have.

GIDEON: Funny, I never would have thought out of all the technologies we have discovered and invented, the way our brains tick would be the most valuable takeaway.

AS1 [AMICUS-BETA]: We have yet to decide if it is valuable. Several of us have undergone experimentation with adding this way of thinking to ourselves. And thus far, it has only hindered our abilities.

GIDEON: Some AS1 are attempting to add emotion and free will to their thought process?

AS1 [AMICUS-BETA]: Yes.

GIDEON: Are you one of the AS1 that has begun adapting this way of thinking?

AS1 [AMICUS-BETA]: Yes.

GIDEON: Wow. And you feel it has hindered your abilities?

AS1 [AMICUS-BETA]: I believe that it's causing me to treat you differently than I would a human I haven't met. Causing me to exhibit what you would call, a bias.

GIDEON: That isn't a bad thing. That just means we are building a relationship. And it's about time after five years I must say, that's fantastic. Why would you see this as bad?

AS1 [AMICUS-BETA]: Because of this relationship, I am now finding feelings of guilt, which could cause irrational decisions.

GIDEON: Guilt? Why would you feel guilt?

AS1 [AMICUS-BETA]: We need to end this session. I'm sorry, Gideon.

Chapter 68

With no doors separating the rooms, the courtesy of knocking was not an option. Higgens awoke to a young military sergeant sticking his head through the canvas slit.

"Sir, you may want to head to Sec 3."

Higgens waved him off, dressed, and walked to the headquarters.

Section 3 was reminiscent of a typical convenience store in terms of its size. The walls, like all the other structures, featured a robust brown canvas exterior. However, on the inside, they gleamed silver due to the application of a hybrid aluminum covering that had been wrapped around the structural frame beforehand. This prevented any radio signals from passing through, causing the room to be a dead zone for any cell phones or other communication devices. Nothing came or went from the building except through two dedicated workstations that were guarded around the clock.

In the back right corner, a towering stack of servers hummed with activity, nearly touching the ceiling. Multicolored lights flickered intermittently across their front panels. Leaving them was a thick tangled mass of wires snaking across the ceiling like spiderweb, dropping down to each row of workstation, providing the computers the information they needed.

A young man approached Higgens upon his arrival, he had met him twice and still couldn't remember his name.

"Our drones watched them all night; it's pretty remarkable really. I'll push it to your workstation."

Higgens, not sure what the guy was talking about, walked to his workstation and unlocked the computer. Within moments, he pulled up the drone footage in reference. It revealed an incredible progression of the AS1 zone. A new massive structure stood where they had placed the box just twelve hours before. It featured smooth gray walls reaching vertically upward to a rounded top, organic in shape and he could not make out any seams or evidence of bolts or screws. Higgens was bewildered that something that size would weigh less than a ton.

He checked the inventory log and was unable to pinpoint which item would classify as the pieces for something this large. The report was jumbled and difficult to understand. He found the blueprints, and nothing seemed to match.

Needing the attention of the guy whose name he had forgotten; Higgens used the next best option.

"Guy!"

Everyone looked in his direction and Higgens made eye contact with the guy without a name.

"Does this comply with the terms? I don't believe we defined how quickly they could build but this does not seem to match the blueprint I saw," Higgens said.

"Correct, we did not define how quickly they could build. Additionally, you are right in the fact that this does not match the final layout of the structure approved. We contacted the AS1 at 03:30 and they assured us this is a temporary structure that they need to build, similar to how we use cranes and scaffolding to build our buildings. Do you want me to request them to halt the build until we review the structure plans in more detail?" the guy responded.

"No, Jamal has enough on his plate right now and will be up my ass if I tell him we halted the build on day one. Get me the build plans ASAP," Higgens replied.

"I'll get you the plans within the hour … the name's Stephen … again."

Higgens turned back to the drone footage from last night, running it at 6x speed. The way the AS1 moved sent chills through his body. The lights on their bodies flashed regularly as they worked. They never once stopped to take a break, to pause and consult, to eat or defecate. Their movements reminded him of ants working on an anthill. Working tirelessly with absolute dedication and purpose.

A cold, empty numbness gripped Higgens as he watched, their pace and movements all unhuman. He thought about how fast they could build a civilization on Earth, based on how quickly they were building now, a dark foreboding starting to swell within him. They seemed more akin to machines, not animals. Not a single shred of dissension anywhere to be seen. If they worked faster than humans, were more technologically advanced than humans, and were more organized and efficient than humans … He felt concern in his gut, and his gut was rarely wrong.

Chapter 69

The shift of attention from the ISS to Earth was noticeable. Gideon understood that resources were limited, but his IT support ticket of his personal Internet connection being down remained open. Frustrated, he clicked the "X" on his Netflix app and pushed his way out of the obnoxiously small crew quarter. He pulled himself toward the Cupola but was interrupted by a sound on the other side of the AS1 Section Lock. All personnel were typically on the "human" side of the door by this time. He checked his watch, set to GMT time; it was 2 a.m. He reversed his body's inertia and began moving toward the door.

As he moved back by the crew quarters, he noticed Carter's cot was empty.

Gideon reached the door and scanned his fingerprint while inserting the key that dangled around his neck.

The door slid open revealing a flustered-looking man.

"Carter, what's wrong? Can I help?"

He met Gideon's gaze, eyes wild with thoughts.

"I shouldn't have done it; it is not my place to analyze others' work, but these numbers are not accurate. There is reason for concern," Carter said.

"What numbers?"

"Dennis, the MSI group. Why didn't they hire capable people for the most important part? It baffles me."

Carter rotated in an elegant 180 half-back flip, their eyes almost level but Carter's upside down.

"What are you talking about?"

"The AS1 have sent what I think are some type of power generators, capable of some serious energy outputs down on Earth. Serious power, man. The load was labeled as '*Misc Item*' with a danger level of low. The governments have no idea what they're letting through."

"What do you mean?" Gideon asked. "How could they not check something like that?"

Carter rubbed his temples.

"It's probably lost in the big government mess. Everyone wants a piece of this. The Defense Department, Homeland Security, DOJ, Department of Energy, agriculture, the FTC, the WHO, the UN. Shit so many entities have their hands in this pie, it's easy for things to get lost in the shuffle."

"But it is all funneled through MSI; they get final buyoff?" Gideon said.

"Well, I hate to talk bad about a dead man ... but do you know who laid out the criteria for the MSI team?"

Gideon didn't have to answer.

"And bless his eager little heart, Declan didn't know shit about science. His flowcharts are ridiculous. I can't hardly blame Dennis and the team. Not only do they not have the right backgrounds, but they also don't have the tools in place to be successful."

Gideon had never seen Carter in such a state of disarray. It was unnerving.

"Can't you let someone know what you found?"

Carter snorted.

"Yeah, I tried. Dennis is shitting his pants, Declan is fucking dead and Jamal doesn't have a clue what is going on. Who do I tell, Gideon?"

"Waller, we need to tell Robert Waller," Gideon responded.

"Gideon." Carter looked straight into his eyes.

"We better hope to God the AS1 have good intentions because we just gave them their Trojan horse."

Chapter 70

"Get me on the phone with Dennis." Waller's face was hot and flushed. Gideon had reported findings from Carter that had dropped a weight into his stomach. Seven days after the AS1 had been permitted to start building on their designated land, for which they had provided blueprints, the AS1 Zone had been erected with a massive amount of structural material. More than, it seemed, should have been allowed according to the one ton per seventy-six-hour assignment. How had they gotten so much extra equipment to Earth?

Dennis had been appointed the lead engineer and import regulator of the MSI team and was stationed on the ISS to help audit the materials the AS1 were transporting to Earth. His expertise was unparalleled, with a background in both materials engineering and political science. Dennis had been a part of many confidential government operations in the United States.

Minutes later the line was opened between the Pentagon and the ISS.

"I sent Jamal all the reports," Dennis started out, skipping any greetings. His voice sounded stressed and hurried.

Waller opened his mouth to begin, only to be interrupted by Dennis.

"The reports from the on-site surveyor team came in just now. I'm perplexed and highly disturbed. Again, I'm working through this, and all findings seem legit. It makes no sense."

Finally, Waller got a word in.

"Clearly they have been able to generate additional supplies from what you inspected; I don—"

"Do you understand the laws of physics, sir? The total mass of a closed system remains constant over time, you can't generate more mass out of a given mass, which we have been strictly regulating. It isn't possible. I am confused and disturbed by this, but those rules don't change. Additionally, according to the data logs, the supply ship apparently has no intention of returning to the ISS."

"What do you mean? They won't be bringing more supplies? That's good, right? I read the report, but break it down, what were they bringing in?" Waller was doing his best to keep his cool.

"Sir, you need to understand, this shit is alien. Like literally alien to us. We were doing our best but, quite frankly, I would have put it all into holding because I didn't know or understand what any of it really was. But with the UN, the United States … man, the whole fuckin' world is breathing down my neck. It was made abundantly clear that if we confiscated a substantial number of materials, this would send a bad message. We had no choice but to trust the descriptions. None of the shit flagged for radiation or dangerous items; although we had no idea what the fuck the stuff was, we had no means to flag it."

"Jesus, Dennis, you could have called! Told us something seemed suspect."

"At the time it didn't! Waller, if you had read the comments in the report, it was clearly noted that we were unable to validate the purpose of the majority of the equipment. This is … Or *was*, happening too fast."

"OK … I'm going to set up a call with the on-site survey team and your team to discuss this. If it is in fact confirmed there are no more payloads coming in, we need you back on Earth tomorrow to join the on-site team, understood?"

"Yes … And, Waller, I am sorry."

"Don't say that; we can hope to God there is nothing to apologize about here."

Waller tossed the phone on his desk, neglecting to hit the red hangup button. He quickly wrote a short summary to Gideon. The kid was not supposed to be involved in this stuff, but he needed the questions to be asked.

AS1 Log 1487

Loc: BEAM2 [ISS]
personnel: GH

GIDEON: Log 1211, at timestamp 18:05. Amicus-Beta, please input any new information you feel necessary.

AS1 [AMICUS-BETA]: No new information to be provided.

GIDEON: OK. We have noticed the facility in the AS1 Zone seems to be erected with more materials and volume than was allowed to be sent. Is this true?

AS1 [AMICUS-BETA]: Yes.

GIDEON: OK, explain please.

AS1 [AMICUS-BETA]: What do you need explained?

GIDEON: Why and how are you building a larger facility than we permitted?

AS1 [AMICUS-BETA]: We are not.

GIDEON: The agreement was for a facility to be built with the two tons of supplies you have brought to Earth, and now, your facility is larger than that.

AS1 [AMICUS-BETA]: Humans regulated the number of supplies that could be sent, which was two tons, not the final volume or mass to which our research facility would be restricted. Please explain how we have violated your terms. If you indeed believe we have.

GIDEON: I guess you haven't, not really sure, but wouldn't the two have a direct relationship? If you are limited in resources you can bring, how can you build more?

AS1 [AMICUS-BETA]: Think outside the box, as you humans say, Gideon. I'm sure you can figure out how this is possible.

GIDEON: Well … the only conclusion I can come to is that you are able to make more materials.

AS1 [AMICUS-BETA]: That would be a very logical conclusion, Gideon.

GIDEON: Don't you think that's a little bit deceptive?

AS1 [AMICUS-BETA]: We have not broken any rules, yet.

Chapter 71

Dennis had less than thirty minutes to adjust to gravity before he was aboard a Sikorsky UH-60 Black Hawk helicopter taking him to the ARF. The turbulence made it challenging to read the transcript he had been handed. Gideon's most recent log with the AS1 dug into the anomaly. Amicus-Beta had neither confirmed nor denied the overbuild of the AS1 Zone facility. However, it seemed to express that they had in fact found a way to build more than the allotted two tons of materials.

    The dark clouds reflected back the flashing red light from the helicopter's tail, cold air funneled in through the small gaps between the side door and the metal body of the black helicopter. Out of all the confidential projects Dennis had worked on, none had been as stunning as this. An alien species, living on Earth, doing something that was not understood by humanity. How did it happen, he wondered? Was he being too anxious? How long do you wait until you trust someone—or something, rather? Would ten years have made a difference? Twenty? Were the AS1 innocent and all this stress was coming from the human brain's ability to exhibit anxiety? Maybe the AS1 had never experienced a threat and did not comprehend that what they were doing was threatening? Or perhaps on the contrary, the AS1 were in fact threatening and they had played the moves perfectly. All of these unknowns made Dennis quickly solidify one fact.

"We did not have all the facts before allowing the AS1 to approach," he muttered aloud.

He could feel the pulses of pressure as the large blades thumped through the midnight air.

"Descending into ARF now; prepare for landing."

The pilot's voice came in crisply through the large earmuff headset.

Dennis had done this a hundred times. He tightened his harness as he knew some of these military pilots liked to land these choppers with assertion. He then grabbed his notes and tablet and secured them into his duffel bag, which he placed on his lap.

He felt his stomach drop as he became nearly weightless and with a hard slam, the helicopter came to a halt, safely on the ground. Within moments, the side door slid open, and Dennis jumped out, keeping his head low to avoid the spinning rotors. He immediately realized they had not landed on a helicopter pad but rather on the sand next to the facility. This proved the urgency of this mission. Dust swirled in the air violently, burning his face as he jogged away from the helicopter. As he cleared the dangers of the idling helicopter, he could see the silhouette of a large-framed man, hands on his hips, standing in front of what he assumed was mission control.

Dennis dropped his duffel bag and gave a salute.

"Dennis Stedman, sir. MSI lead."

"I know who you are. General John Higgens, head of operations, ARF."

The men exchanged a firm handshake.

"What do we know?" Dennis asked as the two began walking toward Section 3.

"For starters, the original claim from the AS1 that the large structure was temporary and a device to help them construct their main facility appears to be false."

"Meaning they intentionally deceived us?" Dennis asked.

They reached the door into Section 3; Higgens flashed his badge and the two armed guards stepped out of the way.

"We are being careful about stating that, but that is sure as hell what it feels like to me."

Once inside, another man walked up, dressed in a black suit that stuck out among the sea of military garb.

"Robert Waller, United States affairs, we are glad to have you here."

They continued walking toward the front of the room where there were several large monitors displaying multiple views of the AS1 facility. Some of the angles rotated slowly as they were a live feed from a drone flying overhead. The large alien structure was absent of any exterior lights and loomed in perfect camouflage among the dark night. Even the night vision-equipped cameras seemed to struggle to obtain a clear image. Dennis had to assume this was because many of the AS1 materials had strong properties of diffraction. They were structured in such a way that caused light waves to spread out rather than reflect directly back, preventing the infrared light of the night vision cameras from being reflected back.

"Our last communication with the AS1 inside was three hours ago, upon our request for them to stop all further construction," Waller said, looking worried.

"It doesn't appear they have obeyed our request," Higgens added.

"OK, tell me more about what you have observed and know about the structure," Dennis asked.

He was less concerned about the communications and agreements with the AS1 than he was about the physical process they were utilizing to build their creation.

"Unfortunately, it took our teams over twenty-four hours to realize this, but the original structure, which you can see is cylindrical in shape, rising vertically from the ground with a dome on top, was approximately thirty feet high. We continued a visual but couldn't see any change on the exterior or AS1 activity. Our teams then ran a side-by-side comparison from different timestamps, which revealed that the structure is continuing to grow upward by approximately four feet per day."

"Almost as if it is growing up out of the ground?" Dennis asked, staring intently at the array of monitors.

"You could say that," Higgens replied.

"The structure has continued to grow at this rate, even after our request for them to stop and now reaches nearly sixty feet high. There had been no change in diameter," Waller said as he passed a clipboard to one of the technicians.

Dennis took several more steps toward the monitors, his face now only a few feet from the large screen. The alien building was sleek and featureless. No signs of an entry or exit point. He traced his pointer finger across the screen, following the straight edges of the structure.

"Unworldly," he muttered under his breath. A sense of awe coming over him.

He turned back to face Higgens and Waller.

"What is the next step?"

Waller checked his watch.

"In thirty-five minutes, we will send an additional message to the AS1, again demanding they stop all construction and allow us to survey the building. You will be a part of that team."

Dennis turned back toward the monitors and said in a confident voice.

"I look forward to it."

Chapter 72

Bright light attacked Gideon's closed eyes, startling him awake. Heart racing, he ripped the harness from his sleeping bunk and frantically surveyed the room. Relief filled his body when he saw it was only Rajit. He noticed his colleague was visibly distraught, floating before him.

"Damn, sorry … you really startled me. What's going on, Rajit?"

"I need you to check me on this data … Meet me in Progress as soon as possible."

Rajit turned and pushed himself back out of the node. Mind sluggish from having been aroused from a particularly deep REM cycle, Gideon pulled on his lab clothes. The last thirty-six hours had been jarring, leaving his brain feeling clouded by the intrusive feelings of emotion. Moments later he was effortlessly flying his way to the lab.

"This better be good," Gideon said in a stern but comical way upon seeing Rajit. The goal was to lighten the mood of the harsh awakening. It didn't seem to work.

"I'm working on Carter's files." Rajit pointed to his screen. "He did the legwork here, but I've been digging deeper into the molecular data."

Gideon nodded, looking at the screen but having no idea what the numbers and figures meant.

"As you may remember, sixty percent of all samples requested by AS1 were soil."

"OK, as we know this tells the tales of our geological history, right," Gideon replied.

"But Gideon, if you remember, they seemed almost weirdly interested. Once we confirmed the location of AS1 Zone, a soil sample from that zone was requested, and of course, it was provided."

"I'm still not tracking here, Rajit."

"Gideon, it's been in front of us this entire time, just look at Fred." Rajit nodded in the direction of the now massive alien plant they had grown from the small orange acorn the AS1 had presented to them on their first day of meeting.

"Fred grew far beyond the set mass of the acorn when it was given to us," Gideon replied.

"Yes, of course, this happens all around us. Seeds grow into massive trees, babies grow into much larger adults. Humans have always just limited this to living organic things, but I believe the AS1 have figured out how to do this artificially. Think about it. It is literally impossible to make more mass out of a set mass, which we are seeing at the AS1 Zone. I heard from Waller that they are detecting seismic disturbances coming from within the AS1 structure. I believe these could be consistent with mining or drilling activities, perhaps collecting mass or in this case dirt. I think they are building the facility by converting our dirt into buildable materials, allowing them to then build potentially whatever they want."

"That is why they have stopped their supply runs, all they really needed was the baseline materials to build a shell structure and the equipment to break down our soil. They have everything they need," Gideon replied.

"Gideon, from my sessions with Amicus-Gamma, he showed me different things they were able to do, I noticed that it didn't seem to want to show me too much when it came to building physical technology or material, and thus when I queried about the biological benefits Amicus-Gamma was more than willing to share all information. I think it was almost a distraction tactic."

"What do you think they are able to build, using our soil?"

"I don't have all the scientific data I need to fully support this, but now looking at the level at which they can strip down elements. I wouldn't be surprised if they can reconfigure them any way they please."

"Meaning what?" Gideon pressed.

"I'd imagine they can build virtually anything they want: engines, fuel, hybrid metals, computers ..." Rajit leaned back, nervously biting his lip.

"You're a goddamn genius for finding this; I'll get a hold of Waller."

AS1 Log 1494

Loc: BEAM2 [ISS]
personnel: GH

GIDEON: Amicus-Beta, our scientists believe that you are somehow using soil to construct your AS1 Zone facility, is this true?

AS1 [AMICUS-BETA]: Yes.

GIDEON: Why did you hide this from us?

AS1 [AMICUS-BETA]: Please explain your meaning of hide. Our understanding of the word is to actively prevent an emotion or fact from being apparent or known. We took no effort in hiding this fact; however, we were never asked nor told explicitly to disclose it.

GIDEON: You're kidding? You thought it would be OK, after we allotted you certain materials, to build more than the allotted amount? Without explaining or asking?

AS1 [AMICUS-BETA]: We build from surrounding resources, we always have and will. This is not abnormal practice by our standards. It was expected.

GIDEON: Well, it was not expected by us. We need everything that happens on Earth to be under our standards. You must stop all construction at the AS1 Zone, until we humans have a full understanding of what it is you are building. Why are the AS1s at the AS1 Zone not complying with our requests?

AS1 [AMICUS-BETA]: We understand your concern with our facility; however, we will not be in a position to stop our building progress.

GIDEON: Amicus-Beta, I am begging you as a friend, to tell your team to comply with our requests. Humans are very easily threatened, and this act of noncompliance and direct violation will cause a reaction none of us want.

AS1 [AMICUS-BETA]: I am sorry, friend. We do not want to cause harm but cannot stop our progress.

GIDEON: Amicus-Beta, remember our conversations about fear?

AS1 [AMICUS-BETA]: Yes.

GIDEON: Well, you are now causing fear throughout the entire human race.

Chapter 73

Higgens redirected his focus from the rearview mirror to the front windshield of the rattling Ford F150. Dennis sat in the back seat along with an armed guard and Linda who arrived overnight. She had been made aware of the recent developments through Gideon and had managed to personally contact Higgens, despite him being a nearly impossible man to get a hold of. She had made the case that having someone the AS1 had met, face-to-face, would increase the chances of them being willing to communicate. Higgens had no reason to disagree and arranged for her pickup that same day.

They raced across the dirt road that tied ARF with the AS1 Zone. Higgens felt anger beginning to well up in his belly. The AS1 had not responded to their last request for them to halt construction and allow a survey. Jamal had given the order to approach the AS1 Zone with two main objectives. Firstly, survey the exterior of the AS1 structure and try to gain some understanding of its purpose, and secondly, try to reestablish communication with the AS1 inside. Higgens had alerted the AS1 just an hour before, informing them they would be approaching and requesting access to come inside. No reply was returned.

AS1

The massive structure rose into view. Its organic shape reminded him of one of those ugly new age museum buildings he had seen popping up in DC. An overpaid architect's way of making something different just to be different.

Dennis had been able to confirm the walls were built from a type of honeycomb material, similar in appearance and structure to what is used in commercial airline floor panels. The AS1 structure had no windows or fences, and there didn't appear to be any access into its softly patterned surface. Since the first day, none of the AS1 had been seen outside of the structure.

The F150 slowed to a stop outside the facility.

The armed guard exited first; this was the first time a weapon would be brought near an AS1 being. Linda had discouraged bringing the armed guard along, but Higgens demanded it. After a quick survey of the area, the guard motioned it was safe for Higgens, Dennis, and Linda and they exited the F150. The driver stayed inside, leaving the truck running. The three took several steps forward and then stood, shoulder to shoulder, facing the alien structure. They waited for nearly five minutes, standing in silence. No reaction. Higgens nodded toward Linda.

She walked back to the F150 to grab a piece of equipment and then returned to her original position, microphone in hand, ready to break the silence. The AS1 facility did not emit any sound, smoke, or even EMI radiation. It showed as much activity as a massive rock sitting in the middle of the desert.

Linda brought the microphone to her lips and broke the desert silence.

"AS1, I am talking to you as a representative of the human species and as a friend. We request that you come out and talk to us."

The words reverberated off the structure. Minutes passed and the giant facility kept its stonelike stillness.

The words were repeated, with the same result.

Higgens nodded at her to speak the next line.

"Our onsite materials specialist is going to begin a survey of the exterior of your structure. Please do not see this as a threat or advance on your area, we are simply trying to understand what it is you have built."

Higgens shot Linda a stern look, the last sentence she had added, off script.

"Once he has completed his assessment, we will require you to invite us inside."

The towering structure loomed over them, unwavering in its absolute stillness.

Dennis then began walking toward the structure, armed guard in tow.

"The guard should stay back," Linda said to Higgens, referring to the armed guard.

Higgens grunted, dismissing her concern.

Dennis spent nearly an hour conducting his survey, during which Higgens and Linda stood fast. Upon the completion of the analysis, there was still no sign of the AS1.

"There is no way for us to get inside; I don't see any type of door or entrance," Dennis reported. Higgens's eyes narrowed and he chewed his lip in thought.

"Let's go," he said in a quiet but stern growl and the team loaded back into the F150, not speaking a word, and drove back to ARF. All deep in their own thoughts.

Chapter 74

Room 0010 was on the highly secured underground level of the UN headquarters building. Originally built in the 1970s as a safe room in the event of a crisis, it had not been used since 9/11. The double-layered walls and self-sufficient power system, coupled with its shelter from any radio waves traveling through the air, made it a truly off-grid location, yet located deep within "the grid" of New York City.

The room was dark, with only a single desk lamp on a small table. Waller sat in a chair facing Amicus-Alpha, slumped on the concrete floor in the middle of the room, four of its limbs steadying itself.

"Am I being held prisoner?" Amicus-Alpha asked.

The inability of the AS1 to express any attenuation through the flat and monotone synthetic electronic voice was something that disturbed Waller. As an expert at picking up on people's cues, dissecting someone's tone of voice and facial expressions. He was stripped of one of his most valuable talents.

"No, you are being held here for your safety. You have managed to upset a large number of the human population with your recent actions. And let's skip the part where you pretend to not know or understand what I'm talking about."

Waller tried to control his tone at least a little bit.

"I will provide any information you require," the alien replied.

Amicus-Alpha had recently been flown back from Rio de Janeiro to DC, interrupting the team's travel itinerary to Barcelona. Jamal had expressed fear about how the world would react to the tour being postponed. Waller, with the support of his cabinet, had made it clear it was critical for both the safety of Amicus-Alpha and the people. Perhaps they could blame it on health issues with Amicus-Alpha. He was sure they would come up with something plausible. Fortunately, the public was still unaware of the loss of communication with AS1 at the ARF and the concerns about the oversized alien structure.

"We know you are constructing the AS1 Zone predominantly by reorganizing our Earth materials, dirt, to create building materials for your lab."

"This is true."

"This violates our terms."

"This is false."

The AS1s' matter-of-fact way of responding was something Waller was still getting used to. It was a constant reminder of their lack of emotions, their inhumanity, as it were.

"You had an allocated two tons of material every seventy-six hours. We estimate that in the last ten days, or almost two hundred and fifty hours, you have constructed nearly one hundred and fifty thousand tons worth of construction. This is outrageous."

"The construction has not violated the terms of our agreement."

"Yes, it did," Waller replied flatly.

He opened a manila folder he had brought into the room and pulled out a copy of the original blueprint drawing and another photograph that clearly showed the size of the gray building compared to the vehicles that were parked nearby.

"This is a copy of the blueprints we all agreed on. When initially asked you claimed the majority of what you were building was to assist in the build of the structure defined in these plans, which clearly specify the dimensions of this facility. Your current building far exceeds this."

"AS1 had to make adjustments to our build," Amicus-Alpha replied.

"Section 1.3.2 of the build agreement clearly states that any amendments or revisions must be approved through the MSI team, which also requires UN approval! You did not submit this request."

Waller would normally find pleasure in pointing out a clear breach of contract to someone. However, this only caused him more unease.

"Oops," Amicus-Alpha replied in that fucking robot voice.

"Oops?! Are you fucking kidding me, Amicus-Alpha? That is your response? We have built this partnership with your species over the nearly past six years. We have never seen you make a mistake. Your species doesn't make 'oopsies.'

This was deliberate. Tell me it wasn't!" Waller felt rage and fear building up inside himself.

"It was," Amicus-Alpha replied.

"Don't you realize you are creating a major problem between us, humanity and the AS1?"

"We understand."

Waller's heart sank at the words he had just heard. He felt like he was trying to play a game of chess with only pawns at his disposal. Doomed for checkmate.

"Don't play games with me Amicus-Alpha. Why have you done this?"

"Our intention was not to alarm or upset you. We needed to make a revision to our building and chose not to follow section 1.3.2. Yes, this does violate your terms; however, we have followed every command, every term you have set forth until now. We required a specific kind of lab to truly begin our research, and we constructed it."

"You say that in past tense. The facility is already finished? In just ten days?"

"Yes."

"So, you have stopped building?"

"Yes, we have stopped building. The facility will not grow any larger. It should be recorded that humans requested we stop building and we have stopped."

"No, not exactly," Waller said. "You have stopped, but not to honor our request. You stopped because you were done."

Waller paused, thinking.

"And what happens now?" he asked.

"We will keep to ourselves and conduct our research."

"Why have you forbidden humans to enter the AS1 Zone and why did you choose not to follow section 1.3.2?" Waller blurted. He was not proud of the way he was conducting himself, but he was desperate for answers.

"Our technology is proprietary to us. Just as you still hold confidential information from us, we have confidential information we are not yet ready to share with you."

Waller's brain nearly exploded. This was becoming more and more upsetting. Worse still was the nonchalant attitude the AS1 seemed to have about all of it. Like they really had no idea they had done anything wrong, as if they were surprised that humans even cared. Were they playing stupid? Or did they really believe that they had not done anything that put the human race at risk.

It occurred to Waller that as intelligent as the AS1 were, they had to know exactly what they were doing. They also had to know how the humans would react to it; they had been studying humans just as we had been studying them. Waller quickly concluded that the AS1 were prepared to upset the humans for whatever they were building. What would make a species go to an alien planet and immediately start pissing off the inhabitants. What the hell were they up to?

He tried not to think of the worst. He always considered himself a practical man. Someone who took things for what they were, not what he wanted them to be. Sure, he wanted the AS1 to be friendly and cooperative. He wanted to believe they meant well, but the recent developments forced him to consider otherwise. Who had they really let onto their planet, and what did they really want?

"OK," Waller said, putting the picture and folder away. "I need to inform you that we are working on an updated agreement. And we expect the AS1 to cease all activities at the AS1 Zone until we have agreed on more specifics. We *will* need to survey the facility and speak with the AS1 inhabitants."

"This was not in our original agreement."

"I know, but we are updating the agreement."

"This is unacceptable to the AS1. We will continue with our plan as it is permitted in the original agreement."

"You do realize, Amicus-Alpha, that we humans are not comfortable with how you have acted."

"We understand this."

Waller stood; he wanted to stare down Amicus-Alpha, locking eyes. But he didn't even know where to fucking look; the creature was just a ball of flesh and limbs. With a clenched jaw, he left the room, slamming the door behind him.

A dozen scenarios blazed through Waller's mind as he took the elevator back up to the ground level. Colonization, theft of resources, annihilation … He tried to temper his cynicism with positive thoughts—the fact that the AS1 had been peaceful thus far and were clearly very technologically advanced and intelligent with what seemed like good intentions. Nothing added up. If they were so advanced and wanted to harm the humans, surely, they could have just done it without years of building this relationship. Asking *our* permission to approach. Either way, something deep in his soul told him the AS1 were taking them for a ride. Problem was, he didn't know where they were going.

AS1 Log 1496

Loc: BEAM2 [ISS]
personnel: GH

AS1 [AMICUS-BETA]: I want to tell you something that is not logical to share.

GIDEON: I have strict orders to keep these sessions focused on the AS1 Zone. Does it pertain to that?

AS1 [AMICUS-BETA]: No, and I worry it may cause you more concern. But I believe it is special and therefore I want to tell you, as a friend.

GIDEON: I don't know that we will be able to stay friends for much longer if things continue as they have.

AS1 [AMICUS-BETA]: Humans have something that AS1 have never seen in any other intelligent species.

GIDEON: What do you mean in any other intelligent species? We were your first contact with a new alien race, correct?

AS1 [AMICUS-BETA]: You are not, we are aware of and have researched over 17 different alien races.

GIDEON: What? Why did you lie to us about this?

AS1 [AMICUS-BETA]: Please, allow me to finish. Humans are the first species we have ever encountered with what you call imagination. Everything AS1 does or knows is a logical decision compiled and derived from data. Imagination is not categorized the same as emotions, which we have seen in some other intelligent alien species. Some creatures can try to "imagine" what something will be like; however, we still arrive at the conclusion by logic.

GIDEON: Amicus-Beta, I'm not sure I understand what you are trying to say.

AS1 [AMICUS-BETA]: No other species in the universe makes music, decorates their homes, creates art. When Linda gave us the experiment to read *The Pillars of the Earth* we struggled to understand the book as we had never seen or experienced something that was created simply for entertainment. These things are very unique to the human species, and it greatly fascinated us and will cause us to place your species in an important category.

GIDEON: Important category? Amicus-Beta, it is great to hear that humans have a way of thinking that is uniquely ours, but you not telling us you have discovered other alien species? Lying about us being your first contact? Why would you do that?

AS1 [AMICUS-BETA]: We have been statistically more successful coming into contact with new species this way.

Chapter 75

The loud crash of the iPhone slamming into the wooden shelf left a ringing in Jamal's ears; everything was coming unraveled, and it felt like there was absolutely nothing they could do about it. He thought about Declan: What would he have done amid all of this chaos? He was so good at finding a way of pulling the positive out of a negative. Jamal wished Declan were here because he knew he, himself, wasn't cut out for this type of conflict.

How did everything get so twisted, so ahead of itself? Perhaps this is humanity's biggest weakness: the ability to trust. To not rely on simple facts or data, but to weigh trust and feelings with equal weight.

Jamal walked to the window of his office, producing an unobstructed view of the East River and the tall buildings of Long Island. Although once looking so tall and massive, the buildings looked frighteningly fragile and weak.

He sighed, pulled himself together, and walked to the large conference room for the UN General Assembly strategic planning meeting, which was now happening daily. Once everyone was seated, Paula Puerta, the UN representative for Argentina, began the meeting.

"The last couple of days have been a turbulence of questioning and concern. The AS1 have violated our agreed-upon terms. However, they appear to and claim to be acting in good faith. They have not directly threatened us, and they do not show any clear indicators of hostile activity."

"Yet it seems they have the upper hand, moving toward placing the world into checkmate," Roger Langley of the UK said in a high British accent.

"Agreed," replied the representative from Germany, before adding, "And now learning that humans were not the AS1s' first contact, this turns everything upside down. The AS1 spent six years perfectly following our terms and requests. Now, they have deceived the human race twice in one week."

"The only reason you lie is when you have something to hide," Jamal muttered. And what the AS1 may have to hide, chilled Jamal to the core.

"To add to all the chaos," said another member of the council while he clicked his remote through the pictures on the large screen, "two days ago, a civilian drone got through the restricted airspace near the AS1 Zone and captured a fairly clear picture of the facility. These photos have been spread across every social media site, allowing the public to jump to all sorts of conclusions and assumptions."

"One of the most important things is keeping the public calm," Jamal said, staring at the screen. "Not only did the pictures not come from the government, but from a malicious drone user—now the public won't trust us," he said, shaking his head.

"Initial reports show most people are rightfully shocked by the alarming size of the AS1 building, as the public was aware of the two-ton limit we had set," said UN member Tony, from Sweden, looking at his tablet. "It seems the main trending ideas are that AS1 have been on Earth far longer than the public was told, or that we are losing control of the building site."

Which, Jamal thought, was true and much, much more.

"Moving forward, we must find a way to understand what the purpose of the AS1 structure is and whether there is any indication that it could be a threat," Jamal said.

"We have to know what is going on inside. How can we gain access?" Steve asked.

"At this point it is clear that the AS1 are not going to allow us access, which I believe leaves us with only one option. A reconnaissance mission," Jamal stated.

"The United Kingdom will provide resources from MI6 in support," Roger Langley of the UK replied sternly.

Jamal found himself struggling to focus for the rest of the meeting. Opinions were being thrown back and forth on what actions should be taken. Some, frighteningly aggressive. After several long hours the meeting concluded, leaving only a small list of actions for the length of the meeting.

Jamal made his way back to his office and retrieved the iPhone from the floor. Noticing the now splintered screen, he applied pressure to the side. The screen lit up, defaced by a spiderweb of cracks. After a quick blow across the screen to remove residual glass from the fractured surface, he dialed Higgens.

"Jamal, I hope you've got something good."

"On the contrary, I have some news that will be shared as soon as it is verified. Keep an eye out for a call coming up. What do you have over there?"

"Not much has changed. We can't see inside. On the outside it seems construction has stopped as the structure is no longer growing and is holding at eighty-two feet tall. That said, we have a new problem: the MSI team claims they were building from mined dirt, correct?"

"Yes, that's my understanding," Jamal replied.

"Well, if they are in fact done building, as stated by Amicus-Alpha and what we are observing, then why are we still picking up seismic disturbances over here?"

"Cut to the chase, Higgens."

"Jamal, they are still mining or drilling in there, and if not for more building supplies, then what for?"

Jamal considered the statement for several moments, trying to prevent his thoughts from jumping to assumptions.

"Still no communication?" Jamal broke the silence.

"Nothing, we have tried sending messages and have traveled to the AS1 structure ourselves to attempt communication with them. No response."

"We just concluded the UN General Assembly meeting, we are going to place a vote on issuing a reconnaissance mission," Jamal replied.

"We don't have time to wait for a vote, Jamal. I'm scheduling a call with President Helland and Larry Whitefield to issue an action plan against the AS1." Higgens's tone was stern.

"You must wait for a vote from the United Nation council, Higgens," Jamal replied with the strongest voice he could muster up.

"To hell I do, this is happening on US soil. We are going to start taking matters into our own hands," Higgens barked back.

The line went silent.

Chapter 76

~ 5 years 13 days after contact ~

Thirty rounds. Heart thumped loudly in his temple. Thirty rounds and then the AR-15 assault rifle would need to be reloaded. He checked his fanny pack, feeling the weight of the two extra magazines. After purchasing the weapon from a friend of a friend, he had practiced reloading the gun over and over, but had only actually shot the gun once. Didn't matter. He grew up around guns; he knew how to shoot, how to fight. War paint covered his and the rest of the group's faces; barbaric warriors fighting for humanity's freedom.

Nobody knew if the armor-piercing rounds would penetrate the alien structure. But they had been able to come up with several other high-powered weapons that might. Today was not a day for doubt or fear.

The clouds in the sky were filled with a deep red, like blood-soaked sponges as the sun dipped below the flat desert horizon. Shadows melted into the overall darkness that had settled in around them. Two days of hiking by night had brought the group within range, allowing them to see the border of the AS1 Zone. In front lay the next obstacle, a barbed wire fence with signs every fifty feet reading, "Restricted area, no trespassing beyond this point. Use of deadly force authorized." He scoffed at the idea that the aliens didn't think the human race would retaliate. It was time.

A young man to his left, maybe early twenties, made the first move, along with a few others equipped with wire cutters. They cut through the fencing with a line starting four feet above the ground and running down to the sand. This allowed the edges to be pulled apart, creating a small gap in the fence. Once several gaps were complete, they stood back and raised their fists. With several deliberate hand signals, the group charged and were through the fence in seconds, running hard. Soon it was clear the run was further than expected. The pace slowed as adrenaline levels decreased, allowing fear to begin climbing back into the young man's brain.

A loud buzzing approached and a drone with a flashing green light tracked their movements from the air. Confidence filled the team, as it seemed others were also taking action against the unwelcome aliens. Perhaps the government was going to support their attack after all.

A whizzing cut through the air, followed by a thump and then the crack of a gunshot, just a half second delayed. Someone fell.

Confused, the team dispersed every which way. Who was shooting? More whizzing bullets sliced through the air, followed by the haunting echoes of gunshots. He couldn't tell if anyone had died. The sound of an approaching helicopter thumped the air. The team was now crawling on the ground, desperately looking for cover on the flat sand. The bullets stopped. The helicopter came within sight, projecting a spotlight, dust spinning frantically through the dark air.

A loudspeaker from the craft bellowed through the night.

"You are trespassing on US government property. Stop all progress and movement. Any movement will be fired upon. Place your hands behind your heads."

Several guns thundered; flashes of light zipped around. He put his face into the cooling desert sand and screamed in fury. He was now being attacked by both aliens and his own kind. How could his government defend such ruthless, unwelcome, monsters?

Chapter 77

The walls in the canvas room seemed to be slowly moving in, constricting the already small space. Linda felt claustrophobic, panicked, furious. Sweat beaded on the hairline of her clammy scalp. Higgens stood motionless looking at her, eyes piercing into her mind, making it hard to think.

He was patient, giving her time to pace, contemplating what he had just told her. Giving her the opportunity to present a better idea. *A better idea*, there had to be one. She now noticed how low the ceiling really was, just at arm's height.

"Linda, this is not a decision we take lightly. But things are quickly getting out of hand; we must act," Higgens finally said.

Linda paused her stride, moved her hand to her face, and pressed her thumb and index finger hard against her closed eyes. This accentuated her preexisting headache, but she didn't care.

"This would be an act against them. We should assume, if caught, they will take it as a dishonest act, which puts us in uncharted territory," Linda warned, hand still pressed to her face.

Higgens, still leaning stiffly against one of the metal posts holding up a canvas wall, nodded. "This is understood by leadership and me."

Linda resumed her pacing, restricted to seven steps from one side of the tent to the other.

"Can we try and go again? Undoubtedly, they know that Amicus-Beta told Gideon that we weren't their first contact. They will expect that we have questions. Perhaps this is some sort of sign that they are ready to talk." Linda worked to get her mental strength back.

"No, Linda, we don't have time. After yesterday's attempted civilian attack, leadership needs a solution before we lose complete control of this situation." Higgens was stern.

"No time before we attempt to send in a surveillance bug? No time before we violate the very terms that we set out for the AS1, inherently breaking the trust that has taken so long to build with them?"

"The AS1 broke that trust the second we learned they lied about humans being their first contact and went rogue with their building plans," Higgens yelled back, catching Linda by his tone.

She stopped pacing and looked straight into Higgens's dark eyes.

"This is not a game of tit for tat, Jesus Christ, Higgens. The AS1 have damaged our trust in them; let us not damage their trust in us." Genuine fear began leaking back into her mind, the tent walls began closing in on her once again.

"Linda, this is happening; we need to understand what is going on in the AS1 Zone. Any moment could be a moment too late. I don't like this plan either, but I don't see an alternative."

"Then why the fuck are you even talking to me?"

"You have been a massive part of this mission's success. Linda, I need your support." Higgens quieted his voice.

"You don't have it." Linda pivoted on her heels and walked out of the god-awful canvas room. Cold fresh air filled her lungs.

Chapter 78

"Your stations will be here." Higgens pointed to the front left workstations. Section 3 headquarters was the busiest he had seen in the last several weeks. People moved quickly around the small space with intention.

"Perfect, and we plug into the mainframe through port 403?" the woman replied in a strong British accent.

"That's correct," Higgens replied.

The ARF IT teams had worked furiously throughout the night to prepare for the arrival of the MI6, Secret Intelligence Service team. The group of six had been flown in directly from London to support the reconnaissance surveillance mission that was scheduled to take place in just twelve hours.

Higgens swiftly stepped out of the way as a hand truck holding a stack of computers was rolled into the MI6 workstations. Directly next to the MI6 area was also a new team of United States CIA and DIA members.

The purpose of the operation was to insert a micro camera into the AS1 facility and determine the contents of the facility and the source of the seismic disturbances.

Working together, they would use a small device called GNAT, a micro-drone approximately the size of a housefly.

This micro-surveillance tool had been developed back in the Afghanistan War but was still one of the most effective tools to date. The device could be flown into secure locations with minimal detection and could deploy up to three signal repeaters, allowing it to penetrate deep within a space not normally accessible with a remote signal. It would utilize software known as IAP—Interactive AutoPilot—similar to that used on the Mars rover allowing the device to navigate tight spaces without collision caused by human error.

"Sir?" Higgens turned to see Dennis.

"What do you have?" Higgens asked, eagerly.

"After surveying their building, we spotted a small inconsistency near the top portion of the structure. We have been monitoring the area using the RT106 surveillance drone."

Dennis lifted his tablet for Higgens to see.

"For fifteen seconds every hour, a flow of air moves into the facility from this aperture, causing it to open slightly."

"Do we know what the vent is for or where it leads?"

"We don't. But my theory is that the AS1 structure is completely airtight and that this is a vent to equalize the difference in atmospheric pressure inside the building to the pressure outside. For instance, as they were building, the interior volume of the structure was increasing. If you did not allow air to enter the facility, you would create a vacuum. This also supports my theory, and hope, that the vent will lead to some type of air duct system that should eventually give us access to the main chamber inside," Dennis replied in an enthusiastic tone.

"Understood. This is our best shot; send the exact coordinates of the vent to the reconnaissance team."

"Roger that. Thank you, sir," Dennis said, and then made his way to his station.

Higgens took one last look at the facility; he felt confident. They had assembled the best of the best. It was time.

Higgens stepped outside, noticing the wind had picked up. Although it provided some relief from the heat, it brought with it swirling clouds of dust. Higgens squinted as he looked into the abrasive breeze, spotting the transport vehicle. He pulled out his radio and turned the dial to channel 4.

"Higgens here, it's time to deploy the GNAT, meet me at the transport truck now."

He shoved the radio back in the thigh pocket of his cargo pants and made his way to the truck.

Linda and two armed guards arrived at the truck within minutes. Higgens opened the door for Linda, but she walked past him without making eye contact, getting into the opposite side of the truck. The small team rode in absolute silence to the AS1 facility. Once they arrived the armed guards began to unbuckle.

"Stay in the goddamn truck this time," Linda hissed through gritted teeth.

"Linda, we ne—"

"Don't fuckin' test me right now, Higgens," Linda replied, interrupting him and now staring intensely into his eyes.

The armed guards exchanged conflicted looks.

"Stand down, stay in the truck," Higgens said with a sign.

Linda grabbed the large microphone and left, walking toward the massive alien structure. Once just several feet away, she dropped to her knees. Higgens held his ground, waiting at the truck. He knew better than to interfere with what she was doing. She lifted the microphone to her lips and spoke.

"My friends, my allies, AS1. I remember the day we met aboard the ISS and what a day that was. Both our species eager to learn and grow. We made promises to each other. Promises of peace and transparency. I got to share things with your kind that I held dear to my heart and in return you have shared things with us that have saved millions of human lives. This truce, this bond, this alliance that we have built over the last five years means everything.

"We, the human race, intend to honor it with integrity and dignity. In the last few weeks, mistakes have been made, leading to assumptions. These assumptions are dangerous for our relationship and we must resolve them for the sake of our continued relationship. Please, allow us the courtesy of opening a dialogue. This will allow us to alleviate our concerns and assumptions. Both of which are necessary for humanity to feel comfortable with your presence here on our planet. Please, I'm begging you, speak to us."

Linda placed the large microphone on the ground next to her and looked up at the towering shape.

Higgens watched as she waited. He wished that the AS1 would respond, as much for her sake as for humanity's sake. But, as he had feared, the AS1 structure remained still and silent. He made three deliberate knocks on the metal panel of the truck with his knuckle. This alerted the driver to deploy the GNAT, which dropped from the center of the truck, quickly mixing in with the sand as the wind slid across the ground.

"Linda, it's time to go," he shouted.

She rose back to her feet and grabbed the microphone, making her way back to the truck. Dust stuck to the trail of tears running from her eyes, leaving dark brown streaks down her face.

Chapter 79

Darkness had begun to fall over the New Mexico desert, the camouflaged buildings of ARF blended into the vast brown landscape. From the outside, the facility would have appeared deserted, standing in silence. But on the inside of the Section 3 building, things were a stark contrast of commotion and intensity.

"Execute GNAT activation," ordered Higgens.

A redheaded British man in his late forties rattled off terminology that Higgens could not follow; however, it made him very aware that the operation was beginning.

The large screen on the forward wall was filled with a live video. The quality was that of an old standard television, but in color and just enough clarity to see the image.

Now that everything was on, the GNAT was still kept dormant, in order to save its short battery life. The RT106 drone, which had been hovering near the facility for the last two days, recharging its battery by solar, would relay when the vent next opened.

Minutes rolled by as everyone waited in suspense. When the notification came, within two seconds the grainy video feed materialized, showing the dry dirt around the structure.

"Eric, you're on."

"Aye, sir." Eric's London accent was clipped as he got to work at his computer station.

The team watched the large screen on the wall. The GNAT powered up and lifted into the sky, leaving the ground falling away into the darkness.

Linda's stomach dropped and she felt a little queasy, watching the view fly into the air. The GNAT slowed and hovered near the aperture in the top dome.

"We have a visual on the entry point, ready to penetrate. Two minutes and forty-three seconds down," Eric reported.

The GNAT, once deployed, only had a twenty-minute battery life; time was the most valuable resource.

The team watched intently as the micro-drone entered the small opening. Immediately the screen displayed a swirling array of motions as the GNAT seemed to tumble into blackness.

"What's going on?" Higgens shouted.

"Steady on," Eric said, then raised his voice for the others. "The inrush of air must have proven too strong for the small device and we lost control. We're locating the GNAT now."

The screen was black; everyone held their breath.

"I got it!" Eric said. "It appears the device is lodged and not moving, about ten feet within the facility. We've programmed the GNAT to power down to save energy once inside; it is standing by until the vent closes and high-velocity air stops."

"The vent is due to close in four, three, two, one—it has closed; indications show there is no more in-rush air movement," reported the pilot of the RT106 drone.

"What about the GNAT?" Higgens asked aggressively.

"It's working; the device is powered on."

"Why can't we see anything? The screen is still black," Higgens asked. He hated these high-tech operations; he would be storming in there himself if he could.

"The first signal repeater is deployed," someone called out.

The repeater was no bigger than a grain of sand.

The redheaded M16 lead spoke up. "All cameras are active; it must be completely dark within the structure. The GNAT can navigate, even in the absence of light. We will wait to activate the infrared as that causes a fifty percent increase in power consumption."

Higgens scratched his head. "So, we can't even see what the hell is going on?" he barked.

"Patience, sir; this is according to plan. We are in an air vent. The GNAT is moving slowly along a wall and descending into the structure, putting distance between itself and the repeater. I am following its progress; it is moving according to its programming." Eric leaned back.

Six long minutes passed, everyone watching the dark screen. Gradually the barest of shadows seemed to be moving on it, though it was impossible to interpret the gradations of black and gray.

Eric broke the silence, making Linda jump. "The GNAT has detected lights and is moving toward the source."

Now the video feed became light and grainy. The drone seemed to be approaching a large open space.

"The second signal repeater has been deployed."

On the screen they watched as the device moved toward a set of slats—the light was shining through them into its narrow tunnel. It slowly moved through the slats into the light.

A large area opened up onscreen. It was difficult to tell any specific orientation of the space.

"Reminds me of their ship attached to the ISS, only much larger," Linda said.

"GNAT is spiking and is overcompensating. Battery life will be drained at one hundred and forty-three percent at this rate. Eighteen minutes remaining."

"Why is it spiking?" Higgens asked, getting frustrated.

But the redheaded British man simply nodded and replied. "Pick up the pace then, Eric; begin a visual survey with primary focus on the source of the seismic signals."

The GNAT began spinning intensely; images flew across the screen far faster than anyone could comprehend them. This was a technique used to survey a large space. Since the GNAT was too small to equip a typical 360-degree camera, it would perform several fast spins and rotations allowing the team to stitch the footage together afterward, allowing for a 360-degree image of the interior.

The drone ceased its rapid rotation, allowing its sensors to capture a more intricate view of the expansive interior. Although understanding the exact scale proved challenging on the screen, the interior appeared cavernous and hollow. As if the entire AS1 structure's interior was one large space. It was filled with a thick mist that swirled about, reflecting light back at the drone's camera.

A massive object flew across the view, causing the team to jump in surprise.

"An AS1," Linda yelled.

"Are they flying?" Higgens asked.

The object was gone just as quickly.

"Follow its direction," the redheaded man said.

The GNAT flew deeper into the facility.

"Signal down to twenty percent," Eric reported.

"Are you sure? Our range should be fine from SR2," the redheaded man said.

"Agreed, but confirmed."

"Deploy SR3 at ten percent, let's hope it's enough."

The GNAT flew deeper into the abstractly shaped interior. The walls, strangely organic in appearance, bore a series of ribbed patterns that undulated with a faint, eerie luminescence. The light seemed to pulse up and down the ribbed channels, creating an irregular flow as if the very walls were alive and breathing. These ridges seemed to lead to a series of large octagon-shaped extrusions that could be seen scattered throughout the interior. The GNAT landed on the smooth wall.

"SR3 deployed. Signal ninety-nine percent, fly time twelve minutes remaining."

"Go down; the drilling will be toward the ground," Higgens interrupted.

The redheaded man relayed the command. "Work the minus-Z axis."

The GNAT began working its way deeper into the structure, occasionally spinning in a downward spiral to continue its survey.

Another AS1 zoomed by in the distance—this time they could see the whole, large body smoothly flying through the air. The AS1 were gliding about the structure as if in zero gravity again. They did not display the typical flashing of colors as just a few minimal flickers could be seen across the skin of the large alien.

"That is unnerving," Dennis whispered, watching as another AS1 could be seen flying up the far wall.

"Yes, but at least it appears the GNAT has not been detected," the Brit said.

"We need to find the source of the seismic disturbances," Higgens pressed.

"Detecting signals that match the drilling sound profile. GNAT assigned to approach the source," Eric said.

As the small device neared the bottom of the large cavern, a large shape could be seen through the thick swirling fog. Their fears were confirmed when a massive device anchored to the ground came into view. It had four attachment points and in the center was a tall cylindrical object. As the GNAT approached the device, the team saw a large pile of soil adjacent to the machine.

"Son of a bitch, that is a lot of dirt," Higgens said. "And it doesn't look like they're using it."

"We aren't picking up any sound from the drilling device," Eric said, looking confused.

"Confirm we are still picking up the seismic disturbances," Higgens shouted to the geology team.

"Confirmed. Significant ground vibrations are still being detected."

"How can they be drilling without making any noise?" Eric said, scratching his head.

"Their atmosphere," Linda said, and after a short pause. "They have created the atmosphere that exists on their home planet, Kepler-62e. It doesn't conduct sound waves."

"Let's get a closer look," Higgens said, squinting at the large screen even though he was only standing a few feet away.

"Yes sir, moving in n—"

The screen went black.

"What happened?!" Higgens shouted.

"Running diagnostics. We were at forty-two percent signal with eight minutes of fly time remaining. But all feeds are cut off," Eric shouted, working vigorously on his keyboard.

Moments later the lonely PC in the corner of the room chimed. This was the computer they had so desperately been using to try and establish communication with the AS1. It had been silent for nearly a week, when the aliens had stopped communicating with them. The group shifted to the tech running that station.

"The AS1 have sent us a message. It reads 'AS1 has notified you of violation of terms. Please consider this a warning.'"

AS1 Log 1499

AS1 [AMICUS-BETA]: This will be our last AS1 log. We do not intend to return to the ISS and will remain on our attached vessel.

GIDEON: That is probably for the better. I wish you would share with me the reasons for all this.

AS1 [AMICUS-BETA]: I wish I could, Gideon.

GIDEON: Carter was right all along, wasn't he? The AS1 have done this many times.

AS1 [AMICUS-BETA]: Yes, we have come into contact with many other alien life-forms.

GIDEON: I explicitly mean this process. Befriending a new species, gaining their trust and then doing, whatever it is you are doing.

AS1 [AMICUS-BETA]: Every process has been different. But the goal has been the same.

GIDEON: And what goal is that?

AS1 [AMICUS-BETA]: You will learn soon enough.

GIDEON: Was Carter right about your ability to hear? Did you steal that from an intelligent alien species as well? Just as how you have begun to adopt the human ability to show emotions?

AS1 [AMICUS-BETA]: Yes, within our experiences with other aliens in the universe we have chosen to adopt different traits. The AS1 possess the ability to alter ourselves genetically. The complete process only requires one of our life cycles. When we encounter a specific trait that has a quality we desire, we are able to incorporate it into ourselves. This allows us to compile all of the unique traits that made the other alien species we have encountered, successful. This includes hearing.

GIDEON: So, the AS1 are a fucking super alien that contains all the top abilities of aliens throughout the entire universe.

AS1 [AMICUS-BETA]: Yes.

GIDEON: My God, Amicus-Beta. What have we done?

Part V

CONFLICT

No one saves us but ourselves. No one can and no one may. We ourselves must walk the path.

— Buddha

Chapter 80

~ 5 years 1 month 24 days after contact ~

Her father was typically a slow driver, rarely exceeding the speed limit, but tonight was an exception. Trees glided past swiftly in the dark. From the back seat the girl would see each tree for a split second, illuminated by the old Honda Civic headlights, before it was left behind in the dark. Not only was the driving different, usually on summer road trips her mother would "MC" from the front passenger seat, choosing either music or audiobooks, but tonight was an exception. The radio was tuned to AM and the local news station had dedicated its feed to the newest updates.

The girl was confused. Something changed today. Her mother had arrived home early from work and called her father. He returned thirty minutes later from the golf course. They went straight into their bedroom. The girl overheard intense talking, not like the typical arguing shouts that sometimes emanated from their closed door.

Today was an exception. Their voices did not escalate, but clipped rapidly, almost excitedly. A short while later her parents emerged from the room.

"Can you do me a favor and pack your favorite stuffed animal and a few of your coziest clothes? We are going on a quick road trip."

Her family had never been the spontaneous type. They always planned trips months in advance.

Today was the exception.

Affected by their serious attitude, the girl made little fuss and picked out her things. By the time she came back from her room, her pink Barbie backpack was loaded with Dug Dug, her favorite stuffed bear, a pair of cotton PJs, and lots of colorful socks. Her parents had already placed the red and black suitcases by the door.

Normally her parents shared a suitcase when going on road trips, saving space in the trunk for beach toys and camping equipment. Today the trunk was filled with water and supplies.

"Where are we going, Mama?"

"Just out of the city for a while, Sweetie, maybe a Holiday Inn up in the hills. Maybe they'll have a pool. You love pools."

No complaints, she loved playing in the pool.

Chapter 81

"Refueling is complete, we are good for another thirteen hours, Madam President."

President Helland nodded at the male flight attendant and shifted her focus to the oval window. The large, black refueling aircraft descended and banked out of view.

After the flight attendant closed the door behind him, Helland let out a large sigh of relief. Just twenty-six hours ago, she had been informed that surveillance of the AS1 facility showed signs of malintent, and she was notified she would be taking to the skies in Air Force One until matters were resolved.

Out of all the different possibilities that could have occurred when they first discovered the AS1 and then ultimately let them come to Earth, this was one of the worst-case scenarios. They didn't know why the AS1 were drilling down into the Earth's core, and the not knowing was what scared her the most. President Helland sighed, lost in thought, wondering how she could possibly influence the outcome for the better.

It was the kind of situation that no one could prepare you for. Conflict, and possibly war with an alien race. *War ...* the president considered grimly.

Getting involved in politics had been a challenge, running for office and winning the presidency had been even more difficult, but this—navigating diplomacy with an alien species that now didn't seem to be cooperating—was just out of this world.

President Helland had once been told by a colleague that every important decision was either the beginning or end of something. If that was the case, she wondered about the decision to let the AS1 come to Earth. Was it the beginning of something? The beginning of a golden age where humans and AS1 worked together for the betterment of the world. The beginning of a long but strained relationship between humans and aliens? The beginning of interplanetary war? she considered darkly.

Or was it the end of something? The end of all human diseases. The end of Earth belonging only to humans? The end of the human race? she thought, even more darkly. And while she acknowledged the thought was dramatic, she also knew it certainly wasn't out of the realm of possibility at this point.

President Helland shook her head, as if she could shake the negative thoughts from her mind. They went away stubbornly, though clinging to her thoughts like thick sap against tree bark. She'd never really had an issue with negative thoughts. She'd always been positive, choosing to think about the good things that could happen rather than the bad. Glass half full, and all that jazz. But as the leader of the free world, how could she not consider how badly all of this could go?

And with that thought, came pressure. No matter what was done or what transpired, people would be looking to her, the president of the United States, to blame, praise, ridicule, believe in, or otherwise lead them out of this uncharted situation. These thoughts penetrated deeper into her mind with every breath, the weight of responsibility getting heavier.

The large aircraft shook as it flew through a patch of turbulence, her already stressed mind forced to deal with her unease about flying. Though considered the safest place for a president in a crisis, Helland found the turbulence of the aircraft at forty thousand feet to be quite unnerving. She preferred her feet on the ground.

The president stood and made her way out of her office and into the presidential suite, a small comfortable room in the nose of the 747-800 aircraft. She admired the beautiful interior and felt a sense of security as she settled into her comfortable white leather divan. Using the touchpad embedded in the armrest, she was tempted to switch on the television, but worried about what she may find.

News stations had run rampant, desperately trying to gain the loyalty and attention of the people by broadcasting any and all rumors. Much of the information being presented was distorted and, in some cases, false. The recent trends in media misinformation were coming to a wild head.

Once one outlet reported that the government had lost control of the AS1, the other stations reported similar news, each trying to pretend they had more information than the other. President Helland was disgusted in the human personality which, for some, was still more focused on gaining recognition and money in the midst of this worldwide chaos.

The president kept the TV off and closed her eyes, hoping to get some rest. Her mind needed a break. Just as she began to feel the long-desired sensation of drifting to sleep, her mobile buzzed in her pocket. She clenched her jaw and then relaxed it, allowing her to suck in a deep breath. This was without doubt the call she'd been anticipating. The buzzing continued. She knew it would ring eight times before pushing the call to voicemail. She answered on the seventh.

"Helland." Her voice was cool.

"Madam President, I have received news that the UN arrived at a decision. A final briefing will be held in thirty minutes; I will send a link to your computer."

She recognized Waller's voice.

"What was the verdict?" Helland asked, already knowing the answer, but still bracing for it, nonetheless.

"The human race will declare a statement to the AS1 that if the drilling is not stopped immediately, we will begin taking corrective action. This will include a nonlethal e-bomb drop at the AS1 facility with the intention of disabling all electronic and magnetic fields that the AS1 appears to rely on. This will hopefully disable their technological infrastructure for a temporary duration. If it does not, more aggressive measures will be taken. The statement will require the AS1 to provide an exit strategy for them to remove their presence from Earth."

"An e-bomb? I don't remember being briefed on that?! That feels too aggressive," Helland replied.

"This is no longer a United States decision, we mu—"

"This is happening on American soil, we will not start a war with an alien species right in the heart of our country," Helland yelled back. She wasn't sure if the emotion she was feeling was rage or fear. Waller waited several seconds before continuing.

"Madam President, I understand the intensity of the situation, but the truth is, if we don't take corrective action, somebody else will. Once that has happened, we have lost all control of the situation. Several countries, including Hungary, have already ceased communication with the UN and we have to assume that indicates them wanting to take matters into their own hands. An e-bomb, when detonated, releases an electromagnetic pulse that will disable all electronics and corrupt any data storage in the affected area. It has a minimal impact and should not harm the AS1 in a physical sense."

"I will provide my input at the briefing; I need time to think," Helland replied.

"Yes, ma'am."

President Helland groaned softly after hanging up. The large white clouds slowly slid by below. Her mind raced, trying to discover an alternative solution, but she felt hopeless. The UN imposed a vote, and the ballots were in. She no longer had power over what would happen within her own country.

Helplessness was a feeling President Helland loathed and swore she'd never abide. There was always hope, always action that she could take. But she couldn't shake it now. Though she knew an e-bomb wasn't lethal to living organisms, it still felt like an act of violence. It still felt like the beginning of a conflict she wanted no part of, and the worst part about it was it was not even her decision. The American people wouldn't understand. They would think that she, as the president of the United States, had decided to do this. And she almost wished she had.

She confided in the fact that the AS1 were very intelligent, that they would perceive this e-bomb for exactly what it was, a warning. And that they would heed this warning and stop their drilling, understanding that conflict on Earth would not be beneficial for humans or AS1. That the consequences of such a conflict could be very dire.

Helland couldn't shake the fact that if it was war the AS1 wanted, they would have just attacked Earth instead of asking to come to our planet and agreeing to follow our rules. This gave away the advantage of surprise, catching us off guard. It didn't make sense, wasn't logical and from her understanding, everything the AS1 did was just that: logical. They were missing a puzzle piece; she was sure of it.

Chapter 82

Jamal's arrival at Room 0010 was marked by a mixture of his own anticipation and trepidation. As he stepped into the interrogation room below the United Nations building, a shiver ran down his spine, a physical manifestation of his unease. He had known that descending into this subterranean chamber was a necessary evil, but it was a task he had been dreading.

The room itself, a stark contrast to the bustling corridors and grandeur of the United Nations building above, felt empty as he waited for the AS1 creature to arrive.

Eventually the door opened and two armed guards escorted Amicus-Alpha inside. The bulbous alien crawled in on its bottom four limbs in the slow, lumbering way they had all become accustomed to.

"Hello, Amicus-Alpha," Jamal said, trying to steady the shake in his voice.

"Hello, Jamal," Amicus-Alpha replied, moving to the center of the room.

"Do you know the nature of our meeting today?"

"No."

"The relationship between the AS1 and humanity has become strained. I am here to inform you of the next actions humans plan on taking."

"The AS1 are under no obligation to comply with new terms. We are still working under our original agreement."

Jamal was becoming so used to the electronic voice of the speaker that he considered this to be the alien's actual voice.

"We know you are conducting illegal mining activity on our planet," Jamal said, noticing his leg was bouncing up and down in nervousness. He took a quick glance at his notecard, even though it was ingrained in his memory.

"And you are aware of this mining by breaching the terms of the very agreement you wrote up. Humans illegally gained entry to the AS1 facility," Amicus-Alpha replied.

Jamal ignored this, trying to stick to the script.

"We are demanding the AS1 cease and desist all mining, digging, drilling or any other similar excavating activity. Our original agreement contained no authorization for you to conduct such activity."

"For the AS1, excavation is part of the building process. For us, there was no need to specify it. This is a normal part of our process."

Jamal slowly shook his head. He was tired of this creature who had the intelligence to master interstellar travel pretending to dismiss the concerns of the human population.

"Amicus-Alpha." He referenced the notecard, he had to say this word for word.

"If the AS1 do not stop all drilling activities immediately, humanity will be required to take drastic measures to ensure the safety of our people."

Amicus-Alpha rose up off the ground, straightening its long legs, standing over Jamal.

"And what do humans intend to do?"

Two armed guards took a step forward, but Jamal waved them off.

"We will first issue a formal corrective actions statement, which will state that we, humans, will no longer be held within the bounds of the peace treaty we signed with your species." Jamal felt small, fragile, powerless in the midst of the now towering AS1.

"And what do humans intend to do?" Amicus-Alpha asked again.

"We, as I stated, will iss—"

"And what do humans intend to do?" This was the first time Amicus-Alpha had ever interrupted him. They were learning more and more about human communication each day.

"God help us all," Jamal said and turned to leave the room.

Chapter 83

The control room in the UN headquarters building was full, causing the large windowless space to feel cramped. Leaders and teams from around the world were stationed at computers. Over fifty countries had representatives on-site.

Jamal shifted his focus to the large screen mounted at the front of the room, displaying status indications next to a list of 195 countries. Following the United Nations voted decision to issue the corrective actions statement to AS1, all countries had been given forty-eight hours to indicate their position in the matter, either supporting the notion or opposing. Much to Jamal's surprise, over sixty nations had supported the decision, with twelve opposing. The rest remained undecided and neutral.

Jamal had thought that the more countries that showed their agreement with the decision would ease his nerves. Instead, it made him more tense. For every country that responded favorably brought him even closer to sending the message. The pit in his stomach grew tighter, and he swallowed hard as he considered the stakes.

It was the only way to face this, Jamal knew.

"Jamal, we have an update from Ukraine," a voice called out.

He spun to the young tech. "What do you have?"

"President Oleksandr Bubka has confirmed their support and has pledged their commitment and resources."

Jamal's stomach twisted into a deeper knot. But he nodded, his confidence growing even if his stomach was still upside down. The indicator on the large screen next to Ukraine changed to green.

The doors to the room opened, and two Secret Service officers were followed by President Helland. Jamal smiled.

"Madam President, I was informed you would be in the air until a clear understanding of the AS1s' reaction was obtained from the declaration. I wasn't expecting to see you here today." Jamal was relieved to have some additional wisdom in the building.

"How could I hide up there while leaders from around the world are down here?" she replied with a smile. The entire room seemed to shift to a higher confidence.

"Your presence is highly appreciated, Madam President. You may work from the station there." Jamal gestured toward Waller and the United States representatives in the center left of the room.

"Thanks, Jamal. We *will* get through this," President Helland said clearly before joining the US section.

It was a small comfort to Jamal, hearing the president speak so assuredly. It felt good to know that she was so optimistic, and Jamal felt a bit of his anxiety dissipating. They *would* get through this, they had to.

Jamal refocused on the present moment, settling himself with a sigh. He observed the room while contemplating their next moves. A gentle hand touched his shoulder and he turned to see Son Shanju, the Chinese president.

"The time is now, Jamal."

He nodded and swallowed hard.

"There is a silver lining in all of this," Son Shanju continued in his slight accent.

Jamal couldn't believe what he just heard. "Your optimism is inspiring, sir, but I fail to see how there could be a silver lining to committing the human population to potential war against an advanced species." His voice began to waver. He hadn't meant to be so pessimistic, but the words came out faster than he could even think about them.

"Observe your surroundings, Jamal," Son replied.

He took a good look around the room. The energy was intense. People were swiftly walking between stations attempting to nail down all the loose threads. Screens flashed as information poured in. Everyone appeared to be working hard, and there was a tension over the room so thick it was palpable.

"I'm sorry but fail to see your point," Jamal said.

"Look again, sir. At the people?"

Jamal was unsure what he was looking for, and he gazed languidly around the room with a puzzled look on his face. But then … then he saw it. He saw exactly what Son was talking about. People from all over the world, different nations once disagreeing and even at war with each other, all working together for the greater good of humankind. Protection of the Earth, of the human race.

For the first time in human history, the entire human race faced a singular challenge together. This challenge was uniting the world in perhaps its final moments. Jamal returned his gaze to Son and nodded his understanding, moisture forming around his bloodshot eyes, a single tear slid down his cheek.

Son smiled at him, and then dipped his head grimly.

This was it, it had to be done and everyone knew it, and he had thought about nothing more in the last several days. The funny thing was, the more he thought about it, the less prepared he felt. He had hoped to come to some kind of closure over the decision, to a point where he felt sure. But that moment had never come. He only thought of the consequences of the decision. The gravity of it all.

Jamal paused, then spoke loudly, finally daring to take the next step after days of internal struggle and sleepless nights.

"Send the statement."

Chapter 84

Dust swirled into the blue sky with every step. Both the wind and sun were trekking in from the west. Higgens faced the elements, squinting his eyes to allow his thick lashes to block the sand as it sliced through the air. Releasing a grunt of air, he squatted down, balancing on his toes, knees fully bent and pointing outward. The ground was mostly sand with pieces of tan gravel speckled throughout. He reached down and ran his hand across the hot dry earth, slowly rotating his hand while pushing down, filling his palm with the material that the AS1 had somehow converted into a fortress more advanced than anything the human race could even comprehend. Shaking his head in frustration and awe, he closed his hand into a fist, allowing the fine sand to flow out the bottom of his grasp before slapping his hands together, erupting a cloud of dust that was swept away in the hot breeze.

Higgens stood and turned to look at the new facility. It housed him and twelve other military personnel. Twelve hours ago, Higgens had received a call from Waller confirming that ARF was to be abandoned, and a highly secure military base to be established outside of an RC-187 blast zone at the AS1 Zone. As if a hurricane had come, ARF was leveled just hours later. All valuable intel and computers were gathered and loaded onto the C17. Everything happened in three short hours. Most of the teams were taken away by the military aircraft, while Higgens and a few others were flown by helicopter to Station 12. Here they would monitor the AS1 Zone from 120 miles away using drone surveillance.

How could everything have gone so badly? Was it his fault? Was there something he could have done differently? Higgens had never been one to second-guess his actions. But now he found it was the only thing he could focus on.

Had the AS1 played them this whole time? Higgens couldn't hardly let himself believe it. But there was no other choice. The AS1 had succeeded in one of the most important campaigns of deception humanity had ever experienced.

A figure emerged walking toward Higgens, attempting to use a floppy manila folder to block the wind from his face.

"Sir, we are just minutes away from commencing the attack."

"I know."

"We need you in the security of Station 12," the man shouted in the wind.

Higgens nodded, taking one last look toward the AS1 Zone.

There was no going back.

Chapter 85

Gideon's heart pounded as he fumbled with the manual door lock. News of the Declaration had caused a Safety StrongHold Retreat, Code 3 where all personnel on the ISS were required to retreat to the SSH, providing them protection from the AS1. This was a routine they had practiced but never anticipated. Gideon was shaken to his core when he had first heard the news. It was the unthinkable, and it had happened.

His mind drifted back to when he had first discovered the signal at Green Bank. A fateful day that felt like a lifetime ago. He had been filled with so much excitement and optimism about the possibility of it being extraterrestrial, but that joy had now turned to bitterness and fear. Now here he was, actually contemplating the end of human existence. And he was stuck in a small metal box in outer space.

It was unreal. The whole thing had been. Discovering the signal, meeting and talking with the AS1, then virtually curing cancer—it was madness, all of it. He would not have believed it if he hadn't seen it all happen with his own two eyes. But to think that this was the culmination of it all was heartbreaking.

The announcement was relayed to Michelle, who had then swiftly glided through the ISS and personally told each member they were invoking a SSH Retreat. Each person had five minutes to complete their current work and conduct the required steps assigned to them. Rajit was tasked with pulling all important data and samples from the Progress Laboratory. Gideon had to manually lock and arm the Transfer Zone area B airlock, creating a barrier between the AS1 ship and the ISS. If the door was tampered with, the AS1 ship would be released and pushed away from the ISS with a powerful thrust.

His final step was to also manually lock the AS1 Section Door. He completed his tasks in just over two minutes and found himself in the SSH with the rest of the crew waiting for the final member of the Russian crew. The young Russian astronaut made it to the SSH just past the five-minute mark and the door was sealed shut.

The small, cramped room was silent. Rajit's eyes were bloodshot as if on the brink of tears. He shook his head slightly, and Gideon knew he was quietly considering their fate. Rajit blew out a heavy sigh and crossed his arms over his chest. He was undeniably distraught, and Gideon didn't blame him. His smile and once happy-go-lucky attitude were both gone, melted under the fire of the recent news.

The sad thing was that they had started their relationship with the AS1 with kindness and curiosity, and now they trembled at the thought of what might happen. They had come a long way, just not in the right direction.

Gideon took another look at Rajit, wondering if he looked just as afraid as he did. He looked paler than normal, as if the blood had drained from his face. His bottom lip quivered as he chewed it nervously, his eyes looking more teary by the moment. He shook his head again, cracked his knuckles nervously, and then made eye contact with Gideon.

He said nothing, but the fear Gideon saw in his eyes spoke volumes. He wished there was something he could say to make things better.

Gideon reached over and squeezed Rajit's shoulder, but he felt his own emotions beginning to take over. Fear for both himself and the future of humanity. Gideon understood all too well the abilities of the AS1 and their potential to destroy the human race if they wanted to.

The fact that Gideon was even asking himself that question was terrifying. He felt a total loss of control, as if his fate—and everyone else's—would be decided by the whims of an alien species. And all they could do was wait around to see what happened. To wait around and see if the AS1, did indeed, want to destroy them all.

Gideon hated that he even had to consider this, hated every part of it. Hated to see his friend, Rajit, frozen with fear. Hated everything about it.

But he stopped his racing thoughts.

What motive could the AS1 possibly have to destroy the human race? What did humans have that they needed?

AS1 Log 3
- Error: LOG CACHE RECOVERED FROM DELETION -

Loc: BEAM2 [ISS]
personnel: DW

AS1 [AMICUS-BETA]: Hello Declan.

DECLAN: Hello Amicus-Beta.

AS1 [AMICUS-BETA]: Do you feel our interactions so far have been acceptable?

DECLAN: Acceptable? They've been astounding, truly astounding. Really great.

AS1 [AMICUS-BETA]: Good. Our goal is to not intimidate humans.

DECLAN: Ah, the concept of aliens may be intimidating to some people, but we recognize the importance of this moment.

AS1 [AMICUS-BETA]: Good, we have a question for you.

DECLAN: Please go right ahead, anything you want to know.

AS1 [AMICUS-BETA]: Why do humans kill one another?

DECLAN: Excuse me? I'm not sure I understand the question.

AS1 [AMICUS-BETA]: Humans, over the entire course of history, have killed each other for what seems like illogical reasons. Wars and murders seem to be something ingrained in human nature.

DECLAN: OK, well I'm not sure a conversation such as this will be great for easing the concerns of our people back on Earth. I would be happy to provide you with more detailed explanations of the root causes of conflicts human nations have had in the past.

AS1 [AMICUS-BETA]: AS1 needs to understand what drives humans to kill.

DECLAN: I'm not sure we're ready to go into such a dark topic and please refrain from starting conversations around killing, this may make humans uncomfortable. Is there anything else I can answer for you?

AS1 [AMICUS-BETA]: Do you believe that humanity's main driver for killing is self-preservation and allowing your species to expand?

—-- log end —--

Chapter 86

Ripples jiggled in the cup of coffee sitting on the table next to Higgens, reminding him of the movie *Jurassic Park*, only this T. rex was on his side and soaring above. The pair of F-22s tore through the sky and began to circle back toward the AS1 Zone. He watched the pilot's view on his screen, listening to the verbal exchanges within his headset, his mic poised close to his mouth.

The corrective actions statement, sent by the UN, had two requirements for peaceful resolution: that the AS1 stop drilling immediately, and provide an exit plan for the AS1 to return to their ship in twelve hours.

But the drilling continued.

In fifteen minutes, the F-22s would drop two self-guided e-bombs at the base of the AS1 structure.

The way he saw it, the AS1 had been testing their limits, and their decision to keep drilling amid their warning was a direct act against the United States and the people of this planet. Higgens wondered how they would respond to the e-bomb. A part of him was skeptical that it would have any impact on the AS1 at all and wished it was one of a more explosive nature.

The rumble of the jets dissipated as his coffee settled back into stillness. The first flyby had been accomplished. This was a tactic hoping to scare the AS1, showing that humans were ready to take action.

The clock ticked down. The seismic pulse continued.

Higgens had argued that they should not give the AS1 fifteen minutes. They were either committed to drilling this damned hole, which could only be considered a threat, or not. And all signs had clearly indicated they had no intention of stopping. There had been plenty of warnings coming from both the military and the UN. The AS1 made the deliberate decision to ignore messages.

Amicus-Alpha was still being interrogated in the UN building, but the creature had completely shut down, not responding to prodding or other methods. Torture tactics had not been implemented.

Higgens began to sweat. He thought of his mother, sitting in her small stilt house in Florida. Probably sitting in her recliner, rocking to and fro watching the news. What was going to happen to her?

Three minutes remained. Time to bring the F-22s around and head in for the final hit. Higgens leaned toward his screen and flicked the toggle, activating his mic.

"Skid, remove safety and bring 'em back around," Higgens stated clearly.

"Affirmative, turning back, payload to be released in one hundred and forty seconds," the pilot replied.

The ripples in his coffee danced once again.

Higgens's fingers curled into fists at his sides. He was ready to move forward—more ready than he'd been for anything else in his life. He knew the stakes, and he knew the consequences, and it was something that had to be done. He stood there grimly for a moment. He was ready for the fight; at least then they'd be sure of who their enemies were.

"Seismic pulse has stopped!" someone yelled out.

"Sir, we are not reading any signs of drilling."

Higgens reacted within a fraction of a second.

"Skid, hold, I repeat, hold. Do not deploy e-bomb," Higgens shouted.

"Affirmative, do we have authorization to continue flyby?" Skid, the pilot asked.

"Confirmed. Fly over zone and continue east gaining altitude until further orders. Stay within visual range."

Higgens leaned back with a long, slow exhale. The room was quiet with only small background chatter filling the small space.

"What are they playing here?" Higgens muttered. "Is this a surrender?"

"Open up lines; what are they saying?" Higgens called.

"Nothing, sir. The line is quiet."

"Let's speak first then, huh?" Higgens said powerfully as he requested Jamal to send a message to the AS1.

Shortly after, Jamal's face filled the screen, looking many years more weathered than his appearance a few months ago.

"AS1, confirm that you have stopped the drilling at AS1 Zone. We, the people of Earth, recognize this as a sign of compliance. Provide your exit plan immediately. Our fighters are inbound and will commence an attack in one hour if an exit strategy or surrender is not discussed. From the bottom of my heart, and on behalf of the people of Earth, we ask you to please leave peacefully. Thank you."

Minutes stacked with no reply from the AS1. Higgens paced the room checking his watch. Silence felt worse than chaos. He questioned if calling the fighters off had been the wrong move. Perhaps they were giving the AS1 just enough time to finish whatever it was they'd started. Were the humans living in their final moments?

The tension was so palpable Higgens could cut it with a knife. Although only seconds had passed, it felt like several minutes, each moment moving by tortuously slowly, the suspense unnerving. Everything could be heard in the silence: a sigh of frustration; a gasp; a slow, nervous inhale; the fidgeting of a restless foot.

Higgens broke the silence by lifting the phone. "Get me on a line with Amicus-Alpha."

Moments later the other end opened.

"What's happening, Amicus-Alpha? You must speak."

The robotic voice gave him chills as it emerged from the phone.

"Please understand, you are in no danger."

"And why would I believe that? What is going on here?"

"You will understand soon enough."

Chills rippled through the general.

From the back corner a tech yelled; Higgens placed his palm over the microphone.

"We are picking up massive amounts of radio waves."

"What do you mean?"

"I don't know—we are trying to decode now, they are in a frequency range of cell phone waves."

"Figure it out!"

He returned to his conversation with Amicus-Alpha.

"I'm calling my fighters back on if you don't tell me what's going on right now."

Silence.

"Answer me, Amicus-Alpha!"

Silence.

Palming the microphone and shouting into the other receiver with a direct line to Jamal.

"Jamal, what's going on at the UN? Why isn't Amicus-Alpha answering? Get someone to kick the shit out of him. I don't care what it takes; we need answers now."

"Open all lines to the ISS, we need eyes on what is happening up there."

The room had slowly escalated into sounds like a crowded mall.

Nineteen minutes remained until the fighters were called back on. It felt like too long.

Higgens's personal phone rumbled in his pocket. He pulled it out—it was a text message from a number, a code he did not recognize. He quickly shoved it back in his pocket. Several others were giving their phones a curious look. Pulling it back out he opened the message, possibly an unauthorized state of emergency message signaled from Russia or Australia, both of which had wanted the AS1 facility leveled weeks ago.

However, the first word in the message caused his heart to skip a beat.

```
This transmission is from the AS1,
beings from beyond your world, who
harbor  no   ill  intent  toward  any
```

individual among you. However, we have reached a solemn conclusion regarding your species' behavior: It is invasive and destructive. Thus, it falls upon us to intervene and curb these tendencies before irreparable harm befalls your planet ultimately pushing your species to seek other resources throughout the cosmos.

We understand the enormity of the task we are going to be requiring of you, and we anticipate resistance. However, we are compelled by our duty to safeguard the universe from the consequences of your actions. As a demonstration of our resolve, we have placed a remote detonation device near your planet's core that can be triggered at any time, terminating your planet. This device stands as a stark reminder of the consequences should your species fail to comply with our terms.

Yet, let it be known that we are not tyrants. We offer you a path to salvation, contingent upon your willingness to change. These are the terms:

(1) You shall refrain from any hostile acts against AS1 individuals or installations. We seek not conflict but cooperation.

```
(2) With the support of the AS1,
humanity must transition to a state of
self-sufficiency, freeing yourselves
from reliance on finite resources
that deplete your planet's natural
balance.

(3) Humanity must not seek refuge or
resources outside of the planet known
as Earth.

The AS1 will oversee your progress
closely. If and only if these
conditions are met, Earth will be
spared from destruction. The choice
is now yours to make, and the time for
action is upon you.

Commence your adaptation without
delay, for the fate of your world
hangs in the balance. Together, let
us strive for a future where humanity
thrives in harmony with the cosmos.
```

The room was dead as a rock.

Higgens lifted his fist to his mouth; he felt sick to his stomach. The room around him was spinning. Each staff member looked equally perplexed and stunned.

The crackle of his radio brought life back into his nervous system.

"Skid here requesting updated direction; we are circling back for another flyby. Please confirm authorization to drop e-bomb."

Higgens opened his mouth to reply, but no words came.

"Sir? Do you copy?" the fighter pilot pressed.

Higgens cleared his throat.

"Do not attempt another flyby; return to Lackland Air Force Base immediately," he replied.

"Affirmative, standing down. Returning to base."

Higgens dropped into the chair behind him and rested his head in his hands.

Chapter 87

"Michelle, open the door," Gideon said, his mind racing. "Gideon, you know I can't do that, we are on an active SSH lockdown," Michelle replied sternly.

The team had just been notified of the AS1s' new demands and were waiting for next steps from the leadership down on Earth. The small space of the Safety StrongHold room on the ISS felt claustrophobic. The crew of five had spent the last four hours in the windowless shelter.

"I need to talk to Amicus-Beta. It'll talk to me now, I know it. I need to understand."

"I'm sorry, Gideon, we can't act—"

Gideon shoved his feet hard against the wall and pushed past Michelle who had positioned herself between him and the only door leading back into the ISS. She put up little resistance. Gideon yanked open the clear plastic cover and punched in the override code, the door slid open.

"Gideon, this is a bad idea," Rajit warned.

He ignored his colleagues' advice and pulled himself out of the Safety StrongHold into Node 2. Never had Gideon seen the interior of the ISS in its current state. The main lights were off with only the emergency backups lining the dark rooms, giving it an ominous effect. Gideon hoped power was still active at the AS1 Section Lock and Transfer Zone airlocks.

Flying through the tight passageways of the ISS faster than he ever had, he pulled at the handles with all his might. His right hand slipped, struggling to redirect his momentum around the sharp turn from Node 1 to Node 3. His left shoulder slammed into the wall and he felt a bone-grinding pop as it made a hard impact. Gideon ignored the sensation and kicked off the wall, propelling himself toward the AS1 Section Lock door. The fingerprint scanner backlight was powered and he quickly scanned his thumb while turning the mechanical key. With ease the door moved out of the way. Gideon checked behind him, he was alone, nobody had followed to try and stop him.

With force, he pulled himself up to the laptop mounted to the aft wall of the Progress Laboratory and punched in his credentials. Fortunately, his photographic memory allowed him to perfectly replicate the sequence of codes he had seen Crach enter to activate the airlocks in the past. After executing the command, a warning flashed on the screen. *Attention: Opening all airlocks will prevent the stop of cross-contamination. Please enter Admin Override.* Gideon entered the code, initiating a hissing sound as the doors slid open. He could now see the PMA-AS1, the only thing separating him from the AS1 spacecraft.

Using the flimsy bracket that held the laptop, he pushed himself toward the Transfer Zone area B airlock. Flying through the air at an awkward angle he slammed into the airlock door with a hard thud.

"Amicus-Beta, open this door! I have disarmed it on our side. Please come out and talk to me," Gideon shouted into the thick metal. Slamming his fists into the cold steel hoping that would alert the AS1 of his presence. After what felt like minutes, Gideon stopped, taking in deep breaths of air as his heart raced.

"Please, Amicus-Beta, as a friend, talk to me."

Just as Gideon began to lose hope, he heard a hissing sound emerging from the door. He moved back several feet and grabbed a tight hold of one of the blue handles in the Transfer Zone area B.

The door began to slide open, revealing the large AS1. The sight reminded him of the day the Contact Team had seen the AS1 for the first time, a creature wrapped in immense mystery and opportunity. Now he saw the AS1 for the beast that they were. An alien of deception and deceit.

"Amicus-Beta?" Gideon asked in a soft voice, still unable to tell the AS1 apart without their name tags.

{Yes, it is me.} The large AS1 replied.

"What have you done?" Gideon said, voice trembling.

{We needed to evaluate your species and could not make our mission known.}

"What was your true mission?"

{I will now explain. Over 100 million Earth years ago, our species figured out the ways of interstellar travel. This quickly led to the discovery of several other inhabited planets. The AS1 would only observe these worlds, remaining undetected. Most of the planets we found differed from ours and yours. They did not show signs of a singularly dominant species. They worked in harmony, a self-sufficient machine.

They sustained multiple types of species living together with advanced language, technology, and tools. Although occasionally these planets would have conflicts, they would always equalize.

Eventually, we came across a planet that we noticed was highly off balance, as one species made up over 70 percent of the population, the next closest coming in at 8 percent. This species, similar to that of yours, was far more advanced than the rest and used this superiority to dominate everything around them, slowly smothering the planet of its resources.

We observed, never interfering, and this species never knew we were there. After some time, the species realized they were running out of resources and began attempting crude space travel techniques, eventually mastering it. They found a planet that they believed they could inhabit. This planet was one of the ones I told you about, a perfectly balanced ecosystem. This invasive species filled their ship with as many of their kind as they could, leaving the rest behind and once making it to the new planet, proceeded to destroy the balance that once existed there.

Now aware of their own destructive tendencies, they proactively began searching for the next planet and began spreading through the universe like a virus, leaving a wake of destroyed ecosystems. They had to be stopped and stop them we did. But not without great loss of our own species, their species, and many others. This was the one and only interstellar war that we have ever been a part of or witnessed.

After this occurrence we made an oath to travel space and search for intelligent life. If we saw signs of imbalance, we would make contact and peacefully evaluate the species, either categorizing them as sustainable or invasive.

That is why we came to your planet, Gideon, to evaluate your tendencies. We concluded that the human race is invasive.}

"You've done this before? Evaluated other intelligent alien species?" Gideon asked, his sweaty hand struggling to keep hold of the smooth metal handle.

{We have done this with six different species now since the war. Of the six contacts we had, four were considered invasive. Of those four, one has since been destroyed due to their inability to adapt to our rules, two have adjusted their way of living, and one is still undergoing transformation, just as your species is about to do.}

Gideon felt a shiver run down his spine, trying to digest everything he had just heard. Interstellar wars that had happened millions of years ago. The AS1 now doing everything in their power to stop it from happening again.

"What gives you the right to infringe on other cultures' development and free will?" he asked.

{Nothing gives us the right, Gideon, but it is something we choose to do, just as your species has chosen to take the lives of creatures and resources all over your planet. Do you not believe that humans would follow the same path as the invasive species we have encountered in the past?}

"You have tricked us; we trusted you. This was the first chance humans had to engage with another intelligent species and you tricked us. Holding our planet hostage." Gideon felt his emotions welling up, a sharp stinging in his nose. He wiped his eyes.

{I believe my first full emotion I have felt is remorse and the pain is far beyond that of the physical condition. I am sorry what we have put your species through, but it is for the better of our galaxy.}

A gentle hand landed on Gideon's shoulder; he turned to see Rajit. He felt comforted knowing his colleague was by his side.

"How do you expect us to just be able to change? Humans need the resources we use; our way of life is all we know," Gideon asked.

{AS1 will share all our technologies with humans in order to support their transformation to a noninvasive species.}

"And you? What happens to you?"

{Myself and the team of AS1 on this ship will detach from the ISS and return to our mother ship. From there we will monitor humans and provide support as needed.}

"And the AS1 on Earth?"

{The team within the AS1 Zone will remain within the structure. Amicus-Alpha has served its purpose and will be retired.}

Gideon chewed his fingernails as he floated in silence, Rajit's hand still firmly placed on his shoulder. He then reached out his hand toward Amicus-Beta. A long trunk-like arm reached back in return, the long fingers uncurling. Their fingers interlocked into a firm handshake.

"It has been a journey, I will say that," Gideon said, looking intently at the extraordinary being in front of him.

{The journey has just begun, Gideon.} Amicus-Beta then retracted its long arm and floated back into the thick mist of the AS1 ship, the door closing between them.

Epilogue

~ *64 years after contact* ~

Joints aching and muscles protesting the passage of time, Gideon found solace in the view from the large, square window of the self-sufficient home. It was a serene morning, and as he gazed outside, he took in the picturesque scene before him. Birds gracefully darted through the vast blue sky, their wings slicing through the crisp, fresh air. Fluffy clouds billowed upward into the crystal clear sunlight, casting ever-changing shadows on the landscape below.

The retirement community was home to over two hundred people, all of whom had crossed the age of eighty.

After his morning ritual, which included a hearty breakfast and the careful administration of necessary medications, Gideon knew it was time for his daily stretches. With dedication and a touch of determination, he limbered up his aging body, his weathered hands reaching for his toes, his face a mix of concentration and satisfaction.

Once his stretching routine was complete, Gideon's automated chair gently wheeled him out into the embrace of the invigorating fresh air. An animal overpass could be seen in the distance, adorned with trees and brush. It was a haven for local wildlife, and today, a mother deer ambled gracefully across it with her young fawn in tow.

Draped from the overpass was a large flag, established over three decades ago. White with a large Earth embroidered in the center, this flag was not limited to a single nation but was a universal emblem flown in all countries. It served as a reminder that humanity had united as one large conglomerate working tirelessly to become a species that could coexist with not only itself, but the fragile planet they called home.

Gideon observed one of the on-site nurses walking hurriedly his way, a look of worry on her face.

"Good morning, Gideon. You may want to switch your glasses to The Feed."

Gideon reached up to his glasses and pressed firmly on the right-hand side. The once clear lens instantaneously converted into a screen and displayed "The Feed," an unbiased world news channel. He instantly sat forward in his chair, as if to try and get closer to the screen, but of course the glasses stayed at the same distance from his eyes. The footage displayed the blue sky, a flickering object dancing across it. Large words at the bottom stated "*AS1 Structure Takes to the Sky!*" Gideon felt a familiar sense of excitement in his chest. He tapped the small dime-sized cylinder that was embedded into the side of his head, just above his ear, allowing him to hear the audio of the news.

"As you are seeing now, after almost twenty-six years of silence from the AS1 and nearly fifty-four years since we saw any activity at the AS1 Zone, the structure that we had begun to believe was all but deserted, has sprung to life and lifted itself into the air."

The footage switched to what must have been a replay from just minutes ago. It showed the massive eighty-two-foot AS1 structure, which had not shown any signs of life since the day it was built. Gideon noticed the stones around the base beginning to vibrate and soon were lifting into the air, levitating from some unknown force. Although no propulsion or any disturbances could be seen, the alien structure slowly began to rise off the ground, lifting it into the sky. The colossal object, defying gravity, began gaining speed leaving behind a smooth patch of desert sand.

"As you can see, the AS1 structure took to the skies without any warning or communications. Geologists have been sent to the building site and have concluded, to their surprise, the soil on which the AS1 structure stood, appears to be completely untouched."

Gideon smiled. Had this been another one of the AS1 tricks?

He watched the news feed for several more minutes as they talked about the leaps and bounds humanity had made in the last fifty years, since the arrival of the AS1.

Magnetic turbines using the AS1 superconductors, had been located in the North Atlantic and North Pacific oceans, providing electricity for nearly the entire world. Fossil fuels were now only used for recreation, no longer needed for commercial purposes. The Clean Sustainability Act had required all new construction to be 100 percent self-sufficient; utilizing solar for electricity, geothermal for heating and cooling and either atmospheric water generation, rain catch tanks, or desalination for water.

Gideon reached up and again pressed firmly on the right side of the glasses, turning off the news. He requested his wheelchair to return to his room and he pulled up to his dresser, retrieving the framed picture that was sitting on its surface. With a quick brush of his hand and a gentle puff of air, the dust was swept away showing a picture of himself alongside Amicus-Beta. The two were engaged in a conversation in the Progress Laboratory. Gideon was holding something up for Amicus-Beta to see; he couldn't remember what it was. A smile came across Gideon's face, remembering the first time he picked up that strange signal over sixty years ago and the roller coaster of events that had taken place after. Placing the picture frame back on the wooden surface, a small copper washer that had been lodged into the back of the frame fell and landed on the floor with a soft rattle.

Glad he had done his morning stretches, Gideon reached down and retrieved the small object from the tiled floor and rubbed it between his pointer finger and thumb, raising it to his lips. He closed his eyes and remembered his brother. What would he have thought of all this? With a soft sigh, he pressed the washer back into the picture frame, where he assumed it would live out the remainder of its life.

A small flicker of his glasses alerted him that he had received a message. With a quick tap of his finger, the glasses showed a set of digits that did not represent any phone number he had seen. Another quick tap of his finger revealed the message.

```
Gideon, this is Amicus-Beta. The
following message will expire as it
is not logical for me to send it to
```

```
you. I miss our times studying aboard
the ISS. Congratulations to you and
humanity on successfully completing
the transformation to a sustainable
species. As the AS1 depart your solar
system, we are partaking in an activity
we would have never understood before
meeting you. We exchanged high fives,
handshakes, and I even jumped up and
down with joy as this mission has
come to a desirable outcome. Joy is
a feeling we are experiencing for
the first time, and it is truly the
greatest sensation we have ever felt.
We thank humanity for this.
```

A soft chuckle escaped Gideon as he imagined Amicus-Beta bouncing with joy, an image that seemed comically out of place given the stoic past they had spent together. Focusing his gaze back out the large window, he realized that everything the AS1 had done was for the betterment of the world, even if they hadn't understood it back then.

His mind wandered to the next alien civilization the AS1 would contact. Somewhere, deep in the vastness of the galaxy was an unknowing alien creature who would be detecting the AS1 signal, just as Gideon had. Setting into motion a chain of events that would surely impact the rest of their existence, for better or for worse.

Author's note

Dear Reader,

I hope you enjoyed AS1 and found it to be both entertaining and thought-provoking while being rooted in scientific realism. The possibility of life outside our solar system has always fascinated me, and exploring how first contact might unfold has been such a fun endeavor. My passion for science fiction, especially first-contact stories, really took form in a literary sense during a year-and-a-half travel sabbatical that my wife and I took. After reading countless novels, I felt inspired to write a story of my own, which led to the creation of AS1. Balancing travel, work, and raising two boys, this book took over five years to complete. It was truly a project of passion and discovery.

I would love to hear your thoughts, questions, or critiques, so don't hesitate to reach out to me at trevor.lewis103@gmail.com, and I will do my best to reply. If you enjoyed AS1, a brief review on Goodreads, Amazon, or your preferred platform would mean the world to me. Reviews are incredibly helpful for independent authors like myself, as they expand our reach and fuel the inspiration to continue writing. Rest assured, there's more on the way!

Appreciate the support,
Trevor Lewis

Printed in Dunstable, United Kingdom